HIS HYPNOTIC GAZE MESMERIZED HER.

"You must find it strange to see someone else in your clothing," Aurelia said. "Do you?"

"Not strange," Clay answered. "Exciting."

His hands caressed her shoulders, slid down her back, and circled her waist. The love he needed, the love she needed—it all became clear when he kissed her. Awash in the power of a dream, Aurelia parted her lips to lure him closer.

Clay unbuttoned the shirt he had insisted she wear. She could scarcely breathe, so powerful was his touch, even though his fingers fumbled with the tangle of satin ribbon that gathered her chemise.

She closed her eyes and clutched his hair between her fingers.

His ragged breath warmed her skin. The fire that had smoldered inside her for months finally exploded . . .

Band
~ of ~
# Gold

Zita Christian

HarperPaperbacks
A Division of HarperCollins Publishers

This is a work of fiction. The characters, incidents, and
dialogues are products of the author's imagination and are not
to be construed as real. Any resemblance to actual events or
persons, living or dead, is entirely coincidental.

HarperPaperbacks *A Division of* HarperCollins*Publishers*
10 East 53rd Street, New York, N.Y. 10022

Copyright © 1993 by Zita Christian

Cover illustration by Diane Sivavec

First printing: August 1993

Printed in the United States of America

HarperPaperbacks, HarperMonogram, and colophon are
trademarks of HarperCollins*Publishers*

❖ 10 9 8 7 6 5 4 3 2 1

To my husband, Dick,
and my daughter, Laurie,
for the faith and encouragement
that comes from love.

To Leslie and Denise,
for brainstorms and bagels
and so much more.

ACKNOWLEDGMENTS

Dull, dry history crackles with excitement and tugs at the heart when one looks at the people behind all those dates and places. My high-school history teacher, Mr. Towles, taught me that valuable lesson. I will forever be grateful.

My gratitude extends to the Alaska Northwest Publishing Company for the diaries and correspondence of many who made the arduous journey described in this book. Among those publications are *Klondike Letters: The Correspondence of a Gold Seeker in 1898*, by Alfred G. McMichael; *The Alaskan Gold Fields*, by Sam C. Dunham; *Along Alaska's Great River*, by Frederick Schwatka; *The Time of My Life: A Frontier Doctor in Alaska*, by Harry Carlos de Vighne; *Gold Hunting in Alaska: As Told by Joseph Grinnell*; *Martha Black: Her Story From the Dawson Gold Fields to the Halls of Parliament*, by Martha Black; and *Chilkoot Pass: The Most Famous Trail in the North*, by Archie Satterfield.

Some of the stampeders knew they were making history and captured it on film. I saw some of the finest photographs in *The Streets Were Paved With Gold: A Pictorial History of the Klondike Gold Rush 1896–1899*, by Stan Cohen, and in *One Man's Gold Rush*, by Murray Morgan, photographs by E. A. Hegg.

My profound admiration goes to the women who were drawn to a career in medicine by their unquenchable desire for instruction. I found their story in *Send Us a Lady Physician: Women Doctors in America 1835–1920*.

Several people gave generous amounts of their time

to answer my questions about porpoises, whales, antique guns, drugs, surgery, and medicine in general. My gratitude goes to naturalist Janna Meyer and Captain Sebby Lovasco, both of the Seven Seas Whale Watch in Gloucester, Massachusetts; to Ralph Morrill, owner of Firearms, Inc. in Vernon, Connecticut; and most importantly, to C. C. Winterberg, HMCM, U. S. Navy (Ret.), my dad.

Finally, to the Visitor Center in Skagway, Alaska, thank you for the exhibit dedicated to the women of the Klondike Gold Rush. It opened my eyes and made all things seem possible.

1

Seattle, 1898

Enslaved by a peddler of the flesh.

Aurelia Breighton shuddered at the thought of her sister's fate. If Violet weren't so innocent, she wouldn't have been so easily tricked. If she weren't so beautiful, she wouldn't have been abducted. If she weren't so helpless, she wouldn't have been forced on a journey from which she couldn't turn back.

Surely, Violet was doomed.

Fighting the visions that had plagued her for months, Aurelia lifted the hem of her simple brown traveling dress to avoid the puddles left by the dreary March showers. Though her quest might not be an easy one, she never considered giving up, not even when she saw the madness on the street. If she did, something horrid might befall her little sister—if it hadn't already.

Aurelia picked her way around the daunting display of canned food and prospecting supplies. The gold rush paraphernalia covered the sidewalk end to end, rose six feet high, and spilled over the edge onto Seattle's busy First Avenue South. Both sides of the thoroughfare mirrored the scene for as many blocks as she could see, creating a maze for the desperate, muddle-minded men who cast aside all sense of decency in their attempts to purchase a Yukon this or a Klondike that.

Hours later, increasingly annoyed by the swarm of anxious buyers buzzing around her and by the ridiculous amount of time she'd already spent waiting for assistance, Aurelia cast propriety aside and raised her voice above the bedlam.

"Over here, young man. Over here!"

The most industrious of clerks came to her aid. "Yes, ma'am," he said, then stared for a moment as though he'd only just realized he was speaking to a lady.

"There's got to be some mistake," Aurelia said. "This list can't be accurate. *Four hundred pounds* of flour, *two hundred pounds* of bacon, a sheet-iron *stove,* and a *tent*?" The list went on with more than seventy-five items.

"Ain't no mistake, ma'am. That's what you need if you're headed for the K-K-Klondike."

Aurelia looked at the potatoes for twenty cents a pound, onions at seventy-five, worse yet, egg yolks for a dollar, all evaporated, all outrageously expensive. She couldn't afford all this, she thought, much less carry it.

The clerk stopped gawking at her long enough to add, "You'll also be wanting lime-juice capsules. Box of a hundred for a dollar. It ain't on the list." He picked up a small cardboard box, rattled its contents, and offered it to her. "For the rot. Turns the l-l-legs to a mass of black pulp. No telling how long you'll be without f-f-fresh fruit."

"Oh yes, an antiscorbutic. To ward off the weakness, anemia, spongy gums, and other symptoms associated with scurvy," she recited from memory.

The clerk appeared impressed, though Aurelia thought he shouldn't be. Compared to the others in her class at the Women's Medical College of Pennsylvania, Aurelia had no cause to boast. Perhaps that was because she was only twenty-four, by far the youngest in the class . . . or simply because school was so much harder than she thought it'd be.

Aurelia returned the box of capsules to the clerk. "You can add them to my order." Scanning the mountains of canned milk, walls of boxed candles, and bricks of bulging flour sacks, she quickly estimated the cost of the recommended items on the list. Five hundred dollars! That'd be half a year's wages once she set up her medical practice. *If* she set up her medical practice.

She grumbled as she tucked a defiant blond curl under the threadbare black velvet bonnet that had once been her grandmother's. "You supply-outfitters are the only ones assured of making a fortune in this gold rush."

"Yes, ma'am," he answered, as though both aware and embarrassed at the fact. "Don't know as anyone told you," he added, "but once you get to Lake Bennett you'll need a boat to get down the Yukon River."

"I have to buy a *boat*?"

"B-B-Build a boat."

She looked at him incredulously, feeling her confidence dwindle. "I'm supposed to *build* my own boat?"

"I hear it's every m-m-man for himself. But I'll wager a pretty woman such as yourself could get a seat in someone else's boat." The lanky young man turned crimson at the boldness of his own words.

His spectacles must need adjustment, Aurelia decided. Men made such offers to Violet, not to her. The thought of her pretty, flirtatious little sister brought a melancholy smile to Aurelia's face.

The clerk straightened his posture and recovered his manner. "Yeah, I been thinking about going to the Klondike myself, stake a few good claims, make myself a f-f-fortune. Course, dock workers here just went on strike and got themselves a jump in pay to fifty cents an hour. Now that's a respectable wage. Then again, maybe I'll just head down to C-C-Cuba to help whip Spain."

"How admirable." Aurelia tried to sound impressed, but she doubted the young man's ability to perform any heavy manual labor. He was so thin, so frail. His shoulders had the sloping arc of a narrow rainbow, no pot of gold at either end, not even a plugged nickel. Violet would brand him a loser, a whey-faced, white-livered flunky. But then, Violet didn't know the first thing about how to recognize a decent man—or an indecent man, unfortunately.

With the eager clerk shuffling close behind, Aurelia moved past the towering cans of meat and sacks of rice and dried beans. Past the wool blankets, sleeping bags, and pyramids of two-quart coffee pots. Past the dogsleds propped against the building like racks of wooden ribs.

She stopped by the table of axes, kegs of nails, coils of oakum, and barrels of pitch. The list issued by the Seattle Chamber of Commerce urged anyone going to the Klondike to purchase every item on the list. But Aurelia knew how much money she carried in her reticule, and it wasn't enough. She'd have to select.

"This is ridiculous. Your fair city may contain the most knowledgable outfitters, but I'm only going to the Klondike to fetch my sister, not pan for gold." With a false sense of bravery, she waved the list in front of the clerk and gave him a stern look.

"Now, ma'am, if you ain't headed up there looking

for The Yellow, you won't be needing the gold pan and some of the other items in our stampeder package." His plaid mackinaw hung on his thin, bony arms as he stretched them over the supplies. Then he looked her straight in the eye. "But it don't pay to gamble. You'll curse the day you didn't provide for yourself when you had the chance. Them Canadians won't let you cross the border without a full year's provisions. Don't want your death on their conscience."

Aurelia hoped that his dire prediction of starvation was part of the sales technique he'd been taught, or that he was merely given to exaggeration, like Violet. She prayed that this time, of all times, Violet had exaggerated.

"Course, if you ain't looking for gold," the clerk continued, "why risk your life getting to the Klondike?" His eyes widened as though he'd just been inspired. "Unless you got some m-m-magic potion to protect you. The Fate Lady two blocks down sells 'em. All kinds. Two bits a bottle. I bought a couple myself."

Magic. Of course. Aurelia tried to dismiss the uncertainties the clerk had fostered. Nana Brooke had given Aurelia all the magic she'd ever need. Even now the powerful silver buckles were fastened tightly to her boots. Their magic had worked three years ago when she left her home in Detroit and went all the way to Philadelphia. But going away to school was nothing like trekking off to the Klondike. Nana Brooke could boast deeds of derring-do, not Aurelia.

Feeling the hand of fate urging her along, Aurelia surveyed the supplies one last time. "With any luck at all, I'll only be in the Klondike for a few weeks, five or six at the most. If I have to take a year's worth of food, so be it. I'll trade some for passage on the river.

But I'm not buying all that equipment." She crossed off numerous items, wrote her name across the top, and handed the list to the clerk. "If you would be so kind as to have everything sent to the steamer *Reliance.* We sail in two days."

The clerk looked at her with admiration. "You want me to call one of the photographers over? Take a p-p-picture of you standing with your supplies? Everybody gets one. Costs one dollar."

"For a photograph?" She rolled her eyes at the absurdity of it all and drew the hood of her red wool cape over her bonnet. "I'm staying at the Sturbridge Boardinghouse. If you send me the invoice there, I'll pay you promptly."

Aurelia gathered her skirt and stepped around the obstacles. "Oh, good luck in your own ventures, whether it's Cuba or the Klondike. 'Remember the Maine' and all that."

The beaming clerk was quickly besieged by dozens of stampeders, holding their lists in one hand and cash in the other. Before he waited on them, he glanced down at the items Aurelia had checked off and called out to her, "Ma'am! You didn't order the m-m-medicine chest!"

"I don't need it. I'm a doctor." Almost a doctor, she corrected herself silently. One more year to go, and then she'd have a fine leather satchel in which to carry her instruments and remedies. Until then, Violet's old converted toilette and manicure case would have to do.

She lifted her skirt just enough to see the end of the sidewalk as she stepped onto the street. Though not as refined as Detroit, which she called home, or Philadelphia, where she had attended school, Seattle in its infancy was still impressive. Stately five- and six-story brick buildings lined the streets, their entries protected by wide, canvas awnings that stretched overhead like circus tents.

The hoopla continued into the street itself, with dozens of horse-drawn broughams and hansoms competing with electric streetcars for the fares of the hopeful who'd descended on Seattle, having been convinced by Seattle's zealous Chamber of Commerce that their fair city was America's gateway to the Klondike.

Aurelia stood waiting for the traffic to clear. It was after four o'clock, not yet dark, but gray and damp. She'd been walking the streets since early morning. Despite her magic boot buckles, her feet hurt. She had every intention of hailing the hansom headed her way until she noticed the commotion at the restaurant across the street.

The activity bore little resemblance to the saloon scenes she had read in the dime novel that had circulated discreetly through her medical college class. The elegant mahogany door of the restaurant opened wide, barely rattling the cut-glass panes. Strains of soft dinner music drifted in the air. Two men shouted obscenities as they emerged.

The first braced his long, muscular arms against both sides of the doorway before he faltered. With the light behind him, Aurelia could see his broad shoulders and trim physique. The cut of his clothes appeared appropriate for a man of business. She estimated his height at nearly six feet, but it was hard to tell. He was staggering. Obviously not a man of temperance.

He fell against a pyramid display of cans and sent the tins tumbling into the street, startling horses and pedestrians alike. He grabbed a lightpost for support.

Aurelia dodged the traffic and made her way

toward the restaurant. A short, round man with a red face and ruffled shirt stood in the doorway. His breath came in puffs. He bellowed to the drunk, who had turned around to face him. "See here, Guardian. I don't care a continental about who or what you used to be. You're nothing now." The round man waddled back inside, closing the mahogany door behind him.

She ventured closer, close enough to see some debris from the street in his black, curly hair. Close enough to smell the whiskey. A far cry from the more refined patient she had assumed her practice would include. But, on the chance he might be hurt, she stepped up behind him, cleared her throat, and tapped him on the shoulder. "Pardon me, I'm a doc—"

He whirled around so fast. She saw his elbow. She felt the pain. First a numbing sensation, then a ringing in her ear. The crowd gasped.

Aurelia stumbled back as an excruciating bolt of agony shot up from her jaw and down to her shoulder. She caught her balance, then pressed her hand to her cheek. Only by biting her lip could she hold back the tears that sprang up instantly.

"Oh, God, I'm sorry." He reached for her with both arms and then pulled back. "I didn't see. . . . I thought you were one of his . . . Aw, hell."

He slumped against the lightpost and hung his head. Covering his face with his hands, he dragged his fingers over the stubble of his cheeks. He took a deep breath and straightened his shoulders. Aurelia knew a shock could induce sobriety, but she'd never seen it happen. Right now she didn't care how restrained and conciliatory he might become.

She swallowed hard and looked straight at him. Despite his condition, he managed to lift his head and

hold it erect. Thick, paintbrush lashes nearly camouflaged the red in his silver-gray eyes. He needed a shave.

The stunned crowd stood still. From the other side
of the street, the clerk who had just taken Aurelia's
order rushed to her side. "Want me to s-s-summon
the authorities, Miss Breighton?"

"No," she managed to say, her lip quivering. "It
was an accident."

"It was my fault," the black-haired man said as he
stepped closer, his eyes pleading forgiveness. "I feel
terrible about this," he said.

She tasted the tears that trickled across her lips.

"Your jaw broken?" the man asked with a sense of
dread.

Aurelia pressed her first two fingers next to her
ear, then examined the line from her jaw to her chin,
opening and closing her mouth like a wooden mari-
onnette. "I don't think so."

"Let me take you to a doctor."

"She *is* a doctor," the clerk said. "And she doesn't
need the likes of you."

Aurelia heard the familiar, critical mumblings
from the crowd, appalled, no doubt, by the idea of a
woman doctor. The dark-haired man was undaunted.
"Let me do something. Anything." He slipped his
hand inside his jacket and took out a fresh, white
handkerchief. "Here."

She stepped back and shook her head. "I just want
to go back to my room." She looked across the street
for the empty hansom, but it was gone.

"Where are you staying?" He quickly ran his fingers
through his hair and brushed the dirt from his dark
suit.

"The Sturbridge Boardinghouse."

"I know the place. Just over a mile. I'll take you."
He hailed another horse-drawn carriage as it rounded
the corner and then offered her his arm.

"I can manage."

"It's the least I can do. Please."

She wouldn't link her arm with his, but she let him
cup her elbow. As they dodged the traffic to get to the
waiting carriage, she forgot to thank the young supply
clerk who remained behind.

It felt good to sit down. She relaxed against the
plush, black leather squabs and kept her eyes on the
man as he took his place across from her and pulled
the door closed. A sense of both propriety and danger
told her she should never have accepted his offer, but
her jaw ached, she was tired, and her feet hurt.
Besides, they would only be together for a few minutes.

The carriage pulled into traffic and rumbled for a full
block before the man spoke. She eyed him carefully.

"You can stop squinting at me like that," he said.
"I'm not some kind of predator. My name is Guardian.
Clay Guardian." He slipped his finger between his
neck and the collar of his shirt and tugged as though
he needed air. "I'm a banker. My neighbor is a doctor. I'd feel a lot better if you'd let him look at your
jaw."

"My jaw is bruised, not broken."

"Right. You're a doctor too. How could I forget?"
After another block of silence, he spoke again. "Tell me,
how does your family, your husband, feel about a lady
going to school and invading—I mean, pursuing—a
man's career?"

"That's none of your business." The audacity of the
man! She closed her eyes and let her head fall back.
Her education wasn't a subject she enjoyed discussing.

According to her father, a woman going out to work was committing moral suicide, particularly when the work was so indelicate. She could picture him ranting and raving.

For heaven's sake, this wasn't sixty years ago when even Massachusetts, one of the most civilized and advanced communities in the world, had only seven industries open to women. This was 1898! There were at least three hundred occupations open to women. They could set type, teach needlework, tend looms, fold and stitch in book binderies, keep bees, keep boarders, and much more.

Aurelia could always argue facts with her father, but she could never silence her mother's tearful warning. "You take up a man's profession and there's not a man in this world who will think of you as a woman."

Clay intruded on her thoughts. "Didn't mean to pry." His apology sounded sincere.

"If you must know, I'm an embarrassment to my parents. They grew up in the ignorant belief that all doctors are addicted to liquor, smoke pipes, and avoid going to church. My sister, however, applauds my efforts. And, Mr. Guardian, in answer to your tactless assumption, I don't have a husband."

Why had she rattled on like that? She sounded just like the shrew her mother had warned her she'd become. She certainly didn't find anything humorous in what she'd just said, nothing that warranted the amused look on Mr. Guardian's face. He was experiencing either some perverse pleasure in knowing her family disapproved of her education or else some equally ill-founded delight in the fact that she wasn't married.

She stared out the window to clear her mind. Why did she care what he thought?

"I understand you had business at Coopers and Levy today," he said.

"The suppliers? Yes. I'm going to the Klondike." Her face reddened as his gaze traveled the length of her body. Unlike Violet, Aurelia wasn't accustomed to being looked at like that.

"I hope you've got something more practical to wear than that getup." The beginnings of a smile revealed his dimples. "You sure don't look like a stampeder. Or a spinster, for that matter."

Aurelia drew her cape closer, despite the warming air. "I'm not a stampeder, Mr. Guardian. I'm simply going to fetch my little sister."

"Alone?"

"Yes, alone. Though from what I've seen these past few days, there will be plenty of others along on the trip."

"Your sister—is she ill?"

"In a manner of speaking."

"She's not alone, is she? The Klondike is no place for a single woman."

"Woman? She's just a girl, only sixteen. And no, she's not alone." Though she'd be better off alone, Aurelia added silently.

"Well, you're a brave woman to be going after her."

Aurelia thought of herself in a number of ways—determined, optimistic, loyal, but far from adventurous and definitely not brave. "She's my sister," she said by way of explanation.

He smiled just a little. Maybe he understood the strength of such bonds and the power of love.

"Your jaw feeling any better?"

"No." Aurelia touched the tips of her gloved fingers

to her swollen cheek. "I wouldn't want to be counted among your enemies, Mr. Guardian."

He looked more embarrassed than proud. The carriage slowed down. In a few moments, Aurelia would say good-bye to him. She felt vaguely disappointed. The accident aside, he'd made such an effort to be a gentleman, hailing a cab, offering to take her to a doctor, escorting her home. Even his questions showed a personal interest in her. Aurelia wasn't used to all this attention.

Of course, she could have had him arrested. That was why he was being so conciliatory. This conclusion left her even more disappointed than before.

Absently, she touched her jaw again. Would he have noticed her under more normal, civilized circumstances? Probably not. Other than her red cape and the silver buckles on her boots, she knew everything else about her was plain. She had a wealth of hair, but it was the color of old hay and difficult to manage. Her eyes were blue, but hidden behind her reading spectacles. Her mouth was large, her lips too full to ever be drawn in a little Cupid's bow. There was nothing exotic about the fresh-faced look of her cheeks. But why did her flaws bother her now? She had accepted them many years ago.

The carriage came to a halt. Clay shifted his weight, as though he couldn't get comfortable. Heaven help him, he looked as nervous as she felt. Perhaps she should assure him she had no intentions of calling the police. She waited for him to open the door, but he lingered.

"The clerk called you by name. It's Miss Breighton?"

She nodded. A nervous tick trembled at the corner of his mouth. He laced his hands together, rested them on his knees, and leaned forward.

"Miss Breighton. In thirty years I've made my

share of mistakes and I've paid the price. But I've never intentionally struck a woman. Never would. I can't tell you how sorry I am."

She looked straight into his bloodshot eyes. She wasn't sure it was physically possible to see sincerity in a person's eyes, but she decided to give him the benefit of the doubt. "Apology accepted."

His dimples deepened as he smiled. He opened the door and stepped out, then waited, hand outstretched to help her. The heel of her boot wobbled as she descended the first step. Only then did she take his hand for support.

He squeezed it lightly before releasing it. She expected him to utter a simple good-bye. Instead, he kissed the tip of his own finger and lay it tenderly against her injured cheek. "My son says a kiss makes everything better. My wife—"

His son? His wife! She shuddered at the thought of being attracted to a married man. One scandal in the family was enough. She didn't want to hear anything else he had to say. "Good-bye, Mr. Guardian." She hurried toward the protection of the boardinghouse.

"Good-night," he called after her.

A fine twilight mist hung in the air. She raced up the steps of the boardinghouse and pulled the brass handle of the heavy oak door. Once inside, she closed it quickly, barricading herself against the dream she'd come close to acknowledging.

She sighed and leaned her body against the solid door, listening for the inevitable. Within several moments she heard the cab pull away, the rhythmic clomp of the horses' hooves taking Mr. Guardian safely back home.

Aurelia took another moment to collect her

thoughts and then asked the desk manager to have an ice bag and a bowl of soup delivered to her room.

"Miss, are you all right?" he asked.

"I'm fine. A minor accident." She felt him stare at her jaw. Her skin flushed anew. If her feelings were as transparent as she feared, she didn't want anyone to see them, at least until she'd had a chance to sort them out.

Alone in her room, she fell across the soft feather bed and gathered the plump pillows close to her heart. His son. Why not? At thirty years old, it would indeed be likely he'd have a family, a child who welcomed his father's healing kisses.

And a wife. Clay Guardian's wife. A lady who surely wouldn't demand a formal education. A lady who would never dare invade a man's career. A lady a man could also think of as a woman. The woman who eagerly welcomes his—

The image blurred. Aurelia closed her eyes and buried her head in the comforting down. With mixed emotions, she recalled the costly bargain she'd made with her grandmother years ago. For the first time, she had regrets.

2

Nana Brooke lay on her deathbed reading the morning paper, her outrageous rings filling the porcelain box on the nightstand next to the cigar the doctor had forbidden her to smoke. She chewed instead.

Aurelia took the white enameled washbasin from the dresser and hugged it to her chest as she hurried from the room. She returned a few moments later, the basin filled with warm, soapy, fragrant water that sloshed back and forth as she tried to keep it from spilling.

"My little nursemaid," Nana called her as Aurelia carefully made room for the basin on the nightstand.

Aurelia beamed at the term of affection. "Do you need the bedpan before I bathe you, Nana?"

"Just my spittoon."

Aurelia held the brass container while her grandmother made use of it, then set it down and began the morning ritual. Just as she'd done for the past three years, Aurelia bathed her grandmother, changed her nightgown, combed and braided her long, gray hair. The routine took hours, because Nana moved so slowly and Aurelia had to be careful not to get the comb caught in the tangles. But Aurelia didn't mind. Nana always made her feel special.

"Fetch my lavender water for me, will you, dear? Not only is it a good cleanser for wounds, it's an aphrodisiac. I'll explain that to you one of these days. You're old enough."

Aurelia took the cut-crystal atomizer from the dresser and passed it to her grandmother, who directed the opening to her bosom. Nana held the bottle in her wrinkled hand and squeezed the bulb.

"I'm an old woman. I only need one shot. But you, come close here and bend down."

This was the part of the morning ritual Aurelia liked best. She knelt down beside the bed, scooped her hair up high, and turned her head first to the left. *Pssst.* Then to the right. *Pssst.* Aurelia giggled. "It tickles."

"It can bring a man to his knees. And, despite what your mother says, fifteen years old isn't too young for you to learn these strategic maneuvers. Just remember now, a fish only sees the hook. And a man who can't see better than a fish isn't worth catching."

"What hook? What man?"

Nana rolled on her side and set the atomizer on the nightstand. "The hook that all men are drawn to—a generous pelvis and a pair of bountiful bosoms. Your mother should have told you all this by now."

Nana took a deep breath. "You'll want to catch yourself a man one of these days. Take your time. Get a good one—one that wants your lifeblood flowing free and not all squeezed into a blasted corset. And just in case, you make damn sure you've got something besides big bosoms going for you." She stared straight at the bodice of Aurelia's dress. "Trust me. You get yourself an education. Education gets you pecuniary independence.

That's a woman's true protection in this harsh world. Don't let anything stop you. You hear me?"

Nana bobbed her head until Aurelia mimicked the gesture. "Yes, ma'am." Aurelia looked down at the budding mounds on her chest, accepting on faith whatever Nana Brooke said, wondering just how harsh the world could really be and how she would be able to recognize the kind of man she'd need protection against. The idea of education seemed silly. But Nana was old, and sometimes old people said things that didn't make much sense.

Nana shook her finger in the air. "Just remember that. Now, go get my treasure chest from the closet. I've been waiting a long time for this day. I'm going to strike a bargain with you."

The hinges squealed when Aurelia opened the door. She pulled the nearly empty wooden trunk from the dark cavern and dragged it across the faded Oriental rug. She thought of the years when the trunk had bulged with finery and, as long as she was careful, Nana had let her play with the contents. So many ensembles, most of them the sporting type. Aurelia remembered feeling adventurous when she tried on Nana's skating outfits and feeling pretty when she slipped into Nana's seaside costumes.

Nana also had a pair of riding breeches and a set of shooting togs, because she used to carry a gun. At least that was the rumor Aurelia had always heard.

"Fetch me the key." Nana's eyes were livelier than Aurelia had seen them in years. "I hid it in your Grampa's urn. On the mantle, dear. Quick. Just reach in. He won't mind."

The fine, gray ashes felt cool and silky. The entire household had thought Nana raving mad when she had had Grampa's body burned, but she had insisted. That way, he could go with her on her travels. Aurelia slowly withdrew her hand from the urn, the cold metal key clutched between her fingers.

"Good. Good. Bring it to me."

With a strength and reverence that surprised Aurelia, Nana Brooke sat on the edge of the bed and leaned over. She took the key and kissed it. Aurelia barely breathed as Nana slipped it into the lock and turned. The simple tumblers announced success. The domed lid creaked as it opened. The chest wasn't empty after all.

Aurelia knelt on the floor and peered inside. The fragrance of the cedar lining wafted up from the deep, dark corners like incense from a magic lamp. She closed her eyes, but opened them quickly when Nana shook her shoulder.

"Pay attention, child. The three things that mean the most to me are in this trunk, and I'm about to give two of them to you."

Aurelia held her breath as Nana's palsied hands reached into the shadows. Mesmerized, she watched Nana retrieve three parcels, one by one, and lay them next to her on the bed. Aurelia feared the effort would exhaust her grandmother, but the old woman swung her legs back up on the bed and briskly rubbed her palms together.

First, Nana dragged a black leather pouch across her lap. She slipped her shaky fingers into the drawstrings and wiggled them lose.

Aurelia leaned closer and gaped as Nana drew forth two large, silver boot buckles and held them up for her to see. They were tarnished in shades of gray, the color of Nana's eyes.

"These were made in Seville by a man who forged

the swords of matadors. Your Grampa." Her voice sounded strong and full of pride, though her face was suddenly filled with longing. "Give me your hands."

Aurelia extended her arms. She gulped as Nana gave her the buckles. They were beautiful.

"These are magic buckles. Wear them. They'll give you the courage to journey where your choices take you."

Aurelia thought she saw tears in Nana's eyes as the old woman pressed Aurelia's fingers around the silver.

"Polish them up."

"I will, Nana. Thank you."

Magic buckles. Aurelia doubted her mother would ever permit her to wear something so valuable. While she wondered how to ask permission, Nana took out the next treasure, contained in a long, wooden box. "What's that?"

"A dangerous matter, child."

Aurelia held her breath as Nana removed the cover and tilted the box to the side. The story was true. Nana did have a gun! Shinier than polished silver, it was covered with curlicues and other fancy designs. The handle was buttermilk yellow with the head of a horned buffalo carved on the side.

"Forty-five caliber, six-shot Colt. The Peacemaker. It's made of nickel-plated steel, and the handle's African ivory." She lifted the gun from the case and pointed it at Aurelia.

"No, Nana, don't!" Aurelia dropped to the floor and covered her head with her hands. She squeezed her eyes tight. Her heart pounded.

"Good. Good."

Cautiously, Aurelia lifted her head and peeked up at the bed. "Nana, are you going berserk? Momma said—"

"Me? Berserk? Hogwash. Get back up here. Didn't

mean to frighten you, child, but you need to know how it feels to stare down that long, dark tunnel. From now on, don't aim it at anyone unless you're prepared to pull the trigger. Here. Take it."

Aurelia dusted her skirt and fussed with her apron before she accepted the present. The sudden weight of it pulled her arm down. She recovered quickly and even surprised herself as her long, slender fingers wrapped themselves confidently around the lustrous handle and slid up and down the cold steel barrel.

"Weighs just over two pounds," Nana said. "Five-and-a-half-inch barrel, as long as an average man's . . . Well, it's long enough to do the job." Nana took a small box of bullets from inside the wooden box. "It's no good unless it's loaded either. Sit down here, let me show you."

The bed creaked as Aurelia sat down. Filled with anticipation, she squeezed her knees together and held her back straight. Her heart still fluttered wildly. She didn't know danger could be so exciting.

She bit her lower lip to keep from grinning. What would her friends say when she showed them the gun? Their grandmothers gave them books of poetry or pictures of flowers. Or hair ribbons or white gloves. Not steel-barrel revolvers. Aurelia couldn't wait to show them. Just for once she'd be the center of attention.

"First, open the loading gauge. Like this. Gives you access to the chambers. Then pull the hammer back to half-cock." *Click.* "That rotates your cylinder. Load the cylinder, one chamber at a time."

Aurelia stood spellbound as she watched Nana neatly drop a brass-cased bullet into each of the six chambers. "If your mother ever finds out I gave this to you, she'll ship us both down to the South Pole."

Nana drew her lips in a mischievous smile. "Now, close the loading gauge and bring the hammer down to safe position. Be gentle." She laid the gun in her lap and looked at Aurelia. "I'm sure you know better than to tell anyone, *anyone,* about this."

"Yes, Nana." Aurelia knew her disappointment showed in her voice. "Not even Violet?"

"Especially not Violet. The girl doesn't have the brains of a gnat. Oh, get that droopy frown off your face. You know she's a spoiled little—"

"She's my sister."

"A biological mystery. Well, let's get on with this. Fetch me one of your Grampa's suits from the closet. I'm partial to the blue plaid, but you pick whatever you like."

Aurelia wondered why as she opened the closet door and reached in but didn't dare question Nana. "Nana, Grampa's clothes all have little holes in them. All in the chest." Aurelia took the blue plaid from the closet and showed it to her. "Moths?"

"Bullets. Target practice. Now go hang it in the window. Be sure it's open. You'll see the nail."

Aurelia did as instructed.

"Let's get to it. Remind me to tell you about my trip to Kenya when we're finished."

Aurelia concentrated as Nana demonstrated how to aim. Elbow to the side. Arm steady. Wrist loose. Squeeze. It sounded simple enough.

She flinched when Nana fired. A black puff of smoke stung her eyes. She and Nana coughed. The air smelled burnt. Aurelia wrinkled her nose.

"Bullseye!" Nana shouted between coughs. "Your turn."

"I don't think I can." Aurelia tried to fan the smoke from her face.

"Hogwash. Do you want the gun or don't you?"

She definitely wanted that gun. She planted her feet, pulled the hammer, recocked, aimed, and fired.

"Good job. Good job." Nana waved the smoke away, then patted Aurelia's knee.

Aurelia sat down on the bed and stroked the tip of the barrel with her finger. It was hot. She sucked her finger to relieve the pain. "Where did those bullets we just fired go?"

"Outside somewhere. Heavens, we're three floors up and the neighbors are on holiday. Stop worrying."

"If that was a real man and not Grampa's suit, what would happen to the man?"

"Why he'd be dead, of course. You're a natural, dear."

Aurelia beamed at her grandmother's praise. She wanted to shoot again, though only at a suit. The idea of shooting a flesh and blood man was . . . well, it was unthinkable.

"That's enough for now." Nana eased herself back against her pillows and tried to blow the dirty, odorous black smoke away. "The years have claimed my body, but not my mind. That's the curse of old age. Seville and your grandfather are long gone." Nana turned her face away.

Aurelia packed the gun in its case, closed the lid, and placed it on the nightstand so Nana could see it. Maybe it would help her dream about Grampa and the wild life they had had together.

"Do you want me to fluff your pillows, Nana? Or get you a glass of sherry?"

Nana's eyes were misty when she turned to answer. "I have everything I'll ever need in this life. Now, come and sit with me one more minute. I'm extracting a promise from you now, child. I give you the buckles and the gun. You give me your word you'll go to college. No, no, no." Nana raised her hand as though warding off a protest. "Don't give me that nonsense about education ruining a good woman. The only thing that can ruin a good woman is a bad man.

"You go to school. Medical school. Oh, I tell you, child, for a woman the worst part of being doctored is having to submit to the hands of a man. It's humiliating. Even for me."

Medical school! Aurelia's eyes widened in disbelief, and alarm. Nana might as well have told her to fly to the moon.

Nana inhaled with visible effort. "I thought of being a doctor myself once, but . . . well, it wasn't in the cards. Your parents won't approve, I'm afraid, though I do believe you'd make a fine doctor. I see how you're always playing with little bottles and how you shadow the doctor whenever he comes to tend your mother, though all she needs is something besides shopping to keep her busy. Your needlework shows promise too. You'd make a good surgeon."

Anxiety squeezed Aurelia's throat. "But all that ugliness. All that blood. I don't think I can, Nana."

"Hogwash! Of course you can. Look at all you do for me. Besides, you're bright. You were reciting your tables when you were ten years old. I know you've been reading your father's newspapers. Oh, you'd make a fine doctor. Makes me proud of you just to think about it."

Aurelia never thought she'd be forced to step beyond the horizon of her home, but such a thought presumed that marriage and family were in her future. Apparently, Nana thought otherwise.

"Goes without saying, you'll have a hard time finding a man who doesn't fear an educated woman. I was a Vassar girl, believe it or not. I didn't find your grandfather till I was nearly thirty, but he was worth the search, God rest his soul. But better an educated, independent spinster than an ignorant, feudal wife."

A spinster? Is that what Nana thought Aurelia would become?

"Look at your mother. Another biological mystery." Nana let her head sink into the pillow. "*You* should have been my daughter, not that squeamish female. She wouldn't even touch the gun, much less fire it." She rolled her eyes in frustration. "Now, back to business. Are you prepared to strike the bargain?"

Fighting her rising panic inside, Aurelia said, "No, Nana, wait. What about the fish and the hook? I thought you said I'd want to catch a man one day."

"You're not following my train here, child. I know you'll *want* to get a man. That's all I ever hear girls talk about. What I'm saying is unless you get yourself a good one—one who can provide for you, one who wants what's best for you—you're better off on your own. And even if you do manage to get a good one, well, chances are he'll die on you. Look at your Grampa." She reached for Aurelia's hand and curled her bony fingers around it. "Don't you see, child. You're going to wind up alone. We all are. You've got to be prepared."

Aurelia tried to make sense of Nana's logic, but her conclusion was the same. She was destined to wind up alone. So when Nana asked again if Aurelia was prepared to "strike the bargain," Aurelia saw no alternative. Even to her own ears, she sounded small and unsure as she said, "Yes, Nana."

Later that night Aurelia found a hiding place for

both her magic buckles and her gun. It wouldn't do to parade them as one would an Easter bonnet. That's what Nana had told her. Most surprising of all, Aurelia discovered she liked the idea of becoming a doctor. She liked knowing her little ministrations made Nana feel better. Maybe someday she could even save somebody's grampa, as long as it didn't involve surgery. She detested needlework.

It was several days later when Nana told Aurelia to bring her little sister, Violet, to see her. Everyone always wanted to see Violet, to stare at Violet, to touch Violet. She had a pale pink complexion, a tiny Cupid's bow mouth, deep purple-blue eyes, and long, shiny hair as black as a stormy sky.

Aurelia often heard her father bemoan the trouble the child's beauty would bring him when she grew up. But right now she was only seven, and she absolutely refused to step into that horrid sick room where everything smelled funny, especially Nana. And she certainly wasn't going to touch Nana's bony hand or kiss her wrinkly cheek. Only when Aurelia confided that Nana had a present for her did Violet agree to visit her grandmother.

Aurelia held Violet's hand as Nana Brooke slipped the third parcel from under her pillow. She twisted the lid of the silver snuff box and, with great ceremony, removed a gold wedding band. She held it up. The afternoon sunlight struck the ring at just the right angle, shooting a burst of light across the room.

Aurelia had never seen anything more beautiful. She watched Nana's eyes brighten as she presented the ring to Violet, who promptly offered it to Aurelia.

"You can wear it first, sister. I have lots of others, and I don't think this one's as pretty as my opal."

Aurelia cupped the intricately carved band in her hand. Engraved orange blossoms circled the outside. The faint image of her grandmother's initials branded the inner rim: LMB. Lucy Maud Brooke. Aurelia wished Nana had given the gold ring to her and the silver buckles to Violet, but everyone always gave Violet the prettiest things.

Maybe it was because Violet was born the year Poppa had finally made it big in the cuff-and-collar business and the family had moved to one of Detroit's handsomest houses. Poppa had bought a fine new carriage and matching black mares. He'd said that from then on his family would have meat for dinner every day, and that in no time at all they'd be hobnobbing with the right people. He'd brought Momma flowers every week for the two months she was confined, and the day Violet was finally born he brought the biggest bunch of flowers Aurelia had ever seen. Violet was cause for celebration. It wasn't her fault; that was just how it was.

Aurelia touched the ring longingly before she gave it back to her sister. "You keep it. Nana wants you to have it."

Nana frowned, as though she expected a greater show of gratitude from Violet. "The ring is magic. Take care of it and it will bring you love. Abuse it and it will destroy you."

Violet nodded and stuck the ring on her thumb. "It's pretty, Nana. Are you going to give me anything else?"

"You won't need anything else." Nana's look was stern.

Violet pouted, then turned and skipped from the room.

"I don't think Violet understands, Nana."

"Do you?"

"If she does something bad with the ring, she'll get in terrible trouble."

"That's right."

Aurelia couldn't bear the thought. It seemed she'd been caring for Violet since the day she was born, though Aurelia was only eight at the time. Momma had always been too sick. She always took a lot of medicine, but it only made her sleepy. So Aurelia had always taken care of Violet.

Aurelia firmed her resolve. "Then I'll make sure Violet doesn't do anything bad. And if she does, I'll protect her."

"You can't do that, child. She'll never learn life's lessons if you don't let her make her own mistakes. You hover over her too much as it is. You're not her mother, though Lord knows, *she* doesn't take the duty seriously herself."

Aurelia thought about what Nana had said, but Violet was the family treasure and worth cherishing. Everyone said so. Even at the expense of her own goals, Aurelia knew she would always hover over her little sister, always protect her, for Violet was to be spared the ugliness of life. Everyone said so.

It all seemed so long ago. Nana and her treasure chest.

Years later Aurelia won a hard-fought argument to attend college, while Violet remained at home. To their parents' dismay, Aurelia read newspapers and studied pharmacology, obstetrics, and surgery. To their delight, Violet played the organ, fashioned shell wreathes and needlepoint pillows, and dabbled in watercolors.

For years, Aurelia kept the silver buckles hidden in her room. She firmly fastened them to her boots when she left her home in Detroit for Philadelphia and the Women's Medical College of Pennsylvania. Now and then she'd lift her dowdy brown skirts, chosen for their practicality, and let the light strike the tempered metal. She took the gun out many times, just to feel its weight in her hand, to practice the rhythm of cocking and firing. She never loaded it until the night she packed for the Klondike.

Violet wore the wedding ring with the other jewelry she'd collected over her sixteen years. It was on her finger the day she disgraced the family and ran away with Fletcher Sculley, that "no-account drifter," according to her father.

Mr. Breighton absorbed himself in his work. His wife turned again and again to her opium-based tonic. After sixteen years, the family had grown accustomed to their financial stability and respectable place in society. Violet's shame threatened their respectability, and that threatened their security. They refused to consider hiring a Pinkerton to bring Violet back. If she could so selfishly turn her back on her family, let her go.

Aurelia took a leave from her studies and, against her parents' wishes, set out for the Klondike. She prayed Violet hadn't abused Nana's ring.

3

Clay Guardian downed another bicarbonate of soda. He set the empty glass on the dresser, on one of those frilly doilies Aunt Liza insisted on scattering about. He was careful not to bump her vase of fresh tulips or her stained glass lamp. His shoes and trousers lay in a heap on the flowered carpet next to the bed. God, he felt awful. He knew better than to drown his troubles in whiskey. He hadn't done anything that stupid in years. Tomorrow morning he'd take care of the damage at the restaurant and apologize to Miss Breighton.

Miss Breighton. Was she really as pretty as he remembered? She was headstrong, and opinionated. But a handsome woman just the same.

His fingers fumbled with the buttons of his shirt. He was about to add it to the pile on the floor when he remembered the ring. He fished inside the pocket for the gold band. Ahh, those beautiful orange blossoms.

The pompous maitre d' had been right. Clay Guardian wasn't anybody anymore. He didn't have his prestigious job at the Seattle Bank and Trust. He didn't have his sterling reputation. He didn't even have his own home. But he had his son, and he had the ring. The symbol of his undoing. The golden joke.

He squinted to see the well-worn initials on the inside of the wedding band: LMB, no V. The ring was probably stolen too.

Clay turned back the pink, ruffled spread and fell into bed. Even if he spent the rest of his life trying, he'd find the con artist, Fletcher Sculley, and his wide-eyed shill, Violet. And when he did, he'd crush them both with the heel of his boot.

Sore jaw or not, Aurelia wanted breakfast. As she dressed and made her way downstairs, she mentally reviewed her list of things to do: post a letter to her parents letting them know she had everything under control, pack her belongings, and read the newspaper for the latest Klondike information. Tomorrow she'd sail on the *Reliance*.

In two or three months, four at the most, she'd be back in Detroit with Violet safe in tow. Then she'd go back to school. Mr. Guardian would be nothing but a memory, their carriage ride the seed for dreams, just as it should be.

Aurelia chose a table by the window. While she waited to be served, she watched the activity outside, so very similar to that of the day before and the day before that. One enthusiast mushed by with four mongrel dogs pulling a child's red wagon. A sign on the wagon said the highly trained Klondike team as well as the genuine Klondike wagon were for sale.

"Pathetic, ain't it?" the waitress said as she poured the steaming tea Aurelia had ordered. "Folks don't dare put their pets on the loose. First time in a decade the leash law gets obeyed."

Aurelia made a commiserating sound as she turned to the window again. Competing for precious dollars were the Klondike Outfitters, the Klondike Hotel, the Klondike Drug Store, the Klondike Barber Shop. Even the signs encouraged the frenzy.

She wasn't surprised. Like everyone else in the country, she'd heard the story about the sixty-eight miners who'd arrived in Seattle on the steamer *Portland* last July, each one bringing down a fortune, some having five thousand dollars in gold, some more, and even a few with a hundred thousand each.

Knowing Violet and Sculley had joined the stampede, Aurelia had read the vivid newspaper account with more than average interest. Caught up in the reporter's descriptions, she pictured the men making their way down the gangplank. Ragged and unkempt, sweat pouring down their bearded faces, the suntanned prospectors hunched over as they struggled to balance the weight of gold stacked high on their shoulders. They'd poured it in leather pouches, packed it in tin cans, and wrapped it in threadbare blankets. Thousands of people crowded the docks to witness the event, to see for themselves the unbelievable hoard of gold. Face to face with the prospectors, their eyes bright with the light of triumph, the crowds were suddenly seized with Klondike fever. Within forty-eight hours Seattle was a bedlam. The fever had the power of a plague. It infected Fletcher Sculley, and he infected Violet.

"Mind if I join you?"

Startled, she turned from the window. "Mr. Guardian!" The unexpected pleasure caused her cheeks to redden.

"May I?"

He took a seat when Aurelia nodded and signaled for a cup of coffee. "Pleased to see you're feeling better. You are, aren't you? Feeling better?" He sounded hopeful, though he winced at the sight of her jaw.

"I am, thank you." Amazing. A shave and a clean suit of clothes could do wonders for a man. "You've benefited from a good night's sleep as well," she said.

He shifted his weight in the chair, apparently embarrassed by her comment. Breakfast and coffee arrived together. Clay inhaled the strong aroma before he drank. "I'll get right to the point. I'm not what you'd call a temperate man, but I'm not a drunk either. Last night, well, last night was a mistake. I know I've already apologized to you—probably made a fool of myself doing it—but I wanted to tell you again, today, when I thought the chances were better that you'd believe me."

"It was an accident, Mr. Guardian. I'd feel less conspicuous if we didn't discuss it further."

Clay ran his finger between his neck and the high, starched collar of his white shirt. Though he looked proper and professional in his dark suit, Aurelia pictured him in leather and boots, a sheriff or a cowboy or an outlaw from a Western novel. Maybe it was his hair, slightly longer than the cut in fashion. She liked it. Even more, she liked his clean-shaven face and the absence of that horrid, droopy walrus moustache so many men had chosen to cultivate. She nibbled her toast and played with the eggs on the plate in front of her, her appetite suddenly gone.

Clay folded his napkin and laid it on the table. "Yesterday you said you were going to the Klondike to get your sister. I'll bet that makes you the only one in this town not going for gold. Everyone wants to find The Yellow."

"No, Mr. Guardian. Not everyone. There are some things more important than gold. Sisterly love. Family honor." Forgiveness, she added silently. "My sister is sixteen years old, innocent, and dangerously naive. Last summer a no-account drifter lured her away from the safety of our family home." Aurelia felt her throat squeeze with anxiety the way it always did when she remembered. She swallowed hard and regained her composure. "She wrote only a few times, but I can tell from her letters that she's in danger from this man. And then her letters stopped coming. I got the last one about five months ago."

"You know where she is now?"

"If I knew for sure, I'd have sent her the money to come home. I know she traveled from Seattle to Skagway, then to Dyea where she crossed something called the Chilkoot Pass. From there, I'm not sure, but her letters mentioned the likelihood of going to the town of Dawson. I think that's where she is. My sister has no means of escape. I intend to find her." Unbidden tears welled in Aurelia's eyes. "Poor Violet. I realize how shallow this may sound, but she hadn't even been presented yet, and that's all she ever talked about."

"Violet? Your sister's name is Violet?"

"Yes. Violet Breighton. Perhaps you've seen her. I have a Kodak of her taken a few months before she met that lecherous Fletcher Sculley." She retrieved the photo from her reticule and handed it to Clay. "Isn't she lovely? So beautiful. So full of life." She looked at him. "Mr. Guardian? Are you all right?"

Clay braced his hands on the table. His knuckles whitened as he pressed his fingertips into the red-

and-white-checkered cloth. Aurelia at first interpreted his reaction as righteous indignation that one of his own sex would deliberately take advantage of such an innocent as Violet. In his eyes flashed another emotion, however, one that Aurelia glimpsed for only a second: suspicion. But then, Aurelia had taken advantage of Violet too, had abused her little sister's trust. Violet might be safe now if Aurelia hadn't . . .

"Please don't stare at me that way, Mr. Guardian. If you have something to say, speak up." Why was this man looking at her as though she'd just fleeced the widows' and orphans' fund?

"I'm going to gamble on your strength, Miss Breighton."

"My strength? That sounds ominous."

He nodded as he slipped his hand to the breast pocket of his suit jacket. "Have you ever seen this ring?" He held the gold band between his thumb and middle finger.

"That's Nana's ring! Let me see that." Even before she took it from him, Aurelia recognized the engraved orange blossoms. Her hand trembled as she tilted the ring to view the carved initials on the inside. Her voice cracked. "Lucy Maud Brooke. My grandmother."

She fisted her hand around the ring and held it to her heart. "This was Nana's legacy to Violet. How did you get it?"

"I'm a loan officer at the Seattle Bank and Trust. Your sister and her friend came to me looking for money, offered her jewelry as collateral. When they disappeared, I acquired the ring from the bank. The ring belongs to me."

"They disappeared? Without repaying the loan?"

Clay simply nodded, as though he didn't want to elaborate.

"I see," Aurelia said as she returned the wedding band to its new owner. She didn't doubt the truth of his words. Violet never attached sentiment to a mere object, especially if the object had monetary value. Violet had mentioned in the letters that she had sold the sapphire brooch her parents had given her on her thirteenth birthday, as well as the jeweled butterfly hairpin. But to sell Nana's legacy? *Oh, Violet, what have you done?*

"Then you *have* seen my sister. The details, please. Whatever you can tell me."

Clay returned the ring to his pocket. "Yes, I've seen your sister. I couldn't forget her. Didn't care for the man she was with. Not at all. Talked like a politician. Confident. Smooth. I got the feeling he was the one who wanted the loan, but he didn't have any collateral. Your sister, on the other hand, had jewelry. Normally, the bank doesn't make loans to women, particularly young, unmarried women."

"Then why did you?"

"Well, let's just say I was persuaded."

Aurelia nodded. "You don't need to explain. I know how convincing my sister can be. Still, I wish you'd talked with her long enough to realize she was merely Sculley's pawn. Then perhaps you wouldn't have loaned her the funds and she wouldn't have left Seattle."

"There are other banks in Seattle."

"You're right, of course. I suppose if you'd turned her down, she'd simply have been forced to go elsewhere."

Clay looked askance. "Forced? Your sister seemed to know what she was doing."

"How could she! She's an innocent child! And *you* have her ring."

"Hold on there. Don't look at me that way. If I were guilty of anything, would I be telling you all this?"

She didn't like the way he stared at her, so intently, so suspiciously. If anyone's motive was worthy of doubt, it was Mr. Guardian's. Before she could say a word, he continued.

"I like to think I'm a good judge of character. I know the look of despair when I see it. These past five years that's about all I've seen. It can make a man—or a woman—resort to things they'd never consider otherwise. Much as I hate to say it, despite her airs and her fancy dress, despair surrounded your sister like a Seattle fog. Or maybe she was just eager to get to the gold fields."

Aurelia felt the battle between fear and courage rage inside her. Her imagination conjured up all sorts of scenarios. "And all because of Fletcher Sculley. He's a base and fearless man, that Sculley." Ruing the day that she led Violet to Fletcher Sculley, Aurelia resolved anew to free her sister. "The *Reliance* sails tomorrow, none too soon."

She took the last sip of her tea and dabbed the corners of her mouth with her mangled napkin. "That ring is a family heirloom. You can understand why I want it back. Unfortunately, I've already spent more on supplies than I'd planned. If you'll hold the ring in safekeeping for me until then—two months, three at the most—I'll pay you whatever you think fair."

"Sounds reasonable, but if the ring is so important, wouldn't your family wire you the funds for it?"

"One would think so. But you see, my parents were both so upset at Violet's actions. No, they weren't upset. They were mortified. No, they wouldn't be willing to wire funds for the ring or for anything else related to Violet's rescue. If it weren't for an inheritance from my grandmother, I don't know how I'd have gotten here myself."

Though she ached inside at the thought of Violet so troubled and lonely, Aurelia felt she'd made more progress in a few minutes than she'd made in months. "You can trust me. I will redeem the ring."

He gave her a crooked smile. "Don't you worry about the ring. You've got enough things on your mind. Somehow I just know you're going to find your sister."

He seemed so moved by her plight and his words were so reassuring. He was so calm and confident— the perfect bedside manner. Because she couldn't diagnose her own sudden discomfort, she grabbed her reticule from the table, eager to leave. "As soon as I return from the Klondike, I'll contact you at the Seattle Bank and Trust and—"

"No." He raked his hand through his dark hair and quickly scanned the room. "I never mix my personal and professional life. Let me give you my home address." He took a fountain pen and a slip of paper from his pocket and wrote down the information. "Here you go. My Aunt Liza lives with me and my boy. If I'm not there, she'll know where to find me."

Aurelia took the slip of paper and tucked it in her bag. "You're not married?" She surprised herself at the boldness of her question. She wanted to ask him last night, but she couldn't think straight last night. Her thoughts were beginning to cloud even now.

"Widower."

"I'm so sorry."

"It's been over five years. Mary died bringing Eli into the world. A life for a life."

Aurelia knew the scenario. Hemorrhage maybe, or puerperal fever. Blood poisoning from lack of sterile technique at the time of delivery. It was typical, horribly painful, and always fatal.

"Great progress is being made in the science of medicine. I'm only sorry it didn't come soon enough to save your wife." She berated herself for the fleeting thought that now he could marry again. It would be better that she left now, before her romantic delusions pained her the way they always did. "My thanks again, Mr. Guardian. You've been so helpful. I have a thousand things to do today, of course. The steamer sails tomorrow." She said good-bye and departed.

Back in her room, Aurelia rejoiced in the knowledge that she was indeed on the right trail. Mr. Guardian was such an honorable man, loaning Violet money, concerning himself with her welfare. How fortunate that both Violet and Aurelia had met him. She wondered if Mr. Guardian felt the same.

A breakthrough at last. Clay dodged the early morning traffic of buyers and sellers and hurried on foot back to the center of town. More than a dozen men were already lined up at the front of the Northern Pacific ticket window when he arrived, but the line was moving fast. He crossed his arms and drummed his fingers while he waited his turn. Preliminary details of his plan took hold.

She was sailing on the *Reliance*, getting off in Dyea. She and Violet would rendezvous in Dawson, either because that was where the dauntless lady doctor would rescue her helpless sister, or because that was where the two of them—no, the three of them— planned to divide the spoils of the Seattle Bank and Trust. This whole lost-sister routine might have been nothing but a ruse to get her through Canadian customs without the usual stampeder's equipment.

Or, he reconsidered, she could be telling the truth, and

she didn't know her sister's full range of "talents." Either way, he needed her to lead him to Violet and Sculley.

Either way, she'd never make it to Dawson on her own. She'd need a man. She'd need *him,* he amended. He'd see to it. Perhaps his luck had finally changed.

Thinking that Aurelia had probably deceived him with her tale of woe made it easier for Clay to accept the fact that he, too, had lied, if only by omission of the details that had cost him everything. He tapped his fingers on his breast pocket and felt the impression of the ring.

A few moments later he was standing at the Northern Pacific window. "Well?" the clerk asked impatiently.

"Dyea. One way. On the *Reliance.*"

"She sails tomorrow. All I've got open is one first-class. Thirty-five dollars."

This was the second time he'd been robbed, Clay thought as he slid the bills under the opening in the glass window.

"Another ticket to paradise," the clerk droned as he exchanged the cash for the sailing voucher.

"No doubt about it," Clay said.

Clay still had a few friends in Seattle, people who believed his story about the missing cash and bonds and would lend him money for supplies. He called on them early.

He spent the afternoon purchasing all he could and arranging for the supplies to be delivered to the ship. He bought the entire stampeder's package, gold pan and all. What better cover for a man headed for the Klondike? He didn't have enough to buy all the food he'd need, but he had a plan.

Exhausted by the end of the day, he'd accomplished what took most people at least a week. He headed for

Aunt Liza's grand gingerbread-trimmed house. The hardest job still lay ahead. He had to tell Eli.

Clay shifted his weight in the rocking chair to make his son more comfortable. At five years old, Eli didn't weigh more than a half-filled sack of oats, but even fifty pounds felt like a lot when it wiggled.

"Tell me again, Daddy. Tell me where you're goin'."

"The Klondike. I'm going to find gold, remember? Let me see if I can draw you a picture."

Being careful not to disturb any of Aunt Liza's fine bric-a-brac, Clay took a newspaper and pencil from the table next to the chair. With Eli curled up in his lap, Clay spread the paper across his knees. He made a dot. "This is Seattle. And this"—he drew a wavy line halfway up the paper—"is the Inside Passage. Lots of little islands and big rocks. This is the route the ship will take to Dyea." He made another dot. "I'll get off the ship there. So will hundreds of other stampeders. We'll all hike over these mountains, cross the border into Canada, and then go down this river. It's called the Yukon River." He made a long, snakey line. "To . . . hmm, I guess right about here." Another dot. "This whole place is called the Klondike. That's where the gold is. Nuggets as big as your fist, just waiting to be picked up. This is Dawson. That's where I'll mail my letters to you and Aunt Liza."

He stroked his son's hair, fine as new cornsilk and just as pale. Just like Eli's mother's. Aurelia's was thicker and warmer, more like honey. Why was he thinking of Aurelia now? "That's where you can send your letters to me, too. Aunt Liza will help you write them. How's that?"

"Are you going to be back for my birthday?"

Clay refolded the newspaper and returned it to the table. He remembered all he'd sacrificed for Eli when the boy's mother died. He remembered feeling helpless. He remembered feeling guilty that if he hadn't gotten her in the family way, she'd be alive today. Most of all, he remembered feeling lonely. He still felt lonely. He hadn't deprived himself of female companionship in all these years, but he wasn't sure he could ever find anyone to replace his loving wife.

Eli had been the center of Clay's life. It broke Clay's heart to think of leaving the boy now, but he couldn't see any other choice. He'd tried finding work at one of the other banks. Hell, he'd tried to hire out as a store clerk, a carpenter, a cook, but no one would hire him. He had been ready to take Eli and move, until he met Miss Breighton. As long as he played his cards right, he'd get back everything he'd lost.

"Are you, Daddy? Are you going to be back for my birthday?"

Clay folded his strong arms around his son and drew him close. The clean smell of soap and shampoo and a sun-dried nightshirt reminded him of so many other nights when he'd tucked the boy in. Sometimes he'd just stand at the bedroom door, watch his son fall asleep, and wonder how he'd ever manage to raise him alone.

Now, he just rocked, ever so slowly, hearing the familiar squeak each time the curved slat touched the wooden floor. "No, partner," he finally said. "I won't be back for your birthday. But I'll be thinking about you." He kissed the boy's forehead. "I'll bet Aunt Liza will have Miss Sophie fix you a grand old cake, chocolate maybe, and when you blow out those five candles—"

"Six candles. I'm gonna be six. I was five last time, remember?"

"Six!" Clay feigned surprise. "Well, I'll be. You're practically a grown man."

Eli sat up straight, and pressed his tiny palms to Clay's cheeks. "Then I can go with you now?"

Clay shook his head. "No, son, you can't."

Just then Aunt Liza, a white-haired, wiry old woman, entered the parlor. She fussed with the photos on the piano and the pictures hanging from their long wires. "You don't want to go off and leave your old Aunt Liza now, do you? You just moved into my house. I haven't had a chance to teach you your letters yet or show you how to cipher. I taught your father, you know. And that was out on that godforsaken place in Kansas."

Clay couldn't resist smiling at her. Yes, she had taught him almost everything, certainly all he needed to survive.

"Who would help me at the market? Who would wind up the cuckoo clock? And who'd lick the bowl when Miss Sophie made her butter cookies?" She fluffed the pillows on the velvet divan, the way she always did when she was fixing to say what was really bothering her.

"But who's gonna take care of my daddy?"

Clay tightened his arms around his son, vowing to become the kind of man the boy needed as a father. "I'll be fine. Promise."

"No need to concern yourself about your daddy, young man," Liza added. "I've seen him break a wild horse and shoot a root beer bottle from a hundred feet. And I know for a fact he can cook up a tasty pot of beans. I taught him. He'll fair far better than most up there. You needn't worry." Aunt Liza reached to take Eli, but the boy squeezed his eyes shut and clung to his father.

"He's all right, Liza. We're just going to rock a little while longer, aren't we, partner?"

"It's after eight o'clock, you know. The boy shouldn't be up so late, and you have a ship to catch tomorrow."

She walked to the far end of the room, then turned back and burst out, "Suddenly you're a stampeder? I know you better, Clayton Ulysses Guardian. There's something else afoot here. You've no need to go traipsing off like a lemming. You've got a boy who needs you right here."

"I know," he whispered, still rocking, never once breaking the rhythm. "I know."

Clay continued to rock, an hour after Eli had fallen asleep against his chest.

Everyone wanted to get on a boat headed north. Only a year ago they had called Seattle's deserted docks the boneyards. Now the docks hummed from sunup to sundown. Rain or shine, the work continued, with at least one boat leaving Seattle every hour.

It poured all morning and drizzled through the afternoon and into the evening. But the early March cold couldn't dampen the spirits of the stampeders, shivering as they boarded the ship, and crying, "Alaska or bust!"

The passengers scrambled up and down ladders and stairs, getting their bearings, looking for their quarters. The steward told Aurelia she was one of only four women on board as he led her down the central passageway to the sleeping room that she and one of the other women would share. The men in first class, she understood, had been grouped in rooms for six.

With the bulk of her belongings stowed in the cargo hold, Aurelia had only her smaller trunk sent to the room and placed at the foot of one of the two sets of bunks.

Sharing the adjacent cabin to the left were a minister's wife, traveling to meet her husband, and a stenographer, traveling with her father, who was a surveyor from a Western mining party. To the right was one of the few fully appointed toilets. Aurelia's roommate was a widow, Lily L'Auberge, traveling with her brother.

Just as Aurelia and her roommate were introducing themselves, the steward came by with instructions for all passengers to disembark immediately and assemble on the dock. A government inspection officer needed to obtain an accurate count of the number on board, as overloading on ships bound for the Alaskan coast had become a common, though dangerous, practice.

"Good gracious," the widow said to Aurelia as they retraced their steps. "It will be nine o'clock before we have dinner."

Huddled under the domes of black umbrellas and pastel parasols, hundreds of well-wishers milled about the dock, waiting to bid a bon voyage to their friends and families on the *Reliance.* Aurelia and her roommate lined up at the edge of the dock, where they could hear the jokes and nervous laughter of those departing and those left behind.

"It's taking you all day just to get out of Seattle!"

"You think she's going to sink?"

"Hope you've made your will."

"Bailing out now?"

"I hear drowning's a piece of cake compared to all that can kill you in the Yukon!"

As the line moved toward the gangplank to re-board after the count, the widow said, "Will you look at that boy toward the head of the line? He looks like a stringbean. And a scrawny one at that."

Aurelia followed her gaze to the young supply clerk from the Cooper and Levy pioneer outfitters. She wondered what had made him decide on the Klondike instead of Cuba.

"And did you happen to catch a glimpse of that rather good-looking man toward the end of the line?" Mrs. L'Auberge whispered as she turned her head slightly to direct Aurelia's attention. "The tall one with the broad shoulders. It's too dark to see his face, but even if it does not equal his physique, he still presents quite an appealing image, don't you agree?"

Aurelia was amazed to hear a seemingly refined widow talk so frankly about a man's physique. Nevertheless, she could not help but look. A tiny breath caught in her throat when she saw the man in question. Clay Guardian! What was he doing traveling aboard the *Reliance*?

"Keep moving, miss." The crewman's directive startled Aurelia, for in staring at Mr. Guardian she had slowed the line of boarding passengers.

When they reached the edge of the gangplank, Aurelia noticed the fortyish widow lift her skirts several inches more than necessary as she took the hand of the crewman and stepped onto the deck. Aurelia thought she even saw her wink at the young man.

"Well?" The widow L'Auberge said as Aurelia stepped unaided to the deck. "Did you catch a glimpse of him?"

"Yes, I did."

"He could certainly bring a little heaven into a woman's life. Or her bed. Wouldn't you agree?"

"Mrs. L'Auberge!"

"Oh, dear," the widow said in a tone that made light

of Aurelia's concern. "I've offended you. From our admittedly brief cabin conversation, I assumed you to be an educated and therefore more worldly woman."

"I'm not offended. I just don't think the open deck of a ship is the place to discuss something so personal."

Two of Aurelia's classmates thought that a man was for pleasure and for procreating, but that otherwise a woman was better off alone. With no frame of reference, Aurelia never knew whether to agree of disagree. One thing was certain, however, she enjoyed hearing her classmates talk about gardens awash in moonlight and men who kissed with their tongues—naked, virile men who had hot blood in their veins instead of formaldehyde.

Once they were inside their cabin, Mrs. L'Auberge hung her coat and immediately began to remove her traveling suit. "I've certainly seen better-appointed ships than this tub."

"I don't know that the fancier lines would get us to Alaska any faster."

"Yes, dear. Well, I understand from the captain that we're the most eligible women on board. I assume he'll invite us to dine at his table this evening."

"How nice."

Half dressed as she was, Mrs. L'Auberge began rummaging through the largest of the three trunks she had brought to the room. With casual abandon, she tossed aside elegant gowns of burgundy and teal silk, frothy white petticoats sprayed with lace, and ruffled taffeta drop-skirts. She littered her own bunk as well as those that remained unoccupied.

Aurelia thought of the sweet, pastel gowns she'd worn for her coming out parties. There was no comparison. Unlike Violet, Aurelia had never really cared a great deal about her wardrobe. That the garments be serviceable was always her prime requirement. But maybe if she'd had a dress like one of these, the young men would have noticed her.

"Oh, here it is!" Aurelia's roommate cried. In grand-finale fashion she lifted from the trunk the most delicious peacock-blue silk gown Aurelia had ever seen. Holding it against her body, she spoke with a confidence Aurelia envied. "I'll have every man's attention—even if it's just for a moment."

Indeed, Aurelia admitted to herself, Mrs. L'Auberge's proportions appeared close to the ideal of the day, thirty-six–twenty-two–forty. She would no doubt do justice to the gown. "It's lovely, Mrs. L'Auberge," Aurelia said, fighting the image that suddenly appeared of the widow and Clay Guardian.

"Please, dear, we're going to be roommates for nearly a week. Call me Lily. You're Aurelia, yes?"

Aurelia nodded as she watched Lily carelessly toss the gown on the bunk, letting it slip off the edge and fall to the floor. Resisting the urge to scoop it up, Aurelia turned her attention to her own bed, straightening the blankets, plumping the pillows, and questioning her earlier decision to wear the same brown wool shirtwaist she'd worn all day. Behind her she could hear the rustle of the taffeta underskirt.

"Dear, can you help me with my corset? This dress requires an eighteen-inch waist. My maid quit rather than accompany me to the Yukon, or the Klondike, or Alaska, or wherever it is we're going. I can't tighten this by myself."

"Contorting the body this way is unhealthy at best, dangerous at worst," Aurelia said, even as she pulled the woman's waist into the required measurement.

"Anything for fashion," Lily said. "Don't tell me those graceful curves of yours are natural?"

Graceful curves?

"You *are* corseted, are you not?"

"Of course," Aurelia replied, still in awe that a woman as glamorous as Lily thought she had graceful curves. "Though I refuse to distort the placement of vital organs."

"A friend of mine had her lower two ribs removed so she could achieve a sixteen-inch waist." Lily laughed. "Even I think that an extreme measure."

"Indeed," Aurelia added as she buttoned the back of the gown.

Lily displayed her white-kid evening slippers with their tottering French heels and pointed toes and her white silk stockings with their lace inserts at the instep.

"I'd be happy to reciprocate the effort, dear, if you'd like. You are going to change for dinner, aren't you?"

"No. I can't. I mean I understood that to save space I was to bring only my smallest trunk to the cabin. I didn't think I needed a change of clothing."

The widow wrinkled her nose and shrugged her shoulders. "That rule doesn't apply to ladies. You're welcome to wear one of my gowns. I believe we're about the same size, or perhaps you're a bit larger on top and smaller on bottom."

"No, thank you," Aurelia said quickly.

"And what about that divinely handsome man we saw earlier? Don't you want to impress him?"

"Not particularly. Why should I?"

The widow dabbed a bit of rouge to her lips. "Because I can tell he's the type of man who appreciates our fair sex. I, for one, wouldn't mind being 'appreciated' by such a man." She licked her lips as she looked at her image in her compact. "But fair is fair. And standing outside in the rain tonight, I couldn't help but notice how often he looked at you, craning his neck to see where you stood in line."

"At me?"

"Yes. At you. I hope your indifference to our Mr. X means you won't mind if I arrange for the captain to introduce me to him. At least the man wasn't dressed as drably as these other goldseekers, but even if he were, it wouldn't matter. I'm not interested in him clothed."

"Surely, you don't mean that the way it sounded."

"Oh, Aurelia, dear girl. Life is simply too short to take oneself so seriously. Never knowing what fate has in store for us should make us eager to squeeze the most out of every single day, not get caught up in what's proper and what's not. Don't wait to learn it the hard way."

Lily cupped the underside of her breasts, then slid her hands down, defining her waist. "Thoreau said it best. 'When it is time to die, let us not discover that we have never lived.' I, for one, intend to live." She emphasized the last word.

Lily winked at Aurelia as she draped a black-seal stole across her shoulders and swept from the room.

Alone in the cabin, Aurelia looked down at her brown wool dress and then at the silk gowns that were still strewn about the room.

How careless of that woman. Aurelia picked up the teal silk, shook it with the no-nonsense attitude of an attendant, and laid it across one of the empty bunks. Then she reached for the burgundy, but, instead of thrusting it away, she hugged the deep wine-colored fabric to her body, pressing its bodice and waist against her own. Violet had always said the color looked good on her. She looked around the cabin for a mirror, but there was none, not even a porthole whose glass might critique her efforts, and she didn't own a compact.

She closed her eyes and hummed a few bars of a waltz Violet had often played on the organ. Hovering on the edge of her fantasy waited Clay Guardian, smiling, offering his arm, then sweeping her across some distant ballroom floor. Had he really been looking for her on the dock?

Aurelia began to dance between the bunks of the cabin, but her steps were clumsy and without grace, and she soon felt like a fool.

The spell broken, she draped the burgundy gown on the bed next to its sister. Looking at it one last time, she straightened the skirt of her serviceable brown dress, tucked the rebellious wisps of her blond hair back in place, and threw her heaviest shawl over her shoulders. She wasn't the type of woman who could sashay and twirl in silk and high heels. She knew it, and Clay Guardian might as well know it too.

At the door of her cabin she stopped to pinch some color into her cheeks.

4

Hoping she'd see Mr. Guardian, and wondering what she'd do if she did, Aurelia braced herself and stepped into the crowded dining room. She was disarmed by the smiles and easy chatter of the men lined up before her with plates in hand. She glanced around the room. If the men weren't waiting for food or for an empty seat at one of the few tables, they were eating while standing. She was disappointed to see that Mr. Guardian wasn't among them.

Though the room was congested, Aurelia did spot the widow L'Auberge. Lily was sitting with the captain, who took his eyes off her only long enough to instruct one of the crewmen to escort Aurelia to his table.

"There you are, dear," Lily said. "I was just telling the captain here how impressed I am with his big boat."

The captain, Big Mike Kegman, grinned appreciatively as he half stood while Aurelia seated herself. "She's no floating hotel, but she's seaworthy. Half of 'em leaving Seattle can't claim that. You slide on over," he instructed Aurelia. "One of the crew will get you a plate."

The widow winked as Aurelia inched to the center

of the rough bench that was bolted to the floor. "It appears that you and I are the only two of our sex immune to seasickness this evening."

"I'm sorry to hear that," Aurelia replied. "Do either of them need medical attention?"

"Negative," the captain said. "Just need to get their sea legs. I'd give 'em a day or two. Besides, we got our own medical man on board." He beckoned to one of the crewmen who was standing nearby. The young boy rushed over. "Fetch the lady here some grub."

Aurelia realized the captain was one of those men who expected all doctors to have whiskers. For Lily's sake, she decided not to challenge the captain's prejudice.

In a matter of minutes the lad returned with a generous amount of the evening's fare and set it before her.

"Pack away all you can now," the captain said. "The sea won't always be as calm as she is tonight. And when the old *Reliance* here commences to pitch and roll, the landlubbers always lose their appetites."

Aurelia looked at the slice of boiled ham and the puddle of creamed corn on her plate and set her fork down.

"Miss Breighton, dear, I was just telling the captain how relieved I am to be away from that giant Klondike warehouse called Seattle. So monotonous. Now we have this lovely sailing vessel and tomorrow, I understand, our view will include spectacular mountains, great birds, and perhaps a whale or two. How astute of you, Captain, to have chosen a career that would afford you such benefits."

Mike Kegman melted with every flowery compliment the widow gave him. Aurelia could never bring herself to flirt so blatantly.

Aurelia nibbled on the corn bread while she listened to Lily sigh and tell the captain about the lonely life she led. Then Lily fluttered her eyelashes and managed a half smile. "Enough of my tale of woe. Tell me, Captain, what do you offer your passengers in the way of entertainment?"

"How's dancing?"

"I simply adore dancing! I remember my first cotillion and all the splendid balls that followed. Indeed, there are precious few activities more pleasurable than waltzing in the strong arms of a handsome man."

"Settled. Tomorrow evening I'll have the boys get their fiddles out and we'll kick up our heels. It's too late for tonight. Electric lights are snuffed at twenty-two hundred." The captain turned to Aurelia. "Them that likes to read can use the kerosene lanterns."

"Marvelous, Captain. Simply marvelous," Lily answered, placing her hand on the table, close enough for the captain to touch.

"How about I bring you?" He moved his own hand a little closer to hers.

"I'll look forward to it."

"Think you'll be wearing that fancy dress again?"

"This?" The widow reacted as though she would hardly consider the peacock silk fancy. "Perhaps."

Aurelia couldn't believe how quickly the widow's charms had affected the Captain. He had praised her attire, asked to escort her to the dance, and very nearly touched her in public. Any moment now he'd use the intimacy of her first name. Aurelia tried to remember exactly what Lily had done. Were all men as vulnerable to such extravagant adulation?

She wondered if she could ever employ Lily's technique successfully. Could she tilt her head just so and lower her eyes? Could she keep her laugh to a tiny titter? Not likely. In talking with men, Aurelia always found it easier to discuss the weather. Fortunately, the occasions that called for such brilliant conversation on her part had been few and far between.

Soon Lily's eyes began to wander, and Aurelia began to feel nervous.

"Looking for somebody, Mrs. L'Auberge?" the captain asked.

"Just my brother. I suppose he's at the card tables."

"Most of the men are. Not much else to do in the evenings. We've got a nickel-in-the-slot music box and a gambling device on the same plan for those willing to try their luck. The men keep both mighty busy. With you ladies on board, though, they'll be wanting to dance every night."

The captain spoke to Aurelia. "And you, Miss Breighton, you'll be coming to our cotillion tomorrow, won't you? We can't all dance with Lily here." He quickly turned to the widow. "My apologies, ma'am. Didn't mean to sound so familiar."

Lily smiled. "I don't think we need to be so formal, Michael. These plunges must be made at some time."

Aurelia was about to say that she had two left feet, when she saw Clay Guardian enter the room. Lily saw him too, and, though she'd just eaten a full meal, her eyes looked hungry.

Clay took his place in line. As he maneuvered his way to the far end of the room, Aurelia watched the warm, coffee-colored folds of his buckskin shirt pull across his shoulders and recalled the widow's words: "I'm not interested in him clothed."

"Yes, Captain, I'll be at the dance tomorrow night."

*   *   *

The sensation felt familiar. Aurelia's heart raced. Her palms sweated. If she were reliving the past, any moment now Professor Sternwell would hand out the soft, blue composition books for the final exam in physiology, and Aurelia would be straining to remember enough to get a passing mark. Instead, Captain Kegman signalled for the music to begin, and the ship's purser asked her to dance as he ushered her to the floor of the social hall.

With two fiddles, a banjo, a guitar, and a wheezy accordion, the lively melody of "Oh! Susannah" sent toes tapping everywhere. The band played the crowd-pleaser over and over again. Dozens of men danced alone or with each other, anything to release the tension that built with every knot the ship put between them and Seattle. Aurelia's sides were poked by flapping elbows, her feet stepped on by zealous hoofers, and her hands clutched by an assembly line of men waiting their turn.

Two agonizing hours later the captain announced the last dance, and the musicians did their best to play "Jeanie With the Light Brown Hair," the only slow number of the evening. Aurelia politely but firmly declined all offers as she made her way through the crowd.

She hadn't seen Clay Guardian all evening, but, considering the crowd of men on the floor and the way she was being whirled around, he could have been right there on the side of the deck and she might not have seen him. If she'd known he wasn't going to attend this soiree, she wouldn't have subjected herself to such torture. She certainly wouldn't have humbled herself and asked to wear Lily's burgundy gown.

The deep ruby silk floated from fanciful puffs on her shoulders down to her full breasts where the fabric draped in waves of tiny pleats, gathered in a wasp waist, then dropped down to the floor. If Aurelia never wore a dress as lovely as this again, at least she had for one night.

She slipped her handkerchief from the buttoned seam of her glove and lightly blotted her forehead. Open portholes on both sides of the room let in the cold night air, but the heat from all the activity was still oppressive. In a few more minutes the haunting Stephen Foster melody and the evening's ordeal would be over. She had survived.

"Miss Breighton?"

The resonant voice could belong to no other.

"Mr. Guardian, what a surprise. What are you doing aboard the *Reliance*?"

"Guess you could say I caught a bad case of Klondike fever. Opportunities to make a fortune don't come along every day."

"What about your employer? How did the bank feel about your sudden departure? More importantly, what about your son?"

"Oh, you might say we all came to an understanding."

"Of course," she said quickly, realizing she shouldn't have asked such personal questions. "Did you just come to the dance? You've missed several rousing renditions of 'Oh! Susannah.' " She silently cursed the perspiration that formed anew on her forehead.

"So I heard." He shifted his weight from leg to leg, as everyone did when the ship rolled. "May I have the rest of this dance?"

Aurelia froze. Palpitations weren't fatal, she

reminded herself. "Yes," she said with the same determination she'd expressed when she convinced herself she could withstand her first autopsy.

"Good," he said, leading her to the center of the deck. "Relax. You're as stiff as a fencepost."

Then, just as Clay pulled her ever so slightly toward him, the *Reliance* hit a swell. It was not enough to upset the equilibrium of the crew, but for Aurelia, the roll of the ship was enough to pitch her forward, into the enveloping arms of her partner.

She found his soap-and-water scent mixed with the aroma of buckskin strangely enticing. "Pardon me," she mumbled and pulled back just as the music stopped. Powerless to control her blush, she felt those dreaded red splotches rush to her cheeks.

Groping for control, Aurelia blurted out, "My, my, Mr. Guardian, how astute of you—" *How astute!* She stopped mid-sentence, her mouth open.

"Yes?"

She didn't know what to say next, and her poise threatened to dissolve entirely. "Do you think we're in for a storm?"

"I see all the signs."

"Do you think the cost of supplies will be higher in Alaska than in Seattle?"

"Couldn't say."

"You dance well. Did your mother teach you?"

"She tried."

Aurelia waited for him to elaborate, but he didn't. Why wasn't he helping her instead of staring at her as though she had warts? If he expected her to carry the entire burden of conversation, they might as well part company now, for she'd exhausted all the topics that had come to mind. She looked down at the deck and the myriad pairs of new and weathered boots that shuffled or skipped past her on their way back to their cabins. She decided to try again. "Your mother must be quite talented."

"She was." As he spoke, Clay led Aurelia to the far side of the room, allowing the crowd of passengers to pass, positioning his body to protect her from being jostled along the way. Aurelia knew it wouldn't look proper for her to stand there for any length of time and converse with Mr. Guardian. Lily wouldn't think twice about appearances, of course. She would tell Aurelia that life was too short to worry about something so trivial.

Lily. Aurelia had spotted her a few moments ago, draped on the arm of the captain, following him off the dance floor, leading him with her smile and her sashay.

A few more minutes wouldn't hurt. There had to be something they could talk about. "Your mother is deceased?"

"Yes."

"Cause of death?" Ugh! She sounded so clinical!

"She had some kind of fever."

"How unfortunate. Was there a doctor in attendance?"

"The nearest doctor was a day and a half's ride away for an able-bodied rider. Four days for a drunk. I was about seven. She'd been showing me the steps so I could waltz with her at the spring dance. She never made it past April."

Though his expression was fleeting, it was so forlorn that Aurelia wished she could do something to help. "I'm truly sorry," was all she managed to say.

She wanted to know more about Mr. Guardian,

but before she could ask, the ship began to roll. She braced herself against the rail this time.

"I'd better escort you to your cabin now," he said. "Queen Charlotte Sound. We're open to the swells of the Pacific here. Could get rough."

She nodded. Apparently he was less than dazzled by her conversational skills. Disappointed, she took his arm and let him lead her toward the sleeping quarters.

When they arrived at her cabin, he thanked her for the dance. Twice, he referred to the coincidence of their being on the same ship. Just after he said goodnight, he added, "If I haven't already mentioned it, you look beautiful this evening."

Behind her cabin door, Aurelia hugged herself as the sound of Mr. Guardian's whistle faded down the passageway.

The widow didn't come back to the cabin that night. Aurelia tried not to think of where Lily was and what she might be doing.

Instead, she thought of Mr. Guardian. He had the kind of life-snap and vigor her classmates admired. They'd say his physique was splendid, ideal for pleasure and for procreating. Aurelia was sure of one thing, at least: Clay Guardian didn't have formaldehyde in his veins.

Strangely agitated, Aurelia prepared for bed. The grinding noise of the steering gear kept her awake most of the night. She tossed and turned as the ship listed from side to side. Lily's evening probably hadn't ended this way, Aurelia would wager her last nickel on that.

A wash of pale yellow preceded the sun's majestic arrival. On deck for her morning constitutional, Aurelia braced her arms on the damp wooden railing, leaned forward, and lifted her face. A spray of salty foam tingled her cheeks. She yawned, filling her lungs with moist, chilly air, hoping that tonight she'd get some sleep.

The ship had hoisted anchor two hours ago, at four-thirty A.M., and the *Reliance* was once again churning through the center trough of the channel. From the gray water's edge rose sloping hills and dizzying mountains, some snow-capped, some ribboned with waterfalls. Their lower halves were covered with stunted growths of spruce and cedar. The malnourished trees were mangy and stiff, stuck upright in the dirt as if defying death. It was such a beautiful but inhospitable land.

Aurelia had never thought herself superstitious, but she could swear the wind from the rugged fringes whispered, "Go back." She shivered.

It wasn't long before crewmen and several other passengers interrupted Aurelia's reverie. She decided to eat before the dining room became crowded. Even an ordinary breakfast menu smelled delightful at sea. Her first-class fare entitled her to a tray of sourdough biscuits and a pot of hot tea in her cabin that morning, but her appetite still called for more. If she wasn't careful, she'd have to pull her corset string even tighter just to fit into her brown shirtwaist.

A moment later she saw the young supply clerk who'd served her in Seattle leaning his lanky body against the railing. In his dark green corduroy suit he looked like one of the scrawny timbers hanging on the mountainside. Aurelia decided to approach him.

"Good morning. I see you've chosen the Klondike over Cuba. Have you spotted a whale? I understand they frequent these waters."

"Miss B-B-Breighton! Good m-m-morning." He grabbed his plaid fore-and-aft hat from his head and held it to his chest as he bowed. "Yes, ma'am. I don't figure I can make much of a fortune in Cuba."

Perhaps he's double-jointed, Aurelia thought, considering his jerky movements. That would explain his absence from the dance last night. She moved alongside him at the railing. "So you've been infected with the gold fever as well, Mr.—I don't believe I ever caught your name."

"P-P-Poyser, ma'am. Waldo Poyser." He bowed again.

Aurelia noticed the round bare spot at his crown—premature balding. The boy couldn't be more than eighteen—two years older than Violet and no more suited to the wilderness than she was.

She peered over the railing. "Oh look, Mr. Poyser, a school of porpoises. Hundreds of them. Look how they frolic in the wave off the bow. They resemble large cod fish, wouldn't you say?"

"I bet they're five feet long. Can jump near as high too. I been watching them. The light gray ones, the ones with the long snouts—those are the dolphins. The porpoises are the dark ones. The whales are way out there. I sure hope they come closer so I can get a better look. They're my favorites."

Just then a trio of the sleek gray dolphins broke the surface of the water and jettisoned into the air.

"Ain't they pretty?"

"Magnificent."

Waldo leaned farther over the railing. "I get the notion they're all smiling at me. Like I was their f-f-friend."

"Why, Mr. Poyser, that's a poetic sentiment. Lovely."

"You fancy poetry, Miss Breighton?"

"Indeed, I do. Emily Dickinson is my favorite. And you?"

Aurelia didn't wait for his answer, but turned her head at the sound of whistling coming from the far end of the deck. She smiled as Clay Guardian drew closer. She hoped her face did not betray the full degree of pleasure she felt at seeing him.

She liked his walk. It was a slow, rhythmic stride, the motion concentrated at the hip. He wore his buckskin over a faded blue cotton shirt, the informal type with the collar attached, open at the neck. The tails of a blue and white bandana knotted at the throat drew her eye down to the patch of fine, black hair on his chest. She tried not to stare.

"Lovely morning, isn't it, Mr. Guardian. Have you met Mr. Waldo Poyser here? Mr. Poyser, Mr. Clay Guardian." There was a moment of hesitation before the men shook hands. "Mr. Poyser was the supply clerk at Cooper and Levy who outfitted me for the trip." She turned to Waldo. "Mr. Guardian is a loan officer with the Seattle Bank and Trust."

"Was," Clay corrected her. "I gave up sitting behind the wire cage. I'd rather work to fill my own coffers."

"The way I heard it, you already did," Waldo said.

Clay glared down at the young man. "You heard wrong, boy. Now, if you'll excuse me, there's a poker table waiting for me. That's a man's game. I'd invite you to play, but I don't take advantage of children. You stay out here and watch the fish."

He turned to Aurelia. "Thank you for last night, Miss Breighton. It's been a long time since I held such a beautiful woman in my arms." With that, he walked away.

Aurelia stood dumbstruck. Before Waldo could say anything, she excused herself and hurriedly returned to her cabin. On the one hand, she felt insulted by

Clay's brazen comment. But on the other . . . well, it was plain as day he was thinking of her as a woman.

Aurelia recalled something Lily had said about the delicious enticement of a shipboard romance. Aurelia wasn't interested in that free and fleeting kind of love. If there was to be any kind of love in her future, it had to be the forever kind, the kind that Nana and Grampa Brooke had had. Disheartened for no reason she could identify, Aurelia spent the rest of the day in a feeble attempt at studying.

At six o'clock that evening there was a knock on her cabin door. She opened it to the man whose image had interrupted her concentration all afternoon. "Yes?"

"I meant what I said earlier today, Miss Breighton," Clay said. "It's been years since I held a woman as beautiful as you. But I never should have said anything so intimate in public."

"You embarrass me in front of a man I hardly know and then simply say you're sorry?" Despite her irritation, she felt elated to hear him say again that she was beautiful.

"Guess I was still feeling the effects of the music and the moonlight." He shrugged as though he didn't know what else to say. "What can I do to make it up to you?"

"Listen here, Mr. Guardian. If you're looking for a shipboard romance—" She stopped herself mid-sentence, an embarrassing blush staining her cheeks. The beguiling look on his face only made her feel worse.

His eyes twinkled with amusement at her sugges-tion. "That's not at all what I'm looking for. Not at all."

"Good." Aurelia composed herself and considered

his earlier offer. "Then why don't you explain the tension between you and young Mr. Poyser."

"Maybe the anxiety of the trip. Look, I didn't come down here just to apologize. I was hoping we could discuss your sister's predicament."

"Violet?" Though Mr. Guardian had only seen Violet and Sculley for a few moments, perhaps he now remembered some piece of information.

"Yes. We could talk about it over dinner, if you haven't eaten yet. You could tell me what you know of her plans. I've read a lot about the Yukon Territory. Maybe I can help you."

"What makes you think I need help?"

"Don't believe all that evangelism of Seattle's fine Chamber of Commerce. Their pamphlets paint a one-sided picture. Oh, the Klondike's filled with gold all right, but getting to it could kill you."

"Really?" He sounded knowledgable, but still, she wasn't convinced.

As though he sensed her hesitation, he added, "We're both headed for the same place. No sense in duplicating supplies. I'll wager you're a better cook than I am. And I can build a boat better, or at least faster, than you can. Won't be many women on the trail, just hundreds of men, some just as bad, maybe worse, than Sculley. You'd be a hell of a lot safer traveling with me. Separate tents, of course. Besides, I owe you. You could have had me arrested back in Seattle."

"I know." Something about his eagerness made her nervous. His offer, however, called for serious consideration. He didn't really owe her anything, but she saw the wisdom in accepting his proposition. The ship should reach Dyea in a few days, and then she'd begin her search in earnest. If she joined forces with

Mr. Guardian, she'd have no difficulty crossing the Canadian border. Mr. Guardian would arrange transportation of their supplies, no small task in itself. He'd serve as a respectable escort to saloons and such, for no doubt that was where Sculley's trail would begin.

Aurelia laid her book on the bunk, peeked over her shoulder, and discreetly took in his measure. Nana Brooke would have called him a good one.

She grabbed her shawl and a small bundle of envelopes from her bed. "You make a convincing argument." She extended her hand. "This could be a fortuitous evening, Mr. Guardian."

"It's Clay." He shook her hand. "I know we've only known each other a week, but I'd like to think it appropriate."

"Clay, then." Aurelia liked the sound of it. Simple. Strong.

He grinned. "Let's get our grub, partner."

An hour later, they joined the crowd in the social hall. Cigar smoke hung in clouds over the bar, the nickel-in-the-slot gambling machine, and the poker tables. Several games were already in progress.

"Hey, Guardian, you son of a bitch, you gonna give us a chance to get our money back?"

"Not tonight," he called to the group of men in the corner. Several of them offered their tables to Clay, but he led Aurelia to an inconspicuous one in the corner instead. "Drink?"

Aurelia thought for a second and decided to celebrate her new partnership with something more bracing than her usual cup of tea. "Sherry, please."

"Sherry it is."

A bartender approached their table, and Clay ordered for both of them.

"Here you are, miss," the bartender said a few moments later as he placed a stein of amber wine on the table.

"Such a large glass?"

"That and tin cups is all we carry on board, ma'am."

Fortunately, it was only half full. "Thank you."

When the bartender left, Clay lifted his frosted glass of beer. "To Violet."

"To Violet." Aurelia gripped the handle of her stein and raised it to his. She sipped. The rich golden brown liquid slid down her throat. "Delicious."

Clay leaned against the back of his chair. "Now, aside from what I told you about meeting Sculley, what makes you think your sister is in danger from the man?"

Aurelia set the bundle of envelopes on the table and untied the white satin ribbon that bound them. "These are from Violet. I can't let you read them in total. They're much too personal." She removed the contents of the first envelope. "Bear with me, please. I'll have to whisper."

Clay nodded. Aurelia took another sip of sherry and began:

My dear Aurelia,
   I'm so lucky to have so quickly found what I'm sure must be true love. . . . Once in Alaska Fletcher and I will cross the border into Canada—the Yukon is not in Alaska after all!—and proceed straightaway to the gold fields to find our fortune. But first we are to be married in Dyea, the gateway to our dreams. It's all so romantic! . . . I've had to pawn the sapphire brooch . . . supplies are so expensive."

This talk of romance. Aurelia felt a blush creep into her cheeks as she folded the letter and put it back into the envelope. Determined to set her emotions aside for the sake of making progress, she opened the second and read.

> *Dearest Sister,*
>   *This boat rolled and pitched for the last five days and I've spent practically every moment sick. Fortunately, I thought to bring a bottle of mother's tonic. There is really nothing Fletcher can do to ease my discomfort, so he spends his time in the bar or at the card tables."*

Aurelia did not try to disguise the concern she felt for her sister. "My mother is a frail and delicate woman. Violet has inherited her constitution, I'm afraid. From what I've heard aboard ship these last few days, the road to the gold fields is not an easy one, regardless of the time of year." As she spoke she opened the third letter.

> *Dearest Aurelia,*
>   *I continue to suffer. I assume I have also contracted the neurasthenia that has afflicted mother for so many years, for like her, I am constantly fatigued. The tonic allows me to sleep, but often leaves me feeling the worse for it when I wake."*

Aurelia sighed and swallowed the last of her sherry.

Clay put his hand over her stein. "Hey, take it easy, partner. I know it's just sherry, but it's powerful if you aren't used to it."

Aurelia shook her head slightly to clear the cobwebs that had suddenly impaired her ability to think. "I trust you can see, Clay, that my little sister is not equipped for the rigors of the trip. And Fletcher Sculley is a scurrilous dog, a loathsome rodent not fit to walk in her shadow." She fanned her cheeks, wondering if anyone else had noticed the change in temperature. "It's terribly warm in here."

"A walk on the deck?"

"Yes." Aurelia fumbled as she tied the satin ribbon around the letters.

"I'd offer you another sherry, but I think you've had enough."

"I think you're right. I feel a bit dizzy. And the advice of the widow L'Auberge is appealing to me."

"Your cabinmate?"

"You noticed her. I knew you would."

"Seems to be a friendly woman."

"Friendly indeed. Would you be interested in her unclothed?" Aurelia had no trouble staring at Clay, as her eyes refused to blink. "She's interested in you unclothed. Told me so herself." Aurelia allowed herself a lingering gaze along his torso.

He raised his eyebrows as he picked up the lopsided pile of envelopes. Slipping his arm around Aurelia's waist, he led her outside to the deck where a chilling night wind urged the ship on its course.

He stopped by an arrangement of small wooden barrels tied to a steel pole. "Here." He dusted off the top of the nearest barrel. "You'd better sit down. Can't have my new partner falling overboard."

Aurelia plopped herself down and fussed with her dress. "I'm cold."

Clay removed his buckskin jacket and covered her with it as best he could. "Better?"

She nodded and snuggled into the leather, warm from the heat of his body. She hadn't had a good night's sleep yet. Surely she would tonight. Her eyelids felt so heavy.

Clay straddled the barrel in front of her to shield her from the wind. He still held Violet's letters. "Aurelia," he whispered in her ear. "Your sister isn't healthy. I understand. But what you read to me doesn't explain your contempt for Sculley. I hope to God it's not just because he frequents the bar and the card tables."

"But you saw him yourself. Trust me. He's a scurrilous dog, a loathsome—" She stopped mid-sentence, yawned, and closed her eyes.

"Rodent," he finished for her. He gazed at the cold, dark sky.

Aurelia's head fell forward, against his chest. The faint scent of lavender teased his nose. The wind had freed small tendrils of her hair, and they dangled across her cheeks and down her neck like golden ribbons. One by one, he coiled them around his finger. She was beautiful. Not with the sultry, sensuous beauty of her sister. No, Aurelia's beauty was fresh-faced and honest, sensual in its own way. She turned her head slightly to the side and nuzzled against his chest.

Satisfied that she was asleep, he untied the satin ribbon and slipped the first letter from the bundle. What else did sweet Violet have to say?

I'm so lucky, my dear Aurelia, to have so quickly found what I'm sure must be true love. I pray that one day you, too, will experience this happiness. Nana Brooke should have bequeathed her magic wedding band to you, not to me. I know how lonely you have been all these years.

Thank heaven for your medical studies; surely they have saved my life. If you had not shown me those anatomy pictures that afternoon in your room, I'm certain the shock of seeing the male physique would have been most frightening. Even now I find the act itself distasteful, but Fletcher says I'd best learn to enjoy it. I will be anxious to hear your impressions of the act when your time comes. Please don't think ill of me for preceding you in this rite of passage. If the painful truth be known, no woman would willingly suffer this ritual, though I suppose it is a wifely duty. I did tell Fletcher I simply must have a diamond solitaire before we marry, especially since I have surrendered my virtue.

Clay looked down at his new partner. Like a thief, he'd helped himself to her secrets. But he needed to know them, he rationalized, trying to ease his conscience.

The moonlight played games with her hair, highlighting strands of gold, casting shadows across her face. She began to shiver. He tucked his jacket around her shoulders.

"Well, Sleeping Beauty, I haven't read anything yet to change my mind. Your sweet sister and her man, Sculley, are a team for sure. But you?" He ran his hands along her arms. "I don't know. Are you part of the scheme? Or are you the virtuous older sister, waiting for the day when you'll perform your 'wifely duties'?"

Just the thought of her so engaged aroused him. "It doesn't have to be painful, Aurelia. It wouldn't be painful with me."

Clay kissed the tip of his finger and placed it

against her lips. They parted easily. He stood up, slid his arms under her shoulders and knees, and lifted her. She nestled her head in the crook of his neck, and again he smelled the lavender as his cheek brushed against her hair. It was so soft, cool, and silky. He wanted to grab a fistful.

"Right this minute I'd give every dollar your sister stole from me to see you unclothed."

He headed for her cabin.

5

The lady was no lightweight, though Clay guessed it was the heavy dress and volumes of ruffly falderal underneath that made his arm feel the strain. The stiff cage around her middle creaked like the hinges on an old barn door. Why a woman would squeeze herself into a contraption like that he couldn't imagine.

Aurelia's arm dangled limply to the side, pulling her dress tight across her chest. She didn't need any contraption to give her curves. She had plenty. He thought of the sidewinding pattern a rattlesnake leaves in the dirt.

His knees tensed as he bent down to reach the handle to her cabin door. The door was unlocked. Pulling her body close to his own, he turned sideways and crossed the threshold.

Light from the passageway cut through the darkness of the room. A cyclone must have hit it! Dresses and unmentionables were strewn everywhere. It was worse than Eli's room ever was. Trunks lay open, filled with feminine toys of slippery satin and barely-there lace—a white embroidered chemise tied with pink ribbons, a filmy blue camisole.

Was that what Aurelia wore under her drab brown dress? Some little silk doodad, thin as a spider web, with lace-edged ruffles he could slip down her creamy shoulders . . . tiny, pearl buttons he could release with one finger and expose what he just knew were firm round breasts . . . narrow, slippery ribbons he could untie with his teeth. . . .

She nuzzled in the hollow under his shoulder.

Would she be so pliant in the heat of passion? Would she surrender to his will? Or would she moan in pleasure, suck his strength, and writhe against him with unsatiable hunger?

Forcing himself to put her down, he laid her on the fresh white sheets of the one empty bed, and turned on the light. With her face framed in golden curls and her eyes closed in sweet repose, she could have been a fairy tale princess from one of the bedtime stories he read to Eli. Of course, Eli was too young for the kind of bedtime stories Clay was thinking of now.

He took a deep breath and wiped the perspiration from his brow. He had to remind himself that he was no prince, and, that with a sister like Violet, Aurelia was probably no innocent princess.

He took a second deep breath to relax the tension still tormenting him. He wasn't proud of having lied to her, but a man did what he had to do.

He bent over Aurelia and tucked the ribbon-bound letters under her pillow. Her lips were so close he could feel the soft whisper of her breath against his cheek. For a few seconds his own breathing mirrored hers as he watched the rise and fall of her bosom, but she was asleep. He was wide awake and needed air, lots of air. As he straightened, he heard the squeak of the cabin door behind him.

"Well, well, what have we here? I had no idea my roommate had become such an accomplished hostess." Lily closed the door and leaned against the lock. Her lip rouge had been smudged, her carefully arranged hair showed signs of distress, and a big black feather plume hung over her ear. She held her shoes in her hand. With the pointed toe of one stockinged foot she drew an arc on the floor in front of her. The look in her eyes dared him to cross it. The obvious pout of her lips promised she would make it worth his while if he did.

There was no mistaking the road signs. He hadn't followed them in a long time, and right now, right this minute, he had the urge to travel. But the destination he had in mind wasn't the widow, it was Aurelia.

Still asleep, she rolled on her side, facing him. Her palms pressed together and pillowed her head. She curled up the way little Eli did when he was cold. Clay reached for the blanket at the foot of the bed and, with movements as impersonal as he could manage, spread it over her sleeping body.

"Your roommate nodded off on deck," Clay said to Lily. "Couldn't very well let her sleep on a barrel."

Lily cocked her head to one side and summoned a pouting tone. "Couldn't have been because of the company."

Clay was silent for a moment. With a poker face he'd perfected over the years, he looked at the woman standing in front of him. Behind the frills and the paint, he saw desperation and loneliness in her eyes. He recognized the signs; he'd seen them in his mirror all too often lately. He also knew the last thing she'd want was the only thing he could give her: pity.

"I'll be going now." There was nothing judgmental

in his voice, just a look in his eyes that made it clear he didn't intend to stay.

"Another time perhaps," she called as he walked away.

Neither Aurelia nor Lily rose for breakfast the next morning. Finally, some time later, Aurelia opened her eyes. The gentle listing of the ship tossed her equilibrium back and forth. The rise and fall of footsteps up and down the passageway pounded in her head the same way Professor Sternwell smacked her long wooden pointer against the chalkboard or on the edge of the desk whenever someone gave an incorrect answer. "Wrong, wrong, wrong," she would bellow to some unfortunate.

Aurelia had no idea alcohol could make a person feel so horrid. She needed some bicarbonate of soda.

She stumbled across the room and turned on the lamp. When she squinted at the silver timepiece she wore on a chain around her neck, she thought it said four o'clock, but was that A.M. or P.M.? She listened to the incessant daytime traffic outside the door. "Oh no," she said with a moan. "I've slept away a whole day of my life.

That's when she realized she'd slept on the bed, not in the bed. She'd slept fully clothed in corset, stockings, petticoats and all. How had she gotten there? Who had covered her with the blanket? Certainly not Lily. From the looks of her, sound asleep, sprawled out on her back, her arms dangling off the bed, her mouth wide open, she hadn't fared any better last night than Aurelia.

Clay. He had to be the one who had put her to bed. A terrible, sinking feeling came over her. She sat on the edge of the bed, cupped her hands together, and let them hold the weight of her pounding head. "I've made a fool of myself."

"No, Miss Breighton," Lily mumbled as she sat up and shielded her eyes from the light. "You were a fool to let him go."

"Who?" Aurelia feigned ignorance.

"Your Mr. Guardian, of course." Lily yawned and rubbed the sleep from her eyes. "Too conservative for my taste, of course, but a fine man nonetheless."

A fine man indeed. Aurelia remembered how interested he'd been when she told him of Violet's predicament. She considered herself lucky to have teamed up with such an understanding man. Then she recalled the comfort of his strong arms around her as he carried her to her room. Adding to the pain of her fuzzy head, she remembered that he didn't even try to kiss her. "Our relationship is strictly business." She stood and began straightening her bed, hoping to discourage Lily from further comment.

"Whatever you say, dear."

Lily spent the rest of the afternoon and evening dozing, while Aurelia tried to study.

The next morning Lily remained in the cabin with a volume of poetry, a basket of hot biscuits, and a pot of tea. Aurelia headed topside. Even before she reached the deck, she heard the deafening crackle of gunfire. She covered her ears with her hands. What was this? A mutiny? An execution? A bunch of hot-headed brawlers? Fearing the worst, she rushed back down to the cabin and grabbed her medical box.

Back through the passageway and up the stairs, she fought to keep from tripping on her skirt as she closed in on the terrifying thunder. As she stepped onto the deck, a sharp, biting wind cut across her cheeks. It stole her breath and stung her lips.

Anchored in the middle of the open channel, the ship bobbed with a quickening pulse. "Why have we stopped?" she asked a passing crewman.

"Captain said the boys needed a bit of fun."

Up ahead dozens of men, rifle butts jammed into their shoulders, crowded the railing. The teak-trimmed fence braced them safely on deck. One after the other, the blast from their hand-held cannons assaulted the peace. In the distance, out of reach, a school of black-and-white orca whales angrily slapped their flukes against the water's surface. In the chaos next to the ship, jumping in and out of the pink-edged foam, hundreds of creatures screamed in panic. The air vibrated with the high-pitched trills of their agony and thundered with the sound of guns.

Aurelia raced along the water-splashed deck toward the bow as the firing escalated.

A thin, gray haze veiled the cheering mob. She recognized the heady, seductive smell of the shotgun blast and the burning-sulfur stench of the rifle shells.

Those who were not shouldering arms swigged beer. Aurelia heard bets from two bits to two hundred dollars. She stopped several yards behind the crowd, looked over the railing, and swallowed hard. From where she stood she could hear the men's profanities clearly. But their language was only mildly offensive compared to what she saw in the swirling waters below: the vivid red blood of injured dolphins.

It was impossible to distinguish porpoise from dolphin. Once hit, some glowed purple against what blue was left of the water, then sunk to the bottom, only to be lifted back to the surface by frantic survivors. Others, their glistening bodies punctured by a rifle's single bullet, drew a trail of blood around them as they swam in circles, turned on their sides, and died. Hundreds of shotgun pellets shattered the flesh of others, scattering a trophy of wet pink confetti.

Aurelia looked up. Horror raced through her as she saw Waldo Poyser raise a rifle to his shoulder. How could he? The man next to him tucked the butt under Waldo's chin and coaxed his fingers around the long, steel barrel. He aimed into the water.

Seconds later, a thirty-five-foot orca pierced the surface and rose majestically into the air. A collective gasp rose from the deck as the men shielded themselves from the spray.

Aurelia froze.

Waldo fired.

The glory of Neptune absorbed the impact and slammed against the water's surface where it floated in defiance. A monument to the dead, it sprayed one last fountain of blood from its blowhole, then sank to its grave. The firing ceased.

Fresh blood smelled distinct. Not rotten like the dried blood in gangrenous tissue or putrid as the stench so powerful on first cutting a cadaver, but thick and warm, almost metallic. She had choked on it the first time she saw it in such quantity. She remembered her first delivery and how the blood had coated her hands. How it had pulled her skin taut as it dried, imbedding itself under her nails. How it had splattered all over everything in the area. But that was nearly three years ago. Blood and death no longer left her squeamish.

Though she could tell none of the men up ahead were injured, she continued slowly toward them. Diffused now, they joked and swore and passed several steins of beer among themselves. She watched one portly dandy roll a fat cigar to the side of his mouth, lick his thumb, and count a handsome pile of bills which he then handed to—to Clay.

He didn't appear to have a gun, and Aurelia hadn't noticed him shooting with the others. Maybe it was some other wager. She was glad her new partner hadn't participated in such a grotesque sport. She found it hard to believe Mr. Poyser had, but she'd witnessed it with her own eyes.

A close-lipped smile crossed Clay's face as Waldo faltered with all the congratulatory backslapping being given him.

"Here's to the Butcher!" one man shouted.

"To the Butcher!" another echoed.

"The Butcher!"

Waldo shook his head repeatedly as he handed the rifle to the man next to him. The boy seemed anxious to get away from the blood-smeared deck. He stumbled as he turned around.

Aurelia looked him in the eye. Oh, merciful God. The boy's torment was so obvious. His eyes were wide at the sight that was too horrible to even try to shut out.

"He was my f-f-friend. I k-k-killed him." He turned toward the railing and leaned over. Even as he wretched, a logjam of carcasses floated in the bloodied water below and thudded against the side of the ship.

Aurelia heard the rumble of the engines as they were fired up. Oblivious to the massacre, the bow of the *Reliance* churned through the water, leaving the slaughter behind.

Her heart ached to see the young man in such

agony. "Why, Mr. Poyser?" she whispered. "Why did you do it?" She moved closer, set down her medical box, and waited for him to regain his composure. There was no longer any substance to his gagging, just the desperate wretching of a grief-stricken boy.

He pulled the new, bright red bandana from around his neck and wiped his eyes and mouth. His lower lip trembled as though even it too had to stutter. "I thought it would make me a m-m-man." He pressed his lips together and looked over the railing at the carnage left behind. Then he crumbled to the deck where he wept openly.

Aurelia summoned a passing crewmember. "A cup of water, please." She retrieved a small amber bottle of tincture of iodine from her box and tried to recall the recommended dosage for seasickness. Ten drops to a wineglass of water. Ten? Or was it twenty? Better to err on the lesser dose, she decided. She measured ten orange-red drops into the cup of water the crewman had fetched.

She knelt down. "Here, Mr. Poyser. Drink this. It will calm your stomach." She held the glass out and noticed his hands were still shaking when he took it from her. "I suggest you abstain from solid foods for the remainder of the day in favor of soup and tea."

He looked from the glass to the deck and back to the glass.

"It's only iodine in water. It will do you no harm, and should restore your spirits in no time." Aurelia tilted her head to encourage eye contact. "Mr. Poyser?"

"Yes, ma'am." Lifting the glass to his lips, he drank it in one effort.

Aurelia took the glass from him and set it down on one of the nearby barrels. "Better?"

He nodded as he stood, though the look on his face said otherwise.

"Now I suggest you return to your cabin, have a cup of tea, and rest. Will you do that for me?"

"It ain't my turn for the b-b-bunk yet."

"I don't understand."

"I'm in steerage. Three to a bunk. We take turns. I been up since t-t-two this morning. I get the bed at five this afternoon."

"How dreadful. When do you eat if you must sleep when the dining room is open?"

"All we get in steerage is stew. Don't mean a whole lot to miss it."

"Oh, you poor boy." She instantly regretted her choice of words, but once uttered, there was no taking them back. "I must be on my way now. Is there anything else I can do for you, Mr. Poyser? More iodine for a later dose? Some biscuits perhaps?"

"You carry anything in that bag for a guilty conscience?"

Aurelia was pleased to see him make an effort to smile, but she shook her head. "I'm afraid not." *If I did,* she said to herself, *I'd have taken it long ago.*

After assuring herself that Mr. Poyser was on the mend, Aurelia set out to find her new partner and discuss their plans. She had, after all, made him privy to portions of Violet's letters. Now that he knew the gravity of Violet's situation, he could appreciate Aurelia's concern for her sister.

She didn't have to look far.

Clay rounded the bow with two other men. One slapped Clay on the back. Another turned the pockets of his own trousers inside out as he tossed his head back in laughter. Though the two men with him were better dressed than Clay, Aurelia decided her new partner was by far the most handsome.

As soon as he saw Aurelia, Clay left the other gentlemen behind and hurried toward her. He smiled and raised his eyebrows in a mischievous arch.

"So, you didn't jump ship on me after all. Didn't see you yesterday. Hope you weren't allergic to the sherry."

Her cheeks colored as her memory of the evening in question returned. "Merely unaccustomed," she managed to say. Goodness, but he had the most attractive face, even with the stubble of several days at sea. His eyes sparkled in a delightfully dangerous way. She tried to mirror his easy smile, though she felt uncomfortable with the way he was looking at her— so playful, so suggestive, and just a little dangerous.

"Mr. Guardian—Clay—the details of our evening together—our business meeting, that is—are unclear to me. I assume we worked out the specifics of our partnership. Duties, responsibilities, financial considerations." She looked away for a second, embarrassed at having to bring up such delicate subjects again. "I didn't make notes. Could you refresh my memory?"

"I'd like nothing better. Shall we?" He picked up her medical case from the deck and offered his arm. She fell into step beside him as she fought to stifle her grin. How she would love for her friends at school to see her now.

They strolled to the other side of the ship. He stopped next to a large wooden barrel and drummed his fingers on the lid. "You fell asleep right here."

She remembered that part. "My apologies—"

"No need," he said quickly. "You were so tired, it was all you could do to keep your eyes open, so I propped you up on this barrel and we worked out the details of our partnership. Let's see if I remember everything." He seemed to think hard for a moment, though the smile never left his face. "We'll pool supplies: I'll arrange transportation of whatever we can't carry, get the horses, the dogs, the sleds, whatever we need. I'll pitch the tents each night, chop the wood, hunt, fish, do all the bull work. Build the boat when we get to Lake Bennett and navigate it down the Yukon. And of course I'll also protect you from wild Indians and grizzly bears. And you, you'll cook and do the laundry."

Aurelia laughed. "I must have been some negotiator."

"You had me eating out of the palm of your hand."

Even through his stubble, she could see his dimples deepen. Aurelia had the notion that if he were a doctor, his practice could thrive on his bedside manner alone.

Before she knew what was happening, Clay slipped his hands inside her cape, around her waist, and lifted her onto the barrel.

The sudden intimacy of his touch stole all her new-found confidence. Her breath caught in her throat, and a wash of crimson colored her cheeks.

Embarrassed at how easily her body betrayed her feelings, she eased herself off the barrel. "I'm in full agreement with the division of work as you've out-lined it," she said, trying to ensure that the conversa-tion remained businesslike.

"Then we're partners," he said, offering her his hand.

She slipped her hand in his. "Partners," she said, ashamed at how eager she was for any excuse to touch him.

Quickly she pulled her hand away. "And now I must check in on my roommate. She hasn't been feeling well."

"Nothing serious, I hope."

Aurelia shook her head. "No, but her confinement

leaves her lonely and I promised to spend the day with her."

"Sure."

"Besides, I'm sure she's anxious to know the cause of all the commotion out here earlier this morning."

"The target practice? That was some shooting match. Did you catch it?"

"Target practice?" Aurelia knew her anger showed on her face. "That was hardly a fair match of anything."

"You don't approve of the sport, I take it."

"To me, a sport implies fairness. What chance did those poor creatures have?"

"They could swim. Away from the ship."

Aurelia took a deep breath. "Perhaps. And what about young Mr. Poyser? Did you see him shoot?"

"Sure did. I didn't think the kid could hit anything, but he surprised me. Surprised a lot of folks."

Aurelia didn't like the way Clay grinned with his last remark. "I think someone put him up to it," she said. "He's too tender a boy to have engaged in such cruelty on his own. He was terribly distraught when it was over."

Clay was silent.

"Do you know anything more about the incident?" she asked.

"Can't think of a thing I could tell you."

"Well, I'm glad it's over. I prescribed a tincture of iodine mixture for him. He should be fine in the morning."

Aurelia wasn't sure what had just happened, but the atmosphere between her and Clay was different. A sober look replaced his grin, and the twinkle left his eyes. "I guess I'd better head back to my cabin now," she said.

On the way back, she huddled in her cloak against a chill that had nothing to do with the weather.

6

The Reliance sliced through the dark waters of the channel at nine knots an hour. Late on the afternoon of the fifth day, she anchored off a crude but sturdy pier leading to one of the dozens of fish-canning villages along the shore. Rough, weathered cabins, perched precariously on barnacled stilts, rose above the beach. The sand glistened from the scales of thousands upon thousands of fish. The pungent air reeked with the heavy scent of halibut and herring.

Jittery passengers watched from the railing while the brawny crew filled their hand carts with cordwood. Aurelia stopped to watch the activity ashore. By now, the other passengers understood she wasn't a woman of questionable reputation even though she was traveling alone. She was Clay Guardian's partner. The arrangement conferred a certain respectability.

The man to her left anxiously opened and closed a pocketknife. The man to her right jingled the change in his pocket. Aurelia could feel the urgency in the air. Underneath her heavy wool cape, she clutched the hobo sack of fresh biscuits she'd taken from the basket she and Lily shared each morning. Fearing the

damage the heavy starch would do to her figure, Lily
had decided to eat sparingly. When Aurelia explained
the plight of poor Mr. Poyser, Lily had urged her to
take all of the remaining biscuits to the young man.

Perhaps it was finally Mr. Poyser's turn to occupy
the cot. He was nowhere on deck. Aurelia decided to
take one last look in the social hall. She didn't want to
spend any time there. The air was filled with smoke
and the language could quickly turn colorful. She just
wanted to find Mr. Poyser and give him the biscuits.

"How do, ma'am. Lookin' for Guardian, are you?"
The grizzled old man who greeted her stretched his
lips over a tooth-gapped smile. "He'll be along. Here,
you have a seat." He'd been twirling a toothpick, and
now he stuck it in his mouth.

"Thank you," she said as she checked the seat for
spillage or spittle before she sat down. "I'll wait for a
moment or two." She was really looking for Mr.
Poyser, but if Clay was on his way, she would wait.
She wanted to discuss a few more details before the
ship docked in Dyea, though business wasn't her only
motive. She simply liked being with him.

"Damn that Guardian—oh, pardon me, ma'am,
but if he ain't the luckiest s.o.b. I ever seen. We ain't
even off the ship yet and he's already made himself a
fortune. Says it was easy on account of his keen judge
of character." The old man grunted. "Hey, Sam," he
called to the bartender, "fetch the lady here a—what'll
you have, ma'am? Beer or whiskey? It's on me."

Aurelia shook her head vigorously. "Nothing.
Thank you."

"Bring me a whiskey, Sam." He grinned again.
"So, tell me, was you up topside for the fishing derby
this morning? Saw some damn fine shootin'."

Aurelia thought of the senseless killing and the terrible effect it had had on poor Mr. Poyser. "Yes, I was there. I thought the entire scene a disgusting display of carnage and not worthy of decent men."

The old man chuckled and widened his yellowed eyes. "Your partner know you to be one of them bleedin' hearts?"

"Mr. Guardian was not a participant in that slaughter."

"That so?" The old man scratched his whiskers and grinned. "He didn't do no shootin' if that's what you mean, but he sure as hell was right in the thick of it. Made a fortune too, if he can collect it before we pull into Dyea."

Aurelia remembered seeing the portly man hand Clay a sizeable amount of money. "Yes, I understand he made a bet of some sort."

"He made a fistful of bets, little lady. And all on that simple-minded greenhorn. Who'd believe Guardian could get that dolt to shoot a gun? Hell, took him an hour just to get the kid to touch it." He took a generous swig of whiskey. "The kid don't drink. He don't smoke. And I'll make my own wager he ain't never had—you know, a woman?" He emptied the shotglass.

"Pardon me, ma'am. I get carried away. As I was saying, Guardian dared the kid to prove he was a man, and I'll be damned if that spineless shitkicker didn't shoot." The old man slammed his fist on the table. "And popped that giant right in the lungs. Damn."

Aurelia crushed the biscuits she held in her lap. Clay was responsible for Waldo Poyser's shooting the whale? Through gritted teeth she called to the bartender, "Sam, I'll have that beer now."

She ran her finger around one of the dozen white

rings on the table while she waited. The top of the thick plank of oak bore the black scars of match heads and had been nicked and gouged over the years by a thousand pocketknives. If the pressure of her fingertip had been any greater, she'd have bored a hole right through the wood.

She took a sip of the beer Sam placed in front of her. Cold yeast and soap suds. The horrid taste brought back an equally horrid memory, but this wasn't the time or place to deal with it. She was about to ask for a glass of wine when she heard Clay laughing with several of the other passengers on the steel stairs just outside. He formed friendships fast enough, she decided. Perhaps one of them would make a better partner for him than she.

As Clay entered the room and sat down next to Aurelia, the grizzled old man stood and gave him an exaggerated wide-eyed look.

"Clear the deck, boys," he said to the others, "We're gonna see some fireworks."

Aurelia sat upright. "Don't look at me with those innocent brown eyes. And save the dimples for someone else. We need to talk."

A little bit of his self-confidence appeared to wane. "Here? With all this noise?"

"Here. Now."

Clay turned to the bartender. "Send a beer over, will you Sam? How 'bout you, partner? Can't say as I ever expected to see you take up the suds." He nodded at the beer in front of her.

"Unfortunately, your keen judgment of character failed you this time. I'm certain you'd have made a sizeable wager on me too if you'd thought of it."

Clay leaned back and folded his arms across his

chest. "So that's what this is all about? Gambling?"

"No!" Her voice rose. "It's not about gambling. It's about Mr. Poyser."

Clay nodded as the bartender slipped a frosty stein in front of him. "The spineless—"

"Mr. Poyser is an awkward adolescent, uneducated, socially disadvantaged, inexperienced, insecure and . . . and . . . unfortunate looking. And for you to take advantage of him as you did was uncalled for."

"Hold it." His dark, heavy brows drew close, and his dimples disappeared. "Number one, I didn't ask for your opinion, and number two, I'm not surprised your puppy dog has you fighting his battles for him. And number three, if he can't shoot, if he won't *kill*, he won't survive."

"Hmph. So you goaded him into that carnage so you could help him survive? Somehow I doubt the nobility of your motive. Besides, *I* don't intend to kill anyone on this trip, Mr. Guardian, and I fully intend to survive."

"I hope you do. You're my partner. Or are you breaking our agreement? Maybe you want to try getting to Dawson with Posey Boy."

All the horror stories Aurelia had heard in Seattle and on the ship—stories about people going blind from the snow, being mauled by grizzly bears, freezing to death, losing their minds to the isolation, their teeth and limbs to the scurvy—all flashed through her mind in an instant. She needed Guardian. "No. I'm not breaking our agreement. I consider myself a woman of honor."

"Here, here," someone at the bar called out as he raised a shotglass in the air. "To women of honor."

Realizing they had an audience, Aurelia rose and swung on her cape. "Good-night." She didn't wait for his acknowledgment, but marched out of the social hall and up the stairs.

Outside on the deck, Aurelia drew her hood up. How was she ever going to work with a man like that? Heavy, dark clouds brewed up in the sky. She didn't remember squeezing the biscuits in the hobo sack, but they must have absorbed all her frustration with Clay, for now she saw that she'd broken them into nothing but crumbs. Not even Mr. Poyser would want these, she decided, as she released the corners of the large dinner napkin and scattered what remained of the biscuits on the open sea. A flock of screeching gulls swooped down in a frenzy. A moment later, the birds and the biscuits were gone.

Aurelia headed for the cabin. Just inside the passageway to the lower decks, Aurelia saw Waldo Poyser, sleeping. Still in his green corduroy suit, his long, lanky body lay stretched atop several shipping trunks.

She cleared her throat. "Mr. Poyser? Waldo?" She tapped him on the shoulder.

Slowly he sat up. He looked like an old man with his face all scrunched up, his eyes squinted. "Huh?" He pulled a pair of spectacles from his breast pocket and hooked the wire rims over his ears, one at a time. "Oh, Miss Breighton, it's you." He raked his hands through his hair. "Are you all r-r-right?"

"Yes, thank you." Aurelia watched him pull at the sleeves of his ill-fitting suit. "I suppose it will soon be your turn to use the cot."

"Not exactly. I mean it's my turn now, but Virgil—he has the turn before me—well, he's sick as a d-d-dog. He still doesn't have his sea legs. So I didn't wake him up. I can sleep just as good out here." He grinned. "Besides, out here I don't have to smell all them real dogs down in the hole. Or listen to them yippin' and barkin' all hours. Got horses and mules down there too."

Aurelia nodded. "And how are you feeling? Did the iodine tonic settle your stomach?"

"Yes, ma'am, it sure did. And I want to thank you." He looked down at the floor. "For everything, you know."

"I'll be happy to mix a tonic for your friend Virgil."

Waldo shook his head. "He won't take it. He don't place no store in lady d-d-doctors." He looked up at Aurelia. "Virgil ain't too smart, but he tries hard."

"I see." Aurelia thought about how smug Clay had acted in the social hall, making fun of such a sweet young man. "Well, Mr. Poyser, I came to see you about a business proposition." She sat on the trunk next to him. "May I call you Waldo?"

"Yes, ma'am!" His eyes widened and his head jutted forward like a turtle poking out of its shell.

"Good. Now, as you may have heard," she began, "Mr. Guardian and I have established a partnership for the purpose of reaching Dawson. Our decision was mutual and based on many practical reasons."

"Yes ma'am, I heard." His voice sounded so soft, Aurelia had to strain to hear him.

"I've decided we need a third partner, and I'm here to offer the opportunity to you. We would pool our supplies and share our labor." She searched for the right phrase. "We would be a team."

His face took on the most stupefied look. "You want me on your t-t-team?"

"If that's agreeable to you."

He pulled at his sleeves again. "What about Guardian? I can't hardly believe he'd want m-m-me around."

"You leave Mr. Guardian to me. I'm sure when he sees the wisdom of my offer, he'll appreciate your joining us as much as I do." She'd never seen a puppy's eyes look more soulful. She stood up and extended her hand. He shook it twice as long as necessary. The strength of his grip surprised her.

"I got me a pair of genuine Arctic g-g-gophers down in the hole. This fellow in Seattle said they was trained special to claw holes in the ice. That should help us."

"Excellent." Aurelia was pleased to see Waldo's spirit return. "I heard one of the crewmen say we'll have to stay put for the rest of the night. Too many rocks. I'd rather we pressed on, full steam ahead, for Dyea, but that's a decision best left to the navigator."

Waldo looked left and right as though wary of being overheard. "I hear the captain's paying four hundred d-d-dollars a month to that navigator. I never seen that much money in my whole life!"

"That does seem excessive for merely steering a boat, but I doubt the captain would agree to the sum unless he felt certain he'd get his money's worth. Who knows, Mr. Poyser, with the advantage of your Arctic gophers, perhaps you'll strike it rich in the Klondike. In any event, unless I see you later, you should plan to meet Mr. Guardian and me when we dock in Dyea." She smiled. "Partner."

As she made her way down the passageway she could hear the anxious sound of Waldo's heels as he tapped them against the side of the trunk.

Lily was asleep when Aurelia arrived at the cabin. Good. She didn't want to answer any questions about how things were going with Clay when she didn't know herself. While she was attracted to the man, she was also upset at his contemptuous attitude

toward poor Waldo. The boy's naivete was abysmal.
Clay would no doubt suggest throwing the boy to the
wolves, but Aurelia couldn't leave Waldo to his wits.
He'd never survive. That much was obvious.

With perverse pleasure she looked forward to
telling Clay about his new partner. She'd explain the
advantages of having another man to help him carry
supplies, pitch the tents, chop the wood, hunt, fish,
and whatever else Clay had agreed to manage. He
should be grateful. And if he wasn't, well, he'd just
have to make the best of it.

Aurelia sat down on the edge of her bed to remove
her boots. *Nana, forgive me,* Aurelia prayed silently as
she bent over and unlaced each boot down as far as the
buckle. *I've let your treasures tarnish. But I still have
them and I still wear them every day.* She pulled the
boots off and paired them on the floor next to her bed.

As she removed the combs and pins from her hair and
placed them in a porcelain container on the dresser, Aurelia
wondered what Nana would think of Clay. Aurelia knew
she needed him. He had common sense and a good head
for business. She wasn't stupid, but she knew very little
about packing supplies or negotiating with Indians.

She inched her fingers up the back of her neck and
loosened the coils of her chignon. Clay was willing to
shoulder even more than his fair share of the load on
this venture. She wasn't weak, but she couldn't picture herself hunting wild game, or building a boat, or
mushing a team of dogs.

Besides, there were more than a few men on board
with that unsavory look that made a woman feel
unsafe, even in a crowded public place in the middle
of the day. Undoubtedly Clay's presence would protect her from unwanted advances.

But was that all she wanted from him? Protection? Sometimes when he looked at her, with his eyes all dark and sparkling, he made her feel scattered, even though she was an educated woman. He was handsome and strong, though he was a drinker and a gambler. And he was so mean to that poor Poyser boy.

Once in bed with the light off, she closed her eyes and listened to the sounds of the night.

Unusually quiet, the *Reliance* bobbed at anchor, a foreigner knowingly trespassing in dangerous waters. She creaked and strained like a rickety barn door as distant waves gathered momentum and slapped her sides. A lonely, ominous wind prowled the decks, howled through the hull, and warned of danger to come.

She thought of Violet. Perhaps Mr. Guardian could help her find her. Aurelia envisioned her sister's once lively purple-blue eyes now sunken and dull, her glossy black hair dirty and matted, her porcelain complexion bruised.

"No!" Aurelia cried as she bolted upright in bed. Her breath caught in her throat. She pressed her hand to her heart, which was beating like a war drum. Sweat plastered her hair to her cheeks. She took a slow, deep breath.

She wasn't aware of her roommate's movements until the hard glare of the kerosene lamp washed over the cabin.

"Dear, are you all right?" Lily sat on the end of Aurelia's bed. "I hope that was merely a dream and not a memory."

Aurelia looked around the room and gathered her bearings. "I'm sorry I woke you, Lily." Aurelia placed her palms next to her cheeks. "Just a dream. That's all."

"Your hands are shaking. Can I get you something?

Order a pot of tea?" The widow walked to the dresser and checked her timepiece. "Oh, dear, I'm sorry. Don't even think about tea. It's nearly three in the morning."

"I'm fine. I'm sorry I woke you." She tried to restore order to the covers on her bed. "Let's try to get back to sleep."

Two hours later, the lonesome moan of the ship's foghorn echoed through the damp, gray mist that cloaked the sun. A rumbling sea and a cold, icy drizzle kept most passengers in their cabins for the day. The following morning they reached Dyea.

7

Aurelia gathered her few belongings and checked the cabin one last time. She couldn't help but smile as she watched Lily exercise uncharacteristic care in packing her trunks. With no maid to attend her, Lily had been forced to care for her own belongings.

"Did your wardrobe survive the trip?" Aurelia asked.

"Better than I expected." Lily folded several petticoats and forced the frothy white lace into the last open trunk. She pulled the lid down slowly as she tucked ruffles right and left. "There," she said, fastening the heavy brass lock, "I did it."

"Lily, wait." Aurelia spied the burgundy silk gown draped neatly across the head of the bed. "You forgot this." She reached for the elegant gown and took one last look at the embarrassingly low décolletage. She thought of Clay Guardian, relishing the memory of his hands around her waist and the beat of his heart against her breast.

"How silly of me," Lily said. "And I haven't a spare inch of room. You'll just have to keep it."

"Keep it? Oh, I couldn't do that. It'll fit in one of

your trunks, I'm sure. After all, there was room for it when you boarded."

"Ah, yes, but I didn't pack the trunks before I boarded. My maid did. And I am obviously not as skilled as she—though I'm far better than I ever imagined." Lily knelt down to buckle the wide leather straps. "If you must know, I never intended to pack the gown. I'd hoped you would accept it as a token of my friendship." She looked up at Aurelia. "I've enjoyed your company. You've listened so patiently to all my troubles, tolerated my teasing, and entertained me with all those amusing stories of college life. I can't believe you're having as much trouble with your studies as you claim. You're much too bright. In any event, I'll miss you." She glanced back at the dress. "Besides, the color is infinitely more flattering to your features. Please, dear. Take it with you."

"But I couldn't. I'm going to the Klondike. I've no need for such a fancy dress."

Lily laughed. "Need? Since when does need have anything to do with acquiring a new dress?" She unfastened the straps of Aurelia's trunk and lifted the lid, then stopped mid-way as though she'd forgotten something. "You finish this, dear. I promised to see Captain Kegman before we docked. He'll be too busy later. See you on deck." She winked and scurried from the cabin.

In just the few moments she'd held the gown, the silk had begun to absorb Aurelia's body warmth. She fingered the tiny pleats across the bodice. If she ever attended a society ball, she'd have the perfect dress. But her future was clear. She'd never be invited to any society balls, even though she'd make her living treating the maladies of the finest ladies. That was the price a woman paid for being a doctor. Aurelia had agreed to it long ago.

She carefully tucked the voluminous skirt into the

trunk. She also knew she'd never marry unless she found a man who didn't give a fig about what people said. She'd agreed to that price too, but she never had known before how dear a price that could be.

She thought of Clay. Bankers of his stature went to lots of balls. No doubt his wife had worn dresses like this. And when she had, had Clay looked at her with admiration? Or longing? He'd only spoken of Mary a few times, but it was always with fondness. It sounded like Mary had been everyone's ray of sunshine.

Aurelia fastened her trunk, stood, and wiped her hands. Who was she to be comparing herself to Clay's dead wife?

Then she joined the other passengers on deck. A cold wind took her breath as she found an open spot near the railing. So this was Dyea. She strained her eyes to see the hodgepodge of tents and wood-frame buildings tucked far back from the shore. The formidable, snow-covered Coastal Mountains rimmed the town on three sides. It was hard to get a clear view, but Aurelia didn't see anything on the mountains that looked like a trail. Just snow—heavy, white, and smothering.

The ship had pulled up next to a wharf. A long, raised, wooden platform tottered on legs of wooden pilings and bridged much of the distance between the ship and the shore.

As chaotic as things had been when the ship left Seattle, they were doubly disorganized in Dyea. The soot-covered crewmen lugged and hoisted to the wharf the precious supplies the ship had carried in her hold for the last six days. There seemed to be no order to the process, the only objective being speed.

"How are we to sort our own belongings?" Aurelia asked the man next to her. "Who's going to move our outfits from the wharf to the town?" The more she observed, the more nervous she became. "Why have we anchored so far from shore?" And why didn't this man answer her questions?

"Good heavens!" Aurelia cried as a sudden noise drew her attention to the ship's aft. "What are they doing to those horses?"

"Shoving them off, lady," the man finally snapped, his knuckles white from gripping the railing. "And if I can't get off this tug pretty damn soon, I'm jumping in after them."

As if the language of the man next to her wasn't bad enough, the crew swore obscenities Aurelia had never heard before. She gaped as they backed the horses and mules to an opening in the railing and forced them over. They also tossed dogs into the icy water below. The splashing never stopped. Both excited and apprehensive, Aurelia leaned over the railing and, with everyone else, watched the animals tred to shore, blazing a watery trail of a thousand rippling chevrons.

"You're next, partner."

She recognized Clay's voice before she turned around. Though she hadn't forgiven his treatment of Waldo Poyser, Aurelia couldn't help but smile. He grinned too, the week-old stubble on his cheeks concealing his dimples. He had an anxious look about him, an eagerness that kept his hands moving, from his pockets to his dark leather slouch hat to his even darker hair.

"You can swim, can't you?" He squeezed in beside her at the railing and gave her a look that said it wasn't his fault they were forced to stand so close to each other.

Panic constricted Aurelia's throat. "No, I can't."

"Good. That means you need me. Unless you want

one of those savages over there to carry you on *his* shoulders."

A group of bronze, broad-faced natives waited on the shore, as a makeshift flotilla of canoes and wide, flat barges headed for the ship.

"Who are they?" Aurelia asked.

"Members of the Tlingit tribe."

"What are they going to do?"

"Carry you to Dyea. You and the freight and the other stampeders who think getting wet is the worst thing that's going to happen to you before you reach Dawson."

This was no time for teasing. Aurelia looked at the town and its awesome mountains again. She knew that as soon as the crew unloaded the *Reliance,* the ship would return to Seattle and take on another load of animals, supplies, and men. Once the ship pulled away and headed back to the world of comforts and luxuries, she'd have no choice but to fall in line and press on. The grimness of her mission sank in.

"This is as close to the shore as the old *Reliance* can get," Clay continued. "Everything that's on that wharf will get loaded on those barges and canoes over there and lightered in closer to shore. I'd say we're about a mile out. A high tide would help, but from the looks of things, I doubt anyone's willing to wait. From there you walk the rest of the way through the mud. Or, like I said, someone carries you."

Aurelia looked at him incredulously.

"Watch the Indians wade in to meet those barges. Water's up to the waist on some of them. Judging from their height, I'd say it should come up to right about here on me." He slapped his hands against his upper thighs. "Course, there may be some deep spots out there. You have to be careful."

"This is ridiculous. No one in Seattle said anything about having to swim to Alaska."

"Didn't you hear the rumor? All men in Seattle are liars."

"Present company excepted, of course?" She felt him stare at her with a sudden, but fleeting, intensity.

"Of course," he said. "After all, only a fool would double-cross his partner. Or her partner."

He must know about Waldo. She slipped her cold hands under her cape and looked right at him. "I suppose you're upset. Even so, I felt it was my duty. But I'm not sorry, and I would do it again."

She saw no response other than a twitch at the corner of his eye. "Well? Aren't you going to say something?"

He hesitated as though trying to fill in missing pieces. "Why don't you give me all the details. Just to make sure I understand." He ushered her away from the railing to a more private area on the deck. "Now, explain."

"I was angry with you for treating Mr. Poyser so shabbily."

"The Butcher?"

"His name is Waldo." Aurelia hoped her tone of voice let him know she didn't appreciate the nickname. "And if you hadn't filled me with all those tales of horror awaiting us on the trail, I doubt I'd have ever done it."

"Done what?"

"Taken him on as our partner, of course. The boy will never survive alone on his—"

"So the gossip mongers were right." He crossed his arms in front of his chest. A coldness she'd never detected in his voice before now punctuated his every word. "You want that sniveling sissy to team up with us."

Aurelia observed his narrowed eyes, his clenched

jaw, and his neck. The tendons behind his blue bandana were tense, strained to their limit. "He'll be able to help you carry the supplies. He can hunt, or at least fish. He can help you pitch the tents and break up camp. Just give him a chance."

He still didn't look convinced. She tried again. "He has a pair of trained Arctic gophers. When the two of you stake your claim, the gophers can dig through the ice. I understand the ground is frozen most of the time up here. Won't that be handy?"

She didn't like the way he stared at her, the way he balled his fists, the way his upper lip curled. "You shouldn't tense up that way. It's not healthy."

"Arctic gophers! Good God, woman," he bellowed so loud that several people at the railing turned to look. "Of all the scams in Seattle, that was the easiest to spot. And the pair of you fell for it." He braced his hands on the wall behind her, caging her with his arms. "I don't want that boy around us. What are you trying to do to me?"

"Clay, try to understand. Please." She felt so foolish. Her words tumbled fast. Her lower lip quivered. "I thought you to be more of a humanitarian. I thought you would welcome the opportunity to help someone less fortunate. I thought Waldo needed guidance and I thought—"

"You think too much."

She caught a glimmer of something wild in his eyes. Suddenly, the possessive stance she'd found oddly romantic turned frightening. "Remove your arms this instant."

He came to his senses and pulled back. A lock of her hair, freed by the breeze, dangled across her cheek. He coiled it around his finger. "The boy's not going with us." He tried to tuck the curl back into place but gave up.

Disturbed by his audacity, Aurelia pinned the lock in place, only to feel countless other wisps of hair flirting about her face and realize how totally disheveled she must appear. The wind was brutal, stinging her eyes.

"Do you always end your disagreements with women this way, acting as though your word is a foregone conclusion?"

"Women don't usually disagree with me."

"But in *this* particular incident," she said, trying to banish the disconcerting effect he still had on her, "*this* one has."

He looked at her with that now familiar fire back in his eyes. "What are you saying?"

"That if you don't accept Mr. Poyser as our partner, I'll be forced to dissolve our arrangement. My conscience won't let me send that innocent young man to certain death."

For a moment he looked stupefied, but the expression didn't last. "Look around. Are you sending all these men to their deaths too? If you think you are, your vanity is bigger than the Yukon. Poyser made his decision to come up here independent of you." Clay folded his arms and looked around at the other men. "You're headed for hell, lady. Any one of these men could protect you better than Poyser. And I can protect you better than all of these men put together."

"Now who has the bigger vanity?"

Clay glared at her. "That weakling doesn't know the first thing about survival."

"But you do. You can teach him while you're teaching me."

"It took him two hours to work up the courage to shoot a gun."

"But he did fire it."

"He's not strong enough to carry even a fifty-pound sack of flour. Hell, the first stiff wind will blow him away."

"He'll toughen up. If you give him a chance."

Clay was momentarily distracted by the increased activity. When he spoke to Aurelia again it was with renewed purpose. "You want to find your sister, don't you?"

"Of course I do."

"Then don't be so stubborn. If you spend your time and energy playing nursemaid to that pantywaist, the best you can hope for is that one of you will survive. If you honor your bargain with me, we'll find your sister."

His words struck Aurelia in the heart. She had to find Violet. That was, after all, the reason she'd come this far. But after what she'd done to Violet, Aurelia knew she could never live with herself if she made the same mistake again. Exasperated, she said, "Have you no conscience? As much as I want to honor our arrangement, I simply can't leave Waldo to fend for himself."

Despite the strength of her conviction, tears welled up in her eyes. "Clay, you and I both know there's not a soul on this ship who wouldn't welcome you as his partner. You're knowledgable. And levelheaded. Usually." She tried to sound light-hearted. "But you and I also know that Waldo isn't—he doesn't have your—Oh, what's the use? I simply couldn't live with myself if I didn't try to help him."

"He doesn't have my what?"

Your masculine form, your dashing style, your

twinkling dark eyes, your inviting smile, your strong arms. "Your self-confidence."

Warmth returned to his eyes, as though he knew the full extent of her thoughts. When had she given him the power to captivate her so?

"I'm an educated woman. I see no reason why I can't make the trip on my own, and certainly with Waldo Poyser. Violet made the journey with Sculley, and though that scurrilous dog has twice the brawn of poor Waldo, he doesn't have half the heart." She'd almost convinced herself of her ability. "Don't worry about us. We'll manage."

The die is cast, she thought as Clay turned his back to her and stepped toward the railing. She prayed he'd reconsider, but if he didn't, she was prepared to go with Waldo, or go alone.

After what seemed an eternity, he turned around. "I don't like it." He shoved his hands in his pockets and came back to her. "But I suppose I can live with it."

Aurelia grinned in relief. "You won't regret it. I promise."

"We'll see."

He ushered her back to the railing so she could see progress below. A short time later, Clay hopped aboard one of the lighters and headed for the shore. He told Aurelia he'd pick out a good spot on the beach to assemble their supplies. Aurelia took comfort in his confident manner. She and Waldo Poyser left the ship several hours later.

"From what I can see, Waldo, every supply outfit in Seattle has found its way to this wharf. Just look at these moldy sacks and broken crates. I'd say many of them have been here for weeks. Wouldn't you agree?" Aurelia called over her shoulder as she carefully picked her way around the haphazardly piled boxes, trunks, and sacks. She'd taken a chance on Waldo. She hoped he was up to the trials ahead.

Behind her, Waldo stumbled every few steps, breaking his fall with whatever trunk or flour sack was handy. "Yes, ma'am." Over his right shoulder he lugged a large canvas sack. Aurelia assumed it contained his personal belongings. He probably couldn't afford a steamer trunk. In his left hand he cautiously balanced a small wood-and-chicken-wire cage.

Aurelia suggested they stop for a moment, not because she needed the rest, but because Waldo was obviously having a difficult time. As Aurelia nodded to the other passengers walking past them on the wharf, Waldo raised the wood-and-wire cage to his face and made soft cooing sounds to its inhabitants.

"Your Arctic gophers?" She retraced her steps to look at the creatures.

Waldo nodded. "James John and Corbett. I named them after the world heavy-weight b-b-boxing champion of a few years back. James John is the boy. And C-C-Corbett is the girl." He squinted behind his spectacles as he peered into the cage. "Hope they'll be all right." He held the cage up for her inspection.

"Fine specimens," Aurelia said, as she wondered how to tell the young man the truth. "Waldo, I've been told by a knowledgable individual that Seattle is full of unscrupulous people who wouldn't hesitate to capitalize on a stampeder's eagerness. Your gophers may not be as useful as advertised."

He looked shocked. "You're saying I been taken for a f-f-fool?"

"Clay seems to feel—"

"Oh. He's the one who t-t-told you. Hmph." He looked inside the cage again and gently scratched his finger against the wire. "I only bought 'em to keep me c-c-company. Shoot. I know they ain't gonna d-d-dig as hard as a man. Hmph."

"Then I'm certain they'll be fine. This country is, after all, their home." Aurelia didn't want to talk about what Clay thought of Waldo and his gophers. "Well, Waldo, I guess we'd better get going. Clay is waiting on the beach for us. He's already started assembling our outfit."

"It ain't gonna work." He fell in step behind her, stumbling only half as much as before.

"What won't work?"

"The th-th-three of us as partners. He don't think much of m-m-me and I don't think much—"

"What was that?" Aurelia turned around to hear all of what he'd said. She used her hands to shield her eyes from the spray of wet snow that lashed her cheeks.

"Nothing."

They finally made it to the end of the wharf. Low tide had exposed the mile-long flats. Each time the barely lapping waters receded, hundreds of tiny crustaceans popped up from bubbles in the sand and mud. Pockets of green vegetation dotted the sticky black earth. Scavenging birds swooped all around.

Old-timers with horse-drawn wagons drove through the mud and water, waist high in some places, to the loaded barges and lighters waiting to be relieved of their cargo. Several dozen Indians waded out to the wharf to carry passengers on their backs. One muscular savage approached Aurelia. He gave her an assessing glance and quoted her his fare for a piggyback to shore.

When she shook her head no, the Indian grunted something she didn't understand and approached Waldo, who declined as well.

"Hold it, partner!"

Aurelia knew the voice. She scanned the crowded beach looking at the horse-drawn wagons. The drivers all had those horrid moustaches, visible for a mile. "Clay! Where are you?"

"Over here."

Aurelia followed the welcome sound of his voice and turned to the side. There he was, wading in water past his knees, his high-topped boots and pants drenched. As he approached the edge of the wharf, he nodded to Poyser in a manner Aurelia determined civil at best. Then he slapped his hand against the last piling. "Let's go."

"Go? How?"

He arched his brow. "I'd prefer to carry you in my arms, but not in this muck. Sit down on the edge here and climb on to my shoulders."

"Couldn't you get a wagon?"

"Not at fifty dollars! I could buy two horses for that amount of money. Now, get down here. My legs are freezing."

Aurelia didn't want Clay to contract an illness on her account. She lifted her skirt, grimacing with the knowledge that her ankles and several inches of her black stockings were visible to anyone who cared to look, though the others on the wharf seemed too concerned with their own problems to pay any attention to her. Thank heavens Waldo had the decency to avert his eyes.

Aurelia sat down on the edge of the wharf. Gracious! It was cold. She clamped her hands on her skirt to keep it from billowing in the breeze and robbing her of any more modesty.

Clay stood in front of her, his chin level with her knees. He didn't look pained at all. In fact, he looked pleased with himself.

Aurelia's pulse quickened as he encircled her wrists and eased her hands aside. It raced as he slid her heavy wool skirt halfway up her legs and spread her knees apart.

"Bet you wish you could swim," he said, reading her thoughts.

Her heart pounded like a war drum as he stepped between her thighs.

He gave her a wicked smile and then turned around. "Grab a hold of my arms and inch yourself to the edge. When I pull, you come. Got it?"

She gripped the buckskin covering his arms. He pulled. She followed. She tried to ignore the hot flush spreading across her cheeks and the tightening down in her privates, but she knew she'd have better luck trying to ignore Alaska. Sitting on his shoulders, she bunched her skirt and petticoat to fill the open space between her thighs and his neck. She tensed her thighs, hoping to keep her balance.

He took two steps and Aurelia could feel the resistance of the water against his legs. She wobbled and wrapped her arms around his neck. The muscles in his neck and shoulders hardened against her inner thighs. She'd rolled her stockings in elastic garters that hugged her thighs several inches above her knees, the same spot where the legs of her cotton combination ended. Her attempt to tuck more modesty between her bare skin and Clay's neck was futile.

She was about to tell him to let her down, that she'd take her chances in the water herself, when one of the Tlingits, with a snappily dressed stampeder on his shoulders, sank to his armpits in a hole in the mud, throwing the man head first into the water.

Clay saw it too. He made half a turn back to the wharf, and Aurelia tensed her legs again and clenched her arms around his neck to keep her balance.

"Poyser, you're on your own."

Aurelia kept her eyes straight ahead. If Clay, the Indians, and most of the other passengers could wade or swim to shore, so could Waldo. After Clay took several more steps, Aurelia heard a splashing sound behind her.

Clay looked back. "About time," he called out.

It took the better part of an hour to reach the shore. By the time they did, Aurelia had adjusted to Clay's rhythm and no longer had to fight to retain her balance. She'd accepted the intimate touch of his hands against her legs. She'd become familiar with the thickness of his hair, as she'd clenched it every time he paused, every time he tried to turn his head to say something to her, every time his whiskers scratched her thigh, every time his warm breath tickled her skin.

With all the activity going on around her, she didn't know how she'd managed to block everything from her mind but the feel of Clay's body, but she had. If she never got this close to him again, she wanted to be able to fetch back this memory. With all his handsome features, her eyes may have betrayed her, but not her sense of touch. He was both firm and gentle, bold and cautious.

"This is it," Clay said as he trudged up the sand and dropped to one knee.

Still surging with wild sensations, Aurelia looked away, feigning interest in the hustle going on around them as she smoothed her skirt and tried to quiet her scandalous thoughts.

"Like some kind of circus, isn't it?"

She nodded, pleased that he hadn't referred to anything more personal.

"One of these days," Clay said as he stretched his arms, "you're going to have to tell me about those silver boot buckles you always wear. I know every little swirl and flower on them by heart." He grinned.

"They were a gift from my grandmother," Aurelia said quickly, relieved that he couldn't read her mind.

Suddenly distracted, Clay looked in the direction from which they'd just come. "Poyser, over here." He waved to get Waldo's attention.

God help him, Aurelia prayed as she watched Waldo make his way across the mud flats. Wet from the waist down, his bony frame appeared even scrawnier than usual. The bottom half of his canvas bag dripped like a running faucet. Several inches of his red and yellow plaid mackinaw were soaked, the weight pulling his sloping shoulders even farther down. At least James John and Corbett appeared safe.

Aurelia rushed toward him. "Waldo, you'll catch pneumonia in those wet clothes. Let's find your—"

"Hold it," Clay barked. "We don't have time for fashion shows. We've got to find our supplies in this madhouse and start stacking them up. I've already found some of yours, Aurelia. They're over there. See the sled propped up with the blue bandana around the front blade?" He gestured to a spot far back from the beach. "That's our cache."

"You could've saved us a l-l-lot of steps by piling them up down here." Waldo jerked his head nervously.

"You want to pile your outfit down here, go ahead. And when the tide comes in, let's see how fast you can move fifteen hundred pounds to dry ground."

Anyone could have made a mistake like that, Aurelia reasoned. She didn't like the way Clay snapped about it, but this was hardly the time to address the issue.

"Aurelia, you come with me. Poyser, you'd better park your wildlife somewhere. You'll need both hands—at least."

Waldo didn't say a word as he carried James John and Corbett to the cache Clay had already started. Aurelia watched him lick his finger and hold it in the air, then reposition one of the smaller sacks and set the wood-and-wire cage protectively behind it.

Aurelia sighed at the enormity of the task ahead.

"We get the cache assembled on the beach," Clay explained, "and then we move it to one of the warehouses in Dyea—that's two miles up the road."

"And exactly how is that to be accomplished?" Aurelia looked around to see what other people were doing. A few were dragging sacks back to the area of the beach where Clay had started their cache. Most of the others, however, were frantically running back and forth among the mountains of supplies tossed wherever the ship's crew had dumped them.

"We get our supplies to town the same way we get them over that mountain over there. What we can't carry on the sled, we carry on our backs. You, too, little lady."

"I have every intention of pulling my share."

"Right. Let's get going. What do your trunks look like?"

Aurelia declined Clay's arm so she could hold her skirt above the mud and sand. She didn't know what had suddenly made him so irritated.

A dozen newsboys from Dyea and nearby Skagway scurried among the crowd. "The latest and most accurate news from the Klondike!" they barked. "Four bits."

"Fifty cents for a newspaper!" Aurelia couldn't fathom such an outrageous amount. She shook her head as she saw how fast they disappeared.

Aurelia noticed some other people working the crowd. Two painted women in ruffled princess dresses and feathered and flowered hats lolled in a horse-drawn hack at the edge of the beach, calling to the stampeders. One soiled dove, her flaming red hair the obvious product of cheap chemicals, waved a white lace hankie at Clay as he added another sack of sugar to the cache.

You brazen trollop, Aurelia thought as she watched the redhead turn sideways in the cab and lean forward, pressing her arms to the sides of her unbelievably ample bosoms. It didn't appear to matter that the woman's face was far from attractive. Not a man on the beach was looking above her neck, Clay included.

8

"*The welcoming committee,*" Clay said, smiling. "You wait here."

"You're not going to talk to them!" Aurelia stiffened with indignation as Clay strode over to the waiting carriage. He put one boot on the step of the carriage and leaned closer to the "ladies." Aurelia couldn't make out the words they said, but she had no difficulty hearing the titters and giggles of the two women as their high-pitched noise mixed with Clay's deep laughter.

What would he want with women like that?

Aurelia had barely formed the question when the answer dawned on her: sexual union. He was, after all, a man. She tried to think of the whole process as nothing more than a bodily function for release and procreation. At least that's the way she used to think of it, before she met Clay.

The redhead brushed Clay's hat off his head and tousled his hair with her fingers. He asked them something, and both women nodded in unison. Clay drew his money clip from his pocket and handed each woman a bill.

That was enough! She wasn't about to let some trollop sap the strength of her partner.

Aurelia marched over to the carriage, the sand slowing her determined stride.

"Excuse me, Mr. Guardian. *Partner.* We have work to do."

"So do we, sweetie," the redhead cooed.

Aurelia stared at Clay. "Perhaps you'd care to introduce me to your new . . . acquaintances." They had charcoal streaked across their eyelids, heavy powder pressed on their cheeks, and lip rouge thickly applied to their mouths. And as if the redhead wasn't bad enough, the other was a blond.

"How rude of me, *partner.*" Clay turned to the women in the carriage. "Ladies, this is Miss Aurelia Breighton of Detroit. And, Miss Breighton, this is Kitty Dundee and Ruby Johnson of the notorious Dyea Dance Hall and Bar."

Aurelia glared at Clay. Rankled by his obvious avoidance of her profession, she turned to the ladies and said with emphasis, "It's Doctor Breighton."

The redhead mimicked Aurelia. "It's Ruby Lips Johnson," she said as she puckered her painted mouth. "Ruby Lips. Don't forget that, honey." Ruby leaned forward and toused Clay's hair one more time. "You won't forget me now, will you?"

"Not a chance." Clay winked at the ladies and gave them the dimpled, sparkling smile Aurelia had come to think of as reserved for her.

Aurelia felt her shoulders sag until Clay slapped her on the back and said in his buddy-to-buddy voice, "Let's go. We've got work to do."

She marched along behind him, though he made no apparent effort to slow down for her. She wasn't naive: He obviously had other things on his mind.

As she tried to keep her skirt above the sand and mud,

Aurelia couldn't resist the urge to look back at the painted ladies. They were repeating their earlier performance to two new men who had approached the carriage.

And just how had Miss Ruby Lips Johnson managed to get her things ashore? Aurelia wondered. She glanced at Clay, whose rhythm never faltered as he hoisted the heaviest sacks and boxes. He would be spending the night, or some portion of it, with one or, heaven forbid, both of those women. What other reason would he have had for giving them money?

The partnership arrangement Clay had offered Aurelia made no reference to the possibility of intimacy, other than the fact that they would have separate tents, which she would have insisted on. He had promised to protect her from the depraved element that would surely be present, but if he had to seek out the services of a harlot on the first day he touched shore, what did that make him?

Aurelia thought of how, barely an hour ago, he'd carried her on his shoulders, and how she'd imagined all sorts of things between them. But, of course, he didn't know her thoughts, and he clearly didn't have similar ones.

Clay worked alone for at least three hours. By ten o'clock that night he'd located and moved half of their supplies to the cache at the high end of the beach. Earlier that evening Aurelia had tried to convince him to let the rest of the work wait until morning, when they'd all had a good night's rest. He said no. He told her she didn't have to keep working, but he couldn't quit now. Another ship was due in after midnight. With two loads of supplies dumped on the beach, finding their own in that mess would be next to impossible.

She had argued that it was too dark. He pointed to the hundreds of campfires on the beach and beside the tents pitched all along the road into Dyea and insisted he'd have plenty of light.

She had complained that she was hungry and had to make use of a privy. He walked with her into town and left her at the Ballard Hotel, where he obtained a room, a bath, and dinner for her.

She had urged him to reconsider and stay in town with Waldo, who had pitched his tent on the outskirts. Clay adamantly refused, shouting that someone had to stay with the supplies to protect them from thieves.

She had warned him that unless he stopped to eat and rest, he would become too fatigued for the task at hand.

The task at hand? What did she know about the task at hand? Clay wiped his brow and slung another sack of something on top of the cache. He could be slinging someone else's supplies at this point: He didn't care. All he wanted to do was work through the puzzle she presented and work off the tension that had tormented his body from the moment he met her.

He liked her lips. They looked soft and full, and he just knew that when the time came to kiss her they'd part on instinct, not experience. He liked her sense of propriety, though he also found it frustrating. He knew he shouldn't have been so aggressive in front of all those people on deck that morning. But he liked letting them know she was his partner, even if she did go around drawing attention to her schooling. He liked letting folks know they had some kind of bond, just the two of them. He liked her spunk. But more than anything, he relished the moment when her arms lost their stiffness and her eyes turned all dark and inviting, because above all, he liked to win.

She wasn't anything like Violet. No, Aurelia was too good-hearted. He could tell by her concern for Poyser, that loser. He thought about how she'd offered to buy the ring. She seemed honest.

But this kind of blindness was dangerous, he told himself. It could make a man careless, and even get him killed. He wasn't making this trip for a chance to bed the woman, though he'd thought about it more times than he wanted to admit. He had to find her sister in order to find his money—the bank's money. If he failed, he'd never be able to hold his head high in Seattle again. Worse yet, little Eli would be shunned by the town's self-righteous community and grow up paying for the sins of his father, just as Clay had before him.

As honorable as Aurelia appeared, Clay still didn't know for sure that she was not involved in her sister's scheme. After what he'd heard that afternoon, he had to be even more careful. Both of the whores he'd met at the beach remembered a young woman who fit Violet's description. But they'd have remembered anything for the money Clay paid them. Anyway, the girl they had described didn't sound as commanding and confident as the seductress Clay had met in Seattle. If what they hinted at was true, Aurelia didn't know half the danger her sister was in. Then again, Violet could have skillfully played the role of victim. It could have all been part of her act.

He needed to clear his head. Until he knew for sure, he couldn't afford to start thinking about Aurelia as anything but a means to an end. One of the reasons he had left the ship alone that morning was to give himself a chance to think. He should never have carried her ashore. That's what started everything, all these feelings about her. He could still picture her standing on the wharf, not knowing where to go, what to do next, waiting for someone to rescue her. Waiting for him.

Things got more complicated when she sat on the edge of the wharf and he shoved her skirts up. He got a glimpse of her garters, rolled just a few inches above her knees, some fancy ribbons and ruffles up a little higher on the thigh, and all that creamy white skin in between.

He tried to concentrate as she grabbed his hands and slipped her legs over his shoulders. She started jabbering about the beautiful mountains and all the snow, but, hell, he didn't want to look at the shore! Not with her long, graceful legs dangling against his chest. He stroked her black stockings, made some comment about helping her keep her balance. Even with that freezing water sloshing against his crotch he got hard.

Then he stumbled and she wrapped her arms around his neck and leaned forward. The fullness of her breasts brushed against the back of his head. Oh, God! How much is a healthy man supposed to stand? Then she had to go and wiggle the way she did and he thought he'd lose it for sure—drop the both of them right into the water. Instead, he grabbed her legs, felt the ruffle on the end of those soft pantaloon things she wore. Felt the silkiness of her bare thigh pressed against his neck.

And did all that touching bother her any? Hell, no. All she was concerned about was Poyser's wet clothes. Damn that boy!

Clay looked toward town, toward the Ballard Hotel where he'd left Aurelia. Determined to dull the ache in his loins, he'd spent the rest of the day in an all-out effort to exhaust himself. Now he was so tired even his toenails ached. He repositioned a few sacks and barrels in the cache to create an alcove and crawled in, only slightly aware of the wind and the sprays of snow blowing off the mountains.

The wind whistled its warning all along the beach, under the flaps of the canvas tents that crowded the road to town, around the doorways to Dyea's dance halls and bars, and through the single-board thickness of the walls and floor of the Ballard Hotel. "Go back," it whispered.

Aurelia's "room," a small corner of the second floor, was partitioned with a faded, whiskey-stained screen depicting Oriental lovemaking. She stared, then quickly turned away, as though caught doing something naughty.

Her bed was a sheet of canvas stretched across a wooden frame, her blanket a large caribou skin. Fully clothed, she huddled under the hide and tried to find a comfortable spot in the middle of the canvas. In her movement, she caught sight of the screen again.

Naked bodies everywhere, one couple romantically tangled in vines and flowers, bathed in the white light of an alabaster moon, another savagely coupling in a position appropriate only for animals.

Again she stared. Would Clay do that?

When had it gotten so warm? Beneath the privacy of the caribou skin, Aurelia unbuttoned her shirtwaist and loosened her corset. Her nipples had grown hard. Knowing she shouldn't, she turned to the screen again, unwilling to fight the temptation to look.

The man had his hands entwined in the woman's long, dark hair, his mouth covered her full, round breast, her legs splayed to welcome him, her hips arched in pleasure.

The man's hair was dark like Clay's. His chest as broad and muscular.

Would a man ever touch her like that? Would Clay? She suddenly felt the pain of her loneliness. For no reason she could explain, she began to sob quietly.

On the other side of the screen the other guests, all men, tossed and turned in their row of crude canvas bunks, snoring like wild animals.

Drying her eyes on the hem of her sleeve, Aurelia stared at the smoke-stained ceiling as she listened to the evidence of deviated septums, postnasal drips, and hacking coughs. She reached for the kerosene lamp and turned it off. For a moment, she wondered if Clay snored when he slept.

Through the window she could hear laughter and the sound of rippling keys on a honky-tonk piano. Why was she even thinking of Clay when he was probably with Ruby Lips? She pounded her pillow, buried her head, and eventually fell asleep.

The rain started sometime after midnight. An unusually warm breeze flung the drops against the dirty hotel window, streaking the layer of dust that served to dim the light of dawn.

Aurelia opened her eyes. Every muscle ached as she sat up and stretched. Oh, what she wouldn't give for a hot bath and a generous handful of epsom salts.

The stench of sweat and whiskey was enough to get her up and out, even if it hadn't been the disgracefully late hour of ten o'clock. She held a handkerchief to her nose and made her way quickly between the bunks and down the stairs to the main room.

A big sheet-iron stove in the center of the room radiated heat and cut the dampness. Aurelia briskly rubbed her hands to stimulate circulation while she scanned the long, crude tables covered with oilcloth.

A man with salt-and-pepper whiskers, wearing black rubber hip boots and holding a long-handled spatula, motioned for Aurelia to sit down. "I'm what you call your waitress. What'll it be?"

Aurelia assumed Clay and Waldo had already eaten and were hard at work on the beach. Feeling guilty for oversleeping, she ordered the corn bread and bacon, which she could see had already been cooked. She gobbled her meal and set out to join her partners.

"Where the hell have you been?" Clay called to her as she reached the spot where their cache was assembled, now twice the size as when she'd last seen it. "The day's half over."

"You look dreadful!" Aurelia cringed at the sight of him. He looked worse than a cat left out in the rain. She swore he'd aged a year overnight. "It's raining. Where's your mackinaw? Your hat?"

"Your concern is touching. Can't you see what's going on here? Another ship pulled in last night, and they say another's due to dock this afternoon. We've got to get our gear off this beach and into a warehouse. Assuming it's worth saving."

Aurelia looked at the mound of supplies in front of her and then at her timepiece. "I'm sorry, Clay. I overslept. It won't happen again." She tried to sound appreciative of all the work he'd accomplished. "When did you do all this?"

"Last night." He drew a handkerchief from his pocket and wiped the rain from his face. "What do you think I did last night? Go whoring all over Dyea?"

Shocked at his language and guilty over her own suspicions, Aurelia covered her lips with her fingertips.

He wasn't finished. "If you and your pantywaist friend had been out here working like you were supposed to, we'd have been finished long ago and, believe me, Miss Breighton, I'd have spent the night spreading the thighs of every whore in town!"

He turned on his heels and yelled to a man approaching the beach in an empty wagon. "Hey you! Bring that wagon over here." As the driver steered the horse toward the cache, Clay again turned to Aurelia. "I don't care how much it costs, we're paying to have the cache hauled to the warehouse. I'm not spending another night on this beach."

She may have felt guilty for her assumptions about where and how he'd spent the night, but it didn't keep her from snapping at Clay when the driver quoted a hundred dollars to haul the load into town. "At that rate," she said, "I'll have to find gold just to pay my way home."

Clay ignored her, paid the driver in advance, and immediately began loading the wagon. Aurelia decided she'd have a few words with Clay later about his dictatorial style. But right now, she'd thank heavens for the wagon. The thought of dragging all those supplies two more miles was unbearable.

She struggled to hoist a sack of flour on her shoulders and then sling it on the open flatbed. Clay was right. She and Mr. Poyser should have been out here working too, if not all night, then certainly earlier this morning. They were, after all, partners.

He probably thought she was one of those frail and

delicate ladies who sat around all day eating bonbons and who wouldn't do anything more strenuous than lift a strand of pearls. She realized it looked like she was trying to take advantage of him. Aurelia looked for the heaviest thing she could find. He was probably all frustrated because he couldn't dally the night away with those two tarts.

A lump caught in her throat at the thought of his sharing such intimacies with someone else. She lifted a sizeable box of nails from the pile and kept her eyes on the ground as she trudged through the sand to the wagon. Her arms strained from the weight and her knees began to wobble. She would show him she could carry her share, she decided, wondering why she felt so close to tears.

"Give me that," he said as he grabbed the box from her arms and shoved it on the wagon. "You ought to know better than to try to lift something that heavy. Strain yourself and you don't have a chance of crossing that pass."

Irritated anew by his harsh words and ungrateful attitude, Aurelia turned back toward the cache, mumbling, "Fine with me, Mr. Muscles. Carry it yourself."

For every three boxes and sacks Clay hauled to the wagon, Aurelia managed one. Each time their paths crossed, she made a point of glaring at him. If he thought she was going to give up, he had another think coming.

Finally, Clay yelled at her again, "Your friend Poyser's down on the wharf checking to make sure we haven't left anything behind. He should be up any minute. You go down on the beach and wait for him. I don't need you here. I can take this to town myself."

Aurelia stiffened. "Need, as in require or want? Of course not. But need, as in 'partner'? Oh yes, you do.

I paid for half these supplies, and you aren't going anywhere without me."

Aurelia turned away so quickly she didn't see the crack in his hardened expression, the hint of a smile that showed that he'd found something gratifying in her words. She marched toward the beach where Waldo waited, muttering as she picked her way through the obstacle course of supplies, "Nothing but a pig-headed, cross-grained mule. Of course you don't need me. You don't need anyone." She pulled her hood forward as far as it would go, bent her head into the wind, and trudged through the sand toward the wharf.

The rain finally stopped. Long, arduous hours later the wagon rumbled toward Dyea, groaning under the weight of its load. Waldo coughed every few steps as the three of them plodded behind, their boots cracking the thin layer of ice beginning to form in the slush.

"Hold it," Clay called to the driver after they'd gone about half a mile.

The driver pulled in the reins. "Whoa, boy." The old horse snorted and a cloud of cold, white vapor drifted in the twilight.

Aurelia didn't have the energy to lift her head to see what was going on. Grateful for the chance to stop, she closed her eyes and felt slightly off-balance. Suddenly, she felt Clay's strong hands circle her waist as a predator would grip its prey. The sudden sensation of pressure and heat jolted her. She opened her eyes. Unnervingly close, his dark eyes appeared to hunt for something in hers as he lifted her in the air.

"Thank you," she whispered, even that taking her strength.

The driver grabbed her under her arms and pulled her up amid the supplies. "Ain't no room to sit, ma'am, so just spread yourself over these sacks and hang on. I'll get you to town in no time."

Why was Clay being so nice to her now? She tried to make sense of the puzzle he presented, but she couldn't. It didn't matter, not now. Flour sacks had never felt so good. She let herself go limp, face down, across a bed of bulging canvas. Already they smelled of mold.

She could tell how close they were to town by the volume of the music. All along the way she smelled smoke, burning wood, and an assortment of strange foods being cooked over open fires. She drifted off to the aroma of flapjacks and bacon and things unrecognizable.

The rhythmic rumble slowed, then stopped as the wagon pulled in front of the warehouse. She'd ridden all the way into town, just like the lazy, lolly-gagging, bonbon-eating female he thought she was. How could she have let that happen? Why had she given in? She tried to avoid eye contact with Clay as he stretched his arms up for her, held her by the waist, and gently set her down.

She limply patted her skirt. "I appreciate the ride, but I could have walked, you know. I'm not helpless."

The sensitivity in his eyes quickly vanished. Back again was the invincible glare. When she did nothing but stare back, he grunted an oath. "Hey, old man," he called to the driver. "Can you see our stove up there?"

The driver turned around and surveyed the load. "Yea. You want it?"

"That and a fifty-pound sack of flour, a can of evaporated eggs, a twenty-pound sack of slab bacon—you see any canned peaches up there?—the cook here's got to make my dinner." He turned to Aurelia, then back to the driver as though he'd just remembered something else. "And utensils." Back to Aurelia.

"What'll you need? A frying pan? A bowl? What else? I'm hungry and I want a big, big supper."

"If you think your primitive masculine attitude is either appealing or frightening, you're wrong. Wrong, wrong, wrong."

Clay scowled, then called up to the driver. "Never mind. I'll be eating in town tonight. I want a decent meal."

"Let me know when you need a boil lanced," she snapped.

Seated in a narrow, false-front building called the New York Kitchen, Aurelia waved the heavy cigar smoke away from her face as she ate her fish and sourdough bread. Waldo ate quickly, then placed a few coins on the table and stood to leave.

"Not so fast," Clay ordered. "Sit down. We've got plans to make. Seeing as how we're all working together." He exaggerated the last few words, as though the concept were in name only. Waldo took his seat.

Clay signaled the bartender for another beer. "While you two were getting your beauty rest this morning, I talked with some men from Skagway, a few miles over. We're still five hundred miles from the gold fields. If we leave from Skagway, we cross the White Pass. If we leave from Dyea, we go by the Chilkoot. The Chilkoot is higher by six hundred feet, but it's twelve miles shorter. Pack animals can't make it to the summit, but, like I said, it's shorter."

"How b-b-bad can an extra twelve m-m-miles be?"

Clay swigged his beer and set the glass down with a sense of determination anyone could see. "How much weight you think you can carry on your back, boy?

Think you can handle fifty pounds? Sixty? Seventy? Indians are packing up to a hundred."

Waldo shrugged his shoulders. "I can c-c-carry as much as you can."

"Good." Clay snickered and gave Waldo a half-smile. "Here's how we'll do it. We each haul a load a few miles ahead, drop it and mark our new cache, go back and get another load. We've got four thousand five hundred pounds to move. That's fifteen hundred pounds each, assuming we're all carrying an even share. The Chilkoot Trail's about thirty-three miles long. By the time we walk back and forth hauling our cache, we'll have stretched that thirty-three miles to nearly a thousand."

Clay appraised Waldo's skinny frame. "You can't carry seventy pounds, boy." He looked at Aurelia, her mouth gaping at his calculations. "And neither can you. So let's figure fifty pounds a load for each of you. When we're on terrain where we can use the sleds, you should each be able to take at least a hundred pounds. How far we move each load each time is another matter, and that depends on the terrain, the weather, and your stamina. I doubt either of you can go more than four or five miles each trip, three round trips a day. Under good conditions, we're looking at six to eight weeks just to get to Lake Bennett, unless we pay the Indians to pack, or we pay to use the tramway. We can't afford to do either one. So now, you tell me, boy. How much of a difference does an extra twelve miles make?" Clay grinned like a gambler who'd just played his winning card.

Waldo fidgeted in his seat. "Well, we could t-t-take the water route."

"Ah!" Clay said with the kind of pleasure that meant he'd trapped Waldo once more. "The rich man's route."

"Are you saying there's an easier way to Dawson?" Aurelia asked.

"I'm saying there's another way, and if the weather's right, it is easier, but that doesn't mean we can take it. Kegman told me about it when we were on the *Reliance*." Clay angled his body to focus on Aurelia and exclude Waldo. "Every now and then you'll find a captain willing to take his boat north through the Aleutian Islands, on to St. Michael, then south on the Yukon River and into Dawson. But, believe me, those captains are few and far between."

"Why?"

"For one thing, the weather. When you're that far north, the river's only ice-free for seven or eight weeks in the heart of the summer. If you have any trouble and have to lay up any length of time, well, you could be stuck for a year—for a *year*—with no more supplies than what you have with you."

"We got p-p-plenty of supplies."

Clay turned to Waldo. "You could run aground and be stuck on a glacier. You could get frostbite and lose your feet, your hands. You could go blind from the glare. You could freeze to death. Understand now, boy?"

Waldo stuck out his lower lip but said nothing.

"What else?" Aurelia asked Clay, drawing his attention back to her.

"The main reason is that there's just not enough passengers to make taking the water route financially sound. In these times, if you own a boat the smart thing to do is make that run back and forth between Seattle and Dyea as many times as you can. You saw how fast the *Reliance* shoved off after the crew dumped our cache ashore. It's a foregone conclusion that every time any ship leaves Seattle it'll be full."

"But if getting to Dawson is easier by water than by land, I would think more people would choose the water route. What possible reason would a person have for taking the more difficult path?"

"Time. Everyone wants to get to the gold fields before all the good claims are staked. Right this minute we're five hundred miles from Dawson and it's going to take us at least three months or so to get there. If we were to go the water route, we'd be looking at almost five thousand miles. Depending on the weather, that could take as little as two months, or as many as four. Kegman said he knew of at least a dozen boats that went up that way and never came back. This place they call Alaska is huge. Sailing around her is not easy. These stampeders won't wait that long to stake their dreams."

"Okay, you've convinced us," Aurelia said. "We'll be ready to leave tomorrow morning."

Clay laughed. "No. You won't be ready tomorrow morning. You won't be ready for at least a week, maybe two. Not if the way you worked today was any indication of your stamina. No." He shook his head. "Only a fool just picks up and climbs that mountain." He looked around the room. "And there'll be plenty of them doing just that. Most of them haven't pushed anything heavier than a pencil." From the look on his face, he had no sympathy for the inexperienced. "We'll spend the next week or so climbing the lower paths around here to limber up, toughen up. Spring's the best time to cross the Chilkoot and—what's today?"

"Thursday, March twenty-fourth," Aurelia answered. "Palm Sunday is April third. Easter the tenth."

Aurelia thought for a moment of how she'd be spending the holiday if she hadn't come to Alaska. Her parents would suggest she stay at school to study; that's what they'd suggested last Thanksgiving. "With Violet gone," her mother had said, "it's not worth the trouble to assemble dinner and feign we've anything to be thankful for." Christmas was the same. Aurelia didn't argue with them or let them know how deeply hurt she felt.

"What is it, Miss Breighton? Didn't pack your Easter bonnet?"

Aurelia wished she had the energy to stare him down, or to respond with some snappy retort that would put him in his place, but she was simply too sad and too tired. "Whatever you say."

Clay nursed the rest of his beer. Once he opened his mouth to say something to Aurelia, then changed his mind. Maybe he was tired of arguing too.

"I'd better get you back to the hotel before they sell your bed," he finally said to her. "It's warmer than it's been the last few days, but it's wetter too. I want to get my own tent pitched before it rains again."

Waldo gulped his beer. "How come you know everything? I thought you was a b-b-banker."

"I am." There was a warning edge in Clay's voice. "But I wasn't born in a bank. If you don't believe what I'm telling you, or you don't have any confidence in my way of handling things, you're free to leave. But if you want to stay partners with me and Aurelia here, you put your money in the pool. I hold it. And you follow my orders."

Waldo picked up a toothpick and tried to roll it on his tongue the way Clay had done earlier. The toothpick fell to the floor.

"L-L-Look here, Guardian. I ain't standing 'round while you trick Miss Aurelia. I know all about what happened at the bank. And you ain't gonna hurt her the way you did that girl."

Clay fixed his eyes on the boy. "You don't know anything."

Unsure of the cause of this heightened tension, Aurelia eyed them both. "Clay, what is this? Waldo, what are you talking about?"

"It ain't the way he t-t-told you. I know the truth 'bout what happened. Whole town of Seattle knows. It was in the paper." He hazarded a quick glance at Aurelia, looking for encouragement. He took an even quicker glance at Clay to gauge the odds of escaping unharmed.

Both hope and dread filled Aurelia. "Go ahead," she said.

Waldo shot another wary look at Clay. "See, Guardian coaxed this girl into the vault, claiming he wanted to show her how safe it was." He hesitated like a man who'd lost his courage. Aurelia nodded, and his words tumbled recklessly. "He gets her in there and goes taking l-l-liberties with her. G-G-Groping at her and all and touching in places only a husband's allowed. He was aiming to have his way with her, but she grabbed a bar of gold and whacked him hard on the side of the head. Knocked him cold. She was running out of the vault all upset and crying. Told the manager what Guardian had done and then, on account of her being so upset, the gentleman friend she come with took her right home."

Aurelia knew the look in her eyes pleaded for a response from Clay, but still he said nothing. Waldo had to be telling the truth.

This can't be happening. Not this. Not Clay.

Desperate to anesthetize the pain, Aurelia searched her mind for some explanation. All she could think of was how yesterday morning on the ship Clay had all but pinned her to the wall, just the way he might have done to the girl in the bank. She knew he had a temper. He'd angered quickly enough when Aurelia told him about their new partner. When she had pointed out how self-centered he was, he had not only admitted he was used to getting his own way, he had bragged about it.

Waldo seemed to draw courage from Clay's silence. "And then the b-b-bank found all that cash gone. Ten thousand dollars. Paper said there wasn't enough evidence to get Guardian on theft, but attacking that girl was enough to get him fired for sure. Paper said her name was Violet. Same name as your sister."

A tremor shook her body. "Clay! No!"

He pounded his fist on the table and leaned forward. "You don't believe this cock-and-bull story, do you?"

She couldn't answer. She didn't know. She remembered how agitated he'd become when she said she'd be back for the ring, how he'd scrambled to make sure she'd come to his home address. Desperate to make sense of this nightmare, she asked, "Why did you leave the bank?"

Pushing back from the table, he glared at Waldo with a loathing that set the boy's lip to stutter even though he wasn't speaking. "I was fired."

"And my sister had to hit you on the head to escape your—"

"She hit me on the head so she could steal ten thousand dollars."

Aurelia curled her fingers in a paralyzing rage. "My sister is not a thief!"

"You weren't there! Your sister stole the money. Stole my job, my house, my reputation—"

"A thief wouldn't simply leave a valuable piece of jewelry behind. How did you really get Violet's ring? Yank it from her finger?"

He hesitated a moment, as though he knew how absurd his words would sound. "She put it on my desk. I don't know when, but I suspect it was just before we went into the vault, just after her friend said he'd wait for her by the door."

"And I suppose you didn't really coax her into the vault."

"She insisted on inspecting it. Said she wanted to see for herself where her jewelry would be kept. But, of course, she didn't leave the jewelry behind."

"She left the ring. Collateral for a loan. That's what you called it."

"That ring isn't worth ten thousand dollars!"

"Your being on the *Reliance*, that was no coincidence, was it?"

"No."

"You're looking for my sister. Aren't you?"

"Yes."

"That's why you wanted me to be your partner. So I could lead you to Violet."

He nodded.

Anger had its own sharp pain, but the agony of betrayal was cold and lonely.

Already grieving a loss she couldn't define, Aurelia asked the hardest question. "Is that still your goal?"

He nodded again.

Aurelia stood. She had to think. She had to get away from both of them and think.

She went outside to where crowds of impatient men jostled each other for space. Numbed to the pain, the shouts and curses that assaulted the air drifted by her. Mules brayed, dogs howled. Deaf to the sounds, Aurelia heard only Clay's confession, over and over again.

In a daze, she headed for her room. No sidewalks, no boardwalks, no randomly scattered planks to bridge the massive brown puddles, she let her skirt drag in the wide swath of mud that was the street. She let her boots sink in the deep ruts of heavily loaded wagons.

Lying on her cot, she fought to still the throbbing in her head, to think objectively, to remember her own goal, to plan. Her loyalty to Violet told her to dissolve the partnership with Clay and stay as far away from that lying bastard as possible. But she couldn't let her personal feelings blind her to reality. She'd never make it to Dawson on her own, and she'd never make it with just Waldo. All the other men she'd seen either frightened or repulsed her.

She turned to the screen, with all its erotic pleasures laid bare for the dreaming.

"Damn you, Clay!"

9

Early the next morning, just as originally planned, the three of them met in front of Aurelia's hotel. The raucous street scene of the night before showed no signs of stopping. With so much on her mind, Aurelia didn't flinch as a passing wagon splattered mud all over her cape.

She looked straight at the two men with her. "And now?" she asked, her hurt and anger from the night before sedated by practicality, "What do the three of us do about our partnership now?"

"Depends on who's still going to Dawson," Clay said. "I am," he added with unmistakable purpose.

"You aren't going without me," Aurelia said with equal determination. "Maybe I can't keep you from finding Violet, but I'll never let you take her back to a noose. I promise you that."

"Then, Miss Aurelia, you'll be n-n-needing me along for sure. To keep Guardian in line."

Clay laughed. "You?"

"That's enough," Aurelia snapped. "We have business to settle here." She'd spent the whole night agonizing over her options. She would go with Clay or without him. Going home without Violet wasn't an option at all.

"This is my assessment of our situation," she said. "I have plenty of food, but no equipment. Clay, you have equipment, but not enough food. Waldo, you have a little of everything and not enough of anything. Much as I loathe to admit this, we need each other."

Waldo nodded, looking relieved to be included.

"And you?" Aurelia asked Clay, expecting some sarcastic retort.

"You're right," he said.

"Good." She was confused by his lack of hostility and disturbed by the penetrating way he looked at her. "I'd like to think we're each mature enough to set our differences aside and work together." Just in case Clay felt as confused as she did, she said to him, "Don't misunderstand me. I'm not saying that I believe you. I'm saying that it's practical for us to stay together. Practical, not desirable."

Clay took her arm to remove her from the path of a harmless drunk. "I understand."

His insincere chivalry bothered her even more. There should be some kind of vaccine against the effect the man had on her. "Your opinion of my sister is based on erroneous information. By the time we reach Dawson, I'll have convinced you of her innocence."

He shook his head. "I doubt that. I'm an excellent judge of character."

Aurelia didn't argue with him. He was too stubborn. She argued with herself instead, ordering her heart to stop aching for a man who would only cause her more pain.

The trio hiked a few miles out of town. Clay barely

broke a sweat. Aurelia and Waldo huffed and puffed all the way back to town. In awkward silence, they spent the rest of the day in the warehouse repacking their cache into smaller loads of thirty to seventy pounds each. They spent every day of the next week doing the same.

The following Saturday started out the same, until Clay insisted on a few changes. He met Aurelia inside the hotel, in the screened corner that served as her room.

"Here. You'll need this," he said as he held out an Arctic fox parka. "Take it."

"I don't want it." She took a step back, feeling the need for distance.

"That's wolf fur on the ruff of the hood. It'll shed the ice crystals that form when you breathe. Take it."

"I don't need it. My cape is adequate." Despite her argument, she took the parka from him and stroked the thick fur, trying to determine how heavy the ice crystals would have to be to pose a health hazard.

"Could keep you from suffocating," Clay said. "Ice freezes on the ruff, builds up, makes a mask. Before you know it, you're gasping for air."

"I'll be careful." Why was he doing this?

"Don't be stubborn. The better prepared you are, the better your chances of reaching Dawson."

She considered his advice, all the while kneading the luxurious pelt.

Clay looked pleased. "The other day, you were the one giving advice, and you were right. The three of us should stay together. Now I'm giving advice. Take the fur."

"It may be months before I can pay you for it."

"I'm not asking you to pay for it."

"I'm insisting."

He seemed annoyed, but he nodded his acceptance of the arrangement. "You'll need these too." He handed her a pair of waterproof elk-skin boots. "The lining is caribou calf. The soles are from the hide of a bearded seal. They'll be a lot warmer and more practical than those boots. You'll be walking more than a thousand miles. Remember?"

"All too well." She laid the coat on the cot and took the boots. "You'll accept a late payment for them too?"

"Sure."

"No need to sound so nettled. You didn't expect me to accept them as a gift, did you? Not from you."

"Of course not."

It was not at all the outburst she expected. Aurelia examined the boots, looking for a way to attach her silver buckles. She couldn't make this journey without them.

Seeing that she'd be able to thread the leather laces through the buckles, she set the new boots on the cot. "Why are you doing this? Are you sure you can trust me? How do you know I'll honor this debt? For all you know, I might be just as deceitful and conniving as Violet."

"I'll take my chances."

"Why?"

"Like I said, I'm a good judge of character."

"You said you were an excellent judge of character. Are you admitting you might not always be right?"

He let out a long sigh as he sat on the overturned crate that served as a chair. "Aurelia, I don't have any quarrel with you. If anything, I . . . I wish you weren't so angry with me."

"It's not that simple for me." She walked over to the window, where she could look at throngs of people and see no one. "I suppose in order to show you Violet's generosity, I could tell you about how she always pestered Poppa for money, then she'd send it to me for books and papers and such. But all you'd see was how she manipulated Poppa."

"Don't you?"

Aurelia ignored his question. "When I told the family I wanted to study medicine, it was Violet who stood by my side. She threw a temper tantrum and screamed at both Momma and Poppa about how I should be praised, not punished, for having a good brain. But you'd likely find something unpardonable with her actions there too, wouldn't you?"

"Just childish."

Tears of frustration filled her eyes. "She knows my favorite color is blue, so she made me a shell wreath of tiny white shells and dozens of blue satin roses and ribbons." Though Aurelia felt a lump in her throat again, she turned to Clay and faced him squarely. "She worked a needlepoint satchel for my books and a small case for my spectacles. She cross-stitched a prayer about sisterly love—"

"How touching."

"Have you no heart!" Aurelia couldn't stop the flood of tears.

Clay jumped up and could barely restrain himself from touching her. "Aurelia, don't cry. Please don't cry."

"Don't you tell me what to do," she snapped. "My baby sister has been victimized, *victimized,* by that loathsome Sculley. And all you can do is cling to your preposterous story." She sniffed and gulped down her tears. "Now you listen to me. I need you to get to Dawson, just as much as you need me. But as soon as we get there, our partnership is over and I never want to see you again."

"Damn it! I'm not some kind of monster. I'm just trying to see justice done."

"I'm warning you. I'll do whatever I have to do to keep you from taking Violet back to Seattle. She's not going to rot in some prison, or hang at the end of a noose!"

For a moment, neither said a word.

Finally, Clay broke the silence. "So you do whatever it is you feel you have to do. And so will I." He shoved his hands in his pockets and walked away.

Aurelia listened to the lonely echo of his footsteps grow faint and disappear. She looked at her new coat and boots. What did he expect from her? Gratitude? No, she would pay him. The thought of being indebted to that insensitive scoundrel was more than she could bear.

Later that morning, wearing her new coat and new, silver-buckled boots, she joined Waldo outside the hotel. Clay was across the street, headed their way.

Waldo gaped at her new attire. "I seen Clay talking to some Indians yesterday. He bought them things for you?"

"We agreed to a loan of sorts." Despite the financial understanding she had with Clay, Aurelia suddenly felt self-conscious wearing clothes he'd picked out for her. It was so personal a gesture. How had he gauged her size?

Clay dodged the slow-moving wagons and joined

them. He didn't look as upset as he had when she last saw him. "Glad to see everything fits," he said to Aurelia. He yawned, stretched his arms, expanded his chest.

It bothered her, the proprietary way he maneuvered closer to her, the sensual way he stroked his beard when he looked at her. Unlike Waldo's thickening peachfuzz, Clay's beard was growing in thick and dark. Was it soft?

She hated the way he invaded all her thoughts. The man was her enemy. Why couldn't she just erase him from her mind? She could shut her eyes, but she'd still see him—she knew, because she'd tried all night.

"Miss Aurelia said you only l-l-loaned her the money for the coat."

"That was her idea," Clay said, looking impatient with the questioning.

"Gosh, Miss Aurelia, next time you need a new coat, I'll get it and you won't have to pay me. Ever. I'll even kill the beast."

Clay rolled his eyes.

"Thank you, Waldo. That's a brave and generous thing to offer."

"I can climb that m-m-mountain right now and go hunting." Waldo grinned, looking like a faithful dog, eager for another pat on the head.

"That's enough, Poyser," Clay said. "You've got a lot more hiking to do before you go hunting."

Aurelia looked up as a drop of rain hit her nose. If only to temporarily relieve the strain among them, she felt as anxious as Waldo to get started.

The Indians refused to pack up the mountain that day, pointing to the sudden warm winds and warning of a slide. But the green stampeders, "cheechacos" the Indians called them, refused to heed the advice and eagerly set out for the climb. In voices low with the threat of disaster, the Indians warned them of the curse. If the white man climbs the jagged peaks, the warm breath of Chinook will melt the snow and hurtle down the swift white death. But the cheechacos continued to climb.

Aurelia, Clay, and Waldo hiked in the rain for several hours. Waldo developed a hacking cough, so alarming that Aurelia told Clay they should cease their drilling for the day in favor of securing dry clothes and much-needed rest. She listened to his lecture on what kind of men make it in the Yukon and what kind don't. They hiked for another thirty minutes, and then Clay said they'd done enough for one day.

Clay's insensitivity didn't surprise Aurelia. When they got back to town, she took Waldo to her hotel and gave him a dose of peppermint essence and laudanum before sending him to his tent.

"I can't seem to do n-n-nothing right," he muttered as he bid Aurelia good-bye.

Clay showed up several hours later. He found Aurelia sitting Indian-style on her cot behind the screen, her head bent in deep concentration, her golden hair hanging loose around her shoulders. In her lap were the new boots he'd bought for her. She'd folded a section of her skirt back to expose the ruffle of her white petticoat. With her index finger wrapped in the soft cotton, she was doing her best to polish her silver buckles.

He cleared his throat. "We should talk," he said when she looked up.

"Yes?" She expected an argument. She was ready.

"We aren't even out of town, and Poyser's sick. You're exhausted. I can see the circles under your eyes."

"Thank you."

"Oh hell, Aurelia, why do you have to be so stubborn? You and Poyser still don't know what you're getting into."

"Waldo might not, but I do." Aurelia covered her petticoat and sat up straight. "I'm going to walk so much my feet will ache even more than they do now, difficult as that is for me to believe. The weight of the provisions will cause muscle strain and give me callused hands. I may strain a muscle or two. I'll have cheek abrasions from the wind. Hypothermia and frostbite are distinct possibilities. What else? Oh yes, my lips will chap."

"That's the first day. And that assumes you know where you're going—which you don't." He paced in front of her cot. "How can I make you see? There are thousands of stampeders out there itching to go to the gold fields, but they don't know for sure where that is. Most don't have compasses. Those that do don't know how to use them. Hell," he threw his arms up in exasperation, "there's no maps anyway. We could all be walking in circles!"

"If this is some ploy of yours to get rid of me, it won't work. For heaven's sake, even I know where we're going. We're taking the Chilkoot Trail to Lake Bennett, then we take a boat from Lake Bennett down the Yukon River to Dawson. Simple."

"We're not on a turnpike here, Aurelia!" Clay shoved his fists in his pockets and glared at her. "We've got a riverbed to follow for part of the way. This time of year it'll either be covered with slick ice or if it dried up last summer it'll be full of rocks. When we're not on the riverbed, we'll be hiking through a trail of loose boulders. Your foot slips once and that could be the end of it."

He began pacing again. "Trees don't grow well around here, if you haven't noticed. Some places they don't grow at all. The ground's frozen. That means I can't just run out every evening and chop down enough lumber for your stove. No fuel means no cooking, no heat, no bath."

Aurelia felt a level of concern she hadn't felt before. "Then how are we to build our boat?"

"Now you're getting the idea." He squatted down next to her cot. "I'm not trying to frighten you, but men are already calling the Chilkoot Trail the meanest thirty-three miles on earth. And when the trail ends at Lake Bennett, we've still got five hundred miles to go."

"Others have made it." She knew she didn't sound as confident as before.

Clay nodded. "That's right. Others have made it. But a fair share of them have lost fingers and toes to frostbite, a limb or two to scurvy. Some have died." He looked into her eyes. "You know how painful it is to look into a mirror when the sun hits it just right? This place is full of glaciers—huge mirrors of ice. The glare from them can make you go blind. And there's more. Dawson's already had an outbreak of typhoid. Measles too."

The frown on his forehead had softened. "I know you're a doctor, and you probably know all about scurvy and typhoid and all, but I don't."

"I know enough."

"I'm just being realistic. I can pitch your tent, hunt

fresh meat for you, build your fires, and keep the derelicts away, but I won't be able to help you if you get sick. Unless you get laid up with something that whiskey can cure."

"You'll do anything to get to Violet first, won't you?"

He winced at the sting of her words, then laughed in a half-hearted, melancholy way. Aurelia wondered if he'd been so protective over Mary. If the issue of finding Violet didn't hang between them, would he still be so concerned about Aurelia?

Probably not. "You needn't worry, Clay. And you needn't feel responsible. I know exactly what I'm doing."

Aurelia didn't feel as confident that night as she lay on her cot. All she felt was lonely.

As she slept, a tepid breeze blew through the town, leaving behind an eerie quiet. The rain that had fallen steadily all day turned to snow, a strange, spring snow, sticky and twice as wet as rain. It floated down in flakes as big as blankets and quickly camouflaged everything it touched.

Deep in the night the mountain rumbled. The steep, rocky ledge on its east wall groaned with the heavy bed of snow already burdening its sides. Halfway to the summit, hundreds of cheechacos had pitched their tents in the snow. They slept soundly, congratulating themselves on their early start.

Twice before dawn the mountain groaned again.

Just before nine o'clock Sunday morning, Aurelia slipped on her new boots and fur parka and went downstairs. She and Waldo had planned to attend the Palm Sunday services being held in the bar next to the Dyea Hotel. The whiskered "waitress" stopped her at the door and handed her a note.

"For you, ma'am. The skinny kid left it. I showed it to your other partner. He went up the mountain to fetch the kid."

Aurelia unfolded the slip of paper.

Tell Guardian I'm getting us a head start on moving our cache up the mountain. Be back tomorrow. Sorry about church. Waldo.

Just as she finished reading the note, the mountain roared. Aurelia looked up. The heavy east face of the mountain broke free and crashed down the side, tumbling over cliffs in leaps of a hundred feet, ridding itself of the heavy white powder.

"Great Skagua, Home of the North Wind, have mercy on us!" the Indians prayed.

"Avalanche!" the stampeders cried.

"Clay! No!"

A second avalanche followed the first and made the mountain a cemetery dotted with headstones of broken barrels, shredded tents, and splintered sleds. The wind moaned a eulogy as the rescuers dug for bodies. Kneeling on the cold floor of a cabin halfway up the mountain, Aurelia held the icy hand of a stranger.

"Love her," the man struggled to say the words. "Tell my wife . . . love her." His voice quivered with the gurgling rattle of death.

Aurelia didn't have either the time or a free hand to

wipe away the tears that wet her lashes. She kept the fingers of her right hand on the man's neck, pressed to his carotid artery, willing the fading rhythm to hold.

"Come on, mister. Try. For your wife, try." Aurelia squeezed his hand, as though she could somehow transfer her health and strength to him. She tried to filter the sounds in the room, the coughing, the crying, the cursing, and listen for the faint breath of life.

He looked to be about Clay's age, though the heavy beard and the massive bruising made it hard to tell. He'd been buried alive for over an hour, his chest crushed by the weight of the snow. When his eyes rolled to the back of his head, Aurelia slipped her hand from his neck and drew his eyelids down. Number twelve. It didn't get any easier.

She stood and stretched her back. The bodies of half a dozen other wounded lay on the floor of the makeshift hospital. They'd been carried in, dragged in, and hauled on sleds. Some had been found frozen stiff in a running position, mouths gaping, eyes wide with fear. Others had been caught sleeping, suffocated under a blanket of white twenty feet thick. Lying amid the dirty puddles on the floor, pellets of rock hard snow still clung to their clothes. The morgue was the nearest snowbank. They'll all wind up out there, she thought with a finality that depressed her.

"He didn't make it," she said to Dr. Bonwitt, an older physician who had left his practice for the lure of gold and who had organized the medical end of the rescue effort.

"This one didn't either." Dr. Bonwitt removed his stethoscope from his ears and straightened. He crooked his finger to the two men standing in the corner by the door. "Take them out, boys."

Aurelia shuddered as the body of the man she'd worked so hard to save was slowly dragged across the room, the heels of his ice-caked boots scraping the wooden floor.

They weren't supposed to die. If she was going to be a doctor, she should be able to save them. At least some of them. Helplessness overwhelmed her, and she began to tremble.

"I know it's hard," Dr. Bonwitt said as he patted her on the shoulder.

She looked into his small, sparkling blue eyes. "I've seen others die, but they were old and frail and had lived a good life. Not . . . like this." She tried to regain her composure, but as she looked around the room the door opened and another body was carried in and laid in the spot just vacated.

"That's the trouble with you women doctors. You don't want to handle the tough cases." Dr. Bonwitt looked down his nose, challenging her to refute his statement.

"That's not true!" Exhausted as she was, Aurelia drew herself up straight. She spoke slowly, but with conviction. "We're rarely given the opportunity to handle the more difficult cases, but that doesn't mean we aren't capable. Or willing. All we ask for is the chance."

Dr. Bonwitt stroked his distinguished-looking white beard and pursed his lips. "Then I suggest you do yourself a great favor and commit the number one rule to memory. You're Dr. Breighton. Not God." He patted her shoulder again, then left her standing in the middle of the floor as he directed the placement of the latest victim.

The one-room cabin was the powerhouse of the

tramway, halfway up the mountain near a place called Sheep Camp, a little over fourteen miles outside of Dyea. Nearly everyone from Dyea had grabbed a shovel and trudged up through the snow as soon the mountain had relaxed. Aurelia had taken her medical box and followed. Hours later, wilted and cold, she'd arrived at the powerhouse to find the first-aid effort organized under the supervision of Dr. Bonwitt.

"Never thought I'd see the day when I'd be working alongside a physician in skirts," Bonwitt had grumbled when she introduced herself. He didn't, however, refuse her help. In a matter of hours they'd easily fallen into a companionable team approach, with the old man not only allowing but expecting her to handle the emergencies she'd only been permitted to observe before. And even though they both knew she wasn't entitled to the title of "doctor" yet, he granted her the honor.

Now, she'd watched more than a dozen men die, and every time the cabin door blew open, she held her breath. Every time the vengeful wind whipped into the small room she bent her back to take its lash. Both Clay and Waldo were still up there somewhere. If she hadn't invited Waldo to become a partner, he wouldn't have started out alone, compelled to prove his manliness to Clay. And if she hadn't made it clear how much she cared for Waldo's safety, Clay wouldn't have risked his own life going up after him.

And what about Clay? Other men, bigger and stronger, had already been brought to their knees by the vengeance of the great North Wind. She thought again of the man who had just died. She pictured Clay buried alive, closing his eyes, resigning himself to his fate, slowly drifting into the heavy sleep that had no end. Or was he, even now, clawing at the snow with his bare hands, calling to her from beneath his white-powder grave?

She had to find him.

Aurelia slammed her medical box shut and reached for her coat. Just as she did, one of the men burst in with news that a woman had been found on the mountain and was being brought down now. A fancy woman.

Dr. Bonwitt caught Aurelia's eye as she hesitated with her coat. "I need you," he said. "In here you're an asset. Out there you're a liability."

Bonwitt was right. She wouldn't know where to dig or how to protect herself in the process. Besides, with Clay's strength and resourcefulness, he'd no doubt survived and was working hard to help rescue the less fortunate. She thought of Waldo again and prayed he'd made it through safely too.

"Here she comes," the man at the door called out.

One man held her under the arms, the other lifted her feet. Even before they had the woman all the way into the room, Aurelia recognized the widow L'Auberge.

"Lily!" Aurelia dropped her coat. "Bring her over here," she directed the two men who carried her.

Aurelia heard the gut-wrenching moan of pain as the widow was placed on the floor. Aurelia knelt down and examined her quickly. Comatose. Heartbeat erratic. Blood pressure barely detectable. White spots on the tip of her nose. Quickly, Aurelia removed the widow's thin leather gloves and examined her fingers. Frostbite.

Again Lily moaned. Her chest rattled. Then nothing. Grabbing her coat from behind her, Aurelia covered Lily's chest and tucked the warm fur around her shoulders. "You'll be all right, Lily," she said, glad her friend couldn't hear the lack of confidence in her voice.

She turned to the men who had brought Lily in. "She was traveling with her brother. Did you find him?"

"He's outside," one of them answered, "dead."

Aurelia cupped her own hands to her mouth, filled them with her warm breath, and vigorously rubbed Lily's arms and legs. No change, except for the beading of sweat on her brow and the twitching of her blue-gray lips. She must have been in terrible pain. Aurelia told herself to stay calm, as she opened her medical case and withdrew a syringe.

"Dr. Breighton," Dr. Bonwitt called to her. "How much more morphine have we remaining?"

Aurelia looked at the needle in her hand, then at Dr. Bonwitt, whose look challenged her judgment. "Very little."

"Let's not waste it on those who don't have a chance. Do you understand what I'm saying?" He stepped over the body of the man he'd been working on and shouted to the men by the door. "We need room in here, boys. Get this one out before he starts to stink."

Bonwitt knelt down beside Lily and examined her. "This woman's dead, Dr. Breighton."

Aurelia shook her head. "No. She can't be." Still kneeling, Aurelia hung her head. "She's my friend."

"I'm truly sorry," Bonwitt offered as he lifted Aurelia's coat from the body and laid it in the corner. "Boys, one more here."

Aurelia sobbed as they carried Lily's body away. She thought of how passionate and full of the joy of life Lily had been and how she had viewed this journey as a great adventure. Once fearless and optimistic, the widow was now just one more casualty.

Wiping the tears from her eyes, Aurelia tried to busy herself by organizing her remaining supplies. She hated to think that Lily, with all her confidence and determination, had been so quickly, so painfully, so finally stopped—and by nothing more than a drop in temperature and an accumulation of delicate, lacy snowflakes.

A sudden shiver unrelated to the cold in the cabin seized Aurelia. Briskly, she rubbed the pebbly goose-flesh on her arms and looked at the tragedy all around her. This was no game. People were dying—men and women whose only crime was wanting a better life for themselves and their families.

She remembered how she'd so cavalierly told Clay she knew exactly what hardships threatened them. What was it she'd said? "My feet will blister, my muscles will ache." And, "oh yes, my lips will chap." How neatly she'd presented her view of the challenges that awaited them. How smug she'd sounded.

She knew better now, and it scared her to death.

Nothing changed for two days, except the death toll. By Tuesday evening, forty-three bodies had been recovered, and another fifteen people had been rescued alive. There was no sign of Clay or Waldo, though Aurelia asked every stampeder who entered the cabin. Aurelia and Dr. Bonwitt kept the emergency room operating twenty-four hours a day, taking turns at two-hour naps.

Too tired to dream, Aurelia huddled in a corner,

her head against the wall, her new fur coat covering her like a blanket. She closed her eyes to fleeting glimpses of Lily's pale, lifeless body and then to frail, sweet Violet, struggling to climb the cannibal path to the summit. *Did you make it, Violet?* she wondered. *Will I?*

Aurelia couldn't remember ever feeling lonelier, except the night Nana died. A night just like this. Windy and raw. So cold, Nana's wrinkled flesh had quivered, even though her bed had been moved close to the fireplace. Aurelia had taken the quilt from her own bed and added it to the mound. "There's no more that modern medicine can do for her," the doctor had said with what Aurelia decided was a fainthearted effort at best. "Don't leave me, Nana. Please don't go."

Aurelia had sat by her grandmother's bed all night and whispered her prayers, now and then kissing the old woman's hand. Somewhere in the early morning hours Aurelia fell asleep. And when she awoke, Nana was gone.

Now Aurelia woke to a rush of cold air and the familiar slam of the cabin door.

10

Like a snow-caked giant, Clay filled the doorway. Barely able to stand, he swayed with the weight of the body he cradled in his arms. Waldo.

Aurelia rushed to Clay's side. "You're alive! Thank God you're both alive!" She longed to enfold Clay, hold him close, keep him warm. The realization startled her, and she stepped back, fumbling with her hands. It was merely the intimacy of those who share disaster, that's all.

"Might have known you'd be up here," Clay said, his lips so cold they barely moved.

Aurelia flinched. "And why shouldn't I be here? I've been able to set bones, treat exposure, bind wounds." Smarting from the sting of his words, she scanned the scraped and bruised body lying deathly still in Clay's arms. "Lay him down by the fire," she said, leading Clay to where she'd set up her examining station.

Energy drained from Clay by the minute. "I just meant I knew you wouldn't shy away from a hard job like this, that's all." Carefully, he laid Waldo's body on the floor, took off his own coat, then sat down on the floor and leaned against the wall. "The boy's all right, Aurelia. Scared, but not hurt." With every word, Clay's eyelids closed a little heavier, and his head hung a little lower.

So he didn't think her foolish, just stubborn. "How did you find him? Where?"

"Followed his whimpering. Found him huddled up next to some rocks. Had that gopher cage of his tucked under his coat."

"But he's unconscious. What happened?"

The sudden, recriminating look in Clay's eyes told Aurelia that despite the fact that he'd carried the boy to safety, Clay thought even less of him now. "He fainted."

"It's not a crime," Aurelia said as she checked Waldo's pulse. After the ordeal Clay had just been through, he should have been grateful to be alive, to find both his partners alive, even if one was a weakling and the other a woman.

Aurelia dipped a cloth in the bucket of warm water and wiped Waldo's face. He stirred, his forehead wrinkling in agony. She turned to Clay, whose eyelids fluttered with the need for sleep. She looked around for a pillow or something Clay could use for a blanket, but there was nothing.

"Clay, wait. Before you fall asleep—the gophers—what happened to them?"

He grunted and huddled down under his coat. "Outside. Left the cage by the door. Leave 'em there."

His show of kindness toward Waldo baffled her, but then, Clay'd been through quite an ordeal too. Maybe the experience had softened his heart. "That was thoughtful of you, Clay."

"Surprised?"

"Well, yes."

He turned his face to the wall and mumbled, "Yea, I guess you would be."

Waldo whimpered and opened his eyes.

"That's more like it," Aurelia said as she wiped his brow. "It's good to see you back with the living. How do you feel?"

Waldo rolled to his side and raised himself up on one elbow. He patted the floor as though searching for something, while he looked straight at Aurelia's nose. "My spectacles, ma'am. I c-c-can't see."

"They're right here." Aurelia drew the wire-rimmed glasses from the pocket of his jacket. Clay must have put them there.

"Am I going to l-l-live?"

"Oh, yes. Thanks to Clay. He's the one who found you and carried you in."

Waldo looked more frustrated than grateful. He sat upright and looked to where Clay had slumped in the corner. "Guess that makes me beholden to him."

"I suppose so."

He pulled his head down. "That sure ain't the kind of d-d-debt I ever expected to have."

"Your fate could have been much worse."

"True enough." Waldo looked at the other victims on the floor around him and began shaking his head back and forth as though trying to rid himself of a bad memory. "See, I couldn't breathe and I commenced to gasping and I thought I was gonna see my m-m-maker, so I grabbed my—" He stopped mid-sentence and looked down at his chest and the gaping pocket of his coat. "James John and C-C-Corbett!"

"Alive and well. They're in their cage, just outside the door. Clay saved them too."

"He d-d-did?" Looking both puzzled and happy, he

scrambled to stand up. This time when he looked over at Clay it was with sincere gratitude, but Clay was asleep.

"I'll be back," Waldo called over his shoulder as he went to the door and stepped outside, passing Dr. Bonwitt, who'd just returned.

Waldo came back in a few minutes, grinning from ear to ear, stomping the snow from his boots, holding the gopher cage out of the draft.

"Hey, kid, where'd you get fresh meat out here?" Butch Rowley, a hulk of a man, one of those who'd helped carry the dead bodies to the morgue, sauntered over to examine the cage. "I'll be damned," he said. "Stoke the fire and get it going good. We're gonna have us some gopher stew." He smacked his lips, then reached for the cage.

"G-G-Get away!"

"You sniveling son of a bitch." With one great hand, Rowley shoved Waldo against the door and grabbed the cage. From a leather sheath strapped to his massive thigh, the man drew a long and shiny knife. "I'll save the skins for you, kid. Your first trophy of the Klondike." He laughed.

"Hold it, mister."

With heavy, deliberate steps, Clay crossed the room. In his right hand he clutched a log from the pile beside the fireplace. "I heard folks hanged a man in Skagway last week for thieving. Stole part of some man's outfit. A sack of flour, as I recall." He stopped three feet in front of Rowley and spoke in a low, hypnotizing voice. "A stampeder can't live without his outfit. Some yellow-bellied swine steals any part of it, the stampeder could die. That makes thieving close to murder. Makes hanging a fit punishment."

With his hand firmly on the log and his gaze fixed

on his opponent, Clay addressed the others in the room. "No law up here but us, boys. What do you say?"

"Kick him out!" someone shouted.

"Here. Take 'em." Rowley shoved the cage back at Waldo, who grabbed them and ran outside.

Clay stared at his opponent a moment longer, then turned his back and headed for what had been his bed.

"Look out!" Aurelia screamed.

Clay spun around to see Rowley lunge at him. He raised the log to deflect the knife, but not before the sharp blade slashed across his left forearm, through his buckskin jacket and his flannel shirt. The blood spread quickly.

Aurelia gasped as she watched Clay grab the log tightly with both hands and sidestep the next lunge. Then, as Rowley came at him again, Clay brought the log down hard and fast on Rowley's hand.

Rowley screamed. The knife fell to the floor. "You broke my hand, you goddamn son of a bitch!"

Dr. Bonwitt called from the back of the cabin. "Rowley, you've caused enough trouble for one day. Now get over here and let me see that hand. Dr. Breighton, you tend to your patient before he bleeds to death and Rowley here has to haul him outside, bum hand and all."

Rowley swore with every step he took. "One way or another, I'll see to it you wind up on the heap, Guardian."

Aurelia's heart finally stopped pounding. She lifted her medical box from one of the two chairs in the room and gestured for Clay to sit down.

"Clay?" she said when he didn't move.

"I'll wait for Doc Bonwitt, if you don't mind."

"I do mind. Dr. Bonwitt is busy. You can see that for yourself."

Still he didn't move, except to press his hand tighter against his bleeding arm.

Dr. Bonwitt called from the other side of the room. "Son, you'll bleed to death before I can tend your wound."

Clay glanced around him, as though he expected a show of support from the men who'd just sided with him in the fight with Rowley, but it didn't appear that anyone was interested in his predicament.

His hand had filled with blood.

Waldo stepped up to him. "Don't be scared, Clay. Miss Aurelia took real good c-c-care of me."

Clay looked anything but comforted. "I should have left you and your rats outside in the snow."

The look of rejection on Waldo's face was pitiful. Aurelia glared at Clay. "How can you be so cruel?"

He matched her stare. "I'm just being honest."

"You're being stubborn. Now sit down here and let me tend that gash."

He sat down hard in the chair. Aurelia smirked. "Now that's more like it," she said.

He winced as she helped him slip his arm from the sleeve of his buckskin jacket. The blood spread a wet crimson stain on the jacket, up past his elbow, down to his wrist. Profuse, but not spurting, and venous, not arterial, she determined with relief.

Though her first concern was his wound, the nearness of him flooded her with provocative feelings she tried to ignore. "The shirt too," she added, embarrassed by the sudden lowering of her voice. "Unless you want me to cut off the sleeve."

"No." He fumbled with the buttons.

"Here, let me help you." She unfastened the buttons on his shirt, noticing how the release of each button revealed more of the soft black hair that covered his sternum. She spread the fabric apart and held her breath at the sight of his naked chest. She eased the shirt back, over his right shoulder and down his arm. Then she peeled back the sticky, wet flannel from his left arm.

Oh dear, she thought as she retrieved several squares of gauze and strips of linen from the jewelry compartment of her case. She'd never worked on such a nasty gash. For the most part, her education had been a matter of observation, with a minimum of hands-on participation, and then only under the careful observation of an instructor. She'd dressed more wounds on her own these last few days than she had in the last three years. According to Dr. Bonwitt, she'd done a good job, but she still lacked experience. It never bothered her more than it did now.

"Hold your arm out straight," she said as she pressed the squares of gauze over the wound. She wrapped the strips of linen around the patch and tied them tight. "That should stop the bleeding." Then she grabbed her fur and draped it over his shoulders. "We don't have any more blankets."

The tremor in her voice betrayed her nervousness as she fumbled to take from her case a small metal cup, a pair of forceps, a spool of black cotton thread, and a needle. She glanced over to see how soon Dr. Bonwitt would be free to help her, but it was clear that he'd be busy for hours.

She turned her face so Clay couldn't see her growing fear. From the side compartment of her medical box, where Violet used to keep her necklaces, Aurelia removed a silver flask, unscrewed the lid, and poured a generous portion of whiskey into the metal cup.

Clay took a whiff, eyed the cup, and smiled for the first time since he appeared at the cabin door.

Knowing her demeanor could either instill confidence or terror, Aurelia assumed her most serious bearing as she cut a four-inch length of thread and dropped it with the needle and the forceps into the cup.

"What in blazes are you doing with that whiskey?"

"Sterilizing my equipment." She knew her actions sounded primitive and less than professional, but she had no other choice. The cut on his arm was a bad one. Her heart climbed right up to her throat as she said, "Clay, you need stitches. But don't worry. The initial trauma deadens the nerves in the area. If I work quickly, you shouldn't feel a thing."

"Stitches! Hold on now. You aren't jabbing me with some needle."

Aurelia placed her hand on his shoulder. One of them had to remain calm. "Relax."

"You're going to hurt me on purpose, aren't you?"

"What?"

"Don't hand me that wide-eyed innocent look. Your sister may have gotten away with it, but you won't. And now you're looking to take your revenge on my arm."

"Of all the idiotic ideas! Fortunately for you, I'm above letting our personal differences interfere with my work."

Aurelia took a deep breath. What kind of brain spawned the thoughts he had? The kind of brain that dreams up cruel insults to hurl at a poor boy. The kind of brain that encourages old-fashioned, narrow-minded thinking about a woman's rights. The kind of brain that shuts out the truth about a young girl's innocence. The more she thought about it, the angrier she got. Maybe revenge was warranted after all.

She put on her spectacles. "The bleeding should be stopped by now." She cut away the linen strips and carefully removed the blood-soaked squares of gauze. "Hmm. Let's hope we don't have to amputate."

He sat there and smirked, as though he could tell she was taunting him.

She immersed several clean squares of gauze into the whiskey, lifted them, and wrung them out directly over the exposed wound. "I need to sterilize the field. You may feel a slight burning sensation."

"Ouch! Goddamnit!"

"Sorry. Now, don't worry. I've watched patients being sutured often enough. I should be able to do it myself."

Still shaken from the sting of the whiskey, Clay dropped his jaw. "You've never stitched before?"

"Only on the dissecting table."

Aurelia held the needle up for inspection, scrutinizing its length, the sharpness of its tip. "That dissecting room was the messiest place. And the smell! Even the purest of girls smoked their first tobacco in that room. Anything to kill the stench." Seeing him squirm, she threaded the needle and held it in her right hand, then slipped the thumb and middle finger of her left hand into the ovals of the forceps. "By the time I finished that class, if I knew nothing else, I knew where not to cut." She studied him. "You looked peeked, Clay."

"Just get on with it."

"As you wish."

Something wasn't right. She needed a vise of some sort, to minimize the movement of his arm. Enjoying the sense of control she felt, Aurelia pointed to the area under her left arm, alongside her upper torso.

"Put your hand here."

He hesitated, as though he couldn't believe the blatant invitation. "You're asking for considerable restraint, doctor. I'm still a man."

"But an honorable man. Correct?"

"Hard as that might be for you to believe, yes." He placed his hand where she directed, then turned his face aside.

She felt a chill as his fingers grazed her inner arm. Barely a heartbeat from the fullness of her breast, his icy fingertips brushed her torso and nestled in her warmth. She felt his large, strong hand tremble for just a second. Its chill disappeared as he absorbed her heat. To quiet the stirrings aroused just by his nearness, she assured herself that regardless of who the patient was, she'd have instructed him the same as she had Clay. But it wasn't true. She knew it the moment he looked up and their eyes locked.

She lowered her arm and tightened the vise. With her thoughts about him suddenly spinning in a thousand directions, she said, "Don't move."

Placing the steel tongs on either side of the gash, she squeezed gently. Said a prayer. Took a deep breath. And inserted the needle.

Clay flinched. Aurelia froze.

He broke out in a sweat and slumped in the chair. She laid the tongs down and touched his forehead. It was clammy.

"Oh, no, you don't," she ordered as she lowered his arm from her side and pressed his head down between his knees. She grabbed a bottle of ammonia, opened it, and passed it beneath his nose. The aroma jarred his senses. He sat up. She felt a thousand times better.

"What happened?" he asked. "I didn't go down for the count like Poyser, did I?"

She didn't know why she wanted to ease his embarrassment, but she did. "I've seen plenty of grown men crumble at the sight of a needle."

"Is it over?"

"No, but I wish it were too."

He took a deep breath and let it out slowly. "Go on then." Slipping his hand back to the tender spot beneath her arm, he closed his eyes so he wouldn't have to watch.

Six stitches later, her own heart still pounding from the ordeal, she laid down her implements and wiped the beads of perspiration from her brow. "None of the tendons were severed. You'll be fine in a week or so."

Clay took the handkerchief she offered and wiped his own brow. He studied the neat row of little black knots, each with two tails of thread.

"I'll take the stitches out next week," she said.

"Good. Looks like a swarm of black flies on a steak."

"Thank you," she said sarcastically, angry with herself for wanting him to say something more positive, more personal. She took a fresh cotton sling from her bag, snapped the white square in the air, and folded it into a triangle.

For all his hardfisted show, his pain was obvious by the way he favored his arm. Despite their opposing views, it was her duty as a doctor to help. What difference did it make that he didn't fawn all over her? That wasn't appropriate for a patient. And wanting him to wasn't appropriate for a doctor.

As she positioned the cloth to cradle his arm, she fussed with the knot. She let her hands linger on his shoulder a moment longer than necessary. Just touching him set in motion a complicated chain of feelings. She hadn't forgotten why he was going to Dawson, and yet she hadn't been able to control her body's response to his touch. With even greater shame, she realized how easily she'd let her personal feelings interfere with her professionalism, just the thing he'd accused her of earlier. What kind of doctor would she be if she could let that happen?

"Clay, I have morphine—"

"Don't want it."

"Then drink this," she said, handing him the cup she'd used to sterilize her instruments. "If your arm isn't throbbing already, it will be shortly."

"Then maybe I'd better," he said, taking the cup from her hands. "Seeing as you've found a way to give me even more pain."

Anger and guilt clashed within her. "I never intended to hurt you. If I did, I'm sorry."

He swirled the whiskey that remained in the cup and swallowed it. Then he sighed and looked for a place to rest. Exhausted and in pain he lumbered to an empty corner, slumped down against the wall, and closed his eyes.

Aurelia turned toward the fire to hide her tears. How could one man have such power over her emotions? She still didn't like the sarcastic way he spoke to Waldo. She didn't like the way he resorted to violence to settle an argument. And the idea of hanging a man for stealing a sack of flour was unthinkable.

But he'd labored himself to exhaustion to establish their cache. He'd spent day after day seeing that she and Waldo were conditioned for the journey. He'd even taken it upon himself to find proper clothing for her. And he'd gone up the mountain to find Waldo before Aurelia had even known Waldo was missing. If he wanted her gratitude, he had it. If only he'd have listened she'd have told him.

There was no risk in admitting gratitude. The risk was in admitting that she couldn't make it to Dawson without him. She may have thought so once, but that was before the avalanche, before she'd seen how treacherous this country could be.

Though it pained her to admit it, Waldo wasn't man enough to inspire her confidence. She needed Clay—but just to get to Dawson, she amended. To need him for any other reason would be to risk rejection. That kind of pain was still too familiar. She thought of that night in Philadelphia the previous spring.

The semester was over, and Violet had come to help Aurelia pack her things. If Aurelia hadn't been so eager to flaunt to Violet the worldly lifestyle of a college student, she'd have never succumbed to the sheer devilry of her classmates. She never would have gone with them to the local bar, and certainly never would have taken Violet there.

Aurelia remembered it all too well. While her friends were dancing, she caught the eye of a young accountant—she never did get his name. But as usual, Violet enticed him away, danced with him, then discarded him as she did everything once she'd finished with it. The accountant's rejection of Aurelia was more embarrassing than painful, nothing compared to the ache in her heart this very moment.

Exhaustion always made everything seem worse. What she needed was sleep. As soon as she took care of the man who was just carried in, she would sit down and rest her eyes for a while.

Six hours later, in the middle of the night, Clay woke up.

Cradling his throbbing arm, he looked around. It took a moment for his eyes to adjust to the dimness. A single, low-flame kerosene lamp burned in the corner where Dr. Bonwitt sat slumped against the wall. The stillness meant no new victims had been brought in for a while, but the moans from those who lay on the floor with bloody bandages around their heads and crude splints on their legs meant the ordeal wasn't over.

Barely a foot away, Aurelia slept, her back against the wall, her head rolled forward. Her face lacked color, except for the dark circles under her eyes. Her golden curls hung in unruly fashion across her forehead, against her cheeks, and along her neck. Blood stained her white-bibbed apron.

He was surprised she'd stuck it out this long. Probably she couldn't take much more. He remembered how quickly Mary had shriveled under the hot prairie sun. Her father, the local banker, had seen to it that she had the bonnets and skin lotion Clay couldn't afford to buy. Mary wasn't to wither and die young the way her mother had.

Clay studied Aurelia. He ought to be angry with her, the way she'd deliberately tormented him with that needle, but he wasn't. He hadn't exactly been a gentleman himself. If he could convince her to stay in Dyea, he would go on ahead, find Violet and Sculley, and bring them back. They'd get a fair trial. Hell, if it'd make Aurelia happy, he'd even take Poyser with him.

Satisfied with his resolution, he moved over to sit on the floor next to Aurelia. He pulled her fur coat back up over her chest and tucked it around her shoulders. He sat there watching her for a few minutes. He wasn't sure why he cared so much about Aurelia's safety, or her happiness, or her feelings about him. But he did.

Clay fell asleep, wondering how he'd ever get her to trust him again.

11

She awoke to the labored tapping of a homemade crutch on the slush-covered floor. Besides Dr. Bonwitt, only the unconscious and those too injured to be moved remained in the cabin.

Dr. Bonwitt helped Aurelia to her feet. "We've got a sunny day ahead of us, Dr. Breighton. We'll be heading down the mountain later. Most of our patients are already out there looking for their belongings."

"Good," she said, surprised at how much effort it took to speak. She opened the door to a welcome feel of fresh air and leaned against the jam. Ahead of her in all directions lay a white wasteland strewn with supplies and collapsed tents. She no longer shuddered at the sight of the snowbank just to her right. Layered between blankets of snow were hats frozen stiff, boots caked with ice. Here and there she saw patches of blue skin.

Dr. Bonwitt came up from behind and patted her slumped shoulder. "Disillusioned, are you?"

"I just feel the hopelessness of it all."

"Good. That'll keep you humble. Now take another look around. Get the full picture. Go on. Look."

Aurelia scanned the landscape again and this time

recognized many of her patients—the broken leg, the dislocated shoulder, the sprained ankle, the gash on the forehead.

"They didn't all die," Bonwitt said. "They may be sore and hobbling, but they're alive. Might not be without you."

Several men grinned when they saw Aurelia and tipped their hats in thanks. Seeing the entire avalanche episode in new light, Aurelia returned their smiles. She'd done a fine job. She might never have the loving companionship she'd dreamed about, but she had a position of usefulness and satisfaction. It ought to be enough.

A few minutes later, Aurelia looked up to see Clay enter the cabin. Even with his arm in a sling and his coat tied around him with a rope, he looked strong. Handsome too, though his dimples were no longer visible beneath his black beard. She winced along with him as the door banged against his arm. It was the doctor in her that felt such compassion for him in his injury, but what explained the yearning she felt?

"How's your arm? I should take a look at it. Make sure there's no infection."

"Not bad," he said, without any of the censure that had marked his speech the previous night. He followed her to the chair and sat down.

She fumbled with the knot on the sling, eager to do what she could to lessen the soreness. She helped him ease his arm from the sleeve of his shirt and reminded herself of how the wound should look, what to do if an infection had set in, and how long it should be before he fully recovered. Entwined with her thoughts was the foolish wish that she were more attractive, more feminine, more like his late wife.

Aurelia's own desires were troublesome enough.

More confusing still was the look in Clay's eyes that suggested his desire to get closer to her.

Dr. Bonwitt joined them. "Let's have a look at your handiwork, shall we?" He looked over her shoulder as she examined the jagged, thin, red ridge, still puffy and raw looking, with a little bit of straw-colored plasma serum seeping out. "Inflamation barely a quarter-inch along each side of the incision. Good sign, no infection. Fine work, Doctor," he said. "Wrap him up. Now I'm going to step outside for a bit. You're in charge." Slapping Clay on the knee, he added, "She's a credit to the profession."

Heady with pride, Aurelia watched Dr. Bonwitt leave the cabin. She finished redressing Clay's wound, helped him with his shirt, and refastened the sling.

"Thanks," he said. "Guess I should have said that last night."

"You're welcome," she said, feeling pleasure far beyond what she'd had with any other patient.

Clay, on the other hand, did not seem happy at all. "Have you looked around outside this morning?" he asked.

"Yes. Inspiring in its own way."

"Inspiring? There's nothing out there but dead and broken bodies." He walked to the single, small window. "I want you to listen to me."

Apprehensive of his tone, she joined him by the window.

"First, I'm sorry about your friend Lily. I heard about her death even before I reached the powerhouse. Word like that travels fast." He studied her face. "And second, this is just no place for a woman. Look at you—dark circles under your eyes—I bet you haven't slept more than two hours at a time."

His concern sounded genuine and not at all deserving of the wariness she suddenly felt.

He continued. "Before you say anything, hear me out. I want you to stay in Dyea. I'll go on to Dawson. If it'll make you happy, I'll even take Poyser with me."

Go to Dawson without her. It was the same goal as before, only he was using a different tactic. "And when you get to Dawson?" Aurelia asked. "What then?"

He hesitated.

"What then, Clay? What about my sister?"

"I'll find her. And I'll bring her back."

"To me? Or to the new electric chair?"

"Aurelia, try to understand. Justice compels me—"

"And love compels me!" She cringed as he reached to touch her.

Clay raised his voice. "So what do you plan to do with Violet when *you* find her? Hide her? Run away with her? You and Violet and Sculley?"

"I don't know."

"You can't make it without me and we both know it. I could dissolve our partnership. Right here. Right now."

"An *honorable* man would stand by his word."

Both knew she'd hit a raw nerve. "You win," he said, "but you'll regret it."

The moaning of a patient called her attention. "Excuse me," she said to Clay and left him standing alone.

She looked over her shoulder as he left the cabin. He was right about one thing. She didn't know what she was going to do when she found Violet. One thing was certain, however. She had to find Violet before Clay did, or she'd have no options at all.

* * *

Everyone left for Dyea later that morning. Their
boots and sleds crunched and squeaked against the
hard-packed snowy trail, a funeral procession of sleds
bearing bodies and mourners bearing grief. One didn't
need to have known the victims personally to know that
with their deaths part of the collective dream had died.

The grueling trip down the mountain had convinced
Aurelia of one thing. She had to prove Violet's innocence
before the three of them reached Dawson. Because even
if the rest of the journey was only half as difficult as the
first step, Clay just might find Violet first.

Sitting on her cot at the Ballard Hotel late that
afternoon, Aurelia carefully removed from her
tapestry satchel the ribbon-bound parcel of Violet's
letters. Clay stood there with his feet spread apart and
his arms folded, looking anything but open-minded.

She took a letter out of one of the envelopes and
glanced over the words she'd read so many times
before. "This is one of the last two." She read aloud:

*It is September now and everyone warns that
winter will be upon us before the month is out.
God's furry creatures are the only ones who can
stay warm in this place. I live on the hope that
any day now I will receive letters in abundance
from you. Once winter sets in, there will be no
communication with the Outside.*

*I hesitate to pen these words, dear sister, for
fear I will cast my own fate; but, I don't think
Fletcher has—or ever had—any intention of marrying me. What am I to do? I have no money for
my return passage and no more jewelry to pawn.*

*Please don't ever let mother know, but I had to
forfeit the pearl ring and the jeweled butterfly pin
she gave me in order to secure our passage
aboard ship. Fletcher seems never to have funds
of his own.*

*Oh, Aurelia, surely you recall the despair I
felt at your leaving home to pursue an education. I remember crying every night for weeks
after you left. My world had suddenly changed;
you—my friend and protector—gone to a far-
away city known for its dance halls and predators.
But as terribly as I missed you then, I miss you a
thousand times more so now. This Skagway is a
lawless and violent town, far worse than
Philadelphia. Painted women parade the
streets. Public drunkenness is common, and
men and dogs are shot daily. I don't belong
here. No respectable woman belongs here.*

Clay looked just as steadfast as he had before
hearing the contents of the letter.

Aurelia folded the paper and slipped it back into
the envelope. "Poor Violet. She didn't expect to hear
from mother and father, especially not after the way
father carried on about how she'd brought shame to
the family. But she expected to hear from me. And I
never wrote. Not once."

"Why?"

Aurelia sighed and looked away, still searching for
the answer to his simple question. "I didn't know
what to say. Like father, I was angry she'd run away.
Like mother, I was hurt to see how easily she could
leave me."

"Sounds pretty lame to me."

"Because it's just half the reason. The truth is I was ashamed to let Violet know her predicament was all my fault. That's why I'm willing to risk my life to find her. I suppose it does sound lame."

Still hoping to soften Clay's judgment of Violet, Aurelia took another envelope and handed it to him. "This is the last letter. Even with my medical training, I would be embarrassed to read it aloud."

Clay removed several sheets of pale pink paper from the envelope and read silently.

And now, dare I tell you the worse? Several days past I searched Fletcher's belongings looking for soiled clothing. There's a laundress in town and I thought to take advantage of her services, though Fletcher insists I learn to do these things myself. What I found has me both troubled and afraid. Advertisements for rubber goods—condoms and womb veils! Are you aware of such things?

And there was more—an advertisement, which Fletcher had circled, for a remedy for gonorrhea, whatever that is, as well as information on pills guaranteed to bring on the monthly flow. I think these pamphlets refer to anti-conception!

I also found several issues of a magazine showing pictures of scantily clad variety actresses, leaving one to wonder about the variety of their skills. Surely, only the most depraved of men would find this rubbish titillating.

I confronted Fletcher when he came home from the bar. He struck me. In my wildest imagination I could never have believed him capable of such violence. I told him I wasn't accustomed to such treatment and threatened to leave. He laughed. As he so accurately pointed out, I've no funds for passage by ship and there is no other way to the Outside. He says we must depart for Dawson before the rivers freeze. I see no alternative but to go with him.

I'm so ashamed. How I wish I'd listened to my family; but this wisdom of mine has come much too late. I know now that Fletcher doesn't love me. I dread the day I learn why he has taken me to this horrid place. Pray for me, Aurelia. I am so afraid.

Aurelia felt her throat tighten as she fought the images that always came to mind when she read Violet's last letter. Surely, now Clay would be convinced of Violet's innocence and would understand Aurelia's need to rescue her.

Clay refolded the letter and handed it back to Aurelia. "This was supposed to make a difference in my opinion?" he asked.

Aurelia's eyes widened in surprise. "Unless you're totally insensitive. I don't understand how you cannot be moved by her plight."

"Moved? She sold all her jewelry for one-way passage and kept nothing for an emergency return. That's financially irresponsible. She takes her clothes to a laundress instead of doing them herself. She's spoiled. That line about her being a 'respectable woman,' now that would have made me laugh if you hadn't looked so serious. I guess about the kindest thing I can say for your sister is she's a poor judge of character. *If* all she says about Sculley is on the level."

Aurelia was desperate to find a way to make Clay see the true picture. "No. You still don't understand.

Violet is sweet and naive. She's pretty and talented and vivacious. She has a magnetism that draws people to her. Everyone admires her. Why, I remember how she'd willingly entertain us by the hour with her elocution and her mimic of accents. And she can act! Everyone always says she should be on the stage."

"Listen to yourself. She can manipulate people and successfully pretend to be someone she's not."

"How dare you twist my words. That's not what I said at all!"

Clay shook his head as though he found the whole conversation useless. "That's exactly what you said. You just didn't listen to yourself."

"Formaldehyde," she said with the vehemence of a curse. "It's formaldehyde that flows in your veins. Not blood. And to think at one point I found you moderately attractive. Now *that's* where I was fooled."

At least that comment broke his armor, the stunned look on his face quickly giving way to one of realization. "And to think at one point I thought you might be in cahoots with your sister and Sculley—"

"You thought what? Clayton Guardian, you are the most suspicious, pig-headed man I've ever met. You get out of my sight this instant."

He walked toward the stairs. "Don't you want to know why I'm so sure now you aren't in cahoots with your sister?"

"Why?"

He stopped and looked over his shoulder. "Because she fooled you too."

Aurelia stared at his retreating form as his words echoed in her heart suddenly throwing a lifetime of conviction into question.

* * *

The Chilkoot Pass was closed for three days while more bodies were brought down for burial or shipment back to Seattle. Though everyone feared there were even more bodies to be uncovered, no one could afford to use up precious food supplies wiling away the hours in Dyea while the rescue teams searched the softening snow.

Easter Sunday found half of Dyea crowded into the makeshift church in the rear of one of the supply houses. Aurelia listened intently while Dr. Bonwitt read from Revelations and said a few words of his own about the meaning of the forces of good and evil. There was no logical reason for her to tremble the way she did, no logical reason to think that Violet was in even more danger than before.

Later that morning, still struggling to dismiss her fears, Aurelia joined Clay and Waldo for breakfast.

Waldo pointed out that it was only the second time they'd had eggs since leaving Seattle. "Forty cents a d-d-dozen? That's three times what we pay at home. I can't hardly believe it." He sopped up the sunny yolk with a chunk of freshly baked sourdough bread. "Yesterday I wrote a letter to my momma. A two-penny stamp cost me a nickel." He gulped his mug of coffee as though he couldn't wait to talk again. "They say the Indians are still packing at eight cents a pound, and when the snow goes, the rate jumps to fifteen cents!"

"You certainly have an affinity for numbers," Aurelia said. "I suppose that's why you were working as a supply clerk back in Seattle."

"Yea, I thought about having my own store, s-s-someday. That is if I don't find my g-g-gold."

"Well, I hope you find everything you're looking for."

"Hope you do too, ma'am."

Clay ate the last of his bread and pushed his chair back as though he'd heard enough sentimental talk. "I hear there's a tramway in operation now. Starts at Canyon City, goes all the way to the summit. Can take loads up to four hundred pounds. That would sure make the trip easier."

"A tramway? Can we afford it?" Aurelia asked, surprised that Clay would even mention something that would lighten their burden.

"Fares are changing by the hour. I won't know till we get to Canyon City. But if we can't use the tramway, we can hire a packer to help us get everything to the summit. What do you two think?"

"You're asking our opinion? Why Clay, what's come over you? An attack of civility?"

Before Clay could answer, Waldo said, "I know how you feel, Clay. My conscience bit me too. Miss Aurelia says I owe you for my life and for James John and Corbett too."

Clay waved his hand to dismiss further comment, but Waldo continued. "I owe you an apology, too. The way I see it, you can't be as rotten as folks back in Seattle was saying."

"Can't believe everything you hear, Poyser."

Aurelia waited for Clay to add some churlish remark, but it never came. Perhaps the fact that Waldo had discovered a more admirable side to Clay's character pleased Clay more than he cared to admit. Aurelia took heart. If Waldo could make such a realization about Clay, then perhaps, in time, Clay could make such a realization about Violet. In time.

* * *

A week had passed since Clay was injured. Aurelia changed his dressing every other day, each time finding the intimate contact between them a little bit easier. Finally, the evening before they set out for the pass, she removed his stitches.

"For a woman as practical as you claim to be, I can't believe you're still aiming to climb in that getup," he said, making conversation in an effort to distract himself from the feel of her hands on his skin.

"And what would you suggest? That I trot around in my bloomers the way those flashy dance-hall women do?"

"I understand the outfit lets them expose their charms."

"Those they imagine they have. I saw Miss Ruby Johnson on the street just yesterday with her dress abbreviated at both ends. One could see her neck, her arms, and her legs up to her knees!"

"Miss Ruby *Lips* Johnson."

"Of course. I wouldn't want to forget her title."

"Trademark."

"Yes, well I'll hold fast to my own wardrobe just the same."

Clay grew thoughtful. "All nonsense aside, the climb won't be easy and those long skirts of yours will just be in your way. You could wear a pair of boy's overalls."

"Overalls? You can't be serious. How would that look?"

"What difference does it make? Anything goes up here."

Aurelia arched her brow. Half in truth, half in jest, she asked, "Is this another of your ploys to keep me from going to Dawson? Because it won't work. I am going."

"No, Aurelia. I've resigned myself to that fact. Finally."

In silence, Aurelia finished dressing his wound. Clay expressed his thanks and left.

Aurelia had to accept her fate. If he'd thought of her as the least bit attractive, he'd never have suggested she wear something so crude as boy's overalls.

The conversation about the overalls replayed with alarming frequency in Aurelia's mind the next morning as she and her partners left Dyea. In a scene reminiscent of Seattle's chaos, hundreds upon hundreds of stampeders bent their backs under the weight of their packs and the pull of sleds and trudged onward. Aurelia, Clay, and Waldo took their places in the upward moving line.

Her fur coat and hood kept her warm, and her elk-skin boots kept her feet dry. Her skirt, however, was definitely in the way. She tried holding it up just enough to clear the ground, but as soon as she hunched forward to walk, which she had to do to carry her load, the skirt dipped deeper in the mud and slush. She hiked it higher. But then, when she straightened, she felt conspicuous—like one of those women who deliberately held up their dresses just to show their handsome underskirts. "More clothes than sense," Nana Brooke used to say.

Clay called to her from his position a few feet ahead. "Ready for the overalls, partner?"

She'd expected that he would have eyes in the back of his head. "No. I'm doing quite well."

Using a canvas-strap contraption of Clay's design, Aurelia carried two twenty-pound sacks of flour on her shoulders. Waldo and Clay each had wider loops of heavier canvas strapped to their shoulders and attached to sleds piled high with supplies. Before them, behind them, and on each side crowded other men with sleds pulled by dogs, horses, mules, or oxen. Still more animals carried loads on their backs, some packed so high and heavy that the animals could barely walk. Aurelia cringed every time a pack animal rolled over in the snow.

Barely a mile out of town, she was breathing hard and had to stop. "This trip wasn't half as hard last week when all I had to carry was my medical case. But loaded down like this—now I understand why so many people have given up and turned back." She paused to catch her breath. "That explains why we saw so many supplies rotting on the docks."

"Giving up?" Clay asked as he showed her how to position the weight of her pack against a boulder to momentarily relieve the strain.

"No, I just need to take it gradually."

Clay dabbed her forehead with his handkerchief, then wiped his own brow. "We don't have time for that. I want to make it to Camp Pleasant before nightfall."

"How far is that?" Aurelia furrowed her brow. "Anything over three feet is too far."

"Seven or eight miles. Come on, let's go." He turned around to Poyser, who was drooping like a scarecrow in the rain. "Buck up, man. You wanted adventure, didn't you?"

Aurelia sighed as she hoisted her pack and fell in step behind Clay. With animal dung all around them, she tried to watch her step, watch the trail, balance her load, lift her skirt, and hide her ankles—Dear Lord, was it this hard for everyone else?

One step at a time. One step at a time. The trail ascended again and then finally leveled off high above the river. Massive granite boulders and scrawny spruce and brush marked the land. They stopped for lunch at a trail-side, tent-covered cookstove called Finnegan's Point Cafe.

Aurelia relished the salty ham sandwich and cup of tea. Not because the ham was fresh or the tea hot—they weren't—but because stopping for lunch meant stopping, period. With the scope of the journey clearer now, Aurelia groaned. This was only their first trip with their first load. How many times would they have to go all the way back down to Dyea and start all over again?

Though she was having difficulty navigating the trail, she knew she was faring better than the pack horses. Puffs of frosty air billowed from their flaring nostrils as they strained to carry the loads tied to their backs while feeling their way on the snow-covered boulders. She saw their legs wobble and their steps fumble.

Beneath her cumbersome skirt her own legs fared no better. Just when she thought her limbs would wither and fall away, the trail entered a canyon. A series of frozen waterfalls hung from the granite walls like ribbons of steel. But it was the cluster of tents, not the beauty of nature, that drew her attention.

"Clay! Isn't that Canyon City up ahead? I remember passing through it on the day of the avalanche." She stepped out of line and let the stampeders behind her and their dogs and mules and oxen pass by.

"It's Canyon City all right," he said, the look in his eyes daring her to drop her pack. "But we're not pitching the tents till we get through the canyon and up to Camp Pleasant."

Aurelia shook her head. "No. We've covered seven miles of agony. I can't go any farther. I can't." One strap at a time, she slipped the pack from her back and let it drop in the snow. Oblivious to the way she looked, she plopped herself down on the pack and hung her head between her knees. "I'm going to die if I don't get some rest."

Waldo slipped his arms out of the straps to the sled, then let his pack fall to the ground as well.

"Hellfire and damnation! Look at the two of you. You're carrying small loads. We're taking a slow pace." Clay paused and looked at the never-ending stream of traffic passing them by. "This is the easy part of the trail, and already you're both ready to quit? No. We're not stopping till we reach Camp Pleasant and that's final. Now shoulder up and let's get moving. I said *now*!"

Tears of fury stung Aurelia's eyes. "Just who do you think you are? *General* Guardian?"

"I'm the one in charge. Remember? And I told you this was no place for women and weaklings. Remember?"

Waldo cleared his throat. "I'll c-c-carry your pack, Miss Aurelia. Then the walking won't be so hard on you." He reached for her pack.

"No, I can handle it." Aurelia hoisted the snow-dampened pack to her shoulders and groaned. "Just dallying these few minutes has made a world of difference. We wouldn't want to interfere with the General's schedule."

"Glad to hear it," Clay said. "Now let's go."

Canyon City's main street was a forty-foot wide swath of mud. Aurelia slumped and let her skirt drag as she trudged past the wood-framed stores, cafes, saloons, and gambling houses. Oh, what she'd give for a warm fire, a hot bath, and a sip—just a sip—of cherry brandy. The hair around her face was plastered to her skin. Her eyes burned from the glare on the snow. Even without a mirror, she knew she'd acquired that scruffy, beaten, wild look that so characterized all the other stampeders.

Clay called them to a halt just outside one of the louder saloons. "You two stay here. I'll be right back." He freed himself from the sled straps and pack and walked into the saloon.

Aurelia was stunned. "How dare he! Going off to quench his thirst for whiskey while he tethers us here in the mud like a pair of mules!" She dug her fists into her hips and turned to Waldo. "I won't stand for this. How about you?"

"W-W-Whatever you say, ma'am."

"Let's go. This twilight will last for hours. I'm sure between the two of us we can find our way to Camp Pleasant. I certainly don't want to stay in this town another minute."

With a renewed level of energy that both sharpened her determination and dulled the feeling of rejection, Aurelia marched her procession of two out of town.

With a smug look on his face, Clay stepped out of the saloon. He felt great. He puffed out his chest and held his head high as he stepped into the street and adjusted his eyes to the deepening shadows. He hadn't meant to get caught up in a poker game, but it had been worth it. He couldn't wait to see Aurelia's face when he told her what he'd done. She and Poyser had probably gone to the cafe across the street. 'Course he'd have to tell her about what he'd done with the ring, too, but she'd understand.

His elation turned to anger, then to fear as he quickly discovered that Aurelia and Poyser hadn't waited for him. The sled and flour sacks in front of the cafe across the street belonged to someone else. In answer to Clay's questions, several people remembered seeing the pretty woman and the skinny kid heading out of town and up the trail toward Camp Pleasant.

"Camp Pleasant," one old-timer said, "now that's a misnomer if ever there was one. Those grizzlies . . ."

12

Beautiful! Aurelia dropped her flour sacks on Waldo's sled and gaped at the bluish glaciers hugging the mountains and the thick blanket of snow that spread itself over the small but blessedly flat, open glen. Camp Pleasant had certainly earned its name. She couldn't fathom why no one else had chosen to camp here. After hours of struggling along a narrow gulch and slipping on snow-covered boulders, she couldn't even think of going on to Sheep Camp, where the evening's trickle of stampeders had trudged.

"Excuse me, m-m-ma'am. You think Guardian'll follow us up here tonight?"

"As long as you can pitch our tents, I'm sure the two of us will be just fine. Don't you think so?"

"Yes, ma'am!" Waldo unloaded the assortment of supplies Clay had packed. "Uh, ma'am, I only got one tent here. Guardian's got the other two and the cookstove."

"What about food? Did General Guardian think to pack food on your sled?"

Waldo rolled his eyes, as if to indicate he shared Aurelia's irritation and then began searching through the carefully packed boxes, cans, and sacks on the sled. "We've got b-b-bacon. Lots of bacon. And flour. And figs."

"Wonderful." She looked at their surroundings. "I don't see much in the way of lumber, but I'm sure I can find enough twigs for a fire—if I hurry. It's getting darker."

Waldo nodded. "I'll pitch the tent." He unloaded a few more items, then stopped. "Ma'am, what about your m-m-medical box? Are you going to be needing it?"

"Here? In Camp Pleasant?" Aurelia stretched her arms wide and looked up at the near-navy sky. "I can't imagine anything going wrong this close to heaven."

"Then I'll leave it r-r-right here on the sled."

"Fine." Aurelia listened to the crunch of her own footsteps as she picked her way through the hard-packed snow to a grove of trees. Spindly and bare, they afforded no protection from the elements. There was nowhere to hide, she realized as an unsettling feeling overtook her. Then she chided herself for her active imagination. There was no reason to hide.

Twenty minutes later she returned to where Waldo was trying to pitch the tent. Though the sun never truly set this time of year, thick black clouds had smothered it, spreading eerie shadows on the snow. "Does it seem unusually quiet to you?" she asked as she dropped her paltry load of twigs.

"Meaning no y-y-yipping and barking and braying?"

"I suppose that's it. And none of that ceaseless *tramp, tramp, tramp* we've all been a part of."

"Yep. Looks like we're in for some good old p-p-peace and quiet for a change."

Peace and quiet. Aurelia worked to clear a place for the fire, trying to shake the feeling that something was amiss. She looked over her shoulder, back toward the scrawny woods she'd just come from. "I didn't realize how accustomed I've become to hearing the birds, even at this hour. I've heard they'll sit deathly still if there's danger nearby. Don't you think it odd that there are no birds?"

"There," Waldo said as he drove the last corner stake into the snow. "That should hold it."

He hadn't heard her. It was just as well. What difference did it make if there were no birds?

Aurelia eyed the tent. Lopsided as it was, it was more than she could have done herself. At least it was shelter. Clay would have erected it properly, of course. He'd have found plenty of wood, even chopped down a whole tree if necessary. He'd have been able to put her mind at ease.

Waldo took the handful of stones and pebbles he'd gathered from the well-traveled portion of the trail and laid them under the pile of twigs. He struck a match and touched it to the wood. The dry twigs hissed, and a thin veil of steam rose from the snow caught in the bark. He grinned as though surprised by his own success.

Aurelia tucked her skirts around her and squatted down next to the fire, determined to quell her misgivings. "I feel like a pioneer," she said as she threaded a thick strip of bacon on a twig and held it to the fire's greedy flames. Drops of fat fell to the fire and sizzled against the stones, sending their scent into the cold night air. "This smells delicious. I'll bet they can smell it all the way back in Canyon City."

Canyon City was nearly three miles and as many hours back. She wondered if Clay even knew she was gone, or if he cared. Well, this should let him know she wouldn't put up with the shabby treatment he had given her in town. Feeling more than a little self-righteous, she plunged her spear closer to the flames.

If the truth be told, she didn't know why he'd gone into the saloon. Maybe to ask about places to camp. Maybe to get a report on activity at the summit. Had she overreacted? It was foolish to pretend she didn't enjoy his company. If it weren't for Violet, she'd be running toward him, not away from him. But it would be foolish to admit that, and dangerous.

Using a pocketknife contraption, Waldo opened the can of figs and spilled the brown juice down his coat, drenching the cloth with the fruit's appetizing scent. He laughed and said this was why he was so skinny, always getting more food on him than in him. Aurelia laughed too, then plucked one of the brown fleshy lobes from the tin and popped it in her mouth. The fruit was sweet and juicy. She licked her fingers and wiped them on her skirt.

Suddenly Waldo lifted his head and grew still. "Did you hear s-s-something?" he whispered.

Aurelia felt the alarm and she, too, grew still. "What is it?"

"Don't know." His eyes scanned the shadowed snow. "But I'm going to light the l-l-lamp, even if it ain't supposed to get any darker." He jammed the cold end of his bacon spear into the snow.

Aurelia cocked her head to one side and listened. All she could hear was the sound of her own breathing. Slowly she stood up, feeling each vertebra straighten and lock, every nerve tingle.

The hard-packed snow crunched beneath Waldo's boots as he hesitantly circled the small camp, all the while holding the flaming beacon in front of him. Neither of them said a word.

He ventured a few yards toward the woods, into the deepening shadows.

Logic told Aurelia to relax, but the sudden sound of crunching snow made that impossible.

"Grizzly!" Waldo screamed as a giant brown bear stood on its hind legs and filled the light. In less than a second the beast closed upon him and seized him with its great paws.

Aurelia raced to the sled. She grabbed her medical box and dumped the contents on the snow. Frantically, she scraped her fingernails against the false bottom of the case.

Waldo screamed again. The huge animal flung him to the ground and straddled him lengthwise. Aurelia could hear the shredding of his clothes.

She released the hidden latch and grabbed the gun. Just as Nana had taught her so many years ago, Aurelia balanced the deadly weapon in her palm, opened the loading gauge, and pulled the hammer back to half-cock. Her fingers fumbled as she dropped the bullets into the cylinders. It took forever. She dropped one in the snow. "Damn!" She closed the gauge and brought the hammer down.

Waldo cried out again, this time sounding fainter and more desperate.

Aurelia held the gun with both hands, aimed it straight ahead, and walked up behind the bear. She bit her lip so hard she tasted blood. *Elbow to the side, arm steady, wrist loose.*

The bear raised its paw, and Aurelia could see its claws dripping with blood.

She aimed at its massive head and fired.

The bear flinched, more irritated than hurt. It turned toward Aurelia and growled, anger flashing from its small, beady eyes. She fired at its head. At its broad chest. Again. And again. And again. Each bullet found its target but only served to enrage the beast.

It moved toward her. She retreated a step. She drew the hammer back one last time and squeezed the trigger. An empty click.

All the madness in the world seemed to fill the bear's lungs as it stood on its hind legs and roared. Aurelia turned to run, but the bear lunged forward and pinned her skirt to the ground. She stumbled and fell to her knees in the snow. In that half-instant before certain death she squeezed her eyes shut and prayed that the end would be swift.

A blast from a rifle shattered the night. Still on her knees, Aurelia felt the ground rumble as the grizzly fell, the heat from its final breath billowing around her legs.

"Aurelia!"

She opened her eyes to see Clay rushing toward her. He dropped the smoking rifle in the snow, yanked her skirt from beneath the bear's paw, and pulled her up.

Pressed against his chest, she began to cry. Sobbing and shuddering, she clung to him. The more her tears fell, the closer he held her.

"Waldo," she said, pulling away. "I've got to help Waldo." She ran over to the motionless figure.

The carnage stopped her cold. Blood covered Waldo's spindly arms, bony chest, and face. All had been raked by the bear's sharp claws. She fought the urge to wretch as she pressed her fingers to his neck to find his pulse.

"He's alive! Clay, he's alive! I'll get my case. Can you carry him back to the tent?"

Clay slipped his arms under Waldo's knees and shoulders and lifted his mangled body. Aurelia ran back to where she'd scattered her medical supplies, thinking how this would never have happened if she hadn't insisted on leaving Canyon City ahead of Clay. She bent to scoop up the precious drugs and equipment.

She pulled back the flap of the tent and helped Clay lower Waldo to the cold canvas of his sleeping bag. Pity welled up within her as she looked at him. Waldo hadn't had a chance against that bear. He didn't have much of a chance now, either.

For once, she was glad she'd been involved in the avalanche; it had given her at least a little bit of the experience she so desperately needed now. She knew what she had to do. She just didn't know if she could.

"Get whatever blankets are on the sled," she said to Clay as she spread a square of cloth on the ground and emptied her medical bag, "and the lamp. I don't know where it is. He was holding it when the bear—"

"I'll find it."

A few minutes later Clay returned with his rifle, the kerosene lamp, and two woolen blankets. With the garish yellow light flooding the small tent, Aurelia instructed him to hold Waldo's flesh together as she stitched. When they finished, she wrapped gauze around his arms, chest, neck, and forehead. She covered his scalp and both ears, praying all the while that God would have mercy on such an innocent young man.

When it was over, Clay spread the blankets over Waldo and gently tucked the edges in around his shoulders. "Any broken bones?"

"No. But only by an act of Providence."

"You think he'll make it?"

Aurelia looked around the tent. With its floor of

packed snow and its canvas walls, it was a useless barrier against the elements. She sighed. "No. Not out here. And if he does, he'll be horribly scarred."

"Then we'll take him back to Canyon City in the morning." He unrolled the second sleeping bag. "What else can we do for him now?"

"Nothing but wait."

"In the meantime, you get some rest." He picked up his rifle.

"What about you?"

"I'm going to watch for bears. They told me back in Canyon City that this place is known for them. If I'd known that before, I'd never have insisted—"

"Never mind that now. The point is you can't stay up all night. You're already exhausted. You'll catch your death—" She broke off at the thought of the all-too-real possibility.

As though he'd considered the possibility as well, he propped his rifle against the side of the tent and opened his arms. "Come here," he whispered. "Please."

Welcomed into his embrace, she nestled against his chest and felt his arms enfold her. He whispered her name. He stroked her hair. She looked up to find his brow deeply furrowed and his eyes filled with pain.

"I saw the bear." He had to swallow hard to steady his voice. "I saw the bear, and I thought I'd lost you." He pulled her close crushing her so much she could hardly breathe. Then he kneaded her shoulders, slid his hands down her back, and cupped her buttocks, pressing her body against the hardened proof of his feelings.

His admission thrilled her, and she gloried in the sudden heat that washed over her. But then she remembered something Nana Brooke had once said about a desire born of danger being the most passionate kind. He was feeling the emotion of the moment, not of a lifetime.

But she felt it too. She tilted her head, knowing she wanted to kiss him but not knowing exactly what to do first. Then he pressed his lips to hers with the urgency of a desperate man, claiming her in some ancient ritual she didn't understand. She forgot all about Nana Brooke.

His breath was ragged when he finally pulled away. As though fighting a magnetic field, he loosened his embrace. "God knows, I don't want to leave you," he said. "Not now. But I don't have much of a choice. We're staying here for the night, and that means I've got some things to take care of." He trailed his finger across her forehead and along her cheek, looking for signs of injury. "I'd better go. I'll be outside if you need me." He bent to kiss her lips once more before he turned and left the tent.

If you need me. Somehow she knew he wasn't referring to his ability to fetch supplies for her, or to chop wood, or even to kill a bear. All her life she'd been the one seeing to the needs of others, and now here was a man not only willing, but eager, to meet her needs. Oddly enough, she couldn't say what she needed, except to rescue Violet. Would Clay help her save Violet? Or was that too much to ask?

She'd talk to Clay about her sister in the morning. Tonight she had a patient to care for. Tomorrow morning she'd also have to find the gun she'd dropped in the snow and hide it back in her medical chest. She had known it was illegal to bring handguns into the Yukon, but she hadn't considered leaving the camp without Nana's legacy any more than she'd considered parting with her silver buckles. Surely, it was Nana's legacy that had saved her life—that and Clay Guardian.

Outside she could hear the sound of an ax chopping what she assumed was wood for a fire. She stepped outside to find his energies and the ax directed to the bear instead.

"You ever had bear steaks?" he called to her. "There's not much fat left on the animal this time of year, but the meat's good. You'll like it."

The sight was gruesome, even for a doctor. Aurelia cupped her hands over her mouth and ducked back inside the tent. Despite the fact that she hadn't eaten anything substantial since noon, she'd rather go hungry than eat bear meat. She could, however, appreciate the justice in the situation.

Sometime near midnight the sounds of slaughter finally stopped, and Clay returned to the tent. The wind had picked up. Blasts of icy air slashed through the canvas. Aurelia had spread her fur over Waldo, taken her boots off, and crawled into the second sleeping bag. She couldn't sleep. Even with her corset loosened, the stays poked her ribs every time she moved. The fullness of her skirt bound her legs. The snow under the sleeping bag was hard and cold. Besides, too much had happened.

"How's Poyser?"

"His vital signs are weak, but steady. I've administered a dose of laudanum. I don't want to hold out hope, but—" She propped herself up on her elbow. "Clay, look at you." The lowered light from the kerosene lamp cast his shadow against the canvas walls. "Your clothes are all splattered with blood."

"I washed my face and hands in the snow. The rest will just have to wait. Don't worry. I'll sleep outside."

"Outside? Where? You'll freeze!"

Clay shrugged. "On the sled. My coat's heavy. I'll manage."

Aurelia sat upright. "No. Wait." Dear God, what was she about to do? "I think it only prudent—in light of the cold, of course—that you and I . . . that you and I share this sleeping bag."

He raised his eyebrows. "Hmm. You want me to crawl in that sleeping bag with you?"

"In light of the cold." Why did he make her suggestion sound so indelicate? "I'm only thinking of your comfort and safety."

His answer began with the twinkle in his eyes and continued with a closed-mouth smile. Aurelia likened his mischievous look to that of a little boy about to steal a cookie. Somehow it took her mind off mountains and bears and pain and dying.

The childlike image vanished when Clay took off his coat and spread it over Poyser's sleeping bag, adding to his warmth. Aurelia couldn't be sure, but Clay's shoulders seemed broader than they had the day before, his arms more muscular, his torso better defined. Or perhaps, she admitted to herself, she was developing a nonscientific appreciation for the male physique.

Knowing her thoughts were absolutely wanton, she hunched down in the sleeping bag and turned on her side, away from him. But the lamp cast a most revealing silhouette on the canvas wall in front of her, and she simply could not close her eyes.

She watched the shadow as he untied his high-topped boots and pulled them off. Quickly he stepped on the bottom edge of the sleeping bag to avoid the cold. Then he unfastened his pants.

"Clay! You're not taking off your clothes, are you?"

"Just the bloody ones. You don't want to sleep next to bear blood do you?" He laughed in that teasing way that both alarmed and excited her. "I'm just thinking of your sensibilities."

She could hear the friction of cloth against skin as he pulled his pants down.

He pulled down the flap of the sleeping bag and crouched down. With her back still to him, she shivered as a rush of cold air stirred the warmth of her cocoon. "The first thing I'm going to do when we get back to Canyon City," he said as he slipped into the pocket beside her, "is buy a suit of long underwear. Look at this. My skin is turning blue already."

This was a terrible idea. The sleeping bag had seemed big enough for two when she was its only occupant, but not now, not with his fidgeting. First his shoulder jabbed her back, then his elbow poked her ribs, then his feet tangled in her skirt.

"That dress of yours is making me itch. I don't suppose you'd consider taking it off."

Silence.

He adjusted his position again. "That was a joke, Aurelia."

"Of course it was a joke. Don't you think I know that?"

But there was nothing funny about this situation at all. Maybe he would be able to fall asleep, but she certainly wouldn't. Not with the way he was gradually shaping his body to hers, matching his chest to her back, fitting his knees to the backs of her knees, cupping his lap to her bottom. They fit together like spoons—two perfectly molded spoons, one with a suddenly stiff handle.

"Sorry," he whispered in her ear. "It's an involuntary reaction. You doctors understand that sort of thing, don't you?"

She tried to inch her body away from his, but there was no room. She could demand that he leave, but he was there at her invitation. Besides, she confessed to herself, she loved the feelings he stirred in her. Her cheeks flushed and her heart began to race. Perhaps she should sleep on the sled.

Just as she was about to suggest it, Clay whispered again, "Before you say anything, I want to thank you. I've known a lot of people who talk a good game about wanting to help a person, but only if it's convenient for them. You're not like that." He sighed, and when he spoke again it was with a tenderness Aurelia had never heard in his voice before. "You're the most caring woman I've ever known. I just wanted to tell you that." He coiled a lock of her hair around his finger. Then he scooped her tresses aside and nuzzled his lips to her neck. "Good-night, Aurelia." He slipped his arm in the curve of her waist and rested his hand on her belly.

She could hear the drumming of her own heartbeat, feel the uneven cadence of her breath. She smelled the faint scent of lavender in her dress and the salty tang of a man's skin. With his hand positioned as it was, she dared not move. For if his hands strayed up . . . or down . . . she wasn't sure what she'd do.

Lie still, she told herself. *Don't move.* She wouldn't look to see if his shirt was unbuttoned, if his legs were bare. If his dark hair spread evenly across his pectorals or if it gathered in a patch like a shield over his heart. If it trailed down his torso, to his navel, to his abdomen, to his—

"Warm enough?" he whispered.

She opened her mouth before the word could come out. "Yes." Even to her own ears the simple utterance sounded breathy and anxious.

"Hmm," he purred.

Lie still, she told herself. *Don't move.*

This situation wasn't totally out of the realm of her imagination. No, she reminded herself, she'd fantasized about it at least a thousand times before. She'd asked Nana Brooke about it once, about how it felt to lie with a man. Nana hadn't been able to explain it. She'd said it'd be easier to explain daylight to a fish that had never been above the ocean's deepest floor. "I can, however, guarantee you this much," Nana had added. "You'll like it."

Indeed.

Clay moaned as he took a deep breath and adjusted his position again. His fingers grazed Aurelia's bosom, and as they did, her flesh pebbled like a million tiny dominoes toppling one atop the other. Even as his hand came to rest on her shoulder, the sensation continued.

Staring at the canvas, she tucked her arm beneath her head and waited for sleep to come.

She wasn't aware that she'd fallen asleep until she thought she heard Waldo moan. She was ready to jump up and investigate, but Clay had her pinned under his arm. She listened carefully. There was no sound from Waldo, just the wind.

Hoping to get a bit more sleep, Aurelia tried to lift the dead weight of Clay's arm, but her movement only served to rouse him. They both moved at the same time and found themselves face to face.

Other than the fine black down that swept across

his pectorals, his chest was naked. Discretion kept her from looking down, but not him. In an effort to loosen her corset, she'd apparently unbuttoned her dress in her sleep. Now her breasts, pink and full, threatened to spill out of her chemise. Defying restriction, her hair billowed around her face and neck and ran in tendrils across her shoulders.

"I know what this is," Clay said, his voice low and husky. "The bear killed me. Now I'm a dead man trying to get to heaven, and you're an angel showing me the way." He yawned and stretched, taking up as much room in the sleeping bag as he could, forcing Aurelia to lie on her back. "I've always wanted to kiss an angel." With that, he slipped one arm under her shoulders, angled his head over hers, and kissed her lips.

All the tension that had tormented her body during the night now surged to the surface. They were both alive, and she knew it. She also knew that with the way things happened in this God-forsaken country, they might not be alive tomorrow. If she was to ever know how it felt to lie with a man, to lie with *this* man, she'd better find out now. She might not have another chance.

She wrapped her arms around his neck, pulling him closer, deepening his kiss. Remembering the scene on the Oriental screen, she arched her body to meet his, pressing her breasts hard against his chest. When she felt his tongue test her willingness, she parted her lips freely.

With one hand he cupped the fullness of her breasts, first one then the other, gently squeezing each pink nipple between his fingers, tugging at the little buds until they ached.

Tangled in his legs, she felt his need as hard and hot as she'd imagined. She reveled in his response. And as she did, she felt her most private parts begin the annointing that signaled her readiness for loving.

"I want you," he murmured as he parted her legs with his knee. "I want you."

If she died this moment, she'd die happy, having known such passion with a man like Clay.

Then she braced her arms against his chest to stay his advance. "Listen!" She took a deep breath and tried to steady her nerves. "It's Waldo. I think he's waking up."

"It's just the wind."

Aurelia pushed Clay's arms aside and struggled to crawl from the sleeping bag. She grabbed her boots and slipped them on, not bothering to lace them up. "I should have been more attentive to my patient's welfare, not my own—"

"Carnal desires?" he said as he sat up. "*Our* carnal desires."

She blocked out his words as she checked Waldo's vital signs. Steady.

"How is he?"

"Holding his own."

"I'm glad. Now come back to me."

The hungry look in his dark eyes devoured her, making her aware of the heat they'd created, of his still heaving chest, and her still-naked bosom. She shook her head, fighting the urge to comply. "I can't."

She'd behaved indecently, offering herself like some depraved, passion-crazed wanton. And he'd behaved no better. She turned her back to Clay to repair her chemise. The stubble of his beard had left her breasts rosy and tingling from his touch. Despite the struggle within her, she allowed herself to picture his hands as they kneaded her breasts, his tongue as it licked her still hardened nipples. She closed her eyes and shuddered, then buttoned her dress, not caring that the buttons and holes didn't match.

"It was the passion of the moment," she said, hoping to convince herself as well as him. "Merely the kind of passion born of disaster. It should never have happened. And it's certainly best forgotten."

"Fine. If you *can* forget so easily, then I guess you should." He scrambled from the sleeping bag and snatched his clothes from where they lay. "I can't."

Aurelia averted her eyes while he dressed, but she turned around just in time to see Clay adjust the bulge in his trousers. With a burning stare, he said, "One thing's for sure, I can't stay here another night. Not with you." He yanked on his boots.

"I don't know why you can't exercise a little more control over your . . . your appetites," she said.

"Because I can't!" He opened the flap on the tent.

"Where are you going?"

"Outside. To roll around in the snow."

Aurelia watched him leave, all the while wishing it had been her sweet charm and her delicate femininity— qualities she didn't possess—that had so intensely aroused him, instead of her shameful lust and aching loneliness—qualities she possessed in abundance.

"Damn," he mumbled under his breath as the cold hit him. He hadn't been wrung out by a woman like that since— He recalled the few women whose beds he'd shared since Mary died. None of them had come close to firing him the way this lady doctor did. He thought about his compliant, gentle wife. He had truly loved her, he thought with the kind of tenderness that meant he wanted to move on.

He rubbed his hands together and tried to warm them with the heat of his breath. What would it be like, he wondered, when he bedded her completely? Because he knew he would, he had to. He couldn't make the rest of this journey alongside her and not think about how she'd warmed so easily to his kiss and how she'd flared like dry kindling when he touched her.

He glanced back at the tent, then grabbed a handful of snow and buried his face in it.

Later, with both his temper and his ardor cooled, he returned to the tent with the half-empty tin of figs that had been tossed in the snow. He also carried a handful of dried moss and a bundle of twigs. "I thought you might need a fire to boil some water for whatever it is you doctors do."

"Thank you."

"Sure. I'll get this going just outside the tent. That'll make it easier for you. I found a small pot in the provisions on the sled. There's not enough wood here for a rip-roaring fire, but—"

"It'll do nicely."

Relieved Aurelia hadn't asked him to explain his subdued attitude, Clay built a fire and boiled some snow for water. He wasn't about to tell her how easily she had reduced him to some kind of savage—not when she could so easily tame her own desires. He pictured the wisps of hair at the nape of her neck, the little hollow at the base of her throat, the softness of her lips, the fullness of her breasts. Then he grabbed another handful of snow.

* * *

Aurelia tended to Waldo. She was amazed at how such a scrawny man could withstand the trauma that the bear had inflicted on him. She checked his dressing. The wounds would definitely leave scars. "I'm sorry I'm not a better doctor, Waldo," she whispered as she pulled the blankets back up and tucked them around his shoulders. "That grizzly has marked you for life."

Why she thought of Dr. Bonwitt now, she didn't know, except that Dr. Bonwitt would remind Aurelia of one very important thing. Waldo was still alive.

She also thought of Bonwitt to keep from thinking about Clay.

She had never claimed to understand men, but to go from ardor to anger so quickly—surely Clay was more complex than most.

"Aurelia!"

It was the angry bellow of General Guardian that drew her attention. He ducked to clear the opening of the tent and marched inside. "Of all the selfish, harebrained schemes—did you know what Poyser was planning to do?"

From his fingers dangled the ivory-handled gun.

13

"*You found it!*" Filled with relief, Aurelia reached for the gun.

"No, you don't want to even touch this thing."

She emphasized her outstretched hand. "I most certainly do."

He shook his head as though he found it useless to try to argue with her. "Well, I guess it's all right. Here," he said, handing it to her. "It's empty. Now be careful. It's heavy. Can you imagine that Poyser trying to smuggle a revolver into the Yukon? He could have had us all turned back at the border. Maybe even arrested."

Aurelia clenched the handle. "No, Clay. Let me explain."

"What's to explain? Poyser was deliberately carrying an illegal weapon—"

"No. For one thing, if it hadn't been for this gun, that bear might have killed both Waldo and me—"

"You don't know anything about guns. That's a Colt Peacemaker. It can drop a man sure enough, but it wouldn't do anything more to a grizzly than pierce its ear, and that's only if you're a damn good shot. Poyser should have been toting a rifle."

Clay reached for his own Winchester propped against the tent. "This'll do the job, and it's legal to carry it. I'm just glad I'm the one who found the Colt, not the Mounties. Maybe we can sell it back in Canyon City. It sure as hell isn't crossing the border with me." He held out his hand for the gun.

Aurelia's voice was firm. "The Colt belongs to me."

"You?"

The way Clay stared at her it was as though she'd told him she was a Mountie in disguise. "That's right. I kept it hidden in the bottom of my medical chest. That's where I'm going to put it right now. And you can rest assured, it *will* cross the border with me."

"How in blazes did you get a gun?"

"My grandmother gave it to me. And as for its ability to down a bear—you're right. For a target of that size, the Colt is ineffective. I trust you noticed, however, I *did* pierce the bear's ear."

"You're protecting Poyser. That's it, isn't it?"

Aurelia shook her head. "The Colt is mine. And it's going with me."

"Damnation, Aurelia! Ladies don't carry guns." His stare took in her disheveled hair and her haphazardly buttoned dress.

"Say what you really mean, Clay. Ladies don't go trekking alone into unknown territories either, or go forming partnerships with strange men. And ladies certainly don't go to school and become doctors. And, as you so emphatically stated, ladies don't carry guns. So I'm not a lady. But I'm not a criminal either. Or some woman of . . . of . . . infinite accessibility."

"Did I say you were?"

"No, but you're looking at me as though I am."

"That's because I don't know you anymore. Hell, maybe I never did."

"Maybe I'm just like my sister. That's what you're thinking, isn't it? Well, I'm not!" No sooner were the words out of her mouth than she realized their implication. Clay did too.

"Meaning what? That your sister *is* a criminal?"

She glared at him. "How skilled you are at twisting words."

"So untwist them. Explain it to me, if you can."

Seeing him gloat the way he did angered her all the more. "For a man who alleges to have been judged unfairly yourself, you're surprisingly quick to censure."

"Come on, Aurelia. Explain."

"I don't have to explain anything to you." With that, she turned and left, shaking inside because she couldn't explain her words. Not to Clay, and not even to herself.

While Clay readied the sled, Aurelia hovered over Waldo, mentally lashing herself for the pain he'd already endured and for the pain yet to come. Violet was not far from her thoughts. It had been her pride that had caused both tragedies. Would Violet ever forgive her? Would Waldo?

With a feather-light touch, she traced his brow. At least his condition hadn't worsened. If they could get him back to Canyon City where there might be a real doctor, he might have a chance. She'd take good care of the gophers for him.

She was checking to make sure she hadn't left anything behind when Clay came into the tent. He looked just as perturbed and just as smug as he had earlier.

"The trail's already filled with stampeders heading up the trail. But that's not where we're going. No. We're going in the opposite direction. I just knew something like this would happen. You had to go running off like some blind fool. If you'd stayed in Canyon City—"

"Well, I didn't," she snapped. She grabbed her medical chest and marched toward the sled. Midway, she stopped and turned around, tears brimming in her eyes. "Don't you think I've thought the same thing? Waldo might die. And if he doesn't, he may wish he had. I know it's all my fault. I don't need you to tell me. So as soon as you can get this tent down, let's go."

She cringed at the pity softening his eyes, then lifted her chin so high that only the most ignorant of fools would dare approach her.

Not a single word passed between them as Clay carried Waldo to the sled. While Aurelia saw to Waldo's comfort, Clay took down the tent and lashed it on the sled along with the bulging oilcloth sacks he'd stuffed with bear meat and chunks of fat. With the morning sun climbing quickly, they headed out of camp.

They hadn't traveled far when Clay asked, "You staying behind in Canyon City with Poyser?"

"Depends on whether or not there's a doctor."

"I'm not staying."

"Now why doesn't that surprise me?"

"Think what you want, but I don't owe Poyser anything. I'm going on to Lake Bennett. The first ones there get the best sites and the best lumber to build the boats. As soon as I get our camp set up, I'll come back for you."

"And the first ones to build their boats are the first ones on the river to Dawson, right?"

"That *is* my destination."

"Mine too, remember?"

"How could I forget?"

He wouldn't come back for her. She knew it.

She looked down at poor Waldo and thought about how much he needed help to make it to Dawson, with or without his injuries. Then again, she wouldn't be surprised if he decided not to go on to Dawson, after the ordeal he'd been through. She prayed that he would live to make the decision.

"Our partnership means nothing to you, does it Clay?"

"*Our* partnership does. As you pointed out back in Dyea, we need each other's supplies and food, but including Poyser was your idea, not mine."

He was right. They did need each other. But it was that righteous edge to his voice that made her bristle, as though God had ordained Clay's mission worthy but not hers. All he cared about was capturing Violet and Sculley and bringing them to what he called justice. He probably wanted to throttle them first. Or maybe he wanted to throttle Aurelia for toting the gun. Or throttle Waldo for not being as manly as Clay. He seemed so eager to see punishment meted out.

Her frustration mounted as they headed back down the trail. She huffed and puffed along, helping to keep the sled upright, praying someone in Canyon City would be qualified to nurse Waldo back to health. She couldn't trust Clay to let him go on without her.

The slush from yesterday's traffic had frozen in the night, only to be softened anew by the morning stream of stampeders. The sled mired down quickly, the wooden runners often disappearing in the muck. Traveling against the flow, Aurelia begged indulgence as she and Clay maneuvered their sled on the narrow trail, explaining to everyone they met how Waldo had tangled with a grizzly to save her life and would survive only if they got him back to Canyon City. Aurelia mentioned Clay's contribution as well, but with less enthusiasm. Indeed, she concluded with satisfaction, conscious or not, Waldo would be a legend by the time they got to Canyon City.

Late in the evening, they reached their destination. After securing two adjacent "rooms," cubicles divided by plaster-covered fabric stretched on wooden frames, Clay pitched his tent on the outskirts of town with the thousands of others. He and Aurelia barely spoke at dinner, except for Clay's accusation.

"You're making Poyser into something he's not."

"By telling everyone what a hero he is for facing that bear? Why, Clay, you sound jealous."

"How can I be jealous of someone who doesn't exist?"

"You don't think Waldo is a hero?"

"It's you who doesn't think he's a hero. If you did, you'd let his accomplishments speak for themselves. He did a brave thing. He was maimed and almost killed. Isn't that enough?"

His words reached deep inside her and found something long buried, something raw and painful. "You're saying I should tell everyone how he trembled, how he screamed, how he cried for his momma?"

"You don't need to say anything. That's the point. Let him tell his own story." His voice softened. "I know you meant well." He reached across the table to take her hand.

She yanked it away. She didn't want his comfort or his platitudes. It couldn't do any harm to embellish the facts surrounding Waldo's ordeal. And if it did, God help her, it was too late.

Waldo regained consciousness the next morning. In between muffled cries of pain, Aurelia told him what had happened, including how his courage had become legendary. "The Indians say there can be no braver deed of man than to stand against the grizzly. To do so and live is a sign of a champion. To be scarred by the grizzly, the ultimate badge of courage."

He didn't look nearly as pleased as she thought he would.

"But I didn't kill the grizzly," he mumbled as he drifted in and out of sleep, "Guardian did."

Five days passed. While Waldo slept, Clay made several trips back to Dyea for more supplies. Aurelia couldn't help but wonder what else he was doing. She asked him how he could have possibly gotten their entire cache up to Canyon City in such a short period of time, but he just shrugged and said something about each of them doing the job he or she was best suited for.

Aurelia assumed Clay didn't care about Waldo, but every night when he came back from Dyea he looked in to see how Waldo was coming along. He sounded genuinely pleased to learn how much Waldo's condition had improved. The day Waldo finally sat up and talked, Clay decided it was time to leave.

Aurelia would have to leave now too. Anxious to find someone to whom she could entrust Waldo's care, she asked everyone she met if there was a doctor or a nurse or a druggist in town. A photographer who came by to take Waldo's picture told Aurelia about the Devines, a missionary and his wife who were in town for an extended period. Mr. Devine had read medicine for several years and might be able to render the assistance Aurelia needed.

The Devines were just the people Aurelia hoped she'd find. Waldo liked them too. Still sore and weak, he knew he wasn't well enough to make the climb. He was, however, able to walk to the huge room that served as a kitchen, sit for hours, and sip cups of hot coffee. Everyone wanted to talk to him about his battle with the grizzly. With each telling, his role in the encounter took on grander proportions. He pointed with pride to the slashes across his face and chest. "I'll be scarred for life," he'd say, holding his head a little higher each time and his shoulders a bit more erect. He told Clay and Aurelia to go on without him. He'd catch up with them at Lake Bennett.

"Hold on, just one big minute," Clay said when he came to Aurelia's room to fetch the satchel of personals. "There's still the matter of your gun."

Her spirits dismal at having to leave Waldo behind, Aurelia couldn't summon the fervor to battle Clay. Instead, she took the gun from the secret compartment and held it in her lap.

"I know this might not make sense to you, Clay, but I don't know of any other way to explain." She stroked the ivory handle as though the touch alone would bring back memories. "Ever since we left Seattle, the talk around us has always been of gold and instant millionaires. I'm not like these thousands of stampeders; I'm not looking for the fairy-tale ending to a sentimental dream. I don't believe in either. Life always exacts too high a price for what people call happiness."

She searched his eyes for a sign of understanding but found only curiosity. "All I have is my grandmother's legacy—my silver buckles and this gun. I could never part with them. Not for any reason."

He didn't say anything at first, and she wondered just how big a fool she'd made of herself, placing so much importance on what he probably considered a trinket.

"You carry that gun and you take an awful chance. For both of us. You realize that?"

"But I'll keep it in my medical chest. In the hidden compartment."

"No, that's the first place the Mounties will look. And you can't keep it in the supplies. They'll be counted and weighed one bundle at a time."

There was panic in her voice. "Then what am I to do?" Her anxiety heightened as Clay maintained his steadfast look. "Clay, please. You've gambled before. Maybe not with anything of this magnitude, but surely you can understand."

Something she said triggered the reaction she had hoped for.

"So what do you want me to do?"

"Help me hide it."

"You're asking me to break the law."

"I'm asking you to preserve a legacy."

With silence hanging between them, Aurelia remembered that Nana used to say the true test of a man's character was to give him power.

"Let me think a minute or two. It's not going to be easy hiding a gun that big and that heavy." He looked over at the medical chest, then at the satchel of personals, then at the gun itself, still lying in Aurelia's lap. "Not even the Mounties would search your person."

"I should hide the gun on my body?"

"It's the only way." His eyes lit up. "Too bad your grandmother didn't give you a neat little derringer. I knew a dance-hall girl once. She kept a derringer strapped to her leg. Said it was to discourage debts, but the way she strutted around showing it to everybody, you'd think it was some kind of ornament."

If she weren't a doctor, she'd have blushed at his free use of the word *leg*. As a matter of anatomy, it was a study in bone, muscle, nerve, and tendon, a well-designed machine for balance and motion. Covered with skin and hair. Warm to the touch.

She suddenly recalled the night they shared in the sleeping bag, particularly the moment when he wedged his knee between her own legs and painstakingly pushed back the barrier of her wool skirt and her cotton petticoats. She had felt the pressure of his bare leg as he separated her thighs, knowing that only the thin barrier of her cotton combination stood between their bare skin.

"I could strap it to your thigh," Clay said, interrupting her vision. "I don't think it would hurt, but it might be uncomfortable. That's a good-sized gun. But with all those petticoats, I doubt it'll show through your skirt." He cocked his head to one side. "Your thigh. Yea, the more I think about it, the better I like it. There's not a Mountie in the Yukon who'd force a lady to lift her skirt."

Aurelia felt a mixture of relief at having found a solution and apprehension at the thought of how it would be carried out. "I'll attach the gun myself."

"Don't be a fool. When we get to the Chilkoot

Pass, you can't afford to be thinking of anything but your next step. The angle is almost straight up. There's no way to climb but on all fours. You don't want to have the gun slide down your leg and fall to the ground. Especially in front of some scrupulous Mountie. So unless you've got some previous experience in smuggling, you'd better let me help you."

"I suppose you're right." She stroked the barrel of the gun. He'd have to touch her again. She slid her finger across the small, pebbly hammer and felt that strange coiling deep inside her, that ache she somehow knew he could cure.

"Unless you've got a better idea," he said.

She avoided looking him in the eye, lest he see her thoughts. Even if she were willing to compromise her virtue outside the vows of marriage—which she wasn't—would she do so with him, knowing the kind of man he was?

"Still think it's a risk worth taking?"

"No!" She jumped up and took a step away from him, releasing the hammer back to its safety position.

"Aurelia?"

"I mean yes." She fanned her cheeks, though the heat still building inside her would not be so easily cooled.

His eyes darkened with a knowing look. "You look flushed. Are you feeling all right?"

"I'm fine."

"You need to roll around in the snow."

She frowned in puzzlement as he approached her, smiling and moistening his lips. She accepted the hand he offered and let him draw her to her feet.

"No, not snow," he said, "I know what you really need."

He pressed his lips to hers in a gentle kiss. Trembling with uncertainty, she welcomed the sweet spray of kisses he left on her eyelids, her nose, and again on her lips. Only a soft moan betrayed her desire for more.

The painful anticipation only worsened as he outlined her lips with his tongue. He pulled back, just a little, and looked at her. Surely, he saw the flush on her cheeks, the beads of moisture between her brows. He placed his fingertips on her mouth and spread her lips. His groan of passion cried inside her as he covered her mouth with his own and with his tongue plundered her darkness. The pulse between her legs hammered.

His hands, their movement at first slow and almost graceful, now bound her tight against him. He freed her hair from its pins, then clutched the golden silk in his fist while his tongue tantalized the soft flesh of her mouth. She opened wider to take him in.

He stroked the column of her neck, then lowered his hands to her breasts. He massaged and squeezed and pressed his thumbs to her hardened nipples. The heat inside her rose all at once, pulling her to a moment of wanting so intense that it hurt. It was the fear of wanting too much that called back her senses.

She struggled with her thoughts as she eased from his embrace, afraid of how vulnerable he made her feel, desperate to know if he too felt as confused and powerless as she did. The strength of his hands as they kneaded her shoulders, keeping her within his grasp, told her he felt very much in control, an imbalance she would have accepted if she had trusted him.

She removed his hands from her shoulders and stepped back. "I think you'd better go now."

He forced the kind of small smile that said he agreed, but only because leaving was what he should do, not what he wanted to do. "We could always talk. You could tell me more about that grandmother of yours. About school. Whatever. Just talk."

Just talk? He made the idea sound absurd, which it was. Her nerves still tingled, as did the air around them. She knew it would be a long time before she regained her composure, an even longer time before she could look at Clay and not see the frightening reflection of her own passion. "I don't think casual conversation is possible right now."

He nodded. "You're right."

"Besides, we've got a big day ahead of us. I can't say I'm looking forward to lugging another load of supplies."

His eyes lit up. "Oh, have I got a surprise for you."

"What kind of surprise?"

"No. I have to go now. Remember?" He placed a kiss on his finger and pressed it to her lips. "You'll find out soon enough."

He wished her good-night and left, leaving her to wonder all sorts of things, including what kind of surprise he'd planned. She ran her finger across her lips, remembering the feel of his kiss, thinking that maybe someday the wish taking shape inside her would someday be granted.

The air at six o'clock in the morning was nothing short of invigorating. Aurelia huddled into the fur of her coat and puffed white vapor clouds as she followed Clay up the side of the mountain to "the surprise." Halfway up the mountain, he stopped and pointed straight ahead.

"There it is."

She looked at the series of tripod-shaped devices, supported along the mountain side with sections of iron pipe bolted together and embedded into rock. "But that's the tramway." Why would he be showing her the tramway? They didn't have the funds to use it.

He pointed to his blue bandana flapping on a pole alongside an enormous pile of supplies sitting cold and frozen in the snow alongside heaps of other supplies. "And that's our cache over there."

"I don't understand. I thought our supplies were back in Dyea."

"They were, but now they're here. And they're going to be trammed to the summit. Every single pound. Every single inch of the way."

She felt a familiar panic, like the one she felt on the day Violet was supposed to board the train from Philadelphia and return home after her visit with Aurelia was over. Instead, Violet laughed and said she was leaving with Fletcher Sculley, and she didn't care how Aurelia explained it to their parents. It was no concern of hers.

"What's gotten into you? We can't afford to use the tramway. We won't have any money left to get to Dawson. What if there's an emergency—"

"Hold on," he said, looking oddly amused by her anxiety. "The fare has been paid in full, in advance, and it didn't cost us a nickel. I even managed to have our cache packed up from Dyea." He tipped her chin, and for a moment she thought he might kiss her, right out there in front of hundreds of people. "Surprise."

The idea that something this good could be happening to her was almost just as frightening, because good things could be taken away so easily. "How?"

He beamed. "Poker. The night you and Waldo took off for Camp Pleasant."

Aurelia groaned at the memory of that horrid night and then listened while Clay explained.

"I went into the bar for news about the summit, and I wound up in a poker game with this slick-haired dandy named No Fold Towles. He owns this tramway. I was only going to put up a couple hundred dollars, play one hand, and get the heaviest things trammed to the summit. But Towles insisted we play for tramming the entire cache, all four thousand five hundred pounds."

Aurelia sensed that not all the news about this story was good. "And how much money did you have to commit?"

He grinned sheepishly. "Fifteen hundred. All I had."

"Oh, Clay, that's insane!"

He looked pleased that she understood the mounting drama. "Right. That's just what I told Towles. 'That's more than two bits a pound,' I said. 'Even the Indians don't charge that much to pack by hand.'"

"And what did Towles say to that?"

"He tried to scare me. 'With those savages you can't be sure you'll ever see your goods again.'"

"So you bet the money—all the money you had—and you won."

"No. I lost."

"Dear God, no!"

"Hold on. Let me finish."

Aurelia didn't like the way this story was going.

"I felt about as low as you can imagine, knowing I'd lost every cent I had."

"You ought to be horsewhipped."

"Could you say that again, only this time smile?"

"You didn't lose my money too, did you? Or Waldo's?"

"No." He laughed nervously, suddenly aware that

Aurelia might not find the humor in his story. "Anyway, I couldn't go back to you and Poyser and tell you I'd lost all my money—"

"So you explained and Mr. Towles gave the money back?"

"No. That's not the way poker works."

"So what did you do?"

"I challenged him to another hand. Double or nothing. So I dealt. I gave Towles an ace, king, nine, and a hole card. I drew a queen, a four, a three, and a deuce—that's a two—in the hole. No chance for a straight. No chance for a flush. Not for either of us. And if neither of us had a pair, he'd win with his ace high."

Aurelia felt bewildered by the summation but understood that the moment must have been tense.

"Then I dealt the last two cards. I gave Towles a jack. And me another deuce."

She gave him a blank look. "Is that good?"

He grinned. "Good? It was great! I won! With a lousy pair of twos."

Aurelia sighed, but her relief was short-lived. "Just a minute," she said. "If you lost all the money on the first go-round, and you didn't bet my money or Waldo's, what did you have to bet when you challenged Mr. Towles to a second?"

"The ring."

14

"Oh, no, you couldn't have—"

"I did. I bet the ring. There, now you know. And there's no need to go looking at me like I'm some kind of monster. I won. Remember? The ring is safe." He fished in the inside pocket of his jacket. "Here. See for yourself." He held it up to her and then dropped it back in his pocket. She didn't look at all appeased.

"How could you have been so thoughtless?"

"Thoughtless? No, you're not pinning that one on me. Now maybe I didn't think long about betting your ring, but I sure thought hard. Are you forgetting how all this turned out?"

"You were thoughtless and reckless."

"Damn it, Aurelia. Don't you listen? I won."

"Sheer luck."

"Skill."

"You jeopardized property that didn't belong to you. My sister's ring. My grandmother's legacy. What gave you the right—"

He raised his voice. "I'll tell you what gave me the right. Responsibility. Four thousand five hundred pounds of it."

"Don't make yourself sound so noble. You're not."

The hard look in his eyes disguised the pain inflicted by her words. Thoughtless. Reckless. Irresponsible. They were all too familiar. Time and place made no difference. He was and would always be the son of the town drunk. He was and would always be the inadequate father of an innocent little boy who deserved better.

She shot again so quickly, she must have had ammunition stored for weeks. "After all we've been through, I thought you were truly interested in helping me. I trusted you."

"So you did," he said, staring into the unrelenting anger in her eyes. "So you did."

"I thought there was some sort of bond between us." Her voice caught, as though the admission itself brought her pain.

His own heart ached as tears filled her eyes. He whispered, lest anyone hear his admission, lest anyone see his vulnerability. "We do have a bond, Aurelia. Something special."

"No. You used me. Again."

She turned her back and walked through the maze of canvas-wrapped dreams, leaving him with nearly five thousand pounds of supplies and an emptiness he couldn't begin to measure.

"Aurelia, wait!" He caught up with her. "You think what you want. I don't have time to waste trying to change your mind. And I didn't bring you all the way up here just to show you the scenery." He pointed to the three burly men headed toward them. "Towles's men. They're going to carry our cache over to the loading platform. About two hours from now our cache is taking a ride to the summit. That's going to save us weeks of hard work, especially now, since it's just the two of us."

"And what am I supposed to do? Watch it?"

"That's right. You stay down here at this end and see that Towles's men load all our gear. As soon as they finish, you go back to town. I'm going up to the Scales. I'll collect our things as they come off the cable and have them weighed. I'll make sure everything's loaded up again and trammed the rest of the way to the summit. I should be back tomorrow or the day after. Think you can handle it?"

"Of course I can."

"Good. We'll leave as soon as I get back. And don't worry. I haven't forgotten about your gun."

She dug her fists into her hips and scowled. "I'll bet you haven't." The frown on her face said she'd rather haul a thousand pounds of rocks than have him touch her.

"See you," he said as he walked away. She didn't wave, and he didn't look back.

Aurelia pressed her fingers to her temple. How could he be so smug? What if he'd lost? Just to contemplate such a disaster brought an ache to her head.

One of Towles's men came closer and eyed her with suspicion. "Folks say you're a doctor."

"That's right," Aurelia answered, no longer feeling the need to defend herself.

The older, scar-faced man spat on the ground. "I seen your kind, always looking for blood and agony to get you fired up. You ain't no woman. You're a butcher. You're harder lookin' than a dock worker and you ain't half as smart as I am."

"Now just a minute," she snapped.

"It's women like you what's bringing down this country." He balanced a barrel across his shoulders. "Women is supposed to be at home keeping their men respectable. Not roaming the world and soiling both sexes."

Another man came over and spoke up. "Quit your harping, Otis. She's the doc what stitched up that man what tangled with the grizzly."

Otis spat again. "Doctor? Hell, she don't look strong enough to stride a mustang or smart enough to mend a bullet hole, and if she can't do that, she ain't no doctor."

"Well, make up your mind, mister! If I'm as hard looking as a dock worker, then I must be strong enough to stride a mustang."

Otis took a breath, just waiting for a chance to throw in his two cents, but the other man pulled him away, saying something about how much work they had to do.

Aurelia screamed after them, "Your arguments are ignorant and narrow-minded! And if somebody ever shoots you, you'd better hope there's another doctor around!"

Her outburst drew a few glances from the hundreds of others around her but hardly caused a stir. Not a day went by that didn't see the breakup of several partnerships, often with the rage of madmen spilling the contents of flour sacks into separate piles, ripping blankets in two, snapping wooden utensils in half.

She fussed with the stray wisps of hair that fluttered around her face, as though that would somehow restore her equilibrium. "And stay there," she grumbled as she tucked the last lock into the tight knot at the nape of her neck.

It wasn't the first time she'd heard the argument that a woman's mission was to hold fast to the sacred altar of the home where she could rear the offspring and fan the flames of piety. Nor was it the first time someone had reminded her of the femininity she lacked. Even Violet used to say she feared all that education would make Aurelia develop a monstrous brain and a puny body, but Violet had encouraged Aurelia to go to school anyway, just as she'd encouraged Aurelia to wear her hair in a more serious and professional, though less fashionable, style.

Aurelia backed into the snow-crusted cache behind her, aware that the acceptance she'd enjoyed during the avalanche was not typical, and might never be. And Clay, what did he really think? If her only ambition were to play the piano and paint bowls of fruit, he might be more solicitous of her feelings, certainly more respectful of her.

The sudden noise startled her. The overhead cable screeched under the weight of its load. She cringed, vowing she'd rather listen to one of Professor Sternwell's chemistry lectures or one of Violet's tantrums. The primitive gas-powered engine chugged and rumbled as its chunky square body belched. Aurelia covered her mouth to filter the noxious fumes and watched as a terrified cow swayed in the air, its belly strapped in a giant sling. Behind the cow, a railroad boxcar dangled precariously from ropes and a mammoth iron hook.

She stood aside while Towles's men loaded sleds with the boxes, barrels, and bundles piled beneath Clay's fluttering blue bandana. The men ignored her now. It was just as well. Her arguments about women being just as fit and intelligent as men would have fallen on deaf ears.

Meanwhile, she heard snatches of conversation carried on the wind.

"Yessir, nuggets big as hickory nuts."

"More yellow than a man could spend in two lifetimes."

"Right there on the sand or the river bottom, pretty as you please, just waiting to be picked up."

Aurelia shook her head at the absurdity of such illusions. Fortunes were not made so easily, not even in the Klondike. Why couldn't these men see the truth?

She stayed to watch Towles's men load the entire cache onto the tramway. She hated to admit it, but Clay was right. It would have taken next to forever for Clay and Aurelia to haul everything to the summit.

With reluctant appreciation for Clay's efforts, Aurelia headed back to Canyon City. Only then did it occur to her that if Clay was so often right about things, could his view of Violet be valid too? A few weeks ago, she would have said "absolutely not." Now, she wasn't so sure.

The following morning, after listening to Waldo hold yet another audience in rapt attention with his tale of the grizzly, Aurelia left the hotel. She intended to show Violet's picture to the local shopkeepers. There were so few women in this country that surely a girl as pretty as Violet would be remembered.

Drawn by the hearty aroma of warm sourdough bread, Aurelia was about to enter the tent marked Bakery, when Otis, the mortally stupid man who had insulted her at the tramway the day before, came running toward her.

"Doc! It's my woman, Jewel. She's having another one of her attacks and she ain't taking to my hot packs or my whiskey." He tugged on Aurelia's coat sleeve. "She's all doubled up in pain, all in the right side. You gotta help her. Come on. Hurry."

Even as Aurelia headed toward the hotel to fetch her medical box, yielding to his plea, she couldn't resist lashing out. "Why me, Mr.—"

"Higgins. Otis Higgins."

"Well, Mr. Higgins, why didn't you fetch the missionary, Mr. Devine. Why me? The butcher. After all, I'm not strong enough to stride a mustang—"

He glared at her, letting her know he'd rather ask anyone else but her, then took her elbow and rushed her on. "Cause my Jewel wouldn't have it. She swore on the Bible she'd die before she let a man look her over. That's cause my Jewel is a lady. Now, come on."

Aurelia couldn't imagine the kind of woman who would be interested in a man like Otis Higgins. Whoever she was, Aurelia doubted the term "lady" was appropriate. Still, Aurelia would do what she could for the woman.

Ten minutes later, apprehensive and short of breath, Aurelia ducked under a row of clean laundry hanging on a sagging line and stepped through the door of the Higgins's cabin, a rough plank structure no bigger than a tool shed, but boasting a clean, wooden floor and one small window. The patient lay curled in a fetal position on a small but sturdy-looking bed in the corner. She stretched out her arm and moaned.

"T'ank you, Otis, t'ank you. You always bein' such a good man. T'ank you for fetchin' the lady doctor."

Aurelia rushed to the woman's side. "Mrs. Higgins, I'm Dr. Breighton. I'm going to help you. Please try to relax."

"I'm so much hurting, lady doctor. So much hurting."

"I know," Aurelia said as she soothed the woman's fevered brow. One hundred degrees, maybe one hundred and one. That meant a localized, not a systemic infection. Fear had dilated the woman's pupils, making her big brown eyes sparkle with striking intensity. "I'll give you something for the pain in just a minute, but first I need to examine you." Hoping to diagnose nothing but a bad case of bilious colic, Aurelia took off her coat and hung it on a nearby wall peg.

"Have you eaten today?" she asked Mrs. Higgins.

"No. Not'ing for two days."

"And your bowels?"

"Not'ing for two, t'ree days."

The answers were not encouraging. Aurelia pressed two fingers to the woman's neck and felt for the carotid artery. A fragile pulse fluttered beneath the pressure. With mortal dread, Aurelia applied two fingers of pressure to a strategic point on the woman's lower right quadrant. She released her fingers. The woman screamed. Along with the other symptoms, such rebounding pain signified intestinal consumption caused by a diseased appendix.

Aurelia looked over at Otis, as though he could give her guidance, then realized how foolish a thought that was. Dear God, what was she going to do? The medical community didn't agree on how to treat such a life-threatening calamity. Some advised starvation. Some enemas. Some morphine and watchful waiting.

Her own school, equally authoritative, advocated immediate surgery. She'd witnessed a dozen such surgeries and had assisted in three, but she'd never been required to recognize the disease, never been responsible for the decision to operate, and had never been held accountable once the operation had been performed.

Tears slid down the woman's lined face as she winced in pain. She could be fifty, fifty-five. Aurelia couldn't tell.

She administered a dose of morphine and sent Otis back to her hotel with instructions to fetch the two books sitting on the floor by her cot: her surgeries. She needed to read them again, and quickly. She also told him to look again for the missionaries, the Devines. Surgery seemed the only viable alternative, and she didn't want to operate alone.

With Otis gone, Aurelia arranged her equipment on one of two straight-backed wooden chairs. Then she boiled some water in a kettle on the tiny stove and poured it into a washbasin that she'd placed on the other chair. An assortment of baskets hung from pegs on the wall. In one Aurelia found a stack of threadbare towels, neatly folded, still smelling of sun and bleach.

She slid her instruments into the boiling water, then sprinkled the floor and lower walls with bichloride solution. All the while, she questioned the patient about the onset of symptoms and their frequency and intensity.

"Da pain, it been coming and going for t'ree days. Sharp like a knife, da pain."

Three days. No doubt, the woman was acutely infected by now. "Mrs. Higgins, I'm going to remove your clothing and bathe you with a carbolic solution."

"You gonna slice me?"

Aurelia looked into the woman's trusting brown eyes. "Yes, Mrs. Higgins. I'm going to have to operate."

Mrs. Higgins made the sign of the cross, clasped her hands in prayer, and closed her eyes. The words she mumbled were in German, but Aurelia could guess their meaning.

"Once more t'ank you, God," the patient said as an afterthought. "T'ank you for sending a lady doctor."

Otis returned with the surgeries. While the morphine eased Mrs. Higgins into a pain-free state, Aurelia read everything she could find on the subject of appendicitis. Then, while Otis watched intently, Aurelia undressed her patient, and draped the operating area with a clean white sheet. Otis took a crocheted throw from a small wooden chest carved with hearts and flowers and draped the colorful modesty across his wife's bosom. "My Jewel's a lady," he said, all the bluster gone from his voice.

"Where are the Devines? They're coming, aren't they?"

He shook his head and looked at his wife with despair. "Went back to Dyea for a few days. Ain't nobody but you."

Aurelia couldn't have been more scared. If he'd threatened her, she might have gotten angry enough to mask her fear, but all he did was pat his wife's forehead while he gnawed at his lower lip.

This was no time for Aurelia's pride to color her ethics. "Mr. Higgins, I'm not really a doctor yet. I have six more months before I graduate."

He didn't look up. "You did good in school?"

"Average."

After an agonizing moment of silence, Otis asked, "My Jewel. Is she going to die?"

"I think her appendix is diseased."

"Is she going to die?"

"Without surgery, yes."

This time he looked up, straight into Aurelia's eyes. "And with your surgery?"

She wanted to assure him, to assure his wife, to

assure herself. But she couldn't lie. "I don't know."

He ran the back of his hand along his wife's cheek in a movement so easy it must have been common between them. "Then do it."

Aurelia nodded.

"Have you a mixing bowl, Mr. Higgins? Something in which we can scrub our hands."

He hesitated a second before leaving his wife's side, then took a blue-speckled bowl from a shelf on the back wall and set it on the small table. "We?"

"Yes. I'll administer the initial chloroform." She flipped through the pages of her *materia medica*. "Proportion of vapor to chloroform: four percent."

"That don't sound like much."

"Oh, but it is. Too much could bring on a seizure." She took a clean handkerchief and laced it with the proper dosage. "As I said, I'll administer the initial chloroform, but should the patient need more—don't look so scared, Mr. Higgins, it's not a difficult task. I'll tell you how many drops to add to the cloth and I'll tell you when. That's it. Oh dear, I almost forgot. Does your wife have dentures—false teeth?"

"Hell no."

"Good." She placed the cloth over Mrs. Higgins's nose. The patient gave a short cry, and her pulse quickened.

"Nothing to be alarmed about," Aurelia said to Otis, who was gripping the bowl so hard that his knuckles were white. "Everything is proceeding as it should."

She waited several minutes and checked her patient's pulse again. It had fallen in frequency and force. Good. She raised the woman's arm to assess reflex action. It fell heavily, just as it should.

Then she looked at the sparkling clean bowl. "Good. Now fill it with boiling water. Then refill the kettle."

When he'd done as she asked, Aurelia prepared a three percent solution of phenol and water in the bowl. She waited a few moments for it to cool. Then she scrubbed her hands and arms with a small white brush till the skin turned red and tingled. "Now you, Mr. Higgins. Scrub up. All the way to the elbows."

He froze.

"Please, Mr. Higgins. We have no time to waste. Your wife is suffering from acute appendicitis. If I don't operate now, she'll die for sure. I can't perform this operation by myself, and you're all I've got. Now scrub."

Moments later, they were ready. Mrs. Higgins, her abdomen draped with towels wrung from the steaming water, lay quietly, her eyes closed, her mouth agape, respiration deep, pulse slow and steady. Otis, sweat pouring down his face, held the chloroform laced cloth over his wife's nose, ready to add more drops on Aurelia's command. Aurelia, her concentration intent, held the scalpel and waited for the trembling in her hand to cease.

Surprised to find her hand suddenly steady, she lowered the blade to the dimpled and stretch-marked skin.

She made a six-inch-long incision in the lower right quadrant, about a quarter of an inch deep.

Otis turned green.

"Pull yourself together, Mr. Higgins," she said. "I need you."

Otis swallowed hard.

"Give me the probes, the ones that look like little screwdrivers."

Otis slipped his hand into the water and retrieved the instruments. "These?"

"Yes," she said, taking them from him. The details of every surgery she'd ever observed came back clearly. Praying she didn't make a fatal mistake, she carefully wedged the first layer of muscle.

When she had finished opening the lining to the abdomen, she stared. And she prayed.

Suddenly aware that her forehead was dripping with perspiration, she turned to Otis. "Wipe my brow, please."

Otis complied and then hazarded a closer look. "You cut the right spot, didn't you?"

"Yes." Thank God.

There it was, the appendix, right where the small intestine joined the large intestine. If healthy, it would be about an inch long and no thicker than a lead pencil. But it was severely inflamed and distended.

Precision was critical. The slightest pressure would cause the appendix to erupt and contaminate the entire abdominal cavity. And if that happened, the patient would die.

Aurelia's heart thundered.

"Mr. Higgins, just how strong is your constitution?" she asked.

"I gut animals all the time, doc. You go on. Do what you have to do." Aurelia didn't doubt the truth of what he said, but the concern that filled his eyes told her he wasn't nearly as strong as he professed.

She took a deep breath, all the while remembering what her instructors had taught her.

Take precautions. "Hand me the sponges please— the rolls of gauze. Right there, on the table."

Counting aloud, she took the white gauze sponges

one at a time, and filled the abdominal cavity. "Six. Seven. Eight. There. Now if the appendix breaks . . ."

To her relief, there was no hemorrhaging as she cut the appendix—just seepage bleeding. She hadn't made any mistakes. She could feel herself grinning, but it was much too soon.

"The phenol," she said.

"The what?"

"The carbolic acid. And a cotton swab."

He handed her the opened bottle and slender wooden stick with a swab of cotton on the end. Sounding just as confident as her instructors, she explained as she dipped the swab into bottle. "This is to cauterize the area and keep it from bleeding. We have to be very, very careful. Full-strength phenol is powerful. It will cauterize everything it touches.

"Now I'm removing the sponges . . . Six. Seven. And eight. Eight in. Eight out."

She stitched the abdominal wall with soluble gut, and then used regular sewing thread to sew skin. "We want to keep scarring to a minimum here. No big ridges."

When she had finished, she looked at Otis and smiled.

He returned the smile. "You did real good, doc."

"Yes, I did." It occurred to her that she'd had a lot of practice lately.

Finally, it was over. The patient's vital signs held steady and grew stronger.

Aurelia stayed with her patient for the next eight hours, still awed by her own success. Otis made a pan of biscuits and a pot of beans. He barely said a word to Aurelia as they ate. Every few minutes he glanced at his wife, now and then going over to kiss her forehead, to whisper something in German. Only late into the night, when Mrs. Higgins had regained consciousness, did Otis step outside.

Mrs. Higgins crooked her finger to beckon Aurelia closer. "Da poison. Is gone, yes?"

"Yes, Mrs. Higgins. I had to remove your appendix."

"I ain't gonna die?"

"There are never guarantees, I'm afraid, but the surgery went well. You're in good health. With proper rest and nutrition, you should be fine."

"Good. My Otis, he will not want me to die, I t'ink."

"Absolutely not."

Aurelia thought of how the man's obnoxious manner of the day before was replaced so quickly by the fear of losing his wife, and how that fear brought out such tenderness in the man. If Aurelia hadn't witnessed the transformation herself, she'd have never believed it.

"I'm t'anking you, lady doctor. Maybe now me and Otis, we go with the others to the gold fields."

The idea of Otis and his wife joining the rush surprised Aurelia. She wasn't sure why, unless it was the permanence suggested by the cabin itself, the wood floor and window in particular. People headed for the gold fields didn't stop to build such lavish structures.

"Why didn't you go before? Your illness?"

"Oh no," Mrs. Higgins said. "The money. That Mr. Towles, he knows the weakness of my Otis for the cards. So now my Otis, he owes all his hard labors to Mr. Towles. And for money I'm taking in the wash. Every day my Otis, he tells me 'bout the rich peoples with their t'ings going up the tramway to the mountaintop, then to the place where is all the gold. He promise someday we gonna go too, easy like the rich peoples, and all our t'ings gonna go on the tramway, but I know is not so. I been knowin' since last spring."

"How? What happened last spring?"

"My Otis build me this cabin." Mrs. Higgins closed her eyes, a sad smile on her lips.

With so few women on the trail, surely Mrs. Higgins would have noticed Violet. Aurelia retrieved the photograph from her pocket. "Mrs. Higgins?"

The patient opened her eyes, but they looked anything but alert.

"Mrs. Higgins, do you recall ever seeing this young lady?" Mrs. Higgins strained and Aurelia held the picture closer. "She would have come through here last spring," Aurelia said.

Mrs. Higgins hesitated, all the while struggling to keep her eyes open.

"Never mind," Aurelia said, ashamed she'd disturbed her patient's rest. As Mrs. Higgins' eyes closed again, Aurelia slipped the photograph back into her pocket. "It can wait."

Otis returned shortly. He stood in the doorway, framed by a midnight sky that was not quite dark. "She's gonna make it, ain't she, doc?"

"I'm optimistic, Mr. Higgins, though I must caution you that infection is the norm. However, your wife's general health is good. Her spirits are good as well." Aurelia looked around. "And your home is spotless. There are still those that believe the cleanliness of the atmosphere has no bearing on the health of the patient, but I was taught the theory of Dr. Lister and—My apologies, Mr. Higgins. I'm sure you aren't interested in the theories on the conveyance of infection."

Aurelia searched for the appropriate words that would assure both Otis Higgins and herself, for as she'd told her patient, the outcome of surgery could never be totally guaranteed. "Your wife needs a great deal of rest. That means she can't do any work for several months. No laundry. Absolutely no laundry. She'll be dependent on you for everything. Can you manage?"

Otis looked solemn and nodded respectfully to Aurelia. "I'll be thanking you, doc."

Aurelia acknowledged his gratitude with the odd feeling that she'd just been privy to a man's transformation, or at least to the opening of his mind. She gathered her things, leaving Otis with strict instructions for his wife's care, and left.

I did it! Aurelia clutched her medical box to her blood-splattered dress as she walked back to the hotel. She glided along the slush-covered street, nodding to the curious who stopped to stare, her mood as gay as the music coming from saloons all along the way. She'd performed surgery, and successfully. Her diagnosis had been correct and her technique flawless. She couldn't wait to get back to her room to make notes that would allow her to relive those scary, empowering moments all over again. Certificate or not, she was a doctor.

The following morning, she stopped by to check on Mrs. Higgins, who was resting comfortably and sipping a cup of tea. After examining her patient, Aurelia prepared to leave, once again feeling that heady rush of pride. But then Mrs. Higgins stopped her dead in her tracks.

"Lemme see that picture again, lady doctor. I'm feeling a little stronger now."

A chill rushed through Aurelia as she produced the photo once again. "Do you remember her being here?"

"Yes. Violet, I think her name was. You know her?"

"Yes. Yes, I do." Aurelia hesitated, ashamed not to acknowledge the relationship immediately. "What else can you tell me about her?"

"Oh, just that she was the sweetest little t'ing. Like a butterfly she was, so delicate, so pretty."

"Did you ever have occasion to talk with her?"

"Many times. She was my customer. And her laundry was the fanciest—like from the old country. Little bit lace and little bit ribbon. She don't have no money and that bother her, so I tell her not to worry. She don't have to pay me, it being my pleasure to touch such pretty t'ings again. She say I do a good job too, better than washer woman in Skagway. That make me feel good."

"But to give your services for free—that was very generous of you, Mrs. Higgins."

The old woman waved her hand, as though dismissing her efforts. "I t'ink for all her fancies, her heart was not happy. Her man—you know him too?"

"Yes," Aurelia answered, the contemptuous look on her face leaving no doubt as to her feelings for Sculley.

Mrs. Higgins narrowed her eyes. "The spawn of the devil, that one." Then she let her head fall back on her pillow. "The little Violet, she was your patient too?"

"Violet is my sister."

Mrs. Higgins didn't look surprised. "You going to fetch her back?"

"Yes."

"Goot."

Though Aurelia was eager for more information about her sister, Mrs. Higgins was obviously tired and needed her rest. Aurelia promised to come again the next day and show Otis how to change the dressing. She would be leaving for the summit as soon as Clay got back.

She closed the door behind her and left. While she was pleased Mrs. Higgins thought of Violet as sweet and delicate, the painful truth didn't escape her. Somehow, despite Violet's anger at how Sculley had used her, Violet herself still found a way to make this poor old woman do her laundry for free. It was hardly cause for a jail sentence. Still, the revelation carried a bitter taste.

15

Time had run out. Pacing her room, Aurelia thanked the power of loud music and watered-down whiskey to empty the hotel and fill the saloon across the street. What she and Clay were about to do was not for the eyes of the public, and the walls of fabric hardly afforded privacy.

He'd come back earlier that afternoon, eager to tell Aurelia about the crowds and the commotion going on up at the Scales where everything had to be weighed before going on to the summit. Thousands of people, some wearing odd-looking clothes and speaking strange languages, trampled every inch of snow while they set up thousands of tents and piled hundreds upon thousands of pounds of supplies. Clay swore the entire world had congregated at the Scales.

Aurelia had thought he might apologize for his careless gamble with the ring, but he said nothing. He did, however, ask about the surgery Aurelia had performed.

He'd found her in her room, sitting on a chair by the window, the lingering sun illuminating the textbook in her lap. He was, to his surprise, happy to see her.

"Is it true?" he asked, after describing the scene at the Scales. "You operated on Otis Higgins's wife?"

Aurelia beamed. She closed her book and hugged it to her chest. "Yes!"

"Do you think you should have? I mean, what if she'd died?"

"She had no chance without surgery. And there was no one but me."

"But how did you know you could—"

"I didn't."

"Were you scared?"

"Terrified. Oh, Clay, it wasn't easy. I tortured myself with doubt. What if I couldn't remember the procedure? What if something went wrong? But I did remember. Everything. And Mrs. Higgins didn't die. Her husband is attentive and eager to be of help. I think she'll make it."

"You sound mighty proud of yourself."

"I am!"

He hesitated before he spoke, lending sincerity to his words. "I'm proud of you, too."

Aurelia could hardly contain her joy. Somewhere along the line, it had become important to her that Clay not just accept her calling, but respect it.

In the hours that followed, Clay asked about Aurelia's decision to study medicine, and she relayed the story of Nana's insistence and the bargain they'd made.

He looked at her with a new understanding when she explained why the silver buckles, the gun, and especially the wedding ring were so valuable to her.

"Well?" he finally asked, "Don't you think it's about time we took care of that gun?"

"Of course," she answered, suddenly feeling somewhat less confident, less successful, and much, much less venturesome.

"Aurelia, what's wrong? You look pale."

"Just tired."

What was she supposed to say? Despite your misguided sense of justice when it comes to my sister, I find you attractive? And the mere thought of what you're about to do shatters my equilibrium? "Just tired," she said again.

Fanning her full skirt around her, she watched Clay withdraw a long strip of beige leather from the sack he'd dropped on the floor.

"Don't know what kind of leather this is, but it's the softest I could find. Here," he said, handing it to Aurelia, "feel it. Thin. But strong."

Aurelia fingered the butter-soft strap and curled the leather around her wrist. She knew Clay was going to use it to bind the gun to her thigh. He would have to see her leg. He would have to touch her. Her voice quivered when she said, "Yes, I think it'll do nicely."

"Good." He took the leather from her and folded it in half, then in half again.

Aurelia cleared her throat, hoping to give her voice a more matter-of-fact quality. "I suppose we should proceed."

Clay looked around the empty room. "We're leaving in the morning. There won't be time then. There sure won't be any privacy." He looked around one more time. "If I do it now, you can walk around with it for an hour or so and see how it feels. And if you decide to change your mind about the whole idea—"

"I won't change my mind." Aurelia swallowed hard. "Let's do it now."

When she didn't move, he asked, "Don't you want to get your gun?"

"Yes, of course," she said as she made her way across the room and retrieved the Colt from her medical box.

Clay slapped his palm on the seat of the chair, indicating that that was where he expected her to brace her foot. "Ready?"

Aurelia thought of how brazenly the painted dance-hall girls showed their limbs and wondered if they felt as embarrassed as she did now the first time they raised their skirts. Well, they obviously got over it. Aurelia would get over it, too.

The floor creaked as she stepped toward him. Still holding the gun, she rested her hand on the back of their chair and raised her right foot to the rickety seat, setting the thin wooden legs to trembling.

Perfectly wanton thoughts made her blush from rose to burgundy as she slowly hiked her drab brown skirt and her once white petticoats past her booted ankles and silver buckles. Clay's eyes followed her moves, seeming to savor her progress. She envisioned the pose she'd struck, as blatantly sexual as that of a saloon girl. "Enjoying yourself?" she asked, half irritated by his smile, half encouraged by his approving look, her skirt now halfway to her knee.

He grinned. "You can't imagine."

How could something that made her feel so vulnerable also make her feel so powerful?

"Don't stop now," he said.

Aurelia concentrated on the wall in front of her as she gathered more fabric in her hand and, in one sweeping move, hiked her skirt past her stockinged knee, past her rolled garter, past several inches of bare skin, and past the lace edge of her combination. "There. Now hurry."

"You don't know what you do to me." His admission added to the dangerously confident attitude she was acquiring.

She heard the quickened rhythm of his breath and felt the slightest tremble in his hand as he took the gun. He knelt before her on one knee, giving her the fleeting and foolish notion of a man about to propose. From the corner of her eye, she watched him drink in the sight of her. Then, just when he sought to catch her eye, she looked away. She continued to stare at the wall until she felt the steel brush against her bare leg. She jumped. "That's cold!"

"Hold still," he said as his rough hands fumbled in the froth of her petticoats. "Almost lost my place. Can't let that happen." He shot her a look that suggested there was another, more proprietary meaning to his statement.

"Just hurry," she said, cautioning herself to stay level-headed, not to shame herself by reading anything so personal into his words.

Meanwhile, the fingers of one hand splayed across the back of her leg and held it steady. She knew exactly where each finger rested. His thumb and little finger braced her kneecap. His three remaining fingers dipped into—oh what was that little soft spot called? She shook her head to clear it, but to no avail. She couldn't remember the anatomical designation, and she couldn't forget the lurid scene she'd created.

"Why, Aurelia, will you just look at all these goosebumps!" He squeezed her thigh gently. "Come on, don't you want to look?"

"What makes you think I want to watch!" She

looked directly down, drawn by the sudden rush of his hot breath against her leg.

"Better?" he asked, then brushed his lips to the back of her knee as he warmed her again with his breath.

He didn't look up, didn't see the admission in her eyes that his touch was deliciously soft, or the yearning that made her feel faint.

"Hmm," he said, as though uncertain of the best place to position the gun. He laid it against her outer thigh, then her inner thigh, then decided on the firm area above her knee. He wrapped and knotted the leather strap.

"Finished," he said at last and tucked the tail of the strap into the leather web he'd created.

Aurelia released the breath she hadn't realized she was holding. Clay stood and stepped back, breaking the spell of his touch. Quickly, Aurelia lowered her skirt and slipped her foot from the chair. "It's heavy."

Clay rubbed his palms against the tops of his thighs as though his hands itched to grab something. "I strapped more than two pounds of cold steel and ivory to your leg. Let's see you walk."

She walked away from him, imprinting in her mind the feel of his hands on her leg.

She ventured into the open room and back. "It feels awkward. But I can manage," she added, lest he insist on removing it. If he touched her again, she'd become even more disordered than she was now.

"Good." He studied her skirt. "Can't even see an outline. Not with all those ruffly things you've got under there."

She supposed she ought to thank him. After the way she'd screamed at him out at the tramway, he could have just told her to take care of the gun herself. And for him to admire her medical work—well, only a modern, enlightened man could do that. In many ways he was such a good man. He was still attracted to her too. She could recognize the signs now. And she felt something for him. In fact, if it weren't for this business about Violet, Aurelia might be tempted to do something crazy.

A powerful urge cast common sense aside.

"Thank you, Clay." She'd barely uttered the words when she flung her arms around his neck and kissed him hard on the lips.

Most everyone had decided to get an early start. Without having to carry much more than the medical box, Clay and Aurelia made good progress, though much of the time they could travel only as fast as the line ahead of them. By eight o'clock they had reached Camp Pleasant. In front of everyone, Clay boldly took Aurelia's hand and held it tight as they walked through the open glade. Evidence of her ordeal with the grizzly had either been covered with new snow or dragged away by animals. Neither of them said a word.

By noon they'd covered only another three miles. The terrain was easy for the first mile, but the horses all around them could barely walk, staggering under the weight of their packs. Mix-matched teams of dogs struggled to pull loads twenty times their weight. The dogs whose owners had fed them that morning were vomiting.

At Sheep Camp, the sight of the avalanche, they saw a large cairn of newly piled stones. "Heard they dug out three more bodies," Clay said to the question she didn't ask. "Expect a few more to surface with the thaw."

"This is not a trail to fortune. It's a trail to heartbreak."

Clay put his arm around her shoulder and urged her on.

The ascent began again, gaining a thousand feet in elevation in the next two miles. Gasping for breath, the climbers trudged upward, one step at a time.

The pitifully narrow trail, pebbled with snow-capped boulders as big as tents, skirted the edge of the mountain. Aurelia cringed at each of the different sounds of distress. Dogs yipped as they became tangled in their lines. Men swore as sleds tipped over. Skittish horses whinnied as the crack of whips coaxed them through what they surely sensed was dangerous ground. Men groaned as they shifted their packs. The weariest horses collapsed and floundered to their bellies in the deep snow, but at least they didn't fall. Those less fortunate struggled to keep their footing, but that was impossible.

Aurelia lifted her head to the bone-chilling sound of metal horseshoes scraping against rock. She gasped. Never before had she heard the shrill scream of a thousand-pound animal as it panicked and fell to its death. She covered her ears to muffle the repeated snapping sounds of breaking branches and the heavy thuds of horses falling on boulders that would not give. Finally there was silence.

"Don't look down," Clay said as the line moved again.

They kept climbing, past piles of abandoned supplies. At first, Aurelia reasoned the owners were somewhere on the pass, taking a load to the summit. Then again, difficult as the realization was to accept, the owners could have simply left all their hopes and dreams to rot. Or they could be buried beneath the snow.

Panting and sweating, Clay and Aurelia made it to the Scales where Clay showed the customs official the receipt for the supplies that had been trammed to the summit.

Outside the customs tent, Clay brushed the snow from the ruff of Aurelia's hood. "You all right?" he asked.

She nodded, her lips too cold to form words.

He removed his gloves, blew warm breath into his hands, and placed them on Aurelia's cheeks. He swallowed hard and pressed his lips together tightly, as though struggling to hold something back. Maybe he was just as shocked, just as afraid, just as uncertain as she was.

"We can't give up now," he said. "We've got to get to Dawson and find your sister." He stopped abruptly. "I'm sorry."

"It's all right." Aurelia didn't want to reopen the wound between them anymore than he did. Their conflict would never change, but neither of them would win until they reached Dawson. In the meantime, they would struggle together, and Aurelia would pretend that the awful void in her heart was filled.

Again, they climbed.

Three more miles and Aurelia saw the final approach to the dreaded Chilkoot Pass. The vision paralyzed her. Before her loomed a nearly vertical wall of ice-covered rock, covered with a single file of ant-sized human animals burdened beyond their limits. Hugging the lifeline that stretched up the mountain, the small, dark figures climbed slowly, toe to heel, mumbling a mournful cadence that made the mountain hum.

Obscenities took on new proportions as hundreds of angry, frustrated men realized the truth of what they'd been told by the Indians all along: Pack animals couldn't make it up to the Chilkoot Pass. A few shook their heads, turned their animals around, and headed back to the Scales. They'd have to take the Peterson Trail, just to the right of the Chilkoot Pass. The Peterson wasn't nearly as steep, but it was much longer and unmarked. One man spoke a few words to his dog, then hoisted the animal on to his own back atop the supplies he was already carrying. Other men, without a moment's hesitation, discarded the veneer of civilization and yanked their supplies off the horses, burros, and oxen, scattering their goods in the snow next to the trail.

The entire march ground to a halt as gaunt, bloody, bare-backed animals stood still in the middle of the trail waiting for instruction, waiting for food, waiting for a gentle hand.

"They can't just turn those animals loose. They'll starve. They're half dead already."

Clay placed his hands on Aurelia's shoulders and, using his body as a shield, ushered her past the tangle. "You can't do anything here," he said as he nudged her along.

"There must be something I can do." She twisted her shoulders free and stared wide-eyed at the horror. "This is inhumane!"

This time he grabbed her shoulders and spun her around to face him. "This is a stampede."

Frustration formed tears in Aurelia's eyes, but

before she could allow herself their comfort Clay urged her onward. She tried to block out the obscenities, the screams, the cracking of whips.

"You can make it, Aurelia. Just don't look back. And don't look down."

She knew he was trying to encourage her, but it was impossible. She felt hopeless, helpless, and she yearned for civilization as she knew it. Clay reached back and grabbed her hand.

One step at a time they trudged upward. Aurelia felt every nerve strain, every ounce of physical endurance dissipate into air that was growing colder by the minute. Her forehead began to sweat and her heart to pound. Panting, she let go of Clay's hand and dropped out of line to one of the turnouts dug into the snow every twenty steps, each with room for half a dozen people to pull out and rest. Clay joined her.

"Here," he said, as he braced himself against the snow wall. "Lean on me and rest."

The precious minutes weren't nearly long enough. "Think you can make it? We're almost there."

"How much farther?"

"I heard one of the Mounties say the mountain's almost four thousand feet high. We're almost there."

"But how long will it take?"

"Hard to say. Most of these men are making it to the top in an hour, depending on how much they're carrying and how often they stop. I heard a man say one trip up took him six hours."

Aurelia groaned as she leaned against Clay's chest again. His jacket was frozen stiff. Patches of ice scratched her cheeks. "Well we can't stay here, can we?" Aurelia summoned every ounce of strength she had remaining. "I'm ready; let's go."

Clay's laughter had an edge of sadness. "Not so fast. Take a look at the line behind us. Unless some kindhearted soul lets us in, we could stand here for hours waiting for a break."

From all the way back down to the Scales, a single stream of dreamers pressed monotonously onward. Single file, single purpose.

"Please," Aurelia shouted to those coming toward them. "Won't someone let us back in line?"

"Here you go, ma'am," one of them said. "Any woman with the guts to make it this far deserves a break."

Aurelia thanked the man and slipped in line, Clay in front of her. Her newfound resolve weakened instantly when she got close enough to the wall of ice to see the ladder of toe-holes. People were crawling on their hands and knees, appearing to hang on by their fingernails.

"The Golden Stairs," Clay explained. "All fours, Aurelia. There's no other way. Dig in and hold on. Don't stop."

Stop? She couldn't stop if she had to. There was nowhere to go but straight up. If she stopped, she'd fall to her death.

Tucking her skirt between her legs, she knelt down and crawled. Ice cut through the leather of her gloves. Shards of icy crystals nicked her cheeks. She counted more than twelve hundred steps while she tucked and cursed her long skirt. She cursed her corset. She cursed the greed that turned sane men into wild animals. She cursed Violet.

"Keep moving," someone behind her yelled. "It's getting dark."

The wind picked up. Snow and grit blew in her face. Her cheeks burned. Her eyes stung. Just when her legs refused to carry her another step, she stumbled into the narrow, level slash that was the summit. Panting for every breath, she looked up. There was the red and blue Union Jack snapping in the wind.

"We made it!" Clay cried as he picked her up in his arms and kissed her. His lips were just as cold and stiff as hers, but she didn't care. She didn't care if anyone was watching. She wanted him to kiss her again. He did, this time sending a blessed warmth through her body and bringing tears of joy and relief to her eyes.

He stepped back, held her at arm's length, and grinned. Ice clung to his beard just as it did to her hair. "You realize how few people in the world can claim to do what we just did? We climbed the Chilkoot Pass!"

She could hardly hear him, the wind was blowing so hard. But she recognized the elation he felt. She felt it too.

Hand in hand, they walked triumphantly into one of the few commercial tents. The sight of a woman on the top of the pass drew everyone's attention. "Two hot meals," he called to the broker, "a whiskey, a cup of tea, and a fire." Looking at Aurelia, he added, "My lady here is cold."

"Wood is two bits a pound up here, mister. You still want a fire?"

"I want a ten-dollar fire! She deserves it."

"I'd like a whiskey too, if you don't mind."

"Atta girl!" the men roared. "You deserve that too."

The bartender loaded one of the sheet-metal stoves and put a match to it. Then he took a wooden crate, turned it over, and placed it next to the stove. "Have a seat, ma'am. I'll bring your whiskey right over. The tea might take a while. Don't know as I got any."

Aurelia sat on the crate and closed her eyes. She

inhaled the smell of burning wood and briskly rubbed her hands. The fire sizzled and popped. The heat felt good. She opened her eyes only to take the whiskey. It burned, and that felt good too.

Clay pulled another crate over and sat next to her. He pulled his boots off and set them next to the stove. He pulled his socks off and draped them on the railing behind the stove designed for the purpose.

"This is no time for modesty," he said as he stood in front of her and raised her foot. "Unless you want to wind up with frostbite, the boots have got to come off. So do the stockings."

"There are Mounties in this tent," she whispered. "You haven't forgotten about my legacy, have you?"

"Couldn't ever." He winked as he slid his hand up her leg to the top of her boot. He pulled first one, then the other. "There. That feels better, doesn't it?"

Aurelia nodded. "I must admit it does." She wiggled her wet toes.

"I'll be glad to get your stockings too, if you want."

"No!"

With all the discretion she could manage, Aurelia peeled her black cotton stockings off and handed them to Clay, who promptly draped them on the rod next to his socks.

After two bowls of bean soup and a big plate of corn bread, Aurelia felt her eyelids grow heavy. Wanting nothing more than a few minutes of sleep, she slumped forward and closed her eyes. The bartender gave Clay a blanket, and he draped it over her shoulders. She slept that way for two hours, with only a random phrase running through her dreams. "My lady . . . my lady."

*   *   *

"Sleepyhead, wake up. Get your shoes and stockings on. We've still got to go through customs."

She hurriedly got dressed, and they went outside to join the hundreds of others on line to pay their customs duties.

Back outside, hundreds of men stood shivering in the twilight. Those who'd identified their own caches among the thousands half buried in the snow were busy setting up tents on the ground, which had been chewed to a muddy pulp. Others, with packs on their backs, shifted their weight from one foot to the other as they waited in line to pay the duty.

"You going to make it?" Clay asked as their turn approached.

"My feet are warm and my stockings are dry. I'm fine."

"That's not what I meant." He glanced at her skirt.

"Next," the official called them into the tent.

The Colt on Aurelia's thigh suddenly felt colder and heavier than ever. She fought the tendency to limp.

"How many in your party?" the Mountie asked as Clay and Aurelia approached the table that served as a desk.

"Three," Clay answered, gesturing to Aurelia. "Our partner, a kid by the name of Poyser, is back in Canyon City. He'll be along in a couple of weeks."

The Mountie looked up. "Poyser? Poyser?" A look of acknowledgment flashed in his eyes. "Is this the Poyser who killed the grizzly with his bare hands and nearly died trying?"

"My heavens," Aurelia spoke up quickly before Clay could comment, though all he did was roll his eyes.

"And you must be the pretty lady whose life he saved. Well, you folks go on and get settled. Don't worry about your friend. We'll see to it he gets the royal treatment when he gets here."

"Thank you," Aurelia said as she nudged Clay to do the same.

The Mountie added, "Got your cache all assembled?"

"Over by the tram," Clay said. He pulled out the paperwork from his pocket and gave it to the official. "That's for all three of us."

The Mountie looked the paperwork over several times. "So you're a medical man," he said as he stamped the papers and gave them back to Clay.

"No. My other partner here is the doctor. Miss Aurelia Breighton."

Aurelia nodded to the official and smiled. This wasn't the time to lecture the man on his assumption. While he continued to write, she turned to Clay, hoping for a commiserating look. He looked preoccupied for some reason.

"I see." The Mountie looked up from the paper before him. "I must say, in this part of the world one can't afford to be too fussy when it comes to finding a doctor." He looked at the paperwork again. "Well then, all I need from you is ninety dollars, that's thirty for each of you."

Clay laid the appropriate amount of money on the table, squeezing the last thirty dollars as he laid it down. He looked like a man in conflict, like a man whose moment of truth was at hand.

The Mountie spoke again. "You aren't carrying any firearms other than a rifle, are you?"

16

Clay hesitated. Aurelia's heart all but stopped.

"No," Clay answered. "I'm not."

"And how about you, ma'am? No derringer in your purse?"

"No."

"Any liquor?"

"*No!*" Clay answered, as though he'd made a decision and intended to stand by it.

"Only what I carry for medicinal purposes," Aurelia added.

The official stamped their paperwork and pointed to the exit. "Next."

The wind slapped them both as they stepped outside. Aurelia's heart still pounded as she pulled her hood up to shield her face. "Thank you," she said, referring to his aid in concealing her gun.

"You're welcome."

"Now what? It's nearly eight o'clock."

Clay took her arm and started walking toward the tram. "Now we pitch the tents and get some sleep."

She nodded at his idea, then stepped aside while

he erected the canvas. Memories of another time worked their own sweet torture in her mind.

She slept soundly that night, exhilarated by her accomplishments, ready to face whatever obstacles lay ahead. Somewhere between dreams she awoke from her warm slumber and turned her ear to the tent next to her. Clay snored, something she hadn't noticed the night they slept in her sleeping bag. Not the wild, thunderous snore she'd often heard from her father when he fell asleep in his favorite parlor chair. Clay's snoring was mellow, more like a low flutter, a sound to which she could grow accustomed.

The sun rose somewhere around four. By four-thirty the summit was alive. Aurelia woke to blinding sunlight, the strong aroma of boiled coffee, and the yipping of hungry dogs. She found Clay outside, loading the sled.

"Now we've got to get all this down the other side of the mountain." He strapped down nearly four hundred pounds of supplies in boxes, barrels, a trunk, and an assortment of sacks.

"Where is my load?"

"Here." Clay pointed to two small sacks of rice.

"But I carried twice that amount before."

"It's enough, believe me. When we start heading down and your legs start shaking, you'll be glad you aren't carrying anything heavier." She didn't argue with him. He'd been right about so many things already.

While Clay continued to pack the sled, Aurelia walked to the edge of the summit and looked down at the trail she'd climbed the day before. Hundreds of ambitious climbers had already threaded their way up the icy wall. Off to the side, the scene resembled a winter carnival. Aurelia shook her head in wonder. Like eager children with new sleds and a newly fallen snow, men who had just reached the summit and unburdened themselves of one load went right back down again for another. Some slid on empty sleds, some on the seats of their pants. Some straddled their shovels and sat on the blade, while others simply walked down the many capillaries of snowy, shoulder-deep ruts, only to pack another load and climb right back up. Only an all-consuming desire could be the reason why a person would willingly repeat such torture. Unfortunately, for those who couldn't afford to have their caches trammed to the summit, there was no other way.

When Aurelia turned around, she saw Clay and an older, grim-faced man walking toward her. The other man, his beaver cap crusted with ice, looked familiar.

"You the doctor?" the man asked.

The anxious look on Clay's face told her the man brought bad news. "Yes," she answered. "I'm the doctor. What can I do for you?"

"For me? Nothing. No sir. You ain't gonna slice into me the way you done Otis Higgins's woman. No sir."

"Mrs. Higgins?" Panic edged her voice as she realized this man was Otis Higgins's friend. "Has something happened to Mrs. Higgins?"

"She's dying is what. Otis sent me to fetch you."

Aurelia nodded. Amidst all the haste and noise, and despite the all-too-vivid memory of the climb, she felt compelled to do whatever she could. "I'll get my things."

"Hold on now." Clay put his hands on her shoulders, focusing her attention on him. "You can't go back down there."

"I have to—"

"The hell you do!"

"Clay, she's dying."

"The missionaries must be back in town by now. They can—" His protest trailed in her wake as she rushed back to their cache. "Then I'm going with you," he called after her. Aurelia barely heard him as she grabbed the medicine case.

Aurelia kept her eyes on the bleak valley below as she hurried down the narrow white crevice. She tried to think: What was the assemblage of symptoms for infection? For fever? More important, what was the treatment? The patient had appeared well on the road to recovery when Aurelia left. What could have caused the sudden transition? A violent emotion of the mind? A suppression of evacuations?

Or maybe Otis, in his zeal to keep the cabin clean, washed it too much and created a dampness, leaving Mrs. Higgins to catch cold. Maybe he opened a window to let in fresh air and created a draft, sending Mrs. Higgins's chilliness below the accepted standard and giving her an inflammatory fever. Maybe her perspiration was obstructed. Or maybe he'd kept the room too warm, destroying the elasticity of the air and rendering it less fit for expansion of the lungs. Any number of things could have gone wrong.

With each thought, Aurelia moved faster. Now and then, her shoulders collided with the white walls on either side. Snow crunched beneath her boots. She would have liked to descend the way so many of the men did—simply straddle a shovel, sit on the blade, and slide down. As it was, it took half an hour. Only when she reached the bottom did she think about having to climb back up. But knowing Clay was at her side helped her relax. Together, they headed for the Higgins's cabin.

Aurelia stomped the snow from her boots before entering the room. It looked just as clean and orderly as the last time Aurelia had seen it—Mrs. Higgins's colorful crocheted throw folded neatly at the foot of the bed, ribbon-trimmed baskets brimming with bleached and mended linens. It was so cozy and full of promise—except for the coffin.

Aurelia fought to hold back her tears at the sight. Otis leaned against the simple box, one arm draped across the lid as though he could still caress the woman inside. He acknowledged Aurelia with an empty stare, through eyes red and swollen with despair. He spoke without emotion while he stroked the rough wood with a gentle hand. "Fellow back in Dyea built a bunch of them after the avalanche, thinking to sell 'em as the snow melted and the bodies surfaced. I was real lucky to get one."

"I'm so sorry. So very, very sorry."

As though her sympathy maddened him, he straightened himself and glared at her. "You ought to be sorry, seein' as it's all your fault. If you hadn't come struttin' in here actin' like you was a real doctor, my Jewel would still be with me."

She knew his lashing was powered by grief, yet she felt compelled to justify her actions. "Your wife didn't have a chance. Not without surgery."

"A one-armed horse doctor could have done more for her than you did!"

Aurelia shook. She wanted to say that she'd done her best and that she was truly sorry her best wasn't good enough, but years of insecurity choked her, and the words wouldn't come.

Clay didn't say a word. His arms hung limp at his sides, his trancelike gaze on Otis Higgins as though it were Clay himself standing over the coffin, his own wife dead inside. Only Clay's eyes, so intent behind their watery shield, betrayed the pain of his own memories and the agony of a yearning so great that only one who had also suffered it could comprehend.

There was nothing Aurelia could do. She hung her head and went outside, where the bright sun all but blinded her. She hadn't been able to save Jewel Higgins's life. She couldn't ease Clay's pain. She'd failed.

That sobering reality numbed her to the torture of climbing the Chilkoot Pass again. This time, there was no joyous celebration when she and Clay reached the pass, just the silent acknowledgment that each knew what the other had lost.

They didn't say much of anything to each other that night. The following morning, amid the usual noise and activity, they packed in silence and headed down the other side of the mountain. The descent was as bad as Clay had said it would be, even worse. With every step she took, Aurelia felt the weight of her body and the weight of the load she carried pound on her knees. Her legs shook, just as he'd said they would. More times than she wanted to admit, her skirt was in the way and got caught on her boot.

Clay struggled with the sled. With the lead rope over his left shoulder, his right hand on the gee pole, and a roughshod rope around the runner, he did his best to guide the sled over the bumpy spots. Pitch holes, some four feet deep, sabotaged the path and sent some sleds speeding down the mountain. A man had been killed the previous week when a gee pole on a runaway sled ran right through him. Everyone had to move slowly.

Halfway down the mountain Clay and Aurelia stopped to prepare lunch: cold bread, cold bacon, and cold coffee. Still weeping inside, Aurelia wanted to stamp her feet, break her utensils, and scream. Instead, she barely said a word as she went through the motions. What had made her think she could successfully perform an operation under the conditions in that cabin? Who did she think she was? No doctor in his right mind would have attempted such a feat. But then she wasn't a doctor. Not a real one.

She had just finished packing up the mess box when she looked up to find Clay coming up behind her, his hunting knife in his hand. There was a determined look fixed in his eye.

"Someday you'll forgive me for this."

"For what? Forgive you for what?" She stood up and backed away. "Clay, what's wrong?"

"Hold still." Before she could say another word, he bent over and grabbed her skirt. "I should have done this before we left Dyea." Aurelia heard the first slash. In less time than it took her to comprehend what was happening, Clay had cut a good ten inches of fabric from the entire hem of her dress.

Aurelia gasped. "What have you done!" She grabbed the shredded edge of her skirt and pulled. Her petticoat poked out shamelessly.

"Maybe saved your life. There's enough other things out here to kill you. I'm not going to have you trip and fall to your death on account of this." He held the fistful of fabric in their air.

Last week she would have railed about her reputation and worried about what people would say seeing a generous two inches of her limbs exposed. But not today. Jewel Higgins was dead, and Otis Higgins was condemned to live without her. Lily L'Auberge was dead. Waldo Poyser was traumatized for life, all because he had wanted to prove himself the man he would never be. And Clay Guardian's long-buried pain had resurfaced, a pain bitter enough to drive him to radical acts, a pain clear enough to remind Aurelia that she was not the kind of woman a man like Clay would marry.

Last week she would have railed, but today she simply shouldered her load and followed Clay down the mountain.

They finally reached the bottom, only to find there was no place to camp within ten miles. A bitter wind blew from the south, bringing so much numbing cold and snow that Aurelia wondered whether she'd survive this trek, whether she'd ever reach Dawson. She had over five hundred miles to go, and it was already April 26.

They plodded on. When they reached the head of Crater Lake, Clay affixed a pole to the front of the sled and attached a blanket as a sail. Billowing with the Arctic breeze, the sled glided easily across the ice. He rigged the sail again at Long Lake and insisted that Aurelia sit on the sled for the mile-long ride.

Beyond Long Lake the trail skirted the rim of a canyon. Aurelia didn't give a thought to the beauty and grandeur of the place, the snow-covered mountains that fanned all around them, the blue glaciers that hung between peaks. She thought only of her foolish pride and her naive optimism that had made her think she could save Mrs. Higgins's life. Was she being just as foolish to think she could save Violet?

The trail dove deep into the scrubby woods. Aurelia continued to lash herself as she tripped over bare roots of trees that curled around rocks and boulders like an octopus. Her gloves ripped and her hands bled from constantly bracing herself against the rocks or from brushing the low-hanging branches away.

Just as she had feared, there was no room at Lake Lindeman to pitch a tent and no place to stay. "It's only a few more miles to Lake Bennett," Clay told her in a voice that sounded foolishly hopeful, especially from him. "There's supposed to be a hotel there. Can you make it?"

Healthy and alive, she had no right to complain. "Lake Bennett? That's where we'll camp, isn't it?"

"For a month or so. Till the ice breaks." He looked concerned. "You going to make it?"

She nodded. The gesture didn't take as much energy as it did to speak.

Clay put his arm around her shoulders and gave them a squeeze. "It's almost over." He harnessed himself to the sled, and they set out again.

"*That's* the Bennett City Hotel?" Aurelia's jaw dropped as she stared at the canvas-roofed wooden affair. It stood next to several more hotels just like it in a tent city no better than the one at Lake Lindeman. Her feet dragged as she and Clay made their way past each of them. They all looked the same: a kitchen, dining room, bar, and dance hall all in one room, and the walls were lined with bunks for overnight guests. All were taken.

They continued to walk until Clay found a spot from which a large tent had recently been moved. "How's this? We won't have to shovel to clear the snow. And look, whoever was here left two piles of spruce boughs to put the sleeping bags on. What do you say?"

"Fine."

Working strictly by rote, Aurelia helped Clay pitch the tents and spread the sleeping bags. She readied the coffeepot and a pan of bacon and beans for dinner while Clay gathered enough wood for a fire. "I *can* cook better than this," she felt compelled to explain, "but not tonight. Not without a stove."

"I'll bring the stove down with tomorrow's load. Don't worry, this smells delicious."

Aurelia stared pensively into the fire. "My mind can't fathom making that trip again."

"You aren't going to make it again, I am. I can travel faster alone. I'll leave in the morning. Should be back by dinner."

She envied his stamina and was about to thank him for his willingness to shoulder the most difficult tasks when she remembered that that was all part of the agreement they'd made—because Clay had his own reasons for wanting to get to Dawson as quickly as possible. Aurelia nodded, accepting the reality of their differences. "Then I'll spend the day unpacking the load we brought down today."

"Good." Clay finished eating and began filling the metal dishpan with snow. Balancing it on the rocks he'd used to rim the fire, it wasn't long before the snow had melted and steam began to rise from the surface.

Aurelia unpacked a fresh cake of Ivory soap and gathered the two granite dishes and utensils they'd used. "That water looks so inviting." She dipped her finger into the pot and made a few ripples. "Just right." She sighed and thought of how long it had been since she'd had a bath.

"Why don't I set the pan inside the tent for you? You can wash up, or whatever." He sounded awkward, as though breeching some rule of etiquette.

"But that's our dishpan."

"It's the closest thing we've got to a tub. The dishes can wait till morning."

Aurelia didn't know quite what to make of it. Though his methods were sometimes questionable, he was as considerate of her feelings as she always tried to be of others'. It felt strange—and wonderful—to be on the receiving end of such kindness. Why did they have to have such a black cloud hanging between them?

He didn't wait for her to answer, but carried the sloshing pan of hot water into her tent and set it on one of the barrels he'd already unpacked. "I'm going to walk a spell. I won't be long. Holler if you need me."

"Thank you, Clay."

"We can take care of that legacy matter when I get back too. I've been thinking about that."

"Yes." She lifted the flap of the tent and was about to go inside. She'd been thinking about that too, and about a lot of other things.

While she still couldn't define her feelings for Clay, she was long past denying their existence. At least one thing was clear, though: the greater the pleasure now, the greater the misery when she reached Dawson. Self-preservation urged her to keep that inevitability uppermost in her mind.

"Aurelia," Clay called over his shoulder as he left, "I'm sorry about your skirt."

She shrugged her shoulders in dismissal. The damage had been done. Picking up her shortened shirt, she ducked inside the tent.

When Clay returned he called her name and then entered the tent. The clean scent of soap and the freshness of lavender water still lingered in the air. Aurelia was kneeling on her sleeping bag, combing her hair, which she had washed. Her skin had a fresh-scrubbed look and her cheeks a rosy glow.

"Clay," she said, not looking him directly in the eye, "I managed to take care of the legacy matter myself. I took the liberty of keeping the leather straps, should I need them again." She spoke in hushed tones that concealed the passion behind her thoughts. "You understand, don't you?"

He looked disappointed, and that in itself made Aurelia ache to have him touch her again. "Sure," he said. Then, as though looking for a way to lighten her mood, he briskly rubbed his injured arm. "You sure did a fine job on my arm. Good as new."

"Be glad you didn't need surgery."

"Hey, come on now." He sat beside her on the sleeping bag. "Guilt and self-pity won't get you through medical school."

"I'm not so sure I'm cut out for medical school after all."

Clay was astonished. She'd been such a crusader for the idea of women in medicine. He couldn't believe she'd turn her back on it now, unless she felt a career would keep her from something else she wanted just as much, or maybe more.

Clay turned so he could look her straight in the eye. "There was a time I'd have agreed with you just on principle. But I can't say that now. Not after all you've done. Yes, Mrs. Higgins died. But you gave her a chance. You tried. It takes a special kind of woman—"

"You don't have to tell me. It takes an independent, assertive, and most of all, unfeminine woman."

"I can't argue about the independent or the assertive part." He winked. "But unfeminine? Never."

"My mother warned me about taking up a man's career. She said there wasn't a man alive who would still consider me a woman."

He shook his head. "Your mother was wrong."

Aurelia's mind raced in confusion. Here in this wild and trying country, she'd found the one man she'd dreamed of. He was also the one man who had to break her heart.

He closed what little distance there was between them. He combed his hand through her damp hair, relishing the feel of it. When he kissed her, she felt his tenderness as well as his passion, and he felt her softness as well as her strength.

He pulled back like a man fighting to gain control of his emotions. "I'll bet there's not a woman in the Klondike whose lips taste as sweet as yours."

"Not even Ruby Lips Johnson?"

"Who? Oh, that woman in Dyea." He shook his head. "She couldn't hold a candle to you."

Aurelia hesitated. "I know it's none of my business, but that day we landed in Dyea, that day on the beach . . . I saw you give her money. I know it's none of my business, but was that . . . was that to purchase the customary services?"

"Oh no," he said. His eagerness to set her straight was quickly replaced by dread. "Oh hell, I knew I'd have to tell you sooner or later. I didn't pay Ruby and her friend for their charms. I paid for information. About your sister. They know her pretty well."

17

"*But they're whores!*" Aurelia had barely made the statement when she realized the implication in his words. She jumped up. "You're calling my sister a whore! How dare you!"

"Your sister is working in a dance hall in Dawson."

"According to whom? Those two tarts?" When Clay didn't refute her statement, she went on. "I don't believe it. Those two harlots have Violet confused with someone else. Plain and simple."

"No," Clay said as he stood. "Ruby described Violet to perfection. Small, delicate, black hair, purple-blue eyes. That combination of innocence and seduction—"

"I've heard enough of your groundless accusations. Violet's always been an excellent dancer, and her voice rivals that of an angel. *If* she's working in a dance hall, it's to express herself. *If* she's chosen a controversial career—just as I have—then I support her wholeheartedly." She lifted the flap of her tent, indicating that he should go.

"Fair enough," Clay said. "We'll just have to wait till we get to Dawson to find the truth."

"That's right, Clay. We'll find the truth. And you'll see just how wrong you are."

He found it useless to argue with her. "Good-night," he said as he ducked beneath the flap and walked away.

If she'd had a real door, she'd have slammed it.

Instead, she hurriedly undressed and crawled into her sleeping bag, muttering all the while. How could Clay have placed any store in what two whores said? Why, they'd have said anything for money! Didn't he realize that?

She tossed and turned, trying to find a restful position. Lying on her back, she stared at the canvas roof overhead while the soft glow of neighboring campfires shed light on her darkness. If Clay was right, Violet was still with Sculley. She'd never stoop to something so low as working in a dance hall unless she was coerced. And if Violet was still with Sculley, she stood to lose a lot more than her morals.

Aurelia buried her head in the fur she used as a pillow. She didn't want the night to see the doubt that was written all over her face or the guilt that brought tears to her eyes. Only one thought consoled her. If Clay was right, Violet was alive, at least for now. All Aurelia could do was pray that her baby sister could hold on. Pray and wait for the ice to break.

Clay left for the summit early the next morning. When he returned that evening he assembled the stove and set it up in Aurelia's tent. She thanked him but said little else.

The following day, he brought down more food, tools, and Aurelia's trunks. Still ready to defend her sister's honor, Aurelia waited for Clay to mention Violet's name. He didn't. No doubt he realized how wrong he had been and would soon offer an apology.

The day after, he carried more food as well as the barrels of pitch, the rope, the whipsaw, and the other items he'd need to build the boat. He had yet to apologize, but at least their conversation was civil, though minimal.

After three more days and three more trips, the entire cache had been moved to Lake Bennett. He continued to honor his part of the partnership—she admitted that. She knew she could never have gotten this far without him.

Since they'd passed inspection at the Chilkoot Pass, Clay could go on without her if he had a mind to. She dared not forget that. For Violet's sake, as well as her own, Aurelia decided not to disturb the tenuous truce that bound them. Besides, she agreed with Clay wholeheartedly on one thing. When they got to Dawson, they'd learn the truth.

In the meantime, she learned to operate the stove, to make dried-apple pancakes, and to bake corn bread. At least once a day someone asked her help in removing a splinter or dressing a burn or treating a number of other minor ailments. In each case, she found her expertise more than adequate and her patients grateful and surprisingly open-minded. Often they wanted to talk of their experiences crossing the Chilkoot, and just as often they wanted to listen to hers.

Clay spent most of the second week building a crude set of shelves, a table, and two benches for Aurelia. While every stampeder had his own folding camp-stool, Aurelia said she needed extra seating when she had more than one patient. Clay also strung a clothesline between her tent and his. He chopped firewood and stacked it on the north side of her tent, where it would help to shield her from the wind. If he intended his hard work to equal an unspoken apology, Aurelia accepted it. She didn't want to fight with the man. She only wanted him to see the truth.

Toward the end of the week he surprised her with a twenty-five-gallon galvanized tub.

"It's not as big as a bathtub, but it's a lot bigger than the dishpan."

"It's beautiful!" she said, grateful yet embarrassed at once again being on the receiving end of his generosity. "Where did you find it?"

"Some folks on the other side of the lake have decided to sell out and go back. A man, his wife, and their daughter. Name's Wabble. From the South."

"There's another woman in this part of the camp? Oh, Clay, this is wonderful news. Do you think they would receive company? I could bring the extra apple pancakes I made this morning."

"Keep the pancakes on the stove. Mrs. Wabble said she'd stop by this evening after supper. Her husband's busy working on their boat. He plans to sell it. He thinks he can get a hundred and twenty-five dollars for it, but that's a lot of money. Anyway, she should be along shortly."

Another civilized woman in camp! Aurelia rushed inside her tent. She'd heard there were several other women in camp, but they traveled in tightly knit families, wore Old World clothes, and didn't speak English. Excited by the prospect of sharing womanly conversation, Aurelia wiped off the table and covered it with the lace tablecloth she'd packed in her trunk. She straightened the lavender quilt she'd spread over her sleeping bag and puffed the white ruffled pillows. From her orderly pantry shelves she pulled out small tins of black tea, cocoa, and dried milk. The teapot sizzled as she set it to boil.

The sound of a woman's voice drew Aurelia outside. Long before her guest came in view, Aurelia could hear Mrs. Wabble. She was singing "Camptown Races," giving added emphasis to the *do-da*s.

Aurelia slipped off the apron she'd worn all day and patted her skirt. As soon as she saw Mrs. Wabble, Aurelia smiled and waved, pleased to see that her new acquaintance had also shortened her skirt, allowing her booted ankles to show.

Mrs. Wabble appeared to be in her late thirties. She was five feet tall and seemed just as wide. Everything about her was round, from the bun on the top of her head to the polka dots on her dress, and even the loaf of bread she carried in her pudgy hands.

"Howdy," she said to Clay and slapped him on the back.

Groaning at the formality of his introductions, she said to Aurelia, "Name's Mabel. Mabel Wabble. So you're the doctor? I heard about you." She shoved the bread into Aurelia's hands. "Baked it this morning. You'll love it."

"Thank you, Mrs.—"

"It's Mabel, honey. Didn't I say that?" The woman looked around. "My girl should be along here any minute." She cupped her hands to her mouth and called out. "Em-ma. Emma!"

Aurelia looked with concern at the crowded canvas town. It was nearly seven o'clock, too late for a girl to be rambling about alone.

Mabel beamed when the girl came in sight. "There

you are, you silly goose. Come on up here. I want you to meet my friend Aurelia. She's a doctor. Hurry up now."

Emma Wabble was barely sixteen, as slight as her mother was stout. Her straight, brown hair hung loose down her back. The only thing that livened her wrinkled dress was a faded blue velvet bow she had pinned to the flat bodice. Mabel slipped her arm around her daughter's waist. "That's my girl. Now, why don't you tell Aurelia about those awful headaches you've been having."

"Momma, please." The girl looked as though the last thing she wanted to do was talk about herself.

Mabel turned to Aurelia. "You fix up females, do you?"

"I had intended to specialize in women's medicine." She turned to the girl. "Emma, I'd be happy to talk to you about your headaches. But why don't we all go inside first. The water should be hot. I've got tea and cocoa."

Aurelia held open the flap of her tent as Mabel and Emma preceded her inside. Clay declined to join them, saying he had wood to chop.

"How do you like that new tub of yours?" Mabel asked. "We got bigger ones, but for its size, it's top of the line."

"I like it very much," Aurelia said as she straightened the small towel she'd draped on the edge of her new tub.

Emma slid to the end of one of the benches and looked wide-eyed around the tent. Her mother walked straight to the shelf on which Aurelia had arranged the refreshments.

"Look it here, Emma, same brands we carry at our store back home." She picked up one of the tins and gave it to Aurelia. "We'll have the cocoa. It's the most expensive."

Aurelia prepared hot cocoa for the Wabbles and a cup of tea for herself. "You have a store back home? Where's that?"

"Chuckatuck, Virginia," Mabel said proudly. "You heard of it?"

"I'm afraid not."

"Right by Calhoun's Pond? Sleepy Hole Corners?"

"No."

"You heard of North Carolina?"

"Yes, of course."

"Well, Chuckatuck's just a few miles north. Dismal Swamp area. Truth is, we packed up the store and moved it with us. We was fixin' to set up in Dawson. Make us a fortune over the counter." Mabel slurped her chocolate and licked her lips. Emma rolled her eyes as though she found her mother's manners unacceptable.

"Your idea sounds promising," Aurelia said. "I hear millionaires are made every hour in Dawson, some by cooking, some doing laundry, running hotels, whatever. Managing a store sounds—"

"I said we *was* fixin' to move to Dawson. Didn't you hear me? We ain't now. We're going home, just as soon as Ed gets the boat finished so he can sell it."

"You're not going on to Dawson?"

"No. See, I'm in the family way again." Mabel patted her polka-dotted abdomen. "I held on to Emma all right, but I done dropped five babies since. Guess my soil ain't too fertile, you get my meaning? Anyway, don't see where I'd have a ghost of a chance keeping this one in the oven out here."

Though Aurelia believed in candid talk between mother and daughter, she thought such subjects were best discussed in private. But Emma appeared to have heard it all before. She seemed more interested in the lace on the tablecloth and the ruffles on the bed pillows.

"You've miscarried five times?"

While Mabel told her her story, Aurelia busied herself making fresh cups of cocoa. Aurelia would have been shocked at the woman's ignorance, except that she'd heard worse in medical school. When she sat down at the table again, she looked at Emma. "Why don't you tell me about those headaches of yours?"

Emma fiddled with a small lock of hair that had fallen in her face. She sifted the hair until she had one single strand pinched between her fingers. Without flinching, she yanked it from her head. "I just get 'em sometimes."

"Would you like me to examine you? You could tell me about your symptoms, and perhaps we could find the cause."

Emma looked to her mother for permission.

Mabel arched her brow and said to Aurelia, "You goin' to charge her for it?"

"No, this would be a courtesy exam." Aurelia turned back to Emma. "What do you say, Emma?"

"Uuh . . . I reckon that'd be okay, but could it be on another day, cause I ain't up to it just now."

Aurelia sensed that the girl didn't want her mother present for the examination. "That would be fine. Maybe some day next week?"

"How 'bout tomorrow morning?"

"That would be fine too."

"Girl, you know I do my washin' in the morning. I can't take the time to come visiting two days in a row."

"I can come by myself, Momma, I know the way."

"My examination won't take long." Aurelia wasn't sure why, but she wanted an opportunity to talk to the girl alone.

"All right then. But mind your manners. I don't want you making a pest of yourself."

After Mabel's third cup of cocoa she and her daughter left. The rest of the day passed quickly. Aurelia was eager to replay the scene for Clay when he came back to camp.

Despite a backbreaking day chopping the trees that he'd have to whipsaw into planks, Clay listened attentively while Aurelia told him of her day.

"Clay, the woman is pregnant." She shook her head in disbelief while she sliced the loaf of bread Mabel had given her. "And she managed to climb that horrid mountain. I don't think she knew of her condition until recently, though. That's why she wants to go back to North Carolina. Seems she's miscarried five times and she's afraid to go on to Dawson. I told her the hardest part of the trip was behind her, but she said she couldn't bear the thought of giving birth to a foreigner."

Clay smiled at the idea of calling a child born in Canada a foreigner. "She was serious," Aurelia said. "And just as serious when she said she'd grown up thinking a woman comes in heat twice a year, just like a hound."

The words had tumbled out so quickly. If she hadn't been so anxious to tell him about her conversation with Mabel, Aurelia would have paused to phrase the details in words more acceptable in mixed company. But Clay just sipped his coffee and smiled.

"Just twice a year?" he asked. "Now that's a shame."

Embarrassment stained her cheeks, yet Aurelia relished the intimacy created by the inuendo. When Clay asked if Mabel knew what had caused her to miscarry, Aurelia heard the huskiness in her own voice when she answered, "Intimate relations."

For a moment, neither said a word. Then Clay, looking more than idly curious, asked, "Do all women dread that first time? I mean, do all women expect it to be so terrible? So painful?"

"I don't know." She knew that Violet had no fondness for that kind of intimacy, but one of her fellow students, a woman twice widowed, claimed that the pleasure of the experience depended a great deal on the skill and sensitivity of the man.

"What about you?" he asked. "Do you think it'll be some kind of awful ordeal?"

His candid question stunned her. She didn't know what to say.

"Maybe you don't think about it at all," he said, then added in a seductive tone, "but I'll bet you do."

"Yes," she admitted, her voice faltering, "I've thought about it."

"So have I." Then he stood, helped her to her feet, and gestured toward her tent. "Guess it's time we went to bed. See you in the morning."

She nodded and moved toward her tent, knowing it prudent to have such a delicate subject dropped.

"Aurelia."

She turned around to look into his dark eyes.

"It doesn't have to be painful."

One way or the other, the man had a knack for disturbing her sleep. In bed that night, Aurelia thought first how easy it had been to discuss such personal subjects with Clay. Then, just as Clay had so accurately guessed, Aurelia tried to imagine what it would be like to make love to a man like Clay. Would she experience those rapturous spasms that some women spoke of?

Warning bells rang in her head. If she and Clay were going to Dawson for any reason other than finding Violet, Aurelia might risk nurturing so wild a dream. But only a fool would deny the truth.

The next morning, Aurelia fixed Clay a hearty breakfast before he set out for the timberline. Like all the other stampeders in camp, in order to build a boat he'd have to chop trees and haul them back to camp where he'd have to set up the whipsaw and work by hand to turn the logs to lumber. Every conversation in the camp already included at least one reference to boat designs.

"I never thought I'd see the day when I'd admit this," he said to Aurelia as he prepared to leave, "but I'm looking forward to seeing Poyser. Can't work a whipsaw by myself." He gulped the rest of his coffee. "Be back around noon," he called over his shoulder.

Aurelia waved good-bye. She was anxious to see Waldo too. It had been over three weeks since the incident with the grizzly. He should be arriving any day now.

Time didn't permit more thought of Waldo. With so few dishes and utensils, she had to wash them after every meal. She had soiled clothes to scrub and clean clothes to mend. This morning, however, Aurelia reviewed the information she had on maladies of the head. Emma would be arriving shortly.

Aurelia took her textbook outside and sat on one of the folding camp-stools. The first week of May in the Yukon was delightful. For at least a week now the sun had been up since four in the morning, and the snow didn't have a chance. Only thin crusty patches of white remained, scattered over the fresh pale green of new grass. The season seemed to change overnight.

"Morning, Miss Breighton."

"Emma?" Aurelia tried to hide her surprise. "Good morning. I'm so glad you could come." Emma wasn't the mousy child she'd met the night before. She'd fashioned her hair in one long braid and tied it with a red ribbon. A pink flower flopped over one ear. Her hips moved in an affected way. She smelled of vanilla.

"My momma's behavior last night was just so uncivilized." She sat down on the stool next to Aurelia and hiked her skirt, testing the limits of how much boot to show. "I picture myself as more like you."

"Like me?"

Emma nodded. "You read *The Cosmopolitan?* Everybody does. Isn't it just the best magazine ever? I buy it regular."

"You do?"

"Got last January's issue in my sleeping bag. I'll let you borrow it. Just don't tell my momma. She had a fit when I sent away for the Vestro bust developer. It's guaranteed to develop the bust six full inches." She straightened her spine and took a look at her bosom. "They'll be poppin' out any day now."

Aurelia stood and gestured toward the tent. "Why don't we go inside?"

"Is that what you used? I wondered 'cause you've got such a great figure. According to the advertisement, the Vestro bust developer fills all hollow places and adds grace, curve, and beauty. It's permanent and it *never* fails. I also bought a can of La Dores Bust Food from the Sears catalogue."

Once inside, Aurelia lifted her medical case onto the table. "You're wasting your money on such things."

The look on the girl's face dropped. Aurelia felt sorry for her. "Emma, you've got expressive eyes, lovely skin, healthy hair, and fine posture. Why is a full figure so important to you?"

"Uuh, well, fashion for one. Momma says there's not enough of me to corset, and everyone knows a woman has to keep up appearances or be neglected. If a woman's big on top, she looks soft and if she's big on bottom, she looks fertile and that's just how I want to look—soft and fertile. That's what gets the men."

Aurelia thought about relaying Nana's lesson about the fish and the hook but decided against it. Emma obviously had her mind set. "If you insist on having a full figure, I'm sure both *The Cosmopolitan* and Sears offer artificial enhancements."

Emma began toying with the shorter hairs around her face, sifting them between her fingers, sorting them down to one strand. She yanked. "I want a man."

Oh, dear. "Have you talked to your mother about this?"

Emma shook her head and twisted her mouth in a ridiculous gesture. "I can't talk to her about that."

"But I'm sure you could. Have you tried?"

"Just a thousand times. She says my time'll come in about five years. In five years I'll be twenty-one! It's impossible for a woman to get a man when she's that old. That's why I want to stay up here. This place is full of men. Oh, there's a few back home, but they ain't the kind I'm looking for."

"I see." Aurelia didn't consider herself qualified to give lectures on attracting a man. That was Violet's talent. "Emma, why don't you tell me about your headaches." Aurelia opened the drawer in her medical chest where Violet used to keep her hair combs and retrieved two chartulas of aspirin. She unfolded the first packet.

"Oh shoot," Emma said, "my head's fine. Sometimes I just tell my momma I have headaches so she'll leave me alone."

"I see." Aurelia hadn't engaged in any "girl talk" since the days when she and Violet had spent Saturday afternoons looking through Mr. Sears's wish book or fantasizing about their ideal husbands. Even at twelve years old, Violet knew what kind of husband she wanted—a rich one who was tall, but not spindly, broad but not rotund like Poppa, and heaven forbid, he should never snivel. Violet despised the idea of a soft man, the kind who had no independent mind of his own, though she said Aurelia might like one of that henpecked kind. Then he wouldn't fight her for the morning paper.

Emma looked impatient. "I thought you said you worked on women."

"That's to be my specialty."

"You ever worked on a man?"

"Yes, I have." She thought of the avalanche, Waldo's injuries, Clay's knife wound, and the dozens of less serious injuries she'd treated here at camp.

Emma leaned across the table. "You ever see a man naked?"

Aurelia closed her medical chest. "Why don't you tell me about the kind of man you're looking for? Is he tall, dark, and handsome?"

"You mean like yours?" Emma giggled.

"Mr. Guardian is my partner."

"He's gorgeous."

It suddenly occured to Aurelia how jealous Violet would be to see Clay by Aurelia's side. The idea brought her a shameful sense of satisfaction. Her thoughts were interrupted by Emma's continued chatter.

"I don't want him too tall, cause I'm not too tall. And I don't really care about the color of his hair, long as he's got some. He's got to have great eyes though. You know, the kind that goes straight to the soul. Color don't matter. But he's got to be sure of himself. I want me a regular hero."

"A hero? That's a tall order."

"I'll find him," she said with the confidence and innocence of a girl who'd never met a scurrilous dog in a handsome disguise.

One cup of hot cocoa later, Aurelia sent Emma back to her mother. The girl returned several times that week just to talk "woman to woman." Mabel stopped by once and invited Clay and Aurelia to join them for coffee that evening after dinner.

Aurelia was amazed when she saw the Wabbles' tent, five times the size of her own. Mabel had a dining room table with six assorted chairs, each one piled high with sacks of flour and sugar and boxes of canned goods. The cache outside the tent was as big as a small building. Mabel had added a string of beads to her polka dot dress, and she twisted them as she held the flap of the tent for Clay and Aurelia to enter.

"Ed should be along shortly. You folks sit down. Take a load off. Coffee's almost ready." Mabel scurried to remove the groceries from the chairs. "I think I hear Ed coming now."

She met him at the door. He looked like a beer barrel, but taller. His shaggy beard was full of sawdust, and the buttons on his plaid shirt were about to pop. His clear blue eyes sparkled with mischief. Ed grinned as soon as he saw Clay. "Hey there, you old

cuss. 'Bout time you let me meet that partner of yours."
Ed grabbed Clay's hand and pumped it, then took
Aurelia's hand and shook it with the same gusto. "Got a
good grip there, little lady, I like that. Don't pay these
days for a woman to be weak, especially in these parts."

Aurelia instantly credited Ed Wabble with having
a progressive attitude. She could see why he and
Mabel made a fine couple.

The entire evening went well, each of them telling
his or her favorite story about crossing the Chilkoot.

"Seems to me," Clay said to Ed late in the evening,
"the hardest part of the trip is behind you. You sure
you don't want to go on to Dawson?"

"Naw, me and the missus are itching to get back
home. I want to try pig farming this time."

"You going to sell the supplies you've brought
with you or haul them back?" Clay asked.

Just then Emma interrupted the conversation.
"You can leave them here with me. I'll go to Dawson
and set up the store. I know how to do it."

Mabel laughed. "Child, you've got a right pleasant
way about you, and that's good for dealing with customers. But you ain't got no head for figures. You can't
remember what beans cost from one week to the next."

"Your momma's right," Ed said. "Besides, we can't
go off and leave you here alone. Not a pretty girl like
you. No sir."

Emma beamed at her father's praise. "But what if I
had me a man. A real hero. Someone who knew
about figures."

Ed and Mabel both laughed. "Oh sure," Ed chuckled a little more as the words came out, "I suppose if
you latch on to a real hero, and he does right by you,
then I guess you can stay here in the Yukon and keep

the cache. Open up a store in Dawson and make yourselves a fortune."

Emma smiled as though she had a plan up her sleeve, then excused herself to go to bed.

Clay and Aurelia did their own share of giggling as they walked back to their tents later that night, talking about what animated characters the Wabbles were. The jovial mood grew serious when they reached her tent.

Clay paused in front of Aurelia's tent. "What do you think Ed Wabble meant about Emma's hero having to do right by her? You think he meant marriage?"

"I'm sure that's what he meant."

"You ever thought about getting married?"

"All women think about it at some point. Most expect to marry and have children."

"Do you? Is that part of your dream?"

Aurelia sat down on one of the stools, and he sat beside her. She rubbed her arms to ward off the night's chill. If any man other than Clay had asked her so personal a question, she'd have declined to answer, but they'd already discussed so many other personal things. Besides, she wanted Clay to know how she felt. She wanted to share her dreams with him, even though they'd never come true. So she shared with him what she'd never shared with anyone.

"When I was a girl Emma's age, I always envisioned myself married. I'd have six healthy children and a comfortable home. And I'd be married to a man who was honest and who asked my opinion on things—not just things going on in my own sphere, but about things going on in the world. He'd kiss me every morning before leaving and every night when he came through the door."

Sounds of other campers walking back and forth intruded. She waited for the footsteps to fade before she continued. "He wouldn't object if I wanted a career. In fact, he'd encourage me, just as I'd support him in his endeavors." She paused as though she had something more to say.

"What else?" Clay whispered.

She searched the sky. What made the stars sparkle so? Knowing she longed for the impossible, she said, "He'd trust me with his dreams."

Having bared her soul, Aurelia closed her eyes and relished a new feeling of freedom. She half expected Clay to take her hand, but he didn't. A moment later, she asked, "What about you? Do you ever think of marrying again?"

"Yea. I guess I do." He seemed to be in his own state of contemplation. He picked up a twig from the pile of kindling and doodled on the ground.

"To provide a mother for your son, I suppose."

"Maybe I should think along those lines, but Aunt Liza does a fine job with the boy. The little fellow's going to be six years old this month. The night before I left all he kept asking was if I was going to be home for his birthday." Clay cleared his throat, as though he found talking about Eli difficult. "I told him no, but that I'd be thinking about him."

"You think about him a great deal, don't you?"

"Sure do." Looking eager for Aurelia's opinion, Clay reached inside his jacket pocket and retrieved a penknife and a small block of carved wood. "It's for Eli's birthday," he said as he handed the wood to Aurelia. "Still got a lot of work to do on it, but I think he'll like it. What do you think?"

"Oh, Clay, it's beautiful." She ran her finger along

the sleek round body, and end to end along the gracefully raised fluke. Her finger froze as she recalled the image of a sea strewn with bloody carnage. "Why did you choose to carve a whale?"

He stared at the ground. "Remember that day on the ship when everybody was shooting?"

"Vividly."

"Me too. Don't think I'll ever forget it."

"You didn't seem upset at the time."

He shrugged. "I wasn't. Not until I saw Poyser heave over the railing after he shot that whale. Then I saw him curl up on the deck like he'd been the one shot."

"I think he felt guilty. I know he felt ashamed."

"What you don't know," Clay said, still focusing his attention on the ground, "is how ashamed I was, how ashamed I am." His voice low and heavy with regret, he chanted, "Butcher, Butcher, Butcher." He swallowed hard, then looked Aurelia in the eye. "I set Poyser up."

"Why?"

"I don't know," he said. "Maybe his weakness. Reminded me so much of my father. Ulysses Guardian, the town drunk, the scum of that God-forsaken prairie hole where I grew up." Pain surfaced in his eyes. "Do you know what it's like to be seven years old, to go to town, and to have people shoo you away from their kids and call you vermin? All because your old man is a loser?"

"No," Aurelia whispered, her heart aching for him.

"Well it's not the sort of thing I ever want my boy to experience." Clay's eyes misted over. He took a few steps into the shadows and stood staring at the stars. A moment or so later he came back with a renewed determination in his eyes. "I don't have much in the way of dreams for myself," he said, "but

what I do have, I'd give up to make sure my boy
never suffers for something I did."

Aurelia understood, but her enlightenment was bitter. Unless Clay cleared his name, Eli would pay the
price. And to clear his name, he had to smear Violet's.

Mid-May. All rhythms of life quickened as spring
claimed the land. The first butterflies with their tiny
gold-and-black gossamer wings fluttered over new
fields of bright pink fireweed, spikes of purple lupine,
clusters of blue forget-me-nots, and a great haze of
white baby's breath.

The mile-high peaks that rimmed Lake Bennett
groaned as huge chunks of white snow and blue ice
freed themselves from winter's grip and tumbled to
the ground. The water's edge became honeycombed
with patches of melting ice. Overhead, geese flew in
ragged arrows heading north, prompting every man
in camp to start betting on when the ice would break.

If they weren't talking about the ice, which was still
at least a foot thick, they were talking about boats. Who
was building what kind? How far along were they? Who
already had his lumber whipsawed? Who was skinning
bark and sapwood? Who was still cutting down trees?

The camp was alive with the hum and the buzz of
saws. The fragile timberline receded a little more
each day. Scows, rafts, dories, and other boats of
questionable design took shape, a dozen at a time.
With sunlight from two-thirty in the morning until
ten-thirty at night, sawdust confetti rained continually.
Excitement ran high.

Tempers flared.

Every day, partners in the sawpits fought over who

did the most work, the hardest work, the best work. Every day, at least one partnership dissolved in a fist-fight, usually over working the whipsaw, seen now as more trying than the Chilkoot Pass. In the midst of this tension, the mosquitos arrived.

"You bloodthirsty carnivore," Aurelia swore as she slapped her cheek, the back of her hand, her leg, her neck. Swarms of giant black pests buzzed around every inch of exposed flesh, leaving her skin marked with itchy red welts.

"For Godsake, Aurelia," Clay yelled as he came up from the sawpit for lunch, "where the hell's your mosquito netting? And why the hell don't you have your gloves on?"

"Oh, for Godsake yourself!" she screamed. "I can't cook or scrub clothes or do anything else with these stupid gloves on, and I can't see where I'm going with my head all covered up in this stupid net." She lifted her skirt and slapped her leg. "Hideous monsters!"

"So rub on some of that oil you gave me this morning. It smells, but it works."

"That was eucalyptus oil, and I'm all out of it!"

Clay slammed his tools down on the ground in front of his tent and stormed away. Aurelia kicked up a cloud of dust with her boot, but there was no stopping the ceaseless buzzing of the insects.

Less than a half hour later Clay returned to find Aurelia removing the freshly laundered clothes from the line. Her head and shoulders were hooded with mosquito netting, and her hands were gloved in cotton. In his own hands he held a bundle wrapped in storekeeper's paper and tied with string. He grabbed one of his own clean shirts from the line, forcing the other clothes to tremble.

"Here." He shoved the clean shirt and the parcel at her. "This is what you're going to wear from now on. And I don't want to hear any form of the word *no.*"

She gasped at the idea of his dictating what she was to wear and at the preposterous notion of her wearing his shirt.

Clay glared at her. "Now get yourself inside and put them on. Now!"

18

Aurelia shredded the wrapping and threw the contents on the table. "Overalls?" she said, loud enough for him to hear. "Have you gone daft?" She stared at the blue denim trousers and canvas suspenders. They were brand new and appeared to be sized correctly, but they were still men's clothing. "I'm not wearing these things."

Clay called to her from outside. "Oh yes you are. They're heavy and they'll cover your legs."

"And this shirt?" She'd laundered it enough times to know that it was his favorite. "I'm not wearing your shirt."

"Come on." he said, the first civil note he'd uttered all day. "Make the mosquitos work to find that tender skin of yours."

His switch in tactics disarmed her. So he thought her skin tender? Pleased with the knowledge, she lifted the faded blue cotton shirt to her face. It smelled of soap, fresh air, and warm Arctic sun. Deep within its well-worn fibers it also smelled of Clay. She inhaled, drawing his essence close to her.

"How 'bout it?" he called. "It's for your own good."

Maybe so, but something didn't feel right. Knowing it would sound like a lame excuse coming from her, she called back to him, "This isn't appropriate attire for a lady."

"We're not in Philadelphia, for Godsake. This is the Yukon. Anything goes here."

Overalls would certainly be more comfortable than her petticoats and skirt. But the thought of wearing Clay's shirt—his favorite shirt—against her skin gave rise to all sorts of tantalizing thoughts. The kind of thoughts shared between couples in love. That was what was wrong.

She clung to Clay's shirt as fiercely as she'd clung to the legacy that for years had numbed her emotions and kept her satisfied with what she had—an education, a career, independence. But maybe, just maybe, Nana was wrong.

Aurelia decided to take the chance. She unbuttoned her dress to the waist and slid it off her shoulders. Her fingers trembled. A paper-thin chemise barely covered her breasts, rounded by the corset she still wore. She held his shirt in front of her. Knowing she invited heartache, she shed her old identity and slipped her arm into his sleeve.

She stepped into the overalls, teetering on one leg at a time. Such a queer garment. She pulled the suspenders up one at a time. Just where were these straps supposed to rest? On the inner curves of her bosom? The outer curves? Right across the nipples?

She spent a few moments fiddling with the straps, then ducked beneath the flap of the tent and went outside.

Scandalous—that's how it felt to wear a garment that so blatantly defined her legs. Scandalous. And dangerously exciting. "Well?" she asked, waiting for Clay's assessment.

He'd just taken the last of the laundry from the line and dropped it in the washbasin that served as a basket. He eyed her appreciatively, then focused on the suspenders that balanced on her full breasts. "Let's go inside," he said. "Quick."

Oh, how she loved his devilish, dimpled grin. She hadn't seen it in weeks, not since the night they'd had coffee with the Wabbles. Knowing he would follow her, Aurelia ducked back into the tent. He wanted to kiss her. She knew it. And she couldn't wait.

Once inside, Clay barricaded the flimsy door with the washbasin. "Now if anyone barges in, he'll trip."

"I can't think of anyone so bold. Present company excluded." She stood by the table and let her hand rest on the edge. She needed to feel something steady and sure. Her knees weren't stable.

He came closer. "I can," he said, his tone more humorous than sarcastic. "Emma Wabble, the love-starved hero-worshiper, or Waldo Poyser, the great grizzly-killer."

Aurelia flinched at the touch of his hands on her shoulders. It simply wasn't her nature to play the saucy flirt. Then again, she reminded herself that she was a new Aurelia now. "You must find it strange to see someone else in your clothing," she said. "Do you? Find it strange?"

His hypnotic gaze mesmerized her. She thought he mumbled something about having to test the suspenders, but she couldn't be sure. The drumming of her heart drowned him out.

"Not strange," he answered. "Exciting." He tucked the middle finger of each hand under the suspenders. With agonizing slowness he grazed the underside of each strap, tugging just enough to pull her closer to him. She shivered when his fingers touched her nipples and blushed at their instant response. "I find *you* exciting," he added.

"Do you, now?" She put her arms around his neck and toyed with the hair that touched his shoulders. "You need a haircut, Clay."

"That's not what I need." He pushed the suspenders off her shoulders.

Yearning filled his eyes. His hands caressed her shoulders, slid down her back, and circled her waist. It all became clear when he kissed her. In a dreamlike state, Aurelia parted her lips to lure him closer. He welcomed her invitation, stroking the sweetness of her mouth with his tongue. Both intimate and provocative, the agonizing play of tenderness and passion strained that now familiar coil deep inside her, squeezing and tightening till she could stand no more.

Then, with a rapid flick of his fingers, he unbuttoned the shirt he'd insisted she wear. She could scarcely breathe, so powerful was his touch, even as his fingers fumbled with the tangle of satin ribbon that gathered her chemise.

"Like this," she said and loosened the knot.

"Beautiful," he whispered as he bared her breasts. Holding their weight in his hands, he lowered his head, drawing each bud into his mouth, torturing her with the tip of his tongue. She closed her eyes. Filled with wanton desire, she clutched his hair between her fingers and pulled him closer.

His ragged breath warmed her skin. Then he sucked harder. The fire that had smoldered inside her for months exploded and threatened destruction.

The laundry basket moved. The tent flap opened.

"Miss B-B-Breighton?" Waldo Poyser stuck his head inside the tent.

Aurelia gasped and turned her back to the intruder. Frantically, she buttoned her shirt while Clay shielded her.

"Poyser, get the hell out—"

Waldo fisted his hands. "What'd you d-d-do to her?"

Aurelia lifted the straps of the suspenders to her shoulders and turned around to face Waldo, her selfish passion already lashing her with guilt. "Waldo, you don't understand."

Waldo took one look at her face, all flushed, at the disheveled shirt she wore, falling off her shoulders and gaping at the neck. He walked straight up to Clay and grabbed the front of his shirt. "You r-r-rotten bastard."

Aurelia screamed as Waldo's punch landed squarely on Clay's jaw. Clay lost his balance for an instant, but quickly recovered. He didn't raise a hand in defense or retaliation.

"I told you what I'd d-d-do if you ever did anything to hurt her!"

Aurelia resisted the urge to run to Clay's aid. Though his cheek looked red and sore, his general appearance was not that of a man in pain. He rubbed his jaw and stared at Poyser with grudging respect. Aurelia waited for Clay to say something, though she doubted mere words could dissolve the tension. Instead, he nodded to Aurelia and left the tent.

Waldo looked as awkward as Aurelia felt. He stared at her with puppydog eyes, as though he'd been waiting a long time to see her again. No doubt, the sight of her so disheveled both confused and angered him.

"Let me explain, Waldo. You don't understand."

"Yea I do," he answered, his voice catching in his throat.

He stepped toward the door, then paused, looking as forlorn and discarded as the rumpled dress and petticoat that lay on the dirt floor.

Aurelia quickly picked the garments up and draped them across the end of her sleeping bag. At a loss for what to say, she fingered the denim of her overalls and said, "I've adopted the uniform of the Yukon. Clay says it will protect me from the mosquitos."

"So what are you gonna wear to p-p-protect you from him?"

Aurelia ached to see the pain in Waldo's eyes. This wasn't how she'd pictured their reunion. She had to talk to him. Hoping to set things right between them, she said, "Let's go outside and sit down."

Once outside, Aurelia moved her folding stool away from its usual spot next to Clay's and sat down. What a strange sensation it was to sit in pants. She was suddenly conscious of her feet and her legs and her hips and her lap, all of which did nothing to ease her awkwardness with Waldo.

A long, heavy pause only emphasized her discomfort.

"So tell me," she said. "How are your injuries? You appear to have made a remarkable recovery." Without touching his face, she scrutinized the marks on his cheeks. Her suturing did leave much to be desired, but the results weren't as bad as she'd expected. "You found someone to remove the stitches?"

"Took 'em out myself."

"I see the scabbing process is nearly complete. That redness will subside in time. I can give you some ointment."

"That's G-G-Guardian's shirt you're wearing, ain't it?"

"Yes, it is." Dear God, she felt so guilty. "You know, Waldo, everyone on the summit was talking about you and your fight with the grizzly. Several people in camp have asked about you. You've become something of a legend."

"Hmph. Is that our cache over there?"

"Yes."

"Guess I'd better get my tent set up."

Aurelia never dreamed she'd find it difficult to talk to Waldo, but this conversation was nothing short of painful. She looked around the camp, seeing everything and nothing in particular. Even before the first word came out of her mouth, she knew she'd wind up rambling. She always did when she was nervous.

"I usually serve dinner around seven. We've been getting up with the sun between three-thirty and four. Then we have breakfast. Clay heads for the saw-pits and I put the dirty laundry to soak. He put this clothesline up for me. Sometimes I have lunch ready at noon, but sometimes not till one o'clock." She stopped, if for no other reason than to take a breath.

"Looks like you two are doing f-f-fine without me."

"Oh Waldo, no! That's not true. Just the other day Clay said he was anxious for you to arrive. He needs your help with the boat. He can't work the whipsaw by himself, and everyone else is too busy with their own boats to offer a hand. The Mounties inspect and number each one, and if a boat's not deemed seaworthy, they won't let it on the river. And I've missed you too."

He didn't blush the way he used to, but then he'd come a long way from his days in the supply store in

Seattle. "Guess I'll go on down to the sawpits then and l-l-look around." He stood and brushed the seat of his pants.

"Yes, that's an excellent idea. Dinner will be ready at seven. Lunch is still on the stove if you're hungry. Clay didn't have time—"

"I ain't hungry."

"As you wish." Aurelia watched as Waldo walked toward the sawpits. His shoulders drooped and his head hung low. Though her mind told her otherwise, in her heart she felt she'd betrayed the young man. But she wasn't experienced in affairs of the heart. And she had never planned to fall in love with Clay.

Late that afternoon, carrying two buckets full of water, Aurelia returned from the river's edge where the ice was already breaking its hold on the shore. The distant grinding and groaning no longer alarmed her, for it signaled the thaw that would allow her to get to Dawson.

She was surprised to find Emma waiting, twirling the hair at her temple, inviting a headache of major proportions.

"Hey, Aurelia! Hey, do you really know Waldo Poyser? He's right here at Lake Bennett. Somebody saw him this afternoon. Said he's got big bear scars on his face and everything. What a man! I'd give anything to meet him. Anything."

Aurelia felt oddly protective of Waldo, then decided it wasn't her place to make decisions for him, especially decisions having to do with girls. "Mr. Poyser should be along shortly. I told him dinner was at seven. You're welcome to join us. I'd consider it an honor to introduce you."

Emma sighed as though she'd died and gone to heaven. "Then it's true. You do know him."

"Yes. He's a fine man."

Emma shook her head in wonder. "How'd you manage to get the two best ones in the whole Yukon? You did order that stuff from *The Cosmopolitan*, didn't you?"

"Oh, Emma, enough of that. Come on, you can help me make dinner." With that, Aurelia ushered Emma into the tent.

Aurelia took her lace tablecloth from the trunk. "Tonight's dinner is very special. What shall we fix?"

"How 'bout sausage and beans and apple short cake? I know you got the makings. I seen your pantry."

"That sounds like an excellent menu for a celebration."

"Yea? What are we celebrating?"

Wishing she could match Emma's enthusiasm, she said, "How about romance?"

"Oh, you have just the best ideas!" Emma crossed her arms and hugged herself. Aurelia started to laugh, until she saw the emptiness in Emma's gesture. An embrace was meant to be shared.

Two hours later dinner was ready. Sausage sizzled in the only frying pan Aurelia had. Beans bubbled in her only pot. The aroma of hot apples and cinnamon filled her tent. Emma had rushed back to her own tent to fetch another dish and set of utensils. She also brought back a small bottle of wine.

"Ssh," she cautioned Aurelia. "It's really raisin jack. Potent stuff. My paw makes it. He keeps it hidden in the flour barrel, but not too far down."

Aurelia held the long-necked bottle to the light. There was a little sediment in the bottom, a little dried foam around the top. The reddish brown liquid appeared harmless enough, but Aurelia knew better. She twisted the cap off and sniffed. Umm, just the way Nana Brooke used to make it. Raisins, sugar, yeast, and time to ferment. Yield, a twelve percent potion. "Guaranteed to cure what ails you," Nana used to say.

"Emma, alcohol is illegal here." Aurelia screwed the lid on tightly.

Emma rolled her eyes. "I ain't suggesting we get drunk. Just a nip or two for celebrating."

Aurelia considered the argument. "I suppose so."

"Good. Now, how 'bout I go out and pick us a bunch of flowers for the table, like you had that other day?"

"Yes, that's a fine idea."

Emma stepped outside and gasped as though she'd just seen a vision. Waldo must have arrived. Aurelia had never heard Emma giggle so much before, but now that's all she could hear. Aurelia set the bottle aside and joined everyone outside.

Clay had arrived too. Waldo appeared dumbfounded as Clay introduced him to Emma. "This is my partner, Mr. Waldo Poyser. Waldo, may I present Miss Emma Wabble. She's here with her parents from North Carolina." Waldo looked unsure of what to do. Not only did Emma make it clear she found him attractive, but Clay seemed to have forgotten the earlier events of the day.

"P-P-Pleased to m-m-meet you." Waldo bowed from the waist. "I'm from North Carolina too."

Emma giggled and began twisting her hair tight as a corkscrew. "You don't say. Well, we just have this little grocery store, is all."

"You setting up in D-D-Dawson?"

"Gosh, how did you know?"

"That's where most f-f-folks are heading, so that's where b-b-business will be the best."

She gazed at him, wide-eyed and blinking. "That's real smart thinking. You going to Dawson too?"

"Yea."

"Me too. But I'm being forced to go alone. See, my momma's in the throes of a life-threatening calamity, and she and my paw have to go back home. So I have to take all the merchandise and go to Dawson by myself. They're counting on me." She arched her eyebrows to emphasize her plight and lowered her voice. "And I don't mind admitting it, I'm scared plenty. What with the dangers and all. A decent girl just don't feel safe without a man to protect her."

"You got any brothers or uncles?"

"No," she sighed, looking far beyond pitiful. "I'm all alone."

"Maybe you shouldn't be going on to D-D-Dawson. Maybe you should go back home with your folks."

She clasped her hands to her heart. "Dawson is my destiny. The Fate Lady back in Seattle told me."

Waldo's eyes lit up. "You went to the F-F-Fate Lady too?"

"Sure did! You too?"

"Excuse me," Aurelia said, "but dinner will be ready shortly and, Emma, I believe you were going to gather some flowers for the table. Perhaps Mr. Poyser would accompany you."

"The flowers—I clean forgot." Emma looked up at Waldo. "You willing?"

"My p-p-pleasure." He offered Emma his arm. "You can call me W-W-Waldo, if you've a mind."

She giggled again as she took his arm. "Let's go

that way," she said, directing his gaze to one of the more populated areas, "I want everybody to see me with you. Waldo."

The two of them headed for the shore.

Emma's flirtation was so obvious, Aurelia first thought it too transparent to be effective, but Waldo seemed pleased. Aurelia turned to Clay. "Have you ever seen Waldo walk so erect? One might call it a strut."

"A woman can have that kind of an effect on a man." He gave her a look that reminded her of the effect they had on each other.

"So I've been told." She traced his jaw with her fingers. Slightly bruised and swollen, but nothing to become alarmed about. "Your attitude toward Waldo surprised me. After what happened this afternoon, I half expected the two of you to wind up in a brawl."

"Probably would have. But I thought about what I'd have done if the situation had been the other way around. If I was the one walking in on you and Waldo."

"And?"

"If I'd thought Waldo was hurting you, hell, I'd have sent him flying all the way to Dawson." Then, taking her hand, he kissed her palm, letting his lips linger on the tender flesh. "But poor Waldo didn't know what he was seeing, a man and woman in the heat of passion. I'd be willing to bet he's never even kissed a woman, much less seen her breasts. Or touched them. Or kissed them."

Aurelia felt her cheeks stain at the memory his words evoked. Though she longed for the experience again, this wasn't the place or the time. She withdrew her hand from his and whispered, "Heaven help Emma when Waldo does."

The forget-me-nots added a festive touch to the table. After dinner, dessert, and coffee Emma nudged Aurelia with her elbow. "Think it's time we got down to celebrating?"

Clay reached for the bottle of raisin jack and poured a small amount in each of the four tin cups. "First, a toast to my partner's recovery, to the man who battled the grizzly."

Emma took a sip of her drink and plunked her cup on the table. "You *did* kill the grizzly, didn't you? I wanted to ask you about it before, but I was afraid it might be too painful for you to recollect. Everyone on the lake's heard the story. How that crazed demon came at you with death in its beady red eyes." She leaned across the table toward him. "In my entire life, I never met a real live hero. Not until today."

Waldo looked down at the table, as though the adulation embarrassed him. "It wasn't really like that, Miss Emma. It was really Clay who k-k-killed the bear. I ain't no real hero." He slid to the end of the bench and stood up. "I ain't the kind of man you thought I was." He started for the door, but Clay stopped him.

"Hold it, Poyser." He slapped Waldo on the back. "Now Emma, I want you to know my partner here is right on one count. I did kill that grizzly, but then I was the one with the rifle. But being a good shot doesn't make me the hero. The hero's the man who faced that monster with nothing but courage." Clay let his hand linger on Waldo's shoulder the way a brother might. "Waldo here offered himself to save Aurelia's life. The world doesn't make bigger heroes than that."

Waldo looked at Clay with a mixture of humility, gratitude, and confusion. "I g-g-guess wild stories make it easy for folks to get the wrong idea about a man."

Emma lifted her eyes to Waldo with increased adoration. "Sounds like the true story's even better, and I'm dying to hear every word again. Right from your own lips."

"Come on, Poyser, let's sit down and entertain the ladies," Clay said.

Emma giggled. "And let's toast romance!" After emptying her cup, Emma leaned toward Aurelia. "Don't you just love his eyes," she whispered. "They go straight to the soul."

Clay and Waldo finished the bottle of raisin jack, and though Waldo swore he felt fine, Aurelia had her doubts. Emma encouraged him to put his arm around her shoulder as he walked her home. Waldo still hadn't returned by the time Aurelia went to bed. She smiled. Perhaps he'd finally found someone who could appreciate him for himself.

Several days later Aurelia invited Emma and her parents to join them for yet another celebration, one she hoped would surprise and please Clay. He and Waldo came up from the sawpits that evening to find all three Wabbles and a circle of folding stools in front of Aurelia's tent. Aurelia held a two-layer cake in her hands.

"Surprise!" they said in unison.

"What's all this?" Clay asked.

"May twenty-fourth," Ed Wabble answered. "It's the Queen's birthday. Everybody in these parts is celebrating. Even us Americans."

Clay looked to Aurelia for an explanation.

"Queen Victoria," she said. "We're in Canada, remember?"

"We're celebrating Queen Victoria's birthday?"

"Everyone else may be, but we're not. Not Queen Victoria's birthday," she said with a broad smile as she placed the cake on a plank between two upturned logs. "Eli Guardian's birthday."

"Eli?" Clay said, his voice suddenly strained. He stared at the white-frosted cake with his son's name and the number six spelled out in raisins across the top.

"You said his birthday was this month, but you didn't say when. I was afraid if I asked you, it would spoil the surprise. So I guessed. How close did I come?"

"It's tomorrow."

"Clay, is something wrong?"

"No. Excuse me. I've got to wash up." He turned his back and walked over to the dishpan of hot, soapy water Aurelia prepared for him and Waldo every afternoon. He immersed his hands, then covered his face with suds. Reminding him of his son's birthday had brought more pain than pleasure.

He turned around to find Aurelia standing behind him. His face looked more wistful than anything else.

"I didn't mean to upset you," she said.

He shrugged. "That was a nice thing for you to do—the cake and all. Makes me remember why I'm here." His lips formed a melancholy smile. "There's nothing I wouldn't do for my boy. I love him. I wish I could say there's nothing I wouldn't do for you too."

Looking rattled by his own thoughts, Clay raked his fingers through his hair. "Well, I guess we'd better get back to our company. I'm looking forward to a big piece of that cake."

Aurelia's feet felt like lead. In some convoluted way, had Clay just told her he loved her? No, he'd only reminded her that Violet would always come between them.

Aurelia tried to banish the fog that had settled over her and recapture the joy and excitement she'd felt only moments before. Back with her guests, she mouthed the words to another chorus of "Happy Birthday" and watched as Clay picked up the knife. Sadness now behind him, he boasted about his son's antics as he lowered the blade to cut the cake.

It wasn't going the way she'd planned. All day long she'd pictured the scene. Clay would look at the cake and realize how much Aurelia cared for him. Willing to admit he was wrong about Violet, he'd say, "Aurelia, I love you."

All day long she'd practiced saying, "I love you too."

19

"*Five dollars says* she'll break at noon tomorrow."

"I've got ten says she's free at six-fifteen tomorrow morning."

"I'll wager eight dollars on ten-thirty Friday night."

"A sawbuck on ten-thirty-three Friday night."

For weeks, men had placed bets on whose boat would be finished first, whose would pass inspection first, whose had the biggest oars, the fanciest name. Now, the bets were on as to when the ice would break. The first twelve miles of Lake Bennett were already free of ice, but the lake was twenty-eight miles long. Even then, there was a series of smaller lakes before a boat could reach the head of the Yukon River. Those lakes were all frozen. But the sun was hot and hovering, if not high, from one o'clock in the morning till eleven o'clock at night. The five-hundred-mile water trip to Dawson should begin any day now.

"You placed your bet, Poyser?" Clay asked as the two of them checked the black pitch they'd applied to the underside of the boat several days before.

"M-M-May thirtieth. I put two dollars on two o'clock in the afternoon."

"Hmm, I'd say that's a pretty good guess." Clay scrutinized each seam one more time. "She looks tight. Think she's ready for a test?"

Waldo nodded and grabbed one of the two lead ropes. Clay grabbed the other. They slung the ropes over their shoulders, took deep breaths, and pulled down the muddy slope to the shore. Buoyed by the water, the boat slid easily into the lake.

"Hey! She floats like a d-d-duck."

"Sure it does. We know how to build a boat." They stood on the shore and watched with pride as their creation rolled with the gentle rhythm of the smooth surface.

"Now let's drag it back up here and give it a name."

"How 'bout the G-G-Golden Girl?"

"I like it." Clay tightened the slack on his rope. Waldo did the same. They pulled together.

"That's what Aurelia means. G-G-Golden."

"Yea? How do you know?"

"I had a L-L-Latin book once."

With the boat on dry land, Clay said, "You're full of surprises, you know that. The Golden Girl it is. We can use the pitch as paint. Here. You can have the honor."

Waldo's brow furrowed as he eyed the boat to determine the best starting point, then dipped the pitch swab in the can. While he carefully lettered the bow of the boat, Clay cleared his throat.

"Poyser, about the other day, the day you walked in on me and Aurelia—"

"What about it?"

"I just want you to know a few things. Number one, if the situation had been reversed, and I was the one who'd walked in, I'd have done the same thing. Number two, for a skinny guy you pack one hell of a punch." He laughed nervously. "And number three—damn, I should be telling her this, not you—I love Aurelia."

Waldo pressed his lips together and looked off in the distance. Clay recognized the pain in the young man's eyes. He had felt something similar when he saw the birthday cake with Eli's name on it. It made for a lonesome kind of sadness when someone you loved was out of reach.

Waldo wiped the sweat from his brow, then shoved his hands in his pockets. "You be g-g-good to her, you hear."

"You can bet on it."

Waldo took on a forced air of nonchalance as he finished the lettering. Setting the brush down, he said, "If it's all the same to you, I'm going to head back up to camp. Got to wash up early tonight. Miss Emma wants me to set down with her folks for s-s-supper."

"Miss Emma? Sure. You go on ahead. I'll clean up here." Clay examined the thick black script and slapped his hand against the wood, proud of the work they'd done. "That Miss Emma's kind of sweet on you. You know that, don't you?"

"That's 'cause she thinks I'm s-s-something I'm not." Absently, Waldo rubbed the scars on his cheek.

"You earned that badge. Don't you ever forget it. Now get going. Doesn't pay to keep a lady waiting."

Waldo nodded and set off for the Wabbles' camp, leaving Clay alone with the Golden Girl.

Word about the dance traveled quickly. All the self-proclaimed experts agreed that the next day, May 30, the entire lake would be free. The next day the gold rush would begin anew, and the fever that had brought everyone this far would rage again. Tonight it was time to dance.

Aurelia had been in a tither for days, packing what had been her home for the last five weeks. She was anxious to get to Dawson. She'd had nightmares all week, horrible dreams in which she'd find Violet crying. They'd reach for each other, but just as their fingers touched, Violet would fade away.

She didn't tell Clay about the dreams. She knew their relationship would never be the same once they reached Dawson and found Violet. All she had was now.

Wanting the night to be special, Aurelia pulled the burgundy silk gown out of her trunk and silently thanked Lily.

Before she began her preparations in earnest, she pinned a note to the outside flap of her tent. Keep Out! Confident of the note's power to assure her privacy, she poured the last pot of hot water she'd been heating for over an hour into the tub, to which she added a capful of rose water from her medical case. Vapors of steam carried the delicate scent to her nose as she shed her clothes and stepped in.

The tub was big enough to kneel in, to bend and wash her hair, to sponge the soap and scented water over her shoulders. It was sheer luxury.

She leaned back and enjoyed the abundance of water until it turned tepid and her fingertips wrinkled. All good things must end, she thought without melancholy as she stepped from the tub. She thought again of Lily. But until they do end, one must enjoy!

Dry and powdered, Aurelia slipped into her laciest combination and held her breath as she looped the small buttons down the front of her summer corset. In the distance she could hear the strumming of fiddles and banjos. What time was it? She certainly couldn't tell by the sun: It dozed for a few hours, but it never slept.

"Aurelia," Clay called from outside the tent, "it's nine o'clock. Let's get a move on. What's taking so long?"

How could it have gotten so late! "I'm almost ready." She grabbed her old black boots and wished she'd thought to buy a pair of evening slippers when she was in Seattle. But then, she rationalized, why would she have done that? Neither her plans nor her dreams had ever included wearing a dress as luscious as this burgundy silk, or going to a dance with a man as wonderful as Clay. She slipped the dress over her head and suddenly realized the tragic error in her timing. Her hair was soaking wet.

"I'm a patient man," Clay called to her again, "and I know you're worth waiting for, but I can hear the music, and my feet are tapping to the beat."

"I'll be right out."

With no looking glass to guide her, Aurelia pushed the sleeves off her shoulders and smoothed her hands over the bodice. She'd remembered the decolletage being low, but she'd forgotten just how deeply the dress cut and how fully her breasts filled the design. At one time she herself would have called such a bodice "scandalously low," had she seen it on another woman, even though it was the fashion. But after all, she wasn't wearing the dress to entice men. She wanted only to entice one particular man.

She brushed her wet hair as best she could and fanned it around her shoulders. The natural curls fell in soft golden spirals along her neck and shoulders, leaving her skin damp. She grabbed a length of thin, black satin ribbon from her toilette. As soon as her hair would permit, she'd tie it back. Normally she'd sooner stay in than appear in public with her hair unbound, but this was the Yukon.

She slipped the delicate black ribbon around her neck and fashioned a small bow at the hollow. The satin tails trailed down her creamy breasts. After two squirts of lavender water from Nana's atomizer, Aurelia released her hatpin from the tent flap and stepped outside.

She expected Clay to flash his flirtatious smile or wink or nod in that slow, approving way that made her think him powerful enough to see through her garments.

Instead he looked scared. His lip quivered. He didn't seem to know where to put his hands. And he'd shaved!

Aurelia stepped closer. She touched his cheeks and drew her hands along the pattern his beard had taken. "I like the change."

"Good."

"Do you think it will be cool by the lake?" she asked, hoping to put him at ease. "Shall I take a shawl?"

"Yea. A heavy one." He looked like he was trying hard to smile and trying even harder not to look beyond her face.

"I'll be right out," she said as she slipped back inside the tent.

The thought that she'd truly rattled him made her feel powerful and deliciously dangerous. For a brief and fleeting moment, she understood how powerful Violet must have felt, with men always so eager for her company and worshipful of her charms.

* * *

Still warmed by the hovering sun, the evening air made Aurelia's shawl unnecessary. She removed it from her shoulders and draped it across her arm. As they walked down the rocky slope to the shore, the music bade them hurry. She heard fiddles being scraped and banjos plucked. She thought she even heard the sweet strings of a mandolin. Aurelia didn't recognize the tune, but it was snappy, and hands were clapping.

As she and Clay drew closer, they saw hundreds of men crowded around a newly built flat scow that had been dragged ashore. Hundreds of men, and only five women—Mabel and Emma Wabble and three other women Aurelia didn't know.

"They came down from the camps on Tagish Lake," Clay said as though he knew what she was going to ask.

The five women and as many men were dancing on the scow, changing partners every few minutes. Men jumped on the scow faster than rabbits, each anxious for a turn to dance with one of the ladies. Aurelia noticed Ed Wabble standing on the ground at one corner. Waldo was either dancing with Emma or standing on the sideline, waiting his turn to dance with her again. Two of the aproned women danced good-naturedly with every man, but each woman made special eye contact with a certain partner. Their husbands, no doubt, Aurelia concluded with a twinge of envy.

Dancing wasn't confined to the scow alone. The celebration spread as far as the sound of the music. All around the scow and for a ways along the shore, men kicked up sand as they danced with other men or by themselves. Crossing the Chilkoot had been a sobering experience, but now, after months of back-breaking work, the mood of excitement had returned.

The anticipation of riches whipped feet to a frenzy with every draw of the fiddle.

The fever was contagious. Aurelia watched the power of the music return Clay's dimples to his cheeks and the twinkle to his eyes.

A voice with a grandfatherly tremor called "Allemande left" and something else Aurelia didn't understand, but everyone on the scow started dancing in a different direction.

"Dance?" Clay offered his arm.

"Oh no, I couldn't. I can't do justice to the waltz, much less this routine."

"Not on the scow, my dear. Not where I'd have to share you with every other man who jumped aboard." He shook his head as though he found the idea abhorrent. "On the beach."

Aurelia had to admit she wasn't thrilled about letting so many strange men hold her hand or link her arm. She appreciated the commanding way Clay nodded to the men who grinned and tipped their floppy hats to her. And the cordial but authoritative way he repeated, "The lady doesn't care to dance right now." She also appreciated the way he placed his arm around her bare shoulder and the way the roughened skin of his palm quickened her nerves. She smiled and linked her arm with his.

The soft southern breeze carried the music with them down to the beach. She'd imagined this scene all day: her steps falling into an easy symmetry with his, a slow romantic pairing of rhythms mimicked by the gentle ripples of the lake as the water kissed the shore. Except for the storm clouds gathering above them, Mother Nature was doing her part. Even the mosquitos had disappeared. Still, the scene wasn't quite playing out according to Aurelia's fantasy.

It was hard to walk on the beach. The heels of her boots kept sinking, making her legs drag. After what had to have equaled a mile of such torture, she welcomed the chance to rest against a cluster of rocks and bolders, their own skirts as sand-crusted as her own.

"The place is deserted," Aurelia said as she looked around her. "There aren't even any tents around here."

"Too far from the timber. Besides, everyone's up at the shindig."

Aurelia looked back at the direction from which they'd come. Dancing flames from a bonfire brightened the dusky night. Now and then the faint strains of a lively fiddle would ride down on the soft breeze.

"Having a good time?" Clay asked as he picked up a stone and sent it skimming across the water.

"A grand time."

"Do you want to walk some more?"

"Truthfully, no. My legs are unaccustomed to the pull of the sand, and the heels of my boots are sinking in."

"Dr. Guardian knows what you need."

Aurelia laughed at the comical way he bowed. "I have competition, do I?"

"I'd like to think we could be partners." He knelt down on one knee. The pose both delighted and disarmed her. "Let me see your boot."

"My boot?" Even as she questioned his reasoning, she lifted her skirt just enough for him to see her worn, black leather high-button shoes, complete with silver buckles. "Clayton! What are you doing?" His dexterous fingers worked quickly to loosen the lacings and slip the boot off her foot. He propped the boot against the boulder.

"The other foot."

Because she trusted him, because the emotions he'd aroused felt so good, and because she was willing to go wherever this odd prelude took them, convention be damned, she complied.

She smiled as she wiggled her toes. The cool sand shifted around her stockinged feet. She'd barely adjusted to the new sensation in her feet when she felt Clay's hands circle her ankles.

"Spread your legs for me." His voice had taken on a slow, hypnotic tone. "Just a little."

Without questioning his command, she eased her legs a few inches apart. Her heart began to pound.

"That's good."

He cupped both hands around one slender ankle and slowly moved his hands along her calf, past her knee, to her thigh. A tiny gasp caught in her throat as he tucked his fingers into the roll of her garters and pulled her stockings down the path he'd just taken, leaving her skin chilled and burning at the same time. He peeled the stocking from her toes and draped it across her boots.

He didn't ask, and she didn't protest, when he bared her other leg.

Anticipation kept her breathing to small, barely perceptible intakes. He appeared to share her symptoms as he stood and worked quickly to remove his own boots and socks.

He reached for her fisted hands and gently relaxed them. "Can you still hear the music?" he asked.

"If I try."

Holding one hand, he led her a few steps closer to the shore. "Aurelia," he whispered as they walked, "do you ever have—I guess you'd call them day-dreams—where you think about how something's going to be? Where it's going to happen. How two people are going to look and what they're going to say. And do."

"A fantasy?"

"Yea, a fantasy."

"Many times," she answered softly.

He looked around as though checking details, then let his gaze linger on her face. "This is mine."

He caressed the silky column of her neck, then ran his fingers through the heavy mane of gold that tumbled down her back. Moving lighter than a feather, he lifted the loops of the thin black satin bow she had tied at the hollow of her throat. Just as lightly, he traced his finger along the path of the ribbon, down to where the frayed satin ends graced the swell of her breasts. He pinched the ribbon between his fingers and pulled till it was taut. Then he let go. "Not yet," he murmured.

He settled his hand at her waist. "I've dreamed of this since that night we danced on the ship. Dance with me now. Please."

Aurelia thought about that night on the ship. "You must have had remarkable foresight to have planned your fantasy so well."

"I've learned not to take chances. The successful man makes his own luck."

He slipped his arm behind her back. She could barely hear the fiddles and banjos, but it didn't matter. He hummed a long forgotten lullaby in her ear, setting the down on her neck to tingle. With his arms to hold and guide her, Aurelia glided across the beach, feeling the cool sand sift beneath her feet and the smooth silk rustle against her bare legs. Now and then he'd increase the pressure of his hand at the small of her back and she'd get a fleeting impression of how well their bodies fit together. Amidst the gray cotton clouds overhead, both the sun and moon rode the sky in tandem, sharing the space Aurelia had always thought reserved for one.

As they danced, the sky darkened enough to cloak their figures. It had to be after midnight.

His steps slowed, as though the melody in his heart had come to an end. He wrapped his arms around her and drew her close, pressing her soft bosom against the hard wall of his chest. Finally, they stood together in stillness.

"Your fantasy was beautiful, Clay. I feel honored to have been a part of it."

"My fantasy has just begun."

He scattered soft kisses across her lips, gently coaxing her response. As she returned his touch in kind, his kiss became harder and she parted her lips eagerly. No longer able to restrain her longing, she relished the duet he'd so skillfully begun.

Her breath was as ragged as his when he pulled away. Without a word, he took her hand and led her back to the cluster of boulders that shielded them from the rest of the world. His usually confident smile trembled as he fingered the satin ribbon again.

"I was going to tie my hair back when it dried," she explained nervously.

"Aurelia, I don't want to scare you. Unless you tell me to take you back to your tent, any minute now I'm going to untie that bow. And when I do, there'll be no turning back. I want you tonight. The way a man wants a woman."

It was what she wanted too. But she *was* scared. She looked over at her boots, flopped against the rocks. The buckles guaranteed to give her courage sparkled in the moonlight, just out of reach.

"You don't need them," he said as though he could

read her mind. "You don't need courage. Not when I'm giving you love."

"Clay?"

He toyed with the hair that fell around her shoulders and wound the golden curls around his wrists. "I do love you."

It sounded more beautiful than she'd ever imagined. The words she'd kept bottled for so long rushed from her lips. "I love you too."

He kissed her again with a sweetness she knew she'd never forget. Then the nervousness he had shown a moment before vanished. He picked up Aurelia's shawl from where he'd placed it on the boulders and spread the heavy woolen square on the sand. Standing at opposite ends of what both knew to be a bed, he unbuttoned his shirt and dropped it in the sand.

Storm clouds overhead swept across the face of the sleepy sun and cast shadows on his darkened skin. Aurelia felt herself smile, even as she bit her bottom lip.

Mesmerized by the sight of him, she watched him unbutton his trousers. All in one movement, he slipped them and his drawers to his feet. He kicked the clothes aside. A dense patch of dark hair shielded his loins. Even though the light was dim, she could see the long, rigid column of his sex rising from the center.

"You're naked." Her flat inflection contrasted sharply with the wild palpitations in her chest.

"It's better this way."

Aurelia swallowed hard at the implication, then before she could argue herself out of her decision, she reached for the satin ribbon around her neck and pulled, dropping the ribbon on the blanket. "No turning back," she whispered.

"No turning back."

"My gown," she said, aware of the breathiness in her voice. "I could use your help with my gown."

"The pleasure's all mine."

He stepped closer, and as he did Aurelia got a better look at the pleasure that awaited her. According to her studies, the female form was supposed to be able to accommodate the male, but she feared the claim had been exaggerated.

"You don't need this contraption," he teased as he worked to free her from the confines of whalebone stays. Over the lacy barrier of her combination he sculpted her breasts, her waist, and her hips with his hands.

"Only a bawdy woman goes uncorseted." She tried to tease back, but with the way he was touching her and with nothing but her combination to stand between her skin and his, she grew more nervous by the second.

As though he sensed her uneasiness, he placed his hands on her shoulders and gently, so very gently, kissed her lips. "I love you," he declared over and over again as he stripped her of the final garment.

Leaning against the boulders, with her dress and petticoats to cushion her against the rocks, Aurelia felt the cool slipperiness of silk on her back and the hot laving of Clay's tongue as he licked the nipple of the breast he held cupped in his hand.

At first, she cradled his head in her hands and moved her fingers to his same gentle rhythm. But as his own need quickened, so did his loving. He kneaded her breasts as he kissed. Aurelia gripped locks of his dark hair between her fingers and squeezed. Knowing only that it felt right, she arched her back and leaned toward him. She wanted more.

She had to feel him. As he had sculpted her body

only moments before, she moved her fingers along his shoulders and down the front of his chest, not stopping until she reached his long column of flesh. He moaned. Instinctively, she slid her hands up and down in a way that obviously pleased him.

He eased her hands away. "I'm only human."

"You don't like it?"

"I love it, but that's not what this night is all about." He led her to the shawl he'd spread on the sand. He knelt down, gently pulling her with him. She stiffened as he drew her back to the ground. "Just relax."

"Impossible."

"Ticklish?" he asked as he slowly stroked her belly.

What he made her feel had nothing to do with being ticklish, except that both were a type of torment.

He lay alongside her as he smoothed his hands down to the soft nest of honey-colored curls. He kissed her gently as his hand parted her thighs, and she shuddered when his fingers found the nub of her pleasure.

She cried out when his finger slipped inside her, but he covered her mouth with his and matched every thrust of his finger with an equal thrust of his tongue.

The rhythm. She'd never been taught it, yet her hips began to pulse against his hand in a way that had to be right.

Desire coiled inside her, winding like a spring, tighter and tighter. She stared up at Clay and knew the tension in his eyes mirrored her own.

"Now," she pleaded. "Love me now."

She spread her legs wide and held her breath as he climbed above her. She could feel the silken head of his sex as it followed the path readied by his hand.

With restraint that made him sweat, he slowly

penetrated her, controlling his movement till he reached her barrier. And then with one quick thrust, the barrier was broken.

She cried out again, even as the rhythm of her hips increased. His face, not the distended clouds above them, captured her vision. His moan, not the strum of a distant banjo, made music to her ears. The salt of his skin roused her tongue, and the firm flesh of his buttocks filled her hands. She closed her eyes and felt the magnitude of his love.

All senses blurred. All thought scattered. The fire he'd built inside her exploded, and his own liquid heat fed the flames.

Her muscles trembled in the aftermath.

With the same hands that had only moments before thrilled her to near delirium, he now stroked and soothed and delivered her to a place more tranquil than she'd ever known.

Then, when the fat, juicy raindrops pelted them, he draped his shirt over their heads and cuddled her in his arms.

20

"*That was some* p-p-powerful storm last night, huh?" Waldo rolled a keg of nails through the sand, righting it at the water's edge.

"Sure was," Clay answered from the boat—but not as powerful as Aurelia made him feel last night. He thought of how vulnerable she'd looked, lying naked on her back, looking up at him with those trusting blue eyes, her hair fanned all around, her skin smelling like soap and lavender. Her sweet lips, soft breasts, and innocent body so sensitive to his touch.

The boat rocked, and Clay shifted his weight to balance himself. Reaching over the side, he took the keg from Waldo and fit it in the boat along with the other goods they'd begun loading that morning.

Waldo hoisted a fifty-pound sack of flour to his shoulders and waded in the water to give it to Clay. "I didn't think it was ever g-g-going to end."

Clay had wanted it to go on forever. He could still feel the rhythm of her hips against his hand and, once he'd fully initiated her to the act, the way she'd arched her body to welcome his.

"For a m-m-minute there, I feared the sky exploded."

Clay had exploded. And it had never, but never, felt so good.

"Hey, Guardian, you're all red!"

"And you're all wet." Clay took the flour sack and turned his back to Waldo.

"I seen you and Miss Aurelia leave the dance last night. You went walking?"

"We did." Clay strained to wedge the flour sack between the boxes and barrels he and Waldo had already loaded. If Waldo had asked him something that personal nearly three months ago, he'd have sworn at the boy and told him to mind his own business. But, to Clay's surprise, he'd learned something about being a man from Waldo, about being willing to admit to having those tender thoughts most men laugh at, except when they're alone.

Apprehension strained Waldo's voice when he said, "I suppose next you'll tell her you l-l-love her."

Clay took his hat off and wiped the sweat from his brow. He knew the day would come when he and Waldo would have to confront their feelings for Aurelia, but he didn't want to risk the camaraderie he and Waldo had finally developed. Then again, putting off an unpleasant task didn't make it go away, it just prolonged the agony. He respected Waldo too much to do that.

"I did," Clay finally answered. "I told her I love her." Saying it again made him feel almost as light-headed as he had the night before.

Waldo lowered the box of canned goods to the ground as though the load and the information were too heavy to bear. "Did it make her h-h-happy?"

"I think so. She said she loves me too." Clay sat down on the barrel. Though Waldo had never claimed to feel anything more than friendship and admiration for Aurelia, Clay suspected that he felt much more. Not so long ago Clay would have been as proud as a conquering hero to know that Aurelia had chosen him over Waldo. Now, all Clay wanted was for Waldo to find happiness, the same kind of happiness Clay had found with Aurelia.

Waldo became fixated on the box of canned goods, intently studying the faded label stamped on the side. After he'd scrutinized all sides, he said, "That's better than finding gold, ain't it?"

"Sure is."

"Then since you found l-l-love, maybe I'll find gold."

"Don't look so glum. Maybe you'll find both."

"And maybe Miss Aurelia will find her sister Violet."

"She will," Clay said, groaning at the mention of Violet.

She and her partner were the only two people who could restore his good name, and she was the only one who could destroy the happiness he'd found. If it weren't for Eli's future, Clay might forget all about finding Violet and Sculley. But he owed it to his son to set the record straight. Someday Aurelia would understand. And he'd find Violet all right. Aurelia would show him the way.

Back at the tent, Aurelia closed her trunk and locked it. Clay had suggested that the cooking utensils, two weeks' worth of food, the tents, and her trunk be the last items loaded aboard the boat. Doing so would make it easier to set up camp each night and would allow her easier access to her personal belongings.

She wished she owned prettier undergarments, the

frilly kind with embroidered roses and pea-sized satin-covered buttons. She'd once thought of herself as a moth, a dull-colored nuisance, always shooed from the light, never sought for its beauty. She didn't feel that way anymore, not after last night. If she closed her eyes, she could relive the transformation.

He'd been powerful but patient, commanding but tender, all at the right time. Never once did he try to force her into submission, to exploit her innocence, to ply her with whiskey or trick her with lies. Clay Guardian would not use a woman to achieve his own ends. He was a far cry from Fletcher Sculley.

The ice creaked and groaned all morning, and by noon, the gray sheet had shattered, clogging the river with flagstones of ice. Nearly four hundred boats loaded to the waterline headed down the lake. Every few minutes another dozen or more shoved off. The eager fortune-seekers tooted horns, waved flags, and shouted "good luck" to each other as the race renewed. Over the next twenty-four hours, another three hundred would depart.

"Ready to leave civilization?" Clay called to her as he came up from the lake.

"Ready," she answered, hating the necessity of showing restraint. She wanted to rush to him and feel his arms around her. The look in his eyes told her that he shared the desire.

"Where's Poyser?" Clay asked.

"I thought he was down at the lake with you."

"No. He took off at least two hours ago. Said he had something important to take care of." Clay looked to where Waldo's tent still stood. "I don't know what's the matter with him. He hasn't even taken his tent down yet."

Suddenly, their attention was drawn to the giggles of Emma Wabble as she and Waldo approached them.

"Hey, Aurelia. Hey, Clay. You'll never guess what." Emma linked her arm with Waldo's and snuggled her head against his shoulder. "Waldo's going with me to Dawson. We're getting hitched."

Aurelia's jaw dropped open. "Married?"

"Paw says that's the only way he'll let me go. Me and Waldo's going to open up the store just like my folks had at home. Waldo knows the prices on just absolutely *everything*. Paw was so impressed. And my momma says he's the kind of man who'll devote himself to one woman for the rest of his life. She can tell." Emma smiled up at her fiancé with adoration written all over her face.

Aurelia looked to Waldo for confirmation, but he avoided her eyes when he answered.

"That's right. And we're going to stay here another day or t-t-two. I'll help Emma's folks get packed to go home, and then me and Emma will head for Dawson. You two can keep my share of the cache."

It took Aurelia a moment to recover from the shock. "I'm happy for both of you. My best wishes." She gave Emma a hug and kissed her lightly on the cheek.

Clay looked genuinely pleased when he said, "You're getting yourself a good man here, Emma."

"I know. I got myself a true hero. He's a romantic too. Gave me a book of poetry by Emily Dickinson, cause her name's kind of like mine."

"A book of poetry?" Clay asked, showing his admiration. "Where'd you find something that special out here?"

"Oh, I g-g-got it back in Dyea. I was saving it."

Clay took Waldo's hand and gave it a hearty shake. "Well, congratulations, you son of a gun. I'm going to miss you."

Waldo looked unsure of what to do but extended his hand to Aurelia. She clutched his hand in her own and squeezed it gently. She couldn't help but remember the day on the ship when she told him Emily Dickinson was her favorite poet. She suspected he'd bought the book of poetry for her.

"Dear Waldo," she whispered. Her throat constricted. Tears filled her eyes. She slipped her arms around his neck and kissed him on the cheek. The stutter that always marked his speech crept to his trembling arms as they enfolded her.

Pulling back, she wiped her tears with the back of her hand, then smiled at Emma. "I hope you don't mind, Emma, but he was, after all, my partner." She turned to Waldo. "And will always be my dearest friend."

Clay cleared his throat. "So tell us, you two lovebirds, when's the wedding?"

"T-T-Tonight."

"Paw met a preacher in camp and he's going to marry us tonight, right after supper. Waldo said he didn't think you could come cause you'd be shoving off this afternoon."

Aurelia looked at Clay. "We could go tomorrow morning instead, couldn't we?"

"I was about to suggest just that. We're not missing our partner's wedding."

Waldo's eyes lit up, then he shifted his weight from one foot to the other as though the situation was still uncomfortable. "Then you suppose you could be my b-b-best man?"

"My pleasure."

"Hey, Aurelia, how 'bout you be my bridesmaid?"

"Thank you. I'd be honored."

"Swell!" Emma squeezed Waldo's arm again. "We gotta get on back to settle a few more details with my folks. And I gotta get all washed up and everything." She nudged Waldo in the ribs. "So do you, honey."

Waldo slipped his arm around Emma's shoulders and said to the others, "Come on down around s-s-seven." With that, he and Emma headed back to her parents' camp.

Clay shook his head. "How 'bout that? Waldo's getting married. Explains why he didn't take his tent down."

Thinking of Waldo sharing his tent with Emma and all that that entailed, Aurelia said, "I just never thought of him as old enough."

"I think you mean man enough."

"That too," she said, the admission a difficult one. "I was always comparing him to you, and that wasn't fair. You're two different people."

"You think Emma really loves him?"

"In her way, yes, I do. She looks up to him. She admires his courage. And she thinks he has the greatest eyes."

"You think Waldo loves her?"

"I hope so," Aurelia said, her voice catching.

"Well, another three hours and he'll be a married man."

And Emma will be a wife, Aurelia added silently, ashamed of the envy she felt.

While Clay returned to the boat to shore it for the night, Aurelia returned to her tent and opened her trunk. She flipped through her small pile of handkerchiefs and selected her best: a pale blue linen square, trimmed with white lace and embroidered with white rosebuds in the corners. She would give it to Emma, she decided as she laid it aside and closed the trunk. Aurelia had something very special in mind for Waldo.

Three hours later the Reverend Gillikin called on those assembled in front of the Wabbles' tent to bow their heads. Emma wore a blue-checked gingham and carried a bouquet of wildflowers. She giggled when she said "I do." Mabel bawled and Ed blew his nose.

Standing right behind them, Aurelia noticed how tight Waldo's shirt fit across his back. She thought his voice sounded deeper than usual when he said "I do." She didn't know where he'd gotten the simple gold ring, probably from the Wabbles' supply, but his hands were steady and sure as he slipped it on Emma's finger. When Reverend Gillikin said, "You may kiss the bride," Waldo slipped his arms around Emma's waist and kissed her with respect and affection and what Aurelia hoped was love.

The Wabbles served cake and coffee after the ceremony. Several other campers in the area stopped by to extend their best wishes to the couple.

Aurelia wanted to stay longer, but Clay reminded her they had to get up at four in the morning and launch the boat. This would be their last night on Lake Bennett.

"One more minute," she pleaded, then called the newlyweds aside.

"Emma," she said, handing her the delicate handkerchief, "this is for you."

"Oooh! Hey thanks, Aurelia. I ain't never seen a hankie this pretty before."

"And Waldo, this is for you." She handed him a small

square package wrapped in old newspaper. Her heart beat wildly as she watched him peel away the layers.

His eyes grew as big as saucers. "This is one of your m-m-magic boot buckles. I can't take this."

"Please." Aurelia could barely speak. "I want you to have it. It was forged in Seville by a man who made swords for matadors, and it's guaranteed to give you courage . . . should you ever need it."

"That's a genuine magic buckle?" Emma piped up.

Waldo nodded. "Real magic. The kind that makes it so a l-l-lady can leave her family if she has to and go off to do something important. And climb mountains if she has to. And build boats. And ride rivers—"

"Like me, honey?" Emma asked.

Waldo looked puzzled, as though he'd been thinking of his admiration for Aurelia. "That's right," he said as he smiled at his new wife, "like you."

Clay and Aurelia said good-bye to the newlyweds, but before leaving, Clay took Waldo aside. Aurelia couldn't hear what they said to each other, but she saw them shake hands.

Aurelia wished Emma's parents good luck on their return trip and urged Mabel to see a woman doctor when she got home.

On their way back to camp, Clay took Aurelia's hand. They walked in a companionable silence.

"They hardly know each other," Aurelia said.

"Don't make it sound so depressing. Emma seems like a nice enough girl, and we both know what a good man Waldo is. They'll make a fine couple."

"I suppose." They walked some more. "I was so surprised to hear Ed and Mabel talking about their businesses. The general store was just one of several enterprises. The Wabbles are wealthy."

Clay chuckled. "Guess that's why they turned their cache over so readily to the newlyweds. Did you see the way they grinned every time they looked at Waldo, like he was a prince. The boy did all right for himself."

They stopped along the way to say good-bye to several stampeders who were loading their cache. Aurelia reminded one to make liberal use of the burn ointment she'd given him and cautioned another to keep his eyes shielded from the sun.

"Another week and this place will be deserted and soon forgotten," Clay said as they moved on.

"I'll never forget it," Aurelia replied. "In some ways I feel I was born on this lake."

Clay squeezed her hand. "I'll never forget it either."

They passed Waldo's tent, where Waldo and Emma would soon spend their wedding night. Aurelia thought about how traditional luxuries weren't important when two people were in love. A sandy beach and a woolen shawl could more than suffice. Still, Waldo and Emma had made a binding commitment to each other, and while that didn't guarantee happiness, it did increase the likelihood.

Aurelia silently bemoaned her fate. Because of Violet, Aurelia and Clay could never make such a commitment, unless he agreed to give up his search. If he did, he'd eventually come to resent Aurelia. How could she ask him to choose between her love and his good name? Or Aurelia could aid in Violet's capture. And if Violet was found guilty, watch her face imprisonment or execution? No, Violet simply couldn't be guilty. Aurelia could never live with herself if she didn't do all she could to save her baby sister from both Sculley and Clay. Not for the first time, Aurelia asked herself how she could be in love with a man who would ask so great a sacrifice of her.

A vision of the only future she could be sure of settled about her like a cold and lonely fog. With hard work, she'd be a good doctor, with a thriving practice and financial independence. Whenever she felt that wasn't enough, which she suspected would be often, she'd have beautiful memories of a night of love in the wilderness with a man who would always hold her heart. She would never, however, wear a band of golden orange blossoms on the ring finger of her left hand.

"Hmm," Clay said when they reached their camp. "Looks like I'm bunking under the stars."

He was hinting for an invitation. Why not? she thought. The only advice her mother had ever given her in such matters was that purity was the chief attraction for a man and that virginal freshness was the best dowry to bring to a marriage. Unfortunately, Aurelia had been only twelve at the time she was given that solitary piece of advice and had had no idea what it meant. Now she did, but it hardly mattered.

"You don't have to sleep under the stars," she said, wishing she'd been able to put more conviction in her invitation.

Clay followed her into the tent. Except for her sleeping bag on the mattress of spruce boughs, the tent was empty.

A night like this might be all she'd ever have. She should make the most of it. She began unbuttoning the shirt he'd given her.

"Let me do that," he said as he eased her hands aside. One at a time he manipulated the familiar buttons between his fingers and released them.

"Wait." Aurelia looked toward the flap of the tent.

"I know more than half the others have already gone, but there are still people around this part of the camp."

"Anyone who's still here is busy packing."

"It's not dark," she said, still keeping her distance. "We might cast shadows, and people might see us. I don't think this is a good idea."

Clay seemed puzzled at her sudden change of mood. "It's as dark as it's going to get. It's as dark as it was last night."

Last night. The music and the beach and the storm and all the passion may have transformed her for that moment, but in reality she was far from the enticing woman she'd been last night. She was practical, old-fashioned, and far too self-protective to allow herself the pleasure of the moment, knowing such indulgence would demand painful payment. Even wanting Clay as much as she did couldn't change that. The price was too high, and her heart already too deep in debt.

"Aurelia, if the light is really worrying you . . . well, I can sleep on the spruce boughs. I've slept on a lot less comfortable beds in my life."

"I'm sorry, Clay. I think that might be better." She refastened the buttons of her shirt.

"Sure," he said as though he wasn't quite sure what was happening. He dragged her sleeping bag off the spruce boughs and onto the ground.

She sat on the edge of the bag and removed her boots. Then, turning her back to Clay, she lay down. He lay atop the spruce boughs and stared at the roof of the tent. After a few minutes of silence, he turned his head in her direction.

"That was some gift you gave Waldo. I know how much your buckles mean to you. Hope he appreciates it."

"I'm sure he does."

More silence.

"I gave him a gift of sorts tonight too. When the two of us stepped aside for a few minutes."

"You did? What was that?"

"Well, let me put it this way. If he does half of what I told him to do, tomorrow morning Mrs. Emma Poyser is going to be one happy bride."

It embarrassed Aurelia to hear Clay talk so suggestively, but not enough to ask him to stop. When he spoke again she could tell he'd rolled toward her.

"First, I told him to take his time, she'd be nervous. I told him to kiss her a lot. Women like to be kissed. They do, don't they?"

"Yes," she answered hesitantly.

"I told him to take her clothes off slowly, with a kind of a reverence. And to be sure to tell her how beautiful he thinks she is. I told him breasts were made for sucking, and if he did it right, she'd really like it. That's right too, isn't it?"

"Yes," she mumbled.

"I told him if she wanted him to suck harder, she'd find a way to let him know. She would, wouldn't she?"

Aurelia didn't answer him.

"You did."

Silence.

"I told him not to feel bad if she gets scared the first time she sees his . . . you know, his—"

"I know," she said quickly, hoping that concluded his lesson. She shifted her weight. The sleeping bag didn't feel comfortable anymore. She could hear the crunch of the dry spruce boughs and knew that Clay wasn't resting any easier.

He spoke again, and his voice sounded deeper, as

though he was sharing a secret. "I told him how important it was for him to use his hands."

Aurelia squeezed her eyes tight, but she couldn't erase the image of Clay's large hands as they roamed over her breasts, gathering their fullness, teasing her nipples, arousing them to a point of aching. She curled up, drawing her knees to her chest. She remembered how his long, thick fingers slowly trailed her body, discovering every curve and hollow, searching for ways to please her.

His voice deepened to a whisper. "I told him about a woman's honey . . . how it has its own special fragrance . . . and how it tastes."

Aurelia held her breath.

"I told him that when he licked her, her bones would melt."

She recognized the restless sound of his breathing. It matched her own.

"I told him not to be surprised if she wanted to taste him too."

Color rushed to her cheeks as she tried to picture what he was referring to.

"When a woman's lips are all soft and moist from being kissed . . . and she takes a man into her mouth . . ." He stopped talking.

Aurelia rubbed her moist palms against her overalls.

"'When you enter her,' I told him, 'give her time to . . . adjust. And when you feel her hips begin the rhythm, and you feel her tilt herself up to meet you . . . then fill her . . . again and again and again . . . until she's satisfied.'"

She could hear him stand up.

"I told him there are lots of ways a man can show his wife how much he loves her, but when they reach for each other in the night, that's the best way."

Aurelia rolled on her back and looked up to find Clay standing beside her, his eyes dark with desire. Knowing the heartache that awaited her, she reached out as she whispered, "Pretend I'm your wife."

He knelt down beside her and looked into her eyes. Aurelia knew he loved her, just as she loved him, but he didn't say romantic things about weddings and golden rings that he might have if getting to Dawson meant the beginning of their relationship and not the end.

Instead, he reached for the buttons on her shirt and smiled. "Come tomorrow morning you're going to be even happier than Emma Poyser."

"Sit tight and wave good-bye to civilization," Clay said as he raised the rope that hung over the side of the boat. The rope was wrapped around a stone as big as a twenty-pound sack of flour. "Our anchor," he said with pride. He checked to ensure her safety, then seated himself and grabbed the oars.

"We've got another pair of oars. I can row too," Aurelia said, wanting very much to keep her hands busy and her mind occupied. In love with the man who would destroy her sister, Aurelia had never felt more torn in her life. Her only hope was that Clay would be willing to listen to the truth, for as selfish and spoiled as Violet was, she was not a thief.

"No, there's no need for you to do this. I'll take care of it. If the wind picks up, we can put up the sail. Right now, you just relax and watch the view."

The cold water fanned against the oars as Clay rowed the Golden Girl away from the shore and into the waterway clogged with boats of all shapes and sizes. The lake alternately widened and narrowed.

Instead of one lake, there appeared to be half a dozen, each one unfolding to present the next, each filled with boats headed north.

The hills to the east were bare of snow, with scrawny patches of spruce and jack pine managing only to grow halfway up the side. To the west, however, the high hills still slept under a blanket of snow, with each successive peak whiter than the one before. Glistening on the slopes on both sides were patches of yellow Arctic poppies, scattered like golden nuggets to lure the seekers onward.

After three hours of hard rowing, the wind picked up, and Clay raised the sail. An eager breeze curled the ivory canvas, and by nightfall they'd covered nearly twenty miles.

Clay rowed the boat as close to shore as he could before dropping anchor. "We'll hit Tagish Lake tomorrow," he said. "Word has it that the place is full of fresh fish and game. Now I'm not faulting your cooking, but I'm looking forward to something other than beans."

"You won't get an argument from me. In fact, if it weren't for our lime juice capsules, we'd both have scurvy by now."

"That, my dear Aurelia, is because you're such a good doctor."

I will be someday, she said to herself. Learning required only that she apply herself totally. It didn't depend on being loved.

Satisfied that the boat was secured for the night, Clay jumped over the side and into the water. "Damn! Hip boots or not, that water's cold! Come on, I'll give you a piggyback." He held his hand out for Aurelia. "I know I'm being selfish," he said as she wrapped her arms around his neck and her legs around his waist, "but I'm glad it's just the two of us now." He carried her ashore, then returned to the boat for the tent and a few other things they'd need for the night.

They'd only been ashore a few minutes when Aurelia heard the familiar and dreaded humming of mosquitos. "Oh blast!" she said as she slapped the back of her hand. "When will we be free of these carnivorous pests?"

"Not until July, and we aren't staying here that long. I'll get the tent closed up tight. We'll be all right."

The mosquitos turned out to be even more of an adversary than Clay had imagined. Despite his best efforts, he and Aurelia spent most of the night swatting and swearing. They didn't dare remove their clothes. In a roundabout way, the mosquitos had done Aurelia a favor. The sooner she learned to live without loving Clay, the better. Her heart had already begun to pay for the pleasure they had shared.

Before noon the next day, they arrived at Tagish Lake to a fanfare of barking dogs. All stampeders were required to stop at the police station there, to let the Mounties inspect their boats for seaworthiness, check their customs papers for accuracy, and search their boats for liquor. Clay explained that the cosmetic case fastened tightly to the underside of the seat was a medical kit, the lady doctor's medical kit. Aurelia was relieved to hear the Mounties accept his explanation.

While Clay and the Mounties continued their inspection, Aurelia wrote and posted a quick letter to her parents. She wrote that she herself was well and expected to reach Dawson in a week or so. She deliberately avoided telling them the rumors she'd heard about Violet, promising to bring her little sister home safe and sound.

All things in order, they set sail again. A stiff breeze moved them along, and by nightfall they'd passed through Lake Tagish, Lake Marsh, and halfway through the Sixty Mile River, covering a total distance of over fifty miles. Along the shore, boulders of white limestone jutted into the water like hedges of granite. Chunks of ice moved sluggishly past them, thwarting a straight passage.

"We'll have to face the Whitehorse Rapids tomorrow," Clay said as he pitched their tent for the night.

"You sound concerned."

"I am. Enough that I've decided we'll unload the boat just before we get to the rapids. I'll have to spend a day, maybe two, maybe three, carrying the load around the canyon. It's the safest way."

Aurelia groaned at the thought of packing their cache again.

Clay looked eager to ease her worries. "*You* aren't going to be doing any packing. I am."

Shaking her head at the absurdity of his thinking, Aurelia said, "No. I'm just as capable as I was when we left Dyea."

"No," he said, with equal conviction. "I don't want you to strain yourself. Now, here's the plan. While we were at the Tagish post, I hired a river pilot named Rider to take the boat through. The going rate's as high as a hundred, but we're only paying forty because the boat will be empty. It'll be worth it. After I haul the cache, you and I can walk around the canyon. It's only about five miles."

Agonizing memories of crossing the Chilkoot Pass came back to her. Aurelia didn't want Clay straining himself either. "No, Clay. As long as we're hiring a pilot to take the boat through the rapids, let's leave the cache on board and go with him. It'll be so much faster."

Clay shook his head. "There's a hundred-dollar fine on the owner of any boat caught taking women or children through those rapids."

Aurelia's eyes widened at the outrageous sum. "A hundred-dollar fine? The rapids are that dangerous?"

"Even if there weren't a fine, I wouldn't take that kind of chance. Not with you."

She softened at his concern.

Clay continued, "One wrong move and the Golden Girl's nothing but a pile of toothpicks. You'll see for yourself tomorrow. Right now let's eat and get some rest. You look tired. I'll get us a fire going."

While Aurelia set about preparing another meal of beans, corn bread and coffee, her heart ached, knowing that as soon as they reached Dawson the intimacy she and Clay had created would have to end.

No sooner had she begun mixing the cornmeal when a small black cloud of buzzing gnats teamed up with a thicker cloud of mosquitos and descended upon her. "Breeders of insanity," she swore as she twirled a wet towel in the air, trying to keep them away.

Clay worked as quickly as he could to anchor the sides of the tent with rocks, burying every inch in the sand. "Let's get inside," he said, "and I'll seal us off."

"Gladly." Aurelia ducked inside. Clay joined her a few moments later. The smoke from the fire helped keep the pests at bay, but the more persistent ones still managed to rob the couple of sleep—and the chance for love.

They'd gone a few miles down the river the next morning when Aurelia noticed that the terrain looked different. "The weather must be warmer here," she said, noticing that the rolling hillsides flanking the river were covered with spruce and pine, now and then breaking to reveal a grassy prairie or a valley densely wooded with poplars and willows of several varieties. In many places the willows grew in such profusion they encroached on the water's edge, heavy veils of tender green fronds making it impossible for a boat to land.

The *plump* sound she heard over and over again came from the plentiful muskrats as they dove into the water from the shore. The crystal clear water turned to a kaleidoscope of figures as the boats and the little animals created wedge-shaped ripples on the silver surface.

How could anything so beautiful be feared? Aurelia rested her hand on the side of the boat, doubtful of Clay's dire predictions about the Whitehorse Rapids still to come.

Then, what had been a vague and distant rumble suddenly vibrated through the wood and into her hand.

21

"Where's Rider?" Clay gripped the oars as he anxiously scanned the riverbanks, searching for the navigator he'd hired. Aurelia, white-knuckled and terrified, held fast to the sides of the boat and saw the panic-stricken faces of those watching from ashore.

"Where the hell is Rider?"

It was too late. The greedy current snatched the Golden Girl and refused to let go.

The thunderous rumble Aurelia had heard for miles now pounded in her ears. She gasped at the frightening sight ahead. The river suddenly narrowed to one-tenth its size, squeezed by sky-scraping columns of dark gray corrugated rock. Towering evergreens on both sides shadowed each other, blocking the sunlight, beckoning the boat forward.

Clay waved his arm. "Get down!"

"Down? There's no room."

"Then we'll make room." As fast as he could, Clay tossed overboard the boxes and barrels and sacks he'd so carefully wedged and packed. The white-capped water gobbled them up.

The boat rocked. Milklike foam sprayed over the sides, wetting Aurelia's hair and face.

"I said get down," Clay shouted. "Now!"

"What about you!"

Clay had grabbed the oars again, but even as his muscles flexed and his knuckles whitened, the river's wrath snatched the oars away and snapped them in two. Hopelessly locked in the current, the boat entered the chute.

Clay took one last look at the nightmare ahead of them before he hit the deck and covered Aurelia's body with his own.

Water splashed over the sides. Aurelia fought to breathe as water and foam filled the bottom of the boat. With a viciousness only the devil himself could have spawned, the water whipped them into the canyon and shot them through with the speed of an arrow.

An eerie calm followed. While the boat rocked gently in a pool of still water, Clay and Aurelia guardedly lifted their heads. If the canyon had been a horror, the sight ahead was hell.

Whirlpools churned all around them, working the water to a frenzy. Waves four feet high smashed against each other and swirled into a seething cauldron of white foam. The boat yielded to the force and was lifted high into the air, only to be slapped down again and again.

"Hold on!" Clay shouted. "Hold on!"

Aurelia coughed and sputtered as the river drowned her screams.

Twenty-six minutes later it was over. The battered Golden Girl drifted toward shore. Clay lowered himself over the side and pulled the boat to dry land.

"We could have been killed," Aurelia said, her fingers still locked on the sides of the boat, her tears blending with the water dripping from her hair. "The boat could have capsized. We could have drowned."

"But we didn't," he said, giving her a shaky smile as he pried one of her hands free. "Come on." He coaxed her to her feet.

Aurelia climbed out, her knees buckling at the feel of solid earth beneath her feet. "You all right?" Clay asked as he helped her onto a warm boulder. "Here. Sit down." Tenderly he touched the bruises on her nose and cheeks where her face had scraped the bottom of the boat.

She nodded. "I guess so. What about you?" Aurelia winced at the cuts and bruises visible through his shirt and pants, which had been torn by the rough edges of boxes and crates as they'd been violently tossed about. His hands were bruised as well, and his knuckles scraped raw. She moved to fetch her medical box. She knew it had survived, as Clay had strapped it to the seat.

"Don't go," he said. He wrapped his arms around her and held her against his chest. "Aurelia, I'm sorry. I should have anchored long before we reached the rapids. I should have waited to find the pilot. I just didn't realize we were that close."

Forcing levity to her words, she said, "I was the one who wanted to take the shortest route." Neither one laughed. Even in the safety of Clay's embrace, Aurelia relived the experience and trembled.

For hours on end, they salvaged what they could, dragging supplies and equipment to shore and spreading them on the mossy bank to dry. They worked in silence, except for occasional comments on how lucky they'd been to survive. Not once did Aurelia question whether finding Violet warranted risking her own life. If Clay questioned his own risk now, he said nothing.

Finally, when they could do no more, Aurelia stretched herself across a sun-baked boulder and relished its soothing warmth. "Now what?" she asked.

"Nothing. We just rest."

"Good," she said and closed her eyes, trying to sort her thoughts about how far she'd come and what she'd left behind. A moment or so later, she asked, "Clay, what brought you to Seattle?"

Looking weary, Clay slumped to the ground and leaned against the boulder. "Eli," he said. "When Mary died, Aunt Liza came out to Kansas to help me with the boy, but she made it clear her stay was temporary. The prairie was too far from civilization for her. She'd come out before, after my paw died. She stayed three years that time, taught me what I needed to know to make it on my own. Anyway, when Mary died, Liza convinced me that if she took Eli back with her to Seattle—got him away from that empty prairie, he'd have a better chance. After the kind of life I'd had out there, I had to agree with her."

"So you let your Aunt Liza take your son?"

"Oh no, I couldn't do that. So I went to Seattle too. See, Mary's father had been the town banker. I'd worked for him for a year or so to get enough money to buy my own place. He liked having me work for him. It meant Mary and I had to live in town. Anyway, I had enough banking experience to get a job at a bank in Seattle. Bought a nice house. Liza helped me find a nanny for Eli. All in all, we had a pretty good life, little Eli and I."

Relaying the story must have made him uncomfortable. He stood up, stretched, then made some excuse about having to check the boat again and walked away. Aurelia heard the part of the story that remained untold, that if it hadn't been for Violet and Sculley, Clay would still have his pretty good life.

That night his contemplative mood still held. Aurelia

watched Clay stare into the dying campfire. For what seemed like forever, he idly poked and prodded the glowing coals, scraping the ashes into neat little mounds. "A penny for your thoughts," she said softly.

"Just thinking about a job I had once."

"Tell me about it."

"I was thirteen."

"Thirteen. I bet you were a handsome young man."

"No, not quite." He smiled to acknowledge her compliment, but the look in his eyes was not happy. My pant legs ended a good three inches above my ankles, and my voice cracked every time I opened my mouth—or at least every time I wanted to say something to Georgia Sweetwater. She was eleven, the storekeep's daughter, and my first true love.

"Anyway, one summer morning the carnival came to town. More than anything in this world, I wanted to ask Georgia Sweetwater to ride the merry-go-round with me. But I didn't have any money.

"So, when Abner Coleman, the blacksmith, offered me a job sweeping ashes, I jumped at the chance. The carnival would only be in town for that one night, so I had to work hard. I kept thinking what it'd be like to ride side by side on those fancy wooden horses. I decided that's when I'd hold Georgia's hand."

Clay looked up to find Aurelia enchanted by his story. "Go on," she said. "Tell me about how you and Miss Sweetwater rode the merry-go-round."

"Never happened," Clay said and turned his gaze back to the fire. "Oh, I shoveled ashes all day. I kept pestering Coleman to tell me the time. I needed at least an hour to scrub the soot off my skin and out of my hair, and I could already hear the snappy organ music of the carnival. Anyway, it was past suppertime when I finally finished. I went to Coleman for my pay. He told me I'd done a good job and handed me a cigar."

"A cigar?"

"That's right," Clay said. "I stammered something about expecting cash. Told him I was hoping for twenty-five cents. 'Course, I'd been dreaming of fifty. He laughed. Said I expected too much, especially for being Guardian's kid."

Aurelia stiffened. "What a mean, selfish, manipulative man! He *owed* you! You didn't let him get away with that, I hope."

"I did then." Clay looked straight into Aurelia's eyes, "But I learned. No one's ever taken advantage of me since."

The next day was blessedly uneventful, as was the day after, and the day after that. Clay didn't mention Violet's name, but he didn't have to. Aurelia knew he was thinking of Violet, and so was she. She also knew that the closer they got to Dawson, the more important it was for her to distance herself emotionally from Clay. That became her assignment. Despite the fact that she loved him, her first duty was to Violet, just as Clay's was to Eli.

Sailing along Lake LeBarge, Aurelia caught herself staring at him, at the man who was once the little boy whose faith had been betrayed, whose hopes had been crushed. No wonder he found it hard to trust anyone. Fate had conspired to throw them together, and for that Aurelia would always be grateful. But fate had also destined them to end up apart, and to live with that Aurelia needed both memories and courage. She stared at him again.

She committed to memory his cheekbones and chisled

jaw and how those rugged features characterized his strength. She had strength as well. She'd finish school, set up practice, and devote herself to helping others. She would remember those dark penetrating eyes and how they had looked at her with love. And the shadow of stubble that was so quick to conceal his dimples.

She felt a stab to her heart. No man on earth could ever give her the pleasure he had. She chastised herself for failing her assignment. The more she tried to think of her life apart from Clay, the more tightly she held him in her heart.

Clay cringed. If she didn't stop staring at him, he was going to, well, he didn't know what he would do. She'd told him about what went on in the dissecting room once. That was probably where she'd like to see him right about then, and he didn't have anyone to blame but himself. He'd been a fool to tell her that story about Coleman and the cigar. Truth was, Clay didn't know what made him think about the old ingrate, but by the time he had come to the end of the story, he knew he was thinking about Violet, not Coleman. Aurelia knew it too, Clay could tell by the pain in her eyes.

Just this afternoon, she'd marveled at the telegraph poles strung all along the river. She had said it was inspiring to see evidence of adventurous pioneers. She hadn't said much in days. And had he seized the opportunity to rebuild the bridge between them? No. He'd pointed out the bleached wooden slabs and simple burial mounds that also marked the trail and, in his own self-righteous way, said that every adventure had its cost.

What he wanted to do was shake her. Force her to

see that her blind devotion to a scheming, manipulative thief would destroy their love.

He turned away so she couldn't see his face. Honor demanded a high price, but what good was a man without it?

Eleven days after leaving Lake Bennett, Clay and Aurelia made camp for the night at a beautiful spot. The gentle hills ran so close to the gravelly shore, there was no room to pitch the tent and barely enough room to set up the stove. A gurgling brook ran nearby, its banks a mattress of soft green moss. Pink phlox, magenta shooting stars, yellow poppies, white heather, and blue forget-me-nots blanketed the hills like colorful patches on a green quilt.

Clay pulled the boat as far ashore as he could and tied it to a tree. They'd seen too many abandoned boats along the riverbanks to trust a rock for an anchor. As he did every night, he strung a sheet of canvas between two trees to afford Aurelia the privacy she needed for personal matters.

"We'll spread the sleeping bags by the brook," Clay said as he unloaded the stove and handed Aurelia the few things they'd need for the night. "Looks comfortable enough."

Awestruck by the gentle beauty of the land, Aurelia gave voice to her private thoughts. "One day I'd like to come back here with Violet, on pleasure bent, of course. The artist in her would marvel at this beauty."

Clay looked angry. "Aurelia, don't you understand? Violet isn't ever coming here for pleasure. She's coming to Seattle with me."

"Why is it always Violet? You never talk about

bringing Sculley to justice. If what you say about Violet is true, then Sculley is just as much at fault. So why do you never talk about bringing him to justice?"

"Because while Sculley may have been the accomplice, it was Violet who robbed me."

"Aren't you going to even listen to her version of the story?"

"Of course I am. She can tell it to both of us. We'll be in Dawson tomorrow."

Tomorrow. Aurelia's stomach clenched. If she wanted him to spare Violet, she'd have to tell him the whole truth. Painful memories slowed her movements while she gathered driftwood for the fire.

Clay busied himself cleaning the fish he'd caught earlier that day. Later that evening, he laid the pink filets in the hot frying pan. "Bet this salmon didn't expect to wind up on our dinner table tonight."

"A fish only sees the hook," Aurelia said.

"What?"

"Something Nana Brooke used to say. She meant that if a fish could see beyond the hook, it wouldn't let itself get caught. But, it can't see beyond the hook, so it gets trapped. People are like that sometimes. They can't see beyond the lure."

"Or won't see," Clay added.

His closed mind was no surprise. If she expected his sympathy for Violet, she'd be disappointed. Undaunted, she inhaled deeply and said, "Clay, what I've told you about my sister and Fletcher Sculley is true. But I haven't told you the entire story. You see, Violet wouldn't be here at all if it weren't for me." The pain of her guilt spawned tears that slid down her cheeks. She wiped them away with the back of her hand.

Clay set the frying pan aside, willing to listen.

"I'd never been to a dance hall before," Aurelia continued, "and I would never have gone that night. But it was the last day of exams, and my classmates kept urging me to throw caution to the wind and celebrate with them. Of course, we all knew that to frequent a dance hall was against the rules of the school. If we were caught, we could be dismissed.

"I didn't have many close friends at school. I spent so much of my time studying. But I did enjoy a feeling of camaraderie with the others in the boardinghouse. I wanted to belong."

Clay sat on a rock opposite Aurelia and leaned forward, bracing his elbows on his legs. "You wanted to celebrate, so you stepped out on the town with your friends."

"No, I mean yes. Yes, I did step out on the town, so to speak, with my friends, but not because I wanted to celebrate. You see, it was the end of the semester, and Violet had come to visit me for a few weeks. I wanted to show off in front of my little sister. I wanted to flaunt in her face the fact that I was strong enough to defy outdated notions about women and obtain an education. I wanted Violet to think I engaged in such worldly escapades all the time."

Aurelia dug the toes of her boots into the sand, needing to be anchored to continue. "I wanted to say to Violet, 'You may be able to attract all the young men you want, but that ability is not important to me.'"

Clay nodded slowly, as though he could accept the honesty of her admission. She continued.

"The dance hall wasn't far from the school. There were seven of us, including Violet. Two of the girls made a point to smile at every man who looked our way. The rest of us sat at the table trying not to stare at the bawdy posters on the walls and forcing ourselves not to grimace at the taste of beer. We had each ordered a whole one.

"As usual, it wasn't long before every man in the establishment noticed Violet. My friends were *thrilled*. There was my sister, drawing to our table the most handsome gentlemen in the room. And then, as though the men were hers to parcel out, she'd say, 'No, I can't dance with you right now, but Amy here would love to.' Or Sara, or Bernice. Thanks to Violet and her immeasurable charms, all my friends were asked to dance. At one point Bernice told me how lucky I was to have such a beautiful sister. Funny, I remember thinking, I never thought of myself as lucky."

Aurelia paused a moment to collect her thoughts. The worst of her confession was yet to come. "Everyone was dancing but me. And then a young man approached the table. I knew he was coming to see me because I was the only one still there. He wasn't particularly handsome, but he appeared clean-cut and somewhat shy. He said he'd just moved to Philadelphia from the Midwest. He was an accountant and had been offered a job with a firm in town. He asked me to dance, something no one had ever done on his own volition. Just as I had mustered the courage to say yes, Violet returned to the table. She took his arm and, in that way she had about her, she made him think he was taking *her* to the dance floor. I heard her giggling as she told him that even after three coming out parties, I still couldn't dance. That was the last I saw of the accountant.

"Later that night, long after we should have all returned to our boardinghouse, Fletcher Sculley arrived. Dressed in his policeman's uniform, he cut a dashing figure. Violet easily dismissed the accountant and turned her attention to what I'm sure she considered a more difficult conquest."

Aurelia stood up and paced behind the fire. "She said she needed my advice. Sculley had held her dangerously close when they danced, and he had asked to see her alone. She asked me what I knew of him, other than the obvious fact that he was older, at least thirty, wielded his authority with a domineering air, spent his money freely on whiskey, and possessed a magnetism that was very seductive."

Aurelia's voice cracked at the painful memory. "I should have set my anger aside. I should have told her the truth, that Sculley had a reputation as a crooked cop who made his money on the sale of chloral and opium. I should have told her, but I thought she'd toy with him just as she had the accountant and then discard him like so much rubble.

"I never dreamed my sister would run away with Fletcher Sculley before the week was out. She was only sixteen. I had to explain to my parents why I hadn't taken better care of my little sister."

"And you felt guilty," Clay said.

"Of course I felt guilty!"

"Why didn't you report Sculley to the authorities for abducting your sister?"

Aurelia stared into the fire. She couldn't bring herself to look Clay in the eye. "That's the worst part of all. If I had reported Sculley, I would have had to explain to the school and to my parents why we were in a Philadelphia dance hall and why we were drinking beer. I would have been dismissed from school. And my parents would have disowned me. So I kept silent." Aurelia sat down on the rock again. "I chose my own ambitions over my sister's welfare. But as God is my judge, I never dreamed it would go this far."

"It was her choice," Clay said with a stinging criticism that surprised Aurelia. "Violet chose to go with Sculley. She could have said no."

"Violet was much too innocent to have made a reasoned judgment."

He looked unconvinced. "Didn't any of the other young ladies in your group tell Violet about Sculley's reputation?"

"How would I know? If they did, she didn't know well enough to believe them."

"And if they didn't, I'll bet it was because Violet appeared quite capable of handling herself."

Aurelia shook her head vehemently. "You don't know her the way I do. There's a part of Violet that is innocent and kind, a part that brought joy to my life and to many others as well. In any event I will have no peace until I find my sister and obtain her forgiveness."

Clay gave her a smile of self-satisfaction, as though he'd just come to a revelation of importance. "So your real motive is a selfish one."

Until that moment, Aurelia had never recognized the self-serving aspect of her quest. Clay's penetrating gaze increased her discomfort. "No more than yours," she snapped.

They ate in silence, with no more mention of Aurelia's need to rescue Violet and obtain her forgiveness or Clay's need to capture Violet and restore his good name. Each spent the night comforted by the thought that he or she was doing the right thing.

Ten miles outside Dawson, Clay rowed the boat ashore and loaded it with as much firewood as it would hold. From other stampeders all along the river he'd heard warnings of the shortage of wood in Dawson. He'd also heard of the shortage of space on shore. Two miles outside Dawson, a medley of boats three and four thick edged both sides of the Yukon River.

Her heart racing with anticipation, Aurelia craned her neck as Clay skirted the small islands that dotted the junction of the Yukon and Klondike rivers. Not fast enough to suit her, they rounded the bend and entered the flat, black mud marsh. They had reached Dawson at last.

For a moment she thought they were in the wrong place. How could this crowding of humble tents and stilt-perched shanties be called the Paris of the North? She'd expected a more permanent, more civilized town, one in which decent people would immediately offer assistance to a young girl in trouble. Feeling a vague but growing sense of uneasiness, she sharpened her focus. Farther inland stood a few frame buildings, plenty of log cabins, and plenty more tents. Halfway up the gently tapering mountain behind the town sat thousands and thousands of white and gray canvas tents.

Aurelia cautioned herself to remain calm while Clay found a small wedge of muddy shore on which to beach the Golden Girl, but the thought of finding her sister made Aurelia restless. "Can't we tend to the usual landing routine later?" she asked.

"Calm down. She's here, we'll find her. All we have to do is check the saloons."

"Don't be so sure of yourself. You may be in for a surprise."

Aurelia climbed out of the boat, not caring how improper she looked in her overalls, and not bothering to see if Clay was coming too. But he was right behind her.

They passed a ragtag group of children playing on

the muddy beach, barefoot little girls in dirty dresses selling apples for a dollar each, and little boys hawking old Seattle newspapers, also a dollar each. "How can people charge such outrageous sums for a piece of fruit or news from home? I pity those who haven't struck it rich. They must be desperate."

"Desperate?" Clay asked, as though he suspected a hidden meaning in her observation. "Already making excuses for her?"

His growing insensitivity rankled Aurelia. "That's enough," she said and turned around.

"What's enough?"

Deaf to his questions, Aurelia marched back to the boat.

"Where are you going?" he yelled.

She retrieved her medical box and small satchel. "It's time we parted company," she said, anger clipping her words. "Don't look so surprised. What did you expect? That I'd simply lead you to my sister, then stand aside while you drag her away?"

"You can't go into that town alone. It's not safe."

"I'm not afraid."

"Where will you stay?"

"I'll find a room. This place can't be as bad as Dyea or Canyon City."

He placed his hands on her shoulders. "Aurelia, be reasonable."

She jerked away. "I am being reasonable! We both knew it would come to this."

Relieved that Clay didn't kiss her or say he loved her or do anything else to make their parting more painful than it already was, Aurelia balanced her belongings on her hips and set out for town. She didn't dare look back.

22

In desperate need of architectural surgery—
that's how the town looked to Aurelia, with row upon
row of rickety one-room shacks, some built of old packing crates, some of tar paper stretched over wooden frames,
and some of kerosene tins opened up and flattened out.
Dozens of amputated trees with stumps three feet high
clogged the main artery, Front Street. Uprooted scrub
brush were left to wither and die.

Experienced now with the riotous movement of stampeders, Aurelia easily dodged horses, wagons, and teams
of dogs to reach the safety of a crudely built wooden sidewalk. Scanning the ornate signs that swung freely over
slapped-together shanties, she found one that said Hotel.

After checking in, she returned to the street. She'd
come to find Violet, and there was no time like the present to begin her search. Though she didn't believe Clay
was right about Violet's working in a dance hall, Aurelia
knew he'd begin his search in Dawson's saloons. Whatever
information he might find there, she had to find first.

There were twenty-eight saloons! Most had elaborate false fronts, but several also boasted handsome
bay windows, carved balustrades, and fancy names

like the Can Can, the Monte Carlo, and the Floradora. Did people do nothing here but drink and gamble? Twenty-eight saloons. It could take weeks to interview the proprietors of all of them.

A hand-lettered flier caught her eye. She stepped around a pile of goods and a sleeping drunk to gain a closer look at the advertisement nailed to the white-washed wall of the Hallelujah Bar. It was closed until eight o'clock when the orchestra would begin its nightly performance. An orchestra! Violet loved classical music. She might frequent an establishment that offered culture. Aurelia made a note to come back to the Hallelujah at eight o'clock.

Then she walked on to investigate the rest of the town and continue her search. The candy-striped pole outside Buddy's Barber Shop assured her that at least some people in Dawson cared about appearances, but no one inside recognized the Kodak of Violet. The tasteful gold-lettered sign outside Madame Rousseau's offered the best in dressmaking and millinery from Paris, but Madame Rousseau was too busy to answer Aurelia's questions. Another shop offered red geraniums, lace parasols, and incense; another, English tea and scones. But no one knew Violet.

The woman in the tea shop suggested Aurelia go to the Mounties. She wished she could, but if—*if*—Violet was as guilty as Clay claimed, Aurelia would be doing Violet more harm than good. No, she had to find her sister on her own.

Aurelia polished her single remaining buckle before leaving her room. *I need courage, Nana,* she said to herself.

Promptly at eight she headed for the Hallelujah Bar. The muddy street was filled with both weary-looking miners and fresh-faced stampeders, most of them too devastated and too drunk to stand. They needed courage too. All afternoon Aurelia had heard the depressing news. Claims in the Klondike gold fields had all been staked the year before. There was no gold for the newcomers. For them, the trip had been in vain.

"I need courage, Nana," she said again as she stepped through the door to hear the last few bars of "Swanee River." Fanning the tobacco smoke, she witnessed a mad promenade to the bar by the couples who had just finished dancing.

The men appeared no different from those she'd seen for the last three months. Many had beards, most had droopy mustaches, all wore hats or caps, and a few wore vests and white shirts. All reeked from free-flowing whiskey and sweat.

But the women! They were amply figured, with painted faces and peroxided hair. They wore the skimpiest, the most decadent costumes, some baring their legs all the way to their upper thighs. And gaudy! Red velvet with black fringe, green satin with purple beads, silver braid, gold tassels, feathered plumes. No lady of Aurelia's acquaintance ever wore such scandalous attire, certainly not Violet. Violet's entire wardrobe was a variation on ivory silk or pink satin.

When she was caught staring, Aurelia turned toward the bar, only to face three seven-foot-high oil paintings of full-figured nudes.

A dark-haired woman with an emerald chip planted in her front tooth plunked a shot of whiskey in front of her. "Evening, sugar. Welcome to the Hallelujah Bar. I'm Glory Glory. You looking for a job?"

"No," Aurelia said quickly.

"Well, if you're looking for gold, you're too late. And if you're looking for a husband, well, you'll have to dip your finger in the rouge pot and shed those overalls. But if you're just looking for a man, well, you've got potential. There's still fortunes to be made here in Dawson."

Aurelia colored at the implication. "I'm looking for information," she said as she took out the picture of Violet. "Have you seen this girl?"

Glory took the picture. Her smile faded. "Never saw her before in my life," she said and handed the photo back.

"Are you positive? It's important that I find her. Here, take another look."

"Don't need to. I'd remember a sweet-looking face like that."

"She's my sister," Aurelia said, fighting the lump that suddenly formed in her throat.

Never in a million years did Aurelia expect to see a woman the likes of Glory Glory take pity on her, but that's exactly what Aurelia saw in the woman's kohl-lined eyes. And when Glory spoke again, it was with compassion.

"Go on back to the Outside while you still can. There ain't nothing here for you to find. Claims have all been staked—"

"I'm not looking for gold! I'm looking for my sister!"

Glory shook her head. She came around the bar, linked her arm with Aurelia's, and led her to the door. "Go on back now. That sweet little girl ain't in Dawson. Go on back."

From out on the street, Aurelia looked back at the swinging door of the Hallelujah Bar. "You're lying, Miss Glory Glory," she whispered in defiance. "Right through your emerald-chipped tooth."

Aurelia needed to learn more about the local population. They were the ones most likely to recognize Violet. Early the next morning, she introduced herself to the druggist at the apothecary and asked if her expertise might be useful. Instead of giving her the down-the-nose look she'd expected, Herb Wilson sounded genuinely thrilled to have her in town.

He took her to the clinic that afternoon and introduced her to the undertaker, Simpson O'Day, who ran both operations. While he too was glad to see another medical professional in town, all he wanted to talk about was the skit he was going to perform when he put on a turn at the Pavilion, the new variety theater opening soon.

Bewildered, Aurelia turned to Herb Wilson. "Has this town always been so topsy-turvy? Tents and pavilions. Saloons alongside Paris fashions. Drunks passed out in front of a tea shop. Strong men who've lost everything in search of some golden will-o'-the-wisp, begging for drinks alongside instant millionaires too busy to bathe?"

"It's just Dawson," Herb said with a smile.

Simpson O'Day slid his slender fingers along the edge of a newly lined coffin. "Miss Breighton, do you sing, by chance?"

"No," she said, confused by his question.

"Well, I don't dare sing at the Pavilion alone. I suppose I'll just have to wait till that lovely sweet voice from Detroit is well enough to sing again."

She froze in both hope and dread. Slowly, Aurelia retrieved Violet's picture and handed it to Mr. O'Day.

"Is this the young lady you speak of? She was several years younger when this was taken."

He studied the photo with a confused look on his face. Then he beamed. "That's her all right. Vera Brooke. Prettiest voice in the Hallelujah Bar."

Excitement overruled manners as Aurelia grabbed the picture back. "Thank you, Mr. O'Day. I must run." Before O'Day said another word, Aurelia was out the door and halfway down the street.

"Tsk, tsk, tsk," O'Day said to Wilson. "If she'd waited half a minute, I'd have warned her not to go snooping around the Hallelujah. That's Sculley's place."

Glory Glory radiated anything but the splendor her name implied. Straddling a barstool, wearing a less-than-modest red nightdress, she hiked her feather boa back up to her shoulder and chugged the whiskey in front of her. She held out her tongue for the last drop, then turned to Aurelia. "So you think I know your sister?"

"Vera Brooke. That's the name she's using. Mr. O'Day—"

"Simpson O'Day is a simple-minded, limp-wristed, stiff planter."

"I'm not interested in your impression of Mr. O'Day. I'm interested in finding my sister. If you don't tell me where she is, I'll be forced to go to the Mounties for help." She prayed the threat would work, for alerting the Mounties was the last thing Aurelia wanted to do.

Glory sneered as she hiked her wayward boa again. "Come on," she said as she led Aurelia to a table in the back of the room. "You a drinking woman?"

"No. Thank you."

Glory rolled her eyes. "Of course not."

Seated at the table, Glory crossed her legs and let her feathered mule dangle off the end of her foot. "So, you want me to tell you where Vera is?"

"Yes," Aurelia said, wishing she could conceal the eagerness in her voice.

"What's it worth to you?"

Aurelia was taken aback. It didn't occur to her she'd have to pay for information, but then that's what Clay had had to do with that Ruby Lips woman back in Dyea. The realization that she had nothing to offer Glory deflated Aurelia's bravado instantly. "I don't have any money. I spent everything I had just to get here."

Glory sighed with impatience. "Jewelry. You got any jewelry?"

"No."

"What about that fancy boot buckle?"

Nana, please understand. Aurelia thought as she fumbled with the straps that held her silver legacy and handed the buckle to Glory. "Here. Take it. Now where's my sister?"

"Hmm." Glory smirked. "Only one buckle. Suppose I could use it on a belt. But I still don't know as that's enough. How 'bout you work for me a few nights? I got customers always looking for something new."

Aurelia recoiled at the thought.

Glory laughed. "You're a priggish prima dona, just like your sister."

"Then you do know Violet!"

"Vera. Two weeks on Fletcher Sculley's magic elixir and she's what you might call a new woman."

Fletcher Sculley. Aurelia's blood turned cold at the mention of his name. "Sculley has enslaved my sister to drugs?"

"Now don't you sound high and mighty? What

makes you think your sister didn't develop her own devotion to the tonic? She certainly took to my wardrobe fast enough. But not as fast as my regulars took to her, if you get my meaning."

Fear made Aurelia insistent. "Where is she?"

"You might say she's in seclusion, her being in the family way and all."

"Violet's pregnant?"

Glory didn't answer but looked over Aurelia's shoulder at the man walking toward them.

"*Was* pregnant," the man said as though he'd been standing there for some time, privy to their conversation all along.

Aurelia spun around to find Fletcher Sculley standing before her, holding a bundled infant in his arms. He looked like a dandy, with his bowler tipped just so, his shirt clean and starched, complete with gold fob and spats. Aurelia jumped up. "You monster! What have you done to my sister?"

"Well, well now. Can it really be? The long-suffering but spirited older sister come to save her sibling from . . . from what?"

"From you, you bastard."

"Look at me," he said, drawing her glance to the baby, "the wholesome image of a family man. I'll bet the ladies will just love it." He laughed a sinister kind of laugh.

"Is that Violet's baby?" She held her arms out, hoping he'd pass the child to her.

"It is," Sculley answered as he stepped back, making it clear he had no intention of even showing the baby to Aurelia. "And it came no time too soon. That disgusting bloated belly kept your sister out of work for weeks. She can't earn her keep that way." He spat on the floor, then smiled wickedly. "Though there is that small depraved segment that loves to burrow into a mare about to foal."

Revulsion swept over Aurelia. Through clenched teeth, she asked again, "Where is she?"

Sculley laughed. "What a little tough you've become. Don't know as I care for the change. I liked you better the last time I saw you. Not so mouthy. Took me a long time to break your sister of that habit, but I managed. Isn't that right, Glory?"

Aurelia looked at Glory and searched her reddened eyes for denial. All she saw was fear.

Sculley sneered. "Go drown yourself in your bottle, you old hag." He shifted the weight of the baby with less care than Aurelia would give a sack of potatoes. "Tell you what, Miss High and Mighty, I'm going to show you just how decent a man I am. You come with me right now, and we'll go calling on your little sister."

Anxious as she was to get to Violet, Aurelia knew she didn't dare go anywhere with Sculley alone. That dog hadn't changed his evil ways. He might have been wearing a respectable suit, but from the way he bared his yellow teeth and the way he pawed the bundle in his arms, Aurelia knew he was still as dangerous as ever.

"How 'bout it, sis? You can hold your new niece too. She's sleeping now. Been acting poorly." He jostled the bundle again, and Aurelia caught a peak of dark hair. "Doesn't cry much though. Just twitches."

Aurelia couldn't bear the thought of this criminal so carelessly holding an innocent child. She had to do something.

"Your sister ain't been feeling too good neither," Sculley added. "Took her three days of screaming to push the thing out. I gave her a blanket, but she still complains about being cold. Hell, I gave her all the opium she wanted. I even gave her some she didn't want." He shook his head "Women," he added with disdain.

"That's enough. I'm leaving here right now, and I'm going straight to the Mounties. I'll have you arrested."

"On what charges?" He feigned an innocent look. "Working hard to take care of my wife and baby?"

Her eyes widened.

"That's right. I married her. She insisted." He toyed with the blankets swaddling the baby. "Hard to say who's the father. For a while there your little sister was the most popular whore in Dawson. Could have been any one of a hundred men." He glanced at the infant again and leered in a manner so revolting it terrified Aurelia.

"Here," he said and offered her the child. "I just brought her along as insurance to get you to go with me."

Aurelia quickly took the baby in her arms. Before she pulled back the blanket covering its face, she knew something was wrong. The child was too quiet, too still.

She lifted the flannel, gasped and felt for the carotid artery. Her eyes brimmed. "She's dead."

"I thought she was asleep," Sculley said. "She was crying just a half an hour ago."

She whispered as she stroked her finger across its cheek. "Poor baby."

Glory came over next to Aurelia and held out her arms. "Give me the babe. Don't worry. I'll bring her over to O'Day."

Aurelia hesitated. Her eyes brimmed anew as she saw Violet's delicate features reborn in the tip of the baby's nose, the tiny mouth, and the few downy wisps of dark hair. Life, with its lure of happiness, lost to both this tiny child and its mother. How devastated Violet would be "Take me to my sister," she said, knowing her desperation showed, as she handed the baby to Glory.

"That's more like it." He gestured toward the door. "Shall we?"

"I need my medical case. It's at the clinic."

"Certainly. Bring pain-killers. Violet's been complaining. It's been four days, and she's not improving the way I'd like. I was almost ready to have old Herb Wilson have a look at her, then I heard you'd come to town. Now I won't have to spend the money."

Four days without medical attention? Violet could easily have contracted an infection. Aurelia thought of her frail sister and prayed that Sculley was painting the picture bleaker than it was. She felt her hatred growing for the man as they went to the clinic.

"One other thing," Sculley added as they approached the door. "It wouldn't do any good for you—or for Violet—to mention my name. Understand?"

She understood all too well. Fortunately, Mr. O'Day wasn't in the clinic, which spared her from having to come up with some excuse for running off so quickly. After checking the contents of her medical case, particularly the concealed compartment, Aurelia latched the case and left.

"No need to draw attention," Sculley said as he squeezed her arm and pulled her through a maze of muddy side streets and lonely, rubbish-strewn alleys.

"You too?" Glory asked the man. She filled her lipstick-smeared glass with whiskey and held it close to his face. "A man as handsome as you comes to see me, he's looking for a pair of soft tits and a hot—"

She laughed when he declined the drink.

"You're saying someone else has already been here looking for Violet Breighton?"

"Her sister, or so she said." Glory downed the drink, then dabbed a handkerchief to her reddened nose and bloated face. "Popular girl, that Violet."

"The sister. When did she leave? Where did she go?"

Clay wanted Sculley too, but the Mounties said he owned the Hallelujah and could be found there every night. The Mounties also said they'd welcome hard evidence against Sculley. The shameless *macques* made his living off the avails of women, none of whom would testify against him. Clay would come after Sculley later. Right now, he wanted to make sure he found Violet before she and Aurelia could get away.

"Information's hard to come by, mister. What's it worth to you?"

Clay pulled out a twenty-dollar gold piece and laid it on the bar.

Glory laughed. "The going rate for *anything's* ten times that, honey!" She parted her silk kimono and drew Clay's attention to the ornate silver buckle at her waist. "You'll have to do better than this if you want to know where Sculley took your lady friend."

Sculley had Aurelia.

He didn't have money, or a claim, or time to gamble. Seeing no other choice, Clay reached into his pocket.

"Oooh! What a beautiful ring," Glory said as slipped the band of orange blossoms on her finger.

A narrow footbridge spanned the Klondike River from the decency of Dawson to the red-light district know as Lousetown. One-room wooden cribs no bigger than a tool shed lined both sides of the center mud thoroughfare. Clay had been in brothels before but hadn't seen anything as bizarre or as pitiful as this. Back and forth from the central hotel to the cribs ran white-coated waiters, balancing trays of beer, stepping in time to the lively notes from a tinny piano. Lousetown's only attraction, the heavily made up, half-naked whores, hung over the half-doors, blatantly describing their services to Clay as he passed by. Fancy-dressed *macques* stood guard. One with a knife strapped to his thigh tried to steer Clay to a young blond who couldn't speak English.

He didn't want to draw suspicion by asking questions. Instead, he looked in one crib at a time. The sights were enough to make a man ashamed of his gender, but this was Sculley's world. Violet was here somewhere. More importantly, so was Aurelia.

Aurelia dug her nails in the palms of her hands as Fletcher Sculley unlocked the door to the crib. She stepped inside, too nervous, too angry, too afraid to even notice the grimy window, the stale smell of tobacco, and the sticky residue of wine and whiskey underfoot.

Her eyes went straight to Violet.

23

Lying on a cot, blood-soaked hay beneath her body, a blood-stained nightgown hanging off her shoulders, Violet moaned and turned her head toward the door. She gasped as though seeing an apparition.

"Aurelia?" she cried. "I knew you'd find me. I hurt so much."

Aurelia rushed to her sister's side and kissed her cheek. "It's all right," she whispered as she caressed Violet's thick hair, now dirty and damp, from her brow. "I'll take care of you. You're going to be all right."

Even as she spoke, Aurelia fought the urge to wretch, so overpowering was the odor in the crib. Gathering her wits about her, she placed her palm then her lips to Violet's forehead. Easily a hundred and three degrees. She picked up the ratty blanket that had fallen to the floor and tucked the frayed edges around her sister's small, trembling shoulders, trying not to betray her own fear at the sight of Violet's horribly swollen abdomen.

She checked Violet's pulse. It couldn't be that fast. She checked it again. A hundred and forty. Lifting the blanket slightly, Aurelia pressed her fingers on the sides and center of the swelling.

Violet screamed.

"There, there," Aurelia cooed, though she knew mere words had no power over the disease that claimed her sister. Overdistention of the bladder— she probably hadn't urinated in days. Possible oophoritis—that would explain the heightened sensitivity in the area of the ovaries. Deep inside, beneath the calm, confident manner Aurelia had been trained to let her face reflect, she shook with dread. The symptoms were unmistakable: advanced puerperal infection. Violet wouldn't live through the night.

"I'm going to die. I know it." Violet's slender fingers locked around Aurelia's wrist. "I've heard the other girls talk. I know how bad . . . I know."

"Hush now." Gently, Aurelia loosened Violet's grip. "Violet, I've got to examine you." Aurelia lifted the portion of the blanket that covered Violet's legs. "It might hurt. I'll hurry as best I can."

Aurelia knew that Fletcher Sculley still stood across the room. For the sake of common decency, she wanted him to leave but knew it was useless to ask. She took her flask from the portion of her medical box where Violet once kept her rose-scented lotion. Wary of Sculley, she unfastened the lock to the secret compartment. Then, after pouring the whiskey over her hands, she began her examination.

The size and condition of the uterus was not encouraging, nor was the profusion of discharge. The blood poisoning was rampant.

Violet released the breath she'd been holding. "Have you seen my baby? Isn't she pretty?"

"Yes indeed." Aurelia forced the words. Across the room Sculley chuckled.

"I named her Lucy Maud. After Nana. Do you think that would make Nana happy?"

"I'm sure it would." Aurelia took out a vial of small pills. "Violet, this is strychnine. I'm only giving you a little, just enough to soothe your muscles and help ease the pain." Ease the pain, that was all she could do.

She looked around the room for a glass. An empty tin cup and a half-empty bottle of red wine sat on the table, which was the only other piece of furniture besides the cot and a chair. Aurelia wiped the edge of the cup and poured in a little wine. She set the bottle back on the table, then held the cup to her sister's parched lips. She knew that for Violet to receive the full benefit of the alcohol, unfortunately, it had to be pushed to the point of intoxication. "One more sip," she said. "Come on, one more sip."

When the cup was empty, Aurelia went to refill it, only to have Sculley grab the bottle.

"You're not wasting good wine on that bitch."

Aurelia slapped him hard across the mouth. In an instant he clamped his hands on her arms. With all her might, she stomped on his foot, then jacked her knee up to his groin.

Doubled over in pain, he staggered backward, gasping for breath. His lips twisted into an evil smile. "You're all the same. Filthy whores, all of you." He grabbed the bottle and smashed it against the edge of the table. "I figured to rid the world of one whore today. Now I'll make it two." He stepped toward her.

"You stay away from me. I'll scream."

"Don't bother. Ain't nobody gonna hear you." He inched closer. "And if they do, they won't interfere."

Aurelia reached for her medical box and took out the gun.

He lunged.

Her movements were lightning quick, though she felt herself in a slow-motion blur.

Elbow to the waist. Arm steady. Wrist loose. Squeeze.

Violet screamed.

Jolted by the gun's kick, Aurelia reeled back.

Sculley's arms fanned to his sides as the bullet buried in his chest. He crashed to the floor in a shower of wine and blood and broken glass.

Violet sobbed, but the sound faded to nothingness as Aurelia slowly stepped up to his body. She stooped down and pressed her trembling fingers to his neck. No pulse. He was dead. She'd killed a man.

She didn't know how long she'd stood there staring at his body, at the bloody froth around his mouth. One minute? Ten minutes? Only when the door burst open and she saw Clay did Aurelia react. "He's dead," she said.

"What about you? I heard the shot—"

"I'm all right." She knew the look in his eyes. He wanted to wrap her in his arms and hold her tight. But comfort from him was not a luxury she could allow herself, not now, not ever. "Please remove the corpse," she said, her voice devoid of emotion. "And bring me some clean water."

Just as Aurelia knew he would, Clay turned to Violet. Her lavender eyes, filled with fear and pain, locked on his. Her dark sooty lashes, once the downfall of many a smitten man, swept across her pale porcelain cheeks, now flushed with fever and damp with tears. "I'm sorry about the money," she said to him. "And I'm sorry I had to hit you. But we needed that money."

Aurelia had to ask one question. "He didn't attack you, did he?"

Violet shook her head. "I needed an excuse to

leave quickly. I knew if I cried and said I just wanted my fiancé to take me home, they'd let me go."

So it was true.

Clay didn't look as victorious as Aurelia would have expected. But then, she didn't feel shocked either.

At least Clay got what he had come all this way for: a deathbed admission in the presence of a witness. He had to feel vindicated. Whatever else he felt, whatever other thoughts he had, he kept them guarded. Without acknowledging Violet's apology, he grabbed Sculley under the arms and dragged the body across the floor.

After the avalanche, Aurelia had hoped she'd never again hear that heavy sound as boots and dead weight scraped against wood. God forgive her, but hearing it now made her smile.

Dislodge the enemy, when possible, and reinforce the resisting powers of the patient. Aurelia mentally recited the remedial treatment for infection as she cleaned up after another bout of diarrhea and vomiting, nature's own way of trying to dislodge the enemy. As for reinforcing the resisting powers of the patient, that was useless. The patient had no resisting powers. Aurelia sat by her sister's side and waited.

Clay, his thoughts still unspoken, sat outside on the step, listening to a piano from somewhere down the street and watching the evening traffic. He'd already alerted the authorities about the death of Fletcher Sculley, and the position of self-defense had been readily accepted.

Aurelia wiped her sister's brow with the clean cloth and fresh water Clay had brought. With an album of bittersweet childhood memories, Aurelia kept her vigil. The future wasn't supposed to have turned out this way. Aurelia was to sacrifice love for an education, and, in a way she'd never expected, that had proven true. But Violet—Violet was destined to be pampered and adored by a loving husband. She was to have cherubs for children and a finely appointed house to showcase her handiwork.

"A penny for your thoughts," Violet mumbled as she opened her eyes. The muscles she needed to smile could barely move.

Aurelia patted her hand. "Nothing of consequence. How do you feel?"

Violet licked her parched lips and struggled to swallow. "A failure."

"Oh no, Violet—"

Violet lifted her hand to ward off Aurelia's protest. "Yes. I do. All my life I felt like some object, polished and paraded. My worth depended on how I fixed my hair, what fashions I wore, how trim I kept my figure." She glanced down at her swollen belly while tears skittered down her cheeks. "When all I wanted was to be loved, to be appreciated for being myself."

She looked up at Aurelia with eyes that begged understanding. "Sometimes I'd dream that I was bright enough to go to college too. Then I could be like you. Confident and independent, so when a man grew tired of me, I could make my own way."

Violet's disclosure opened Aurelia's eyes. Violet saw Aurelia's loneliness as independence, while Aurelia viewed the smothering to which Violet had been subjected as love and attention. All these years each had coveted what had caused the other pain. Worst of all, Violet had never believed in a kind of true and lasting love, the kind Aurelia could have had with Clay.

Suddenly, Violet gathered strength and tried to lift herself. "Where's my baby?"

"In good hands. Don't worry." Aurelia eased Violet down. The truth would only bring pain. Violet already had more than she could stand.

The fever gave Violet's eyes a mystical glaze. "Show me Nana's silver buckles. The ones that give courage."

"They're gone," Aurelia said, knowing that if she could, she would give Violet anything she asked. "I gave one to a very dear friend who had less courage than I. And I used the other to pay for something very important."

"Poor Nana. You don't have her buckles. And I don't have her ring." Violet looked toward the door. Clay's back was visible as he sat hunched over on the step. "I gave it to him. But you know all that, don't you? That's why he's here."

"Clay," Aurelia said, "Can I see the ring? Just for a few minutes."

He turned to her, his face drawn and weary. "I'd give it to you, Aurelia, but it's gone."

Her eyes pleaded for an explanation.

"I spent it," he said, "To find you."

"You mean Violet."

He shook his head. "The Mounties told me I'd probably find your sister somewhere in Lousetown."

"Then why didn't you just take your time and look?"

"I'd planned to, until that woman at the bar said you'd gone off with Sculley." He looked to the ceiling, as though the intensity of his emotions threatened to overwhelm him if he didn't gain control. "Information doesn't come free around here. I couldn't take a chance on your getting hurt. I'm sorry. About everything."

"I understand. So am I."

Aurelia turned back to her sister.

"Oh Violet, if only I'd told you about Sculley that night at the dance hall . . ."

Violet shook her head, the effort obvious. "You didn't have to. I knew. I've always been able to see a man's true colors." She paused. "Nana knew I didn't need the buckles. I was too foolish to be afraid. She knew you didn't need the ring to find love." Violet looked toward the door again and labored for breath to continue. "He does love you, doesn't he? I can tell. And you love him too."

What did it matter? "You rest now," Aurelia whispered, registering Violet's deterioration, knowing the end would come soon.

Just before dawn, with a wash of pale sunlight waiting to celebrate a new day, when the only music was that of chirping birds, Violet moaned.

The sound startled Aurelia. She jumped, realizing she'd fallen asleep.

Violet moaned again. Her face contorted in pain. She tried to pull her legs toward her chest but screamed at the effort. "Aurelia! I hurt!"

"I know, I know," Aurelia said, rearranging the blanket Violet had tossed aside, feeling more helpless by the minute.

"Give me something. I know you have it. Please!"

"I've given you too much already. If I give you any more, it'll kill you."

"Aurelia! Please!"

"It'll *kill* you. Don't you understand?" Aurelia slipped her arms around her sister's tiny shoulders and pulled her close.

When Aurelia finally eased her sister back to the pillow, Violet looked deep into her eyes. "I'm dying anyway," she whispered. "Aren't I?"

Aurelia's only words were the tears that ran down her cheeks.

"How much longer?" Violet asked.

Aurelia opened her mouth to speak, but the words just wouldn't come out.

"Am I going to see tomorrow?"

"No."

A deep calm settled over Violet's face. "And my baby?"

"I held her in my arms. She was a beautiful little girl."

"I don't want to see tomorrow." Violet turned her head. Only by the weakened heaving of her shoulders could Aurelia tell she was crying.

The tin cup and the tincture of laudanum were on the table. Aurelia measured by the eye and poured the powerful opiate into the cup. One swallow and the pain would be gone, but Violet might never regain consciousness again. Aurelia had just found her little sister. She wasn't ready to say good-bye.

"Help me!" Violet cried out. "I hurt! I hurt!"

Her own desires aside, Aurelia slipped her arm under Violet's head and lifted her up so she could swallow. Fighting back her own tears, Aurelia held the cup to her sister's lips. "Easy now. That's good. One more sip."

A look of relief softened Violet's eyes, a look that said if not at this instant, surely in a moment or two, the pain would be gone. Then suddenly, as though aware of her final moments, Violet grasped Aurelia's hand. "Don't tell anyone about me, about what I did in Seattle. About this. Swear you won't tell."

"Oh no, don't ask that of me. Clay needs a witness—"

"But Momma and Poppa. The truth will kill them. Please. Please don't tell."

Aurelia didn't know what to do. She hadn't been able to spare Violet the ugliness of life, but she could spare Violet's memory. Tenderly, she whispered, "I won't tell."

Violet struggled against the tranquil sleep that beckoned her. "*Promise!*"

"I promise." She kissed her sister's forehead. "I love you, Violet."

Aurelia held her sister's hand until she died.

Clay had dug both graves: one for Violet, one for her child. Every day for six weeks he climbed the peaceful hillside with Aurelia. Every day he stood back while she knelt beside the freshly mounded earth and struggled alone with her grief. He'd tried to comfort her and told her he was sorry things had turned out this way, but she'd just nod and turn away. It didn't take much to see that all she wanted to do was put distance between them, but he was counting on her changing her mind. And so, while he was anxious to get back to Seattle, he didn't want to leave without her.

Now, a patch of red fireweed, always the first flowers to appear after disaster, covered the two mounds. Though with August drawing to a close, a killing frost could come any night, and soon it would be snow that blanketed the graves.

Clay opened the sack he'd carried with him and took out a hammer and two long wooden markers. On the top of one he'd carved a cherub, its innocent face turned toward Heaven. On the other he'd carved the name Violet and surrounded it with orange blossoms.

Carving had kept him occupied, kept him from confronting Aurelia, but now he'd run out of time.

Aurelia started when he came up behind her, though she had to know he was there. He was always there.

Kneeling at the head of each mound, he drove the markers into the ground. Each pound of the hammer summoned fresh tears to Aurelia's eyes. Helplessly, he watched as they ran in silence down her cheeks.

"Thank you," she said when he'd driven the last one deep into the earth. She accepted his handkerchief and wiped her eyes. "The markers are beautiful."

He stood and helped her to her feet. Not knowing if this was the right time, afraid that there would never be a right time, he took her hand. "The last boat leaves day after tomorrow.

"Funny, isn't it? Just a few months ago it was almost impossible to get a boat to take the northern route. It would take too long. It would cost too much money. Do you remember your telling me all that?"

"Yes, I do. But it's all supply and demand. With no more claims to be staked, the stampede's over. All the great town of Dawson has now are thousands of men who just want to go back home—the easy way."

"Easy?"

"Until the river freezes. Like I said, the last boat leaves tomorrow. I wrote and told Eli I'd be home soon. If we want to get to the Outside any time soon, we have to go now."

She looked at him wide-eyed, as though the idea of leaving Dawson was unthinkable. "We?" she said, knowing the word implied a couple, a pair, a union of two, and knowing it was not meant to apply to her. "No, I'm not leaving. Between Herb Wilson and Simpson O'Day, I have plenty of work to keep me busy. This country needs medical professionals. And here, no one minds that I haven't graduated. Or that I'm a woman. All they care is that I can dress a wound and splint a broken bone."

"Don't you want to finish school?" He wanted to tell her how much he admired her and loved her, that he'd be proud to tell people his wife was a doctor, but he knew his praise would sound hollow to her ears.

"You mean don't I want to stitch without leaving scars? Or perform surgery that isn't fatal? Or save a woman from puerperal fever? Of course I do!" She turned to look back at the graves.

"She's dead," Clay said, wanting Aurelia to release the hold Violet still had over her.

"That's all the more reason why I have to honor my promise. It's too late for Violet to redeem herself."

"Violet wasn't looking to redeem herself. Don't you see? Her last act—the promise she exacted from you—that had to be the most selfish thing she ever did!"

"How can you say such a thing? All she wanted was to spare our parents the shame of having the family name sullied. I don't know how you could misconstrue such a noble gesture."

"Noble?" Clay said, raising his voice. "Violet couldn't die without taking your future with her. What's noble about that?"

She looked stunned by his attack. "My future? What are you talking about?"

"Your future with me. She knew we loved each other. Don't try to deny it."

"So what if she did?"

"She forced you to make a choice, Aurelia. Defend her lie and turn me away, or admit the truth and embrace our love. She knew you'd choose to protect her in death, just as you always tried to in life."

"She was my sister."

Clay retreated. As though it was a final effort, he asked, "What about us?"

He was glad to see the struggle in her eyes. That meant he still had a chance. He'd sat alone for too many nights, his eyes closed, afraid that only in this kind of darkness would he ever again know the powerful love she'd awakened in him. Even now he wanted to hold her and kiss away her sorrow. He wanted her to know how much he treasured her. He wanted to make love to her and free her to dream again.

"We're alive," she said. "We each have a future ahead of us. I have my medicine. You have your son."

"That's not what I'm asking, and you know it."

"I know what you want me to do—go back to Seattle and let the newspapers turn my sister into an object of scorn. I can't. I owe it to Violet."

"*No.*" He held her by the shoulders, afraid she'd slip away. "Don't you owe something to yourself? Don't you owe something to us?"

Before she could reject him again, he kissed her. He wanted her to remember how good they were together.

Her lips parted easily, as though she, too, remembered. His shoulders felt broader, his arms stronger, as she leaned into him, sharing the anguish she'd carried alone all these weeks.

But he knew he'd failed when she broke from his embrace and ran down the hill.

Outwardbound. The steamboats that had made it to Dawson from the long northern route were all headed in one direction now. Word had it that ice had already begun to form up ahead. Like everyone else in Dawson, Aurelia had only two choices: leave then or stay until next spring. But for her, the choice really was between leaving then with Clay and helping restore his reputation or staying in Dawson alone and keeping her promise to Violet.

Loyalty had forced her decision. With a heavy heart, she joined the evening pilgrimage to the wharf to wave and watch the last boat leave town, the ending ritual of the dying season.

Waldo and Emma met her outside their store. They'd arrived several weeks earlier and were already known for the variety of merchandise they carried and for the two friendly gophers that had the run of the store. It was Emma who'd convinced Aurelia to have her photo taken and Emma who'd put the likeness in the silver frame Aurelia now clutched so tightly in her hand.

Cold nights had already hardened the muddy shore, still claimed by a hodgepodge of tents, boats, and sheet-iron stoves. Praying for the courage to say good-bye, Aurelia stepped as close as she could get to the gangplank and scanned the deck, crowded with those who would never come back.

"Twenty minutes," a uniformed man shouted.

The lights on the steamer came on, and Aurelia suddenly ached with a desperation she'd never known. She felt Clay's presence behind her, even before she turned around.

"I'm here to change your mind," he said.

Too choked up to speak, she shook her head.

"Listen to me," he said, his voice sounding desperate. "I've had a lot of time to think. I can't say I don't want your testimony. I do. But if you can't testify, I'll accept that. What I won't accept is leaving you behind."

Seeing the pain in his eyes didn't make her choice

any easier. "It wouldn't work," she said. "You know that as well as I do. You'll come to resent me. Maybe not next month, or even next year, but eventually you'll blame me for what Violet did to you."

"No—"

"*Yes.* But even if you don't, I'll always know how you feel about my little sister. And no matter what she did, I'll always love her." She gave him the photograph. "Just as I'll always love you."

With unabashed longing, Clay looked down at her picture. Resignation weighted his words. "Violet wasn't the only victim of the gold rush."

A small glimmer of hope flickered inside Aurelia's heart. That Clay could see her sister as something other than a thief brought her a kind of peace.

His face looked both determined and strained, as though he'd rehearsed his words again and again, but was still afraid of getting them wrong. "She robbed me, Aurelia. And she took a lot more than the money that was in my care. She took my good name. That's a truth that will never change. Even so, it's not as simple a truth as I once thought. Your sister was a victim too. Her beauty, her youth, her boredom, it all worked against her. I can see that now."

The truth had worked its own magic on Aurelia too, as had the last few dark and lonely nights, predictions of dark and lonely years to come. Feeling less of a traitor for admitting her true feelings, she said, "Violet wasn't the naive innocent I once believed either."

The steamboat whistle blared. "Five minutes," the uniformed man shouted.

Clay stuck Aurelia's picture in the satchel at his feet, freeing his hands to stroke her hair one last time, to tenderly kiss her lips.

"You'd better go," she said, silently adding, *before I change my mind.*

"I guess we're all victims of something," he said. "Someone's gossip, our own guilt, blind loyalty, even society's outmoded ideas. But we don't have to remain victims. We don't have to give up our dreams."

His optimism was contagious. What would happen if she did go with him? She'd have to stand before a court of law, break her promise, and admit knowledge of her sister's guilt. Her parents would be devastated, and Aurelia would have to live with an action that could never be undone.

But an honest man would be vindicated. And what about Eli? An innocent little boy would inherit a legacy of honor and a future untainted by someone else's shame, unlike his own father. Selfishly, Aurelia also admitted that the happiness she longed for might finally be hers.

So attuned to her thoughts, Clay reached into his pocket and withdrew one of her silver buckles. "I won it," he explained and handed it to her. "I want you to have enough courage"—he paused and looked into her eyes—"to go home with me. And be my wife."

Paralyzed by indecision, Aurelia struggled to think clearly.

Just then, Waldo stepped up and touched her arm. Slowly and clearly, he said, "Maybe this can help you decide." He pressed the matching buckle into her hands. "I don't need it anymore." He smiled at Aurelia, then looked lovingly at Emma, who mirrored his devotion.

With Nana's strength in her hands, urging her to follow her heart, Aurelia glanced at the boat, then at Clay. "Do you think Eli would like me?" she stammered.

"Eli will love you. Just as I do."

She looked at Waldo and Emma and at the town where she'd buried her sister. "Do I have time to get my things?"

Standing on the deck next to Clay, Aurelia leaned over the railing and waved good-bye. With Dawson receding in the background, Clay reached into his pocket one more time. "Here," he said, taking her hand. "This really belongs to you." He slipped the ring on her finger.

"Nana's ring," she said with the joy of finding something she had thought was lost forever. "You won this back too?"

"I'm a lucky man."

She held her hand up and studied the band of orange blossoms, remembering both Nana's happiness and Violet's sorrow. "When I was a girl, I used to dream that someday this would be my wedding band."

"You wouldn't mind that the ring belonged to someone else first?"

"In this case I would treasure it all the more."

"Then that's one dream I can make come true. If you'll let me."

She said yes with a kiss. She would always treasure her band of gold. It would always symbolize their love.

COMING NEXT MONTH

ONE GOOD MAN by Terri Herrington
From the author of *Her Father's Daughter*, comes a dramatic story of a woman who sets out to seduce and ruin the one good man she's ever found. Jilted and desperate for money, Clea Sands lets herself be bought by a woman who wants grounds to sue her wealthy husband for adultery. But when Clea falls in love with him, she realizes she can't possibly destroy his life—not for any price.

PRETTY BIRDS OF PASSAGE by Roslynn Griffith
Beautiful Aurelia Kincaid returned to Chicago from Italy nursing a broken heart, and ready to embark on a new career. Soon danger stalked Aurelia at every turn when a vicious murderer, mesmerized by her striking looks, decided she was his next victim—and he would preserve her beauty forever. As the threads of horror tightened, Aurelia reached out for the safety of one man's arms. But had she unwittingly fallen into the murderer's trap? A historical romance filled with intrigue and murder.

FAN THE FLAME by Suzanne Elizabeth
The romantic adventures of a feisty heroine who met her match in a fearless lawman. When Marshal Max Barrett arrived at the Washington Territory ranch to escort Samantha James to her aunt's house in Utah, little did he know what he was getting himself into.

A BED OF SPICES by Barbara Samuel
Set in Europe in 1348, a moving story of star-crossed lovers determined to let nothing come between them. "With her unique and lyrical style, Barbara Samuel touches every emotion. The quiet brilliance of her story lingered in my mind long after the book was closed."—Susan Wiggs, author of *The Mist and the Magic*.

THE WEDDING by Elizabeth Bevarly
A delightful and humorous romance in the tradition of the movie *Father of the Bride*. Emma Hammelmann and Taylor Rowan are getting married. But before wedding bells ring, Emma must confront not only the inevitable clash of their families but her own second thoughts—especially when she discovers that Taylor's best man is in love with her.

SWEET AMITY'S FIRE by Lee Scofield
The wonderful, heartwarming story of a mail-order bride and the husband who didn't order her. "Lee Scofield makes a delightful debut with this winning tale . . . *Sweet Amity's Fire* is sweet indeed."—Mary Jo Putney, bestselling author of *Thunder and Roses*.

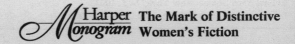 **Harper Monogram** The Mark of Distinctive Women's Fiction